Pentru the "Crofty"

MW01322752

Womb Town

Enjoy, Live, Love!

Banea
July 2016

WOMB TOWN

Cover: Raluca Fratean

ISBN-13: 978-1519775870
ISBN-10: 1519775873

Chapter 1
Incredibly fast and painfully real

A man must prove himself at all times, you said.

We paddled in the milky mist that hovered over the waters like peeling skin after a sunburn. The Lake was packed with trout. There was heart-wrenching silence. The mist cleared just enough so we could see the trees on the shore.

Father, why did we stop?, I asked.

You did not say anything. Your face was sober like on the day of my first violin lesson.

Give me your hand, you said.

Your face was peaceful and majestic.

Your eyes were calm and sunk in thoughts.

You took my hand and put it on your heart. This is your future, Tim, you said.

Then I saw your last smile.

Then the blood on your hand gushing from the hole.

I slipped. The water was freezing cold. It was crushing my skull. Thousands of needles pierced my skin. You shouted my name.

My thighs burned, my cheeks burned, Father.

Come on, Tim, focus!, you screamed at me.

I couldn't move.

Lie on your back, son, use your arms!

Then the second bullet entered your left temple and exited through the right. The impact threw you into the water.

I could have saved you.

Chapter 2
The first attempt to determine the depth of the rabbit hole

My name is Tim Tolstoy.

I was born in a white room where my mother, held by two nurses, pushed me out. They laid me on a white tray and fed me a spongy liquid through tubes, for seven days. Then they all left and I smiled, alone in my beautiful white room where it was quiet and peaceful.

A childhood later, one evening, my mother asked me to come to dinner.

Tim, dinner is ready.

I smell the boiled vegetables through the walls. I can tell that she has put too much salt on them. They are bleeding, salted wounds. Lettuce cries for the roots left behind in the ground, cucumber cries for the peel that is thrown into the compost, the endives cry for the chives with which they shared a glass jar, in a long, claustrophobic hibernation.

The spinach is the muscle of Zeus, Mom tells me.

Mom teaches history. Zeus was son of Chronos, Chronos had big muscles, like the Soviet steel workers in the middle of the twentieth century, Marx, Lenin, Stalin had beards or moustaches. Is there divine strength in the follicle? All gods have beards, and all aliens are totally bald. We see ourselves into a future of baldness and spongy soft bodies, like organic mayonnaise.

Would you like some spinach?

No, thank you.

Chapter 3
Travel guide to the theatre at the end of the Universe

At 7:13 the school bus stops down the road, by the Church. Eleven students get on. She is not among them. I close my eyes and think of an atom smasher buried into the ground, arched to the infinitesimality of a quantum sleep. What keeps sheep together on this planet? Gravity. What a strange word. Maggots transform the energy into mass and traverse the whole of Shakespeare to wind up at the end of the Universe, where language stops, where there is nothing but melted clocks.

We arrive right when Mr. Popp, our science teacher, begins his lecture.

Mr. Popp draws a big circle on the blackboard. He is fascinated by black holes. He would jump into one just to take a walk through the entrails of the most crowded space in the whole Universe, yet he knows that such a thing is not possible and would make him throw up.

What is time?, he continues, and sliced the circle in two. Time is—

—a dream, I say.

Yes Tim, exactly, a product of our mind, but what-does-it-mean?, he underlines imaginary floating words. We need a brain to understand this, and he scribbles quickly the long version of Einstein's field equations while humming some Beethoven. He writes fast, he has done it many times, before generations of curious young students. He knows the rhetoric of modern physics by heart.

I hear the echo of a fire truck from outside, a harpsichord in a cave, mingled with cold drops from the hanging icicles, or Mr. Popp's finger as it taps on the blackboard around the cosmological constant like it was a blueberry muffin. He frowns, he is frustrated because he is an old man. Science does not advance fast enough for me, he mumbles to himself. I'd better lie in hay and watch the stars and think I'm a Tsar, ha, ha, ha. His laughter is copious and jolly. Then he rubs his pipe and scratches his head with it and dandruff falls slowly on the desk.

Tim, what is a superstring?, Mr. Popp asks.

I look away and see her. She smiles. I am sure she can see the redness in my cheeks.

A superstring is a shoelace tied in a spiral around itself, I say, vibrating like a noodle, curly as a poodle, smaller than a flea on the head of an atom. A superstring makes a bridge between the incomprehensible smallest with the stupendous large forces in the cosmos.

Chapter 4
A thought of freedom and ice cream marks

I smell cows and yellow five-point stars spiraling around my head. My dad has been dead for a decade, my mother teaches history, Henry 8th was an asshole, Louis 16th lost his head out of naiveté, there is no such thing as a nuclear bomb, or starvation out of pure choice. We still have blood flowing through our jugulars, but soon it will be pure lead. Read me a story, Mr. President, with fairies and magic sticks and Pinocchios turned into real North Korean boys, smiling and happy like a rainbow drawn on the classroom's door. A Moor, drawn on the flag of Spain, chuckles in disdain and rubs his curved sword. All I need is a word, in the name of my god, how can a name cause so much action?, Fight!, I say, and millions will jump out of their beds and dart upon the first city and hack everybody to pieces. Steal their cookie jars, their jewelry, burn their houses and set the pianos on fire, symbol of pure desire, yes Sire, mission accomplished. I thank thee for this tree of tranquility by which I shall rest my horse and my pouch with gold coins.

You have ice cream marks right there, in the corner of your lips, I tell her.

Show me, she says.

There.

No, silly, put your finger.

There.

Ha!

Her name is Iris.

Chapter 5
The irony of a hole into an iron-reinforced wall

They say that the Church has a crack in the wall. History seems to be in reverse, and soon we'll hear that the Church grew wings and lifted into the air and popped like a balloon.

This can't be right, Tim, mom says. We never had earthquakes in Town. I know this area very well, before your father brought me here.

Mom carefully arranges the honey jar and the milk bottle along the axis of the table.

Your father, Tim, remember, he always wanted us to live in a safe place.

Dad died many years ago.

Iris fixes her eyes on my mouth.

How did he die?, she asks.

I feel her hand on my back, like a torch, violet crepuscular light melting on willows, lying low under an artificial horizon, the smell of a creek through the ozone of my thoughts. I remain quiet and Mom does the same. Iris keeps her smile arched. Mom stretches out one arm, holding the apron with the other. She turns up the volume on the radio. Beethoven's Piano Concerto No. 5, at two minutes and twenty-two seconds into the first movement, right when the horns dance on their heels, like swans on Viennese lawns. Iris recognizes the piece and starts drumming her fingers on the table, on an imaginary piano. I look at Mom, she looks at me, Iris looks at both of us.

I know this piece, Iris says, and plays a few notes on my left hand.

We ran out of milk, Mom says.

The bus is here. Let's go Tim, let's go!

Iris can be unexpectedly feisty. We both jump from the table and dart out the door.

We walk fast down the road.

Our hearts were pounding. I haven't properly swallowed the last piece of pie. Iris pinches the skin of my waist, still chuckling and, while I try to fend her off, I remember something.

Iris, I just remembered where I was three days ago.

On the moon?, she teases me.

No, stop it. I push her hand back. I've been to Church.

No kidding.

Father Frank asked me to go there to pick up the scores for Handel's Messiah. I went into his office, with those big brown oak windows. He showed me the bell tower. The bell was made during the war. It can fit three people under it. He handed me a pile of musical scores bound with a cotton string and took me outside. These walls are made of stone, he said. Feel them. I put down the papers and touched the Church wall with my palms. I felt an electrical discharge through my spine. I jumped back and stepped on the Messiah. Don't step on Handel, son, he said. Take it easy. Are the walls cold?, I asked. Of course they are, it's stone from the river. That was it.

Bizarre, Iris says.

Bizarre is the crack that appeared in the same spot on the wall, I say.

Iris pulls the radio from her pocket and switches to the music station, lowers the volume. For the remainder of the piano concerto, we remain quiet.

I'll see you Saturday, at the rehearsal, she says.

Okay, and I wave good-bye.

Chapter 6
Handel at the helm of the space shuttle named Providence

The rehearsals are at 9 a.m., in the school auditorium.

Father Frank enters with a stick in his left hand and the score in his right.

It's the hour, people. Stage is yours, please, chop, chop!

Boys in the back, girls in the front.

Father Frank is very precise when he gives instructions.

There is this quiet boy in our class. Nobody is really sure about his name, because he never says it, and writes only his initials on the test papers. We call him The Quiet Boy. He sings in a crystal-clear tenor, fully formed for a teenager. He goes to his place in the second row from the back, opens the score, looks at it for a couple of seconds, closes his eyes and squeezes them. He sings the part in his mind. I look at Iris, she looks at me, we both shrug.

Father Frank reminds us of the key: D major.

Every year we begin the rehearsals with this song. Father Frank calls it a hymn, not a song. It is an ode of adulation, he says, when mankind bends its knees in front of God and rejoices in respect and love. Father Frank is a good shepherd, a good man. He arranges us in rows, with a kind of well-tempered severity and discipline. Fill your lungs with air, you are birds. Then he hits the stand with the stick.

Invisible metronome, fifty voices in unison. Hal-le-lu-jah! Hal-le-lu-jah! Father, your stick is parting the seas, and you let us cross to the other side of the Earth, men are atoms in marmalade, cascade of arpeggios, voices chasing each other, on two, three, four tracks, passing hallelujahs at each other, like a ball filled with sand, we are training our stomachs, we are training our muscles, our souls, like boxers, fists hitting steel, octaves at thousands of degrees when everything becomes vapor, outpour of vibrating air rushes at the audience, patience my friends, one soul at a time through the gates of heaven, one owl at a time through the beak of the raven, one amen per second, count the syllables, god omnipotent takes a nap with me, in a tent, I do not fear the bears nor the wolves of the dark forest, crack this crust off my eyes, let light come in, let light come in, this planet is spinning too fast, this room is spinning too fast, vertigo atlas, father wears indigo, hallelujah, halle—

Stop, stop, stop!

Tim, are you okay?

Tim?

Tim!

He's fainting.

Don't touch him.

Give him air.

Give me air, my lungs crave their food. I need to run, I need to escape, I need the room between me and the fabric of space-time, where is the door, I'm hot in this skin, they call my name, the door, the curtain behind the stage, my legs, the soft tired eggs after conception.

Tim, where are you going?

Let him breathe!

I need air, this curtain has no doors, no windows, it's illusion.

I am going through.

Chapter 7
Giza plateau of smiling white camels

My room is clean and quiet and the air is fresh. The whiteness of the space seems transparent, translucent like a clean, tropical lagoon. My things are in their places. Through the window I see the Giza plateau in the middle of a green sea, and my father is paddling on a canoe in the distance. He is waving at me. I wave back. He disappears into the reflection of the sun, in the waters, a fata morgana, an optical transition to irreality. I uncover the mirror and look at my face. I can see the clock on the wall behind me. It is 12:13. I can see a microscope on the floor, where Iris left it, and a red scarf. It must be hers. I can see the curtain fluttering, the pandanus touching the lamp, books on the table, mostly unopened, and the curvature of the wooden globe, turning white as its light touches my retina. White bed sheets, white pajamas.

I cannot feel my face.

Chapter 8
Tension in the muscles before the jump

The Quiet Boy lived with his father, a well-known lawyer, his mother, a museum curator, and a sister, who was three years old. They had a big house with a big front yard, where The Quiet Boy usually went out and read thick books, in a rocking chair. Sometimes on late Saturday afternoons his father called him inside and they closed the blinds. The next day, they came out all at once, quietly. The boy's mother had dark eyes and wore a pearl necklace. Later in the day they were seen at the Synagogue, sitting in silence in the third row, then shaking the hands of acquaintances after the sermon, nodding their heads. The Quiet Boy has been seen smiling only once, when he was five and saw the ice cream man driving by on their street. He seemed very peaceful. He must have a peaceful family.

He met Tim at school, in a science class, and liked him immediately. He liked Tim's curiosity, his imagination, his passion for nature and his ability to understand the correlation between matter and mind. The Quiet Boy barely spoke with Tim, but when he did, they always had pleasant words to exchange about some project or some happening in the world. When Iris joined their class, it felt like a burst of energy. She's a rocket, The Quiet Boy thought. When he saw her become interested in Tim, he felt she was interfering with his friendship. But it's okay, he told himself later, Tim and I have a strong connection.

One day The Quiet Boy's father took him to an outdoor shooting range and put noise-canceling headphones on him. They were too big for him and fell off, but the father picked them up with a grim face and told him in his grating, firm voice, Hold this, and gave him the pistol. I'm going out for a smoke, don't play with that. The Quiet Boy didn't play with the pistol, but he stretched out his arms and aimed at the target, without shooting. He thought that was a serious thing to do. Later that day, his mother asked him how his day was and he looked at his father and his father said, Did you get my mail today?, She handed it to him, then looked again at her son. The Quiet Boy raised the imaginary pistol and aimed at her. She put her hand on his head and smiled briefly. She was a good mother. Lunch is ready, she said.

Chapter 9
The angular momentum of the jump

Lunch is ready, Tim.

I cannot feel my face. Mom works until four. The air in my white room becomes dense like flour. The air is trying to escape. I fear that it might be nailed to my lungs. My stomach rumbles, I live in a giant gingerbread house, I rip a piece from the wall, it looks like a pistol, it tastes like bread. I read *War and Peace* two summers ago and it still shoots vivid images through my dreams, the rims of this planet are a curvature that falls unto itself. I need to run.

Chapter 10
All praise is due to god

His name is Gregoire. He owns an ice cream truck, and he works part time at the aquarium. I bet he has a torture room in his basement and forces his hostages to watch soap operas, and stuffs them with ice cream and fast food and—

Please don't say that, Iris, I tell her.

Tim, I have an idea, she says. Have you been into a Mosque before?

I look at Iris's face opening like the horizon after a dark storm, orange rays of light piercing the skies and awakening the meadows. I always wanted to see them bowing their heads in unison, Mosque, all echoing in one voice, bare feet, perfection, discipline.

Through the crowd we make our way, we walk through the park and greet some schoolmates. Where were you going?, they ask. To the Mosque, we say. They elbow each other and perform a mock bow that was more like a Buddhist salute. Iris knows them well, and before I can utter a word she bows back. Namasté, she says. Whatever, they say, and carry on with their business and we carry on with our business.

Do we take the bus?, I ask.

We have time, Iris says.

She seems very relaxed.

There were a lot of cars parked on the road. It is prayer time. *Salah*. Iris tells me to relax, of course they'll let us in, first we have to take our shoes off, second we need to cover our heads. She gives me a khimar. When others forget theirs at home, she explains. Does that happen often?, Oh yeah.

Bismi-llāhi r-raḥmāni r-raḥīm. In the name of God, the most kindly merciful.

Shush, someone tells us.

Our faces are of stone.

Beautiful large hall, white marble and granite, thick pillars with discreet carvings mingled with liquid letters flowing, bowing and rising like the thousand heads perfectly synchronized. Do what they do, Iris instructs me with whispers. Our foreheads touch the floor. Odor of jasmine covers us like a mist and settles in the nostrils. I play the Scheherazade in my head. Her curly hair is covering my hand, she seems to be kissing the floor.

Lift your head!, she says. She pokes me subtly. We lift our heads and listen to the sermon, uncommon echoes bounce off the inert bodies, transfixed into meditation or thoughts about redemption or family left at home, worries about tomorrow, or simply some undefined sorrow, or an effusion of optimism hearing about the peaceful teachings of the prophet, courage gained at the end of a sentence, when no hope was in sight at the beginning of it, a verb that moves your pulse into your toes and fingers, an adjective that makes you think for a moment about everybody else, except yourself, *Al ḥamdu lillāhi rabbi l-'ālamīn*, all the praises and thanks be to Allah, the lord of mankind, this is my own little Nirvana, my nails are not sharp enough, not long enough to cut into my palms, and my teeth are not sharp enough to carve my lips. I'd better play the Scheherazade again from the beginning, elongating my rubber arms around the equator to grab the whole planet, shake it well, dry it up, hang it on a string with laundry clips, give me a place to stand and with a lever I will move the whole world. I am my own talking tortoise, sitting on my own back, in an infinite array of tortoises to the Big Bang and back, *Ar raḥmāni r-raḥīm*, the most gracious, the most merciful, where are you, Dad? Can you get a good sleep where you are? Are they treating you well? Do they bring you water when you are thirsty, or bread when you are starved? You do not need these things, you are immaterial, you are dark energy, you are bright energy, can you hear music if you don't have ears and a gelatinous brain to decode the vibrating air, can you feel the gravity or do you permeate space and time like an abstract noodle?

Tim, are you okay?, Iris asks.

Chapter 11
Family breakfast breaks fast

The Quiet Boy woke up the next day, got out of bed, put his glasses on, walked to the window and opened it. The doves that were piling up straws on the ledge did not pay him any heed, so he shooed them with his hand. As the doves soared away, he aimed at them with two fingers that took the shape of a pistol barrel.

It was Shabbat. His parents were downstairs quarreling about priorities in the family and financial planning. The father mentioned his wife's parents and she mentioned his golf buddies. They only agreed on the fact that the weekly socializing at the Synagogue that used to extend their social network and business connections has become a chore. They thought it was stereotypical and counterproductive. You're such a hypocrite, she said. It was your idea in the first place, he retorted. The Quiet Boy heard a set of porcelain plates shattering against the wall. From the sounds they made, he could tell they hit Grandpa's portrait above the fireplace. His sister started crying in the next room, but nobody except him heard her. Her cry was covered by the sound of the loading of a gun. His father grabbed his shooting gear and was ready to storm out of the house. Run away, run, like you've done your whole life, this is the truth, this, right here, the mother said, crying. The father threw some more stuff in his bag and yelled back, Maybe I'll find some Muslims, that'll keep me calm. And then he stormed out. The Quiet Boy didn't understand what Muslims his father was talking about, nor what they had to do with all this. The people emerging from the Mosque came to his mind: Tim's pale face and Iris patting his back. He could hear his mother's cry fading, while she picked up the shards. He walked to his sister's room and put his index finger on her lips. She stopped crying. He wiped her tears, gave her a doll and put her on the bed. She lied down, sobbing. The Quiet Boy closed the door, then went to the window and shooed the doves away.

Chapter 12
The violin lesson violently lessens

The walls in my room are soft today. They shiver like ferns ransacked by a sudden ocean breeze. Snails freeze on my floor, it is cold today, much colder than yesterday, maybe Mom is saving on heating, but that's okay, in my drawers beehives are still untouched, no production of honey yet, and it still smells like jasmine and Iris's skin, I am going to tell her about my pulse how I feel when she's around, about my silence when I'm spellbound and the sight from my window towards the north.

I open my window and the cold pierces my nostrils. I feel small icicles forming in my lungs. From the ledge to the horizon there is a vast sea of turquoise waters and gigantic menhirs of ice, the winds are still, tiny waves break onto the ledge, I can hear somebody whistling as the waves grow bulkier, frothier. A boat is approaching, a sailor in an Eskimo outfit, paddling on a canoe. My father.

Son, go inside, it is cold today.

I am fine, Dad.

Has your mother turned down the heat again?, he chuckles. I like his smile, his dimples, his wrinkles like Norwegian fjords.

I am not cold, Dad. I lost my bees.

Your bees? Nonsense! Why do you keep bees in your room?

His voice is rusty, thick, old and open like the sky.

Here, I brought your violin, he says. Take it.

My violin. I haven't touched it since you died.

Take it, it's no good here, the wood will crack, the strings will snap, I'll scare the whales with it.

Thank you, Dad.

Be good, son, be good. Scratch that old barrel, make some noise, make some music! Go out, play!

He paddles away, chuckling and whistling, Play son, play. His echo becomes ice, phantom in frozen winds. I close the window.

The violin smells like an old barn. Its body is smooth, perfect and glossy, like a newborn covered in dark red blood, Mr. Bach, I am in the mood for a partita, the bow under my pillow, elbow horizontal, straighten my back, chin up, andante, slow, I can close my eyes, music is a mechanical transformation, inauguration of wound in blood and closed by sound and opened again by the next phrase, another phase, another voice, paragraph, autograph yourself on the eardrum with a pen of air, a thin gavotte, lustrous redingote, the air warms up and through a crack in the window a thread of water sneaks inside. Tim, are you up? Breakfast's ready.

I'm coming, Mom.

I lay the violin on my bed, carefully. I run downstairs. Scrambled eggs and apple pie. The pot is full of fresh milk.

Were you playing the violin?

Yes Mom.

After all these years, Tim. She squeezes my cheeks and kisses my forehead.

There's somebody at the door, Mom. I'll get it.

Wait, wait, wipe your mouth.

I recognize the silhouette through the distortions of glass in the front door. Iris.

Want to go on a bike ride?, she asks. She takes a bite from a big green apple.

Umm, sure.

She waves at Mom. Hi, she says.

She's in the kitchen, she can't hear you, I say.

Chapter 13
Yet another opening of the womb

Leaves and straws fall from nests, bounce off our hands as we race down on the road. Where are you taking me?, I ask.

I don't know, Iris replies, taking the lead on her bike, gliding through the passersby gracefully, avoiding car mirrors by the width of a hair, finally slowing down when the crowd of people thickens not far from the Mosque. The area was surrounded with DO NOT CROSS yellow tape, a good distance around a mobile crane and the trucks from the fire department. Luckily there were no reporters to make pointless noise. She shows me an enormous crack in the wall, from the ground to the highest point, through which we see people inside with safety hats, looking at blueprints, scratching their chins, and jumping back when a boulder falls from the ceiling. A pillar detaches itself from inside the Mosque and leans on the crack, making a deafening echo. Acting like an oversized wedge, it widens the opening at the top, spits a few bricks towards the watching crowd and rolls a perfectly round stone at my feet. Iris's eyes find mine. Before she says a word, I hear her in slow motion, like in the movies, when all other noises are blurred, when time is dilating, when pelvic muscles contract and relax before a conspicuous protuberance that comes out or goes in.

It is the pillar you leaned against, she says.

I know.

The lines in my palms look like canyons dug by archaeologists or gold seekers. Iris grabs my hands and turns them with the dexterity of an old gypsy woman. She looks carefully at the signs, Hmm, she says, you're fine, you're going to be a great man, ha! She jumps on the pedals, turns briskly and accelerates at greyhound speed. Come on, let's go!, she says.

Chapter 14
Cause, caucus and pointed cactuses

Ladies and gentlemen, please, may I have your attention! Citizens of our beloved Town, everybody, especially our friends in the back of the room, Father Frank, Mr. Popp, Imam, Rabbi, everybody welcome to this gathering at our Town Hall. To remain encapsulated within the realities of social, cultural and political correctitude, I shall say that *unusual events*, well debated by the media, have befallen us in recent days. Some have argued that the events rely solely on the causalities of the physical nature of things. Others, most of them present here, and whom I thank for honoring my invitation, are claiming that the roots of the subject in question go beyond geophysical explanations and have to do with ethnic and religious frictions within our community. I, your elected Mayor, have the duty to recognize the realities, affirm them and, if they do not benefit the wellbeing of our community, come forward with solutions and pacifying, umm, initiatives. The facts are these—

Mr. Mayor, allow me to interject and present the facts from the first observer's perspective.

By all means, Imam.

Our Mosque has suffered conspicuous damage, which has affected the whole structure of the edifice. The pillar that crushed the wall and created the enormous crack has now caused a chain reaction and other cracks have appeared in other pillars and elements of structural resistance. Our preliminary investigations have concluded that criminal human factors are behind all this.

Preposterous, You are the criminal, We don't want you here, Absurd, Yes, he's the criminal, Let the man speak, Nonsense, Where were you on that day?, He was praying on a stack of hay, Ha, ha, Gentlemen, please, we're a civilized town, Look at him, is that civilized?, Go and fly airplanes in your desert, Sue the bastard, Gentlemen, we have no proof and he is the victim, What victim, look at his face, He's all lies, lies.

Citizens, please, let the Imam finish, the insults and brawling do not help. Let us continue in an orderly fashion. Thank you.

Thank you, Mayor. As I was saying, criminal human factors. Yes Rabbi, you can hide behind a smirk, we all know your allegations and your claims, that land is *our* land, we have papers, we have rights, we have developed a community around the land, rightfully purchased by our forefathers, we have suffered persecution in the past, we have endured, we will not accept malicious attacks, duplicitous politics and subterfuge, we *know* you were behind all this, tearing down a building does not tear down a soul.

Mr. Mayor, beloved citizens. Imam. These despicable accusations are absolutely ridiculous, counterproductive, worrisome and—

Hypocrite Jew, Shut up, What do you know?, That man would drill for oil under his own Church, gentlemen!

—worrisome and instigative! Not only—

Yeah!

—not only is it beyond our imagination and interests to cause damage to the Muslim community in our Town but it is our desire to live in peace with our neighbors for the mutual benefit and prosperity. Imam's vehemence proves one thing—

Prosperity, oh, please!

—his vehemence proves one thing. Facts and history show the tendency of the Muslim community to isolate itself—

Not true!

—to isolate itself and sabotage the peace around us. It is obvious now that those criminal factors Imam is talking about come from nowhere other than their own congregation, for the sole purpose—

Liar, Let the man talk, Outrageous!

Gentlemen, please, order!

—for the sole purpose of disrupting our society and create an excuse for conflict.

That is absurd, Rabbi!

Imam, our Synagogue has not been affected. What other better excuse you need to blame us for the damage? You did it to yourself!

I am obliged, Mr. Mayor, to respond.

Yes Imam, please proceed.

Thank you. I am obliged to respond to these ludicrous statements with yet another fact. We all know how, in the early years of this century, the land on which the Jewish Synagogue is erected was forcefully expropriated from hardworking, honest Muslim families, to be used for the erection of a power plant, which—

Instigator!

—which, mind you, was never built because of political attritions and lack of interconfessional consensus. And—

Saboteur, Please, please, the man is right.

—and was auctioned back to the community by the next administration and no Muslim bidders were accepted. Isn't that Machiavellian? Isn't that sabotage? And who bought the land? Who did? The Jewish Council, of course. They were behind these machinations, it was all their plan from the beginning, the power plant was never their intention, it was all a plan to marginalize us, the community of Allah.

Do you think we prefer to keep the old plant, which runs on your oil? I didn't vote against the new plant, it was Town Council, which we all elected—

Yeah, Well said, Rabbi!

—freely and democratically, by your people as well.

Oh, please!

Gentlemen, gentlemen, this is no way to channel our efforts towards consensus. Father Frank, please, I invite you to say a word to this gathering.

Thank you, Mr. Mayor. Citizens of all confessions, we are all aware of certain dissensions among us, but let us remember that *our* Church has always spoken the truth and we never blamed anybody for any unfortunate happenings. Our Church too has suffered structural damage quite recently, it was also in the media, and the crack that appeared in the exterior wall has widened and is now affecting the structural integrity. We did not blame anybody. Our investigations, with the collaboration of Mr. Popp and a group of geologists and geophysicists, are making progress, although we have not reached a conclusion yet, since the tectonic characteristics of The Valley are extremely stable. No earthquake can be suspected and, at the same time, no *criminal human factors*, as was mentioned here, can be suspected either. Engineers have confirmed the soundness of the construction plans and established that the crack has no architectonic explanations. It is, so far, a mystery.

Thank you, Father.

We are all Jonahs in the belly of a huge whale.

Thank you, Father.

Let us repent and pray for peace.

Yes, thank you, Father. Umm, yes, that is good advice. My beloved citizens, we need to remain calm until the investigations come to an end. I promise that my administration will provide a timely report and we will find the necessary resources to undo the damage suffered by the two churches, umm, establishments.

Well said, Mr. Mayor, Bravo.

My friends, no need for applause, it is our duty to serve our community well. Thank you all for coming.

Chapter 15
Stake-out after significant heavy purchases

Tim, over here. She waves at me and rings the bell on her bike.

We cross the park. She still has a good lead, her wheels spit gravel and dust. You must keep up, she says. Light is shredded into fringed rays through the spokes. We are chasing spooks in East Berlin, everything morphs into a black-and-white film, punctured by editing marks and clapperboard jaws, sound booms visible in an imperfect take, Everybody from the beginning, take five, take nineteen eighty-nine, the wall is behind us, the sentries watch us through the rifle scopes, passersby in grey trench coats drag their feet impassively, grey taxis slow down and do not honk when we cross the street, because honking is illegal and subversive, the baker shows his license to two officials in uniforms, we furrow the sea of extras, the director yells, Cut!, reality washes its face and regains color.

We pedal down the road for a minute and stop across the street from a hunting gear store. We see the black sedan of The Quiet Boy's father, The Lawyer. The Lawyer comes out of the store with significant heavy purchases, looks left, looks right, then throws the stuff in the trunk. He drives off slowly.

We follow him at a safe distance.

He stops in the back of a Turkish restaurant, where he meets somebody.

It's Gregoire, the ice cream man.

The Lawyer gives Gregoire one of the heavy bags, and they shake hands. After The Lawyer leaves, Gregoire writes something on the back of his hand with a ballpoint pen. Then drives off in a different direction. We follow him.

He seems involved in something more than selling cold sweets to children, I say.

You think?, she asks me.

We stop at his house, not far from the exit sign at the edge of Town. He parks his old truck on the driveway, with the back towards the garage, unloads the stuff quickly and shuts the door behind him. A minute later, we hear the sharp loud noise of a circular saw. We decide to tie our bikes to a pole some distance from his house and wait until nightfall.

Chapter 16
Scenery with purple sun at dusk

The Quiet Boy did not get out of his room the whole day. He watched birds from his window, then the local news on his small television. With a magnifying glass, he looked at faces of Middle Eastern people in an atlas, then circled them with a red marker. He didn't hear when his mother called him to lunch, but he did hear when his father came home and dropped the bags on the floor. His mother raised her voice and asked the father in a loud rhetorical tone if he thought that bringing those things in the house every other day was a good example for the children. The father did not say anything and everything went quiet for hours. Later in the day, The Quiet Boy opened the window and watched the purple sun at dusk.

Chapter 17
Clear juxtaposition of the good and the bad

Behind us, the purple sun is melting the horizon into a stew of earth and air. Iris is listening to her radio, at low volume. I take the binoculars from her and I zoom in on Gregoire's house. Sparks are jumping from the circular saw.

What's he doing in there?, she asks.

I can't see. He's cutting some metal. He's wearing a welder's mask.

What's that blue light?

It's the TV upstairs. I think his cable got disconnected.

What's he doing now?

He's pouring a thick liquid into a metal can. Or some powder. I don't know.

I want to see.

The window is too dirty and too small.

Let's go there.

Tim, don't!

She turns off the radio.

Stay here. Watch the bikes, I say.

I cross the street. The last light bulb on a street pole burns out. I tiptoe by his car and stop under the garage's window, on the side of the house. I feel my heart hitting my chest. I smell formaldehyde and the stench of sulfur, with gasoline and some organic material. I put my back against the wall. An electric pulse passes through my spine as the wall melts and warps itself around me.

I seep into the brick wall as through an oozy placenta, tumbling into an enormous uterus, with light inside, bright and blinding. I am in my white room. Gregoire is fiercely cutting buckshot shells with the rotor saw and collecting the powder in a jar. On the wall I see a map of The Valley, The Mountains, red pins marking the entrance to the old coal mines. He is building something, doesn't really mind me. How did he get in here, what was that smell, the whole Red Army could choke in here, I hope he didn't touch my violin or my microscope, how did he get in here, he stops the rotor saw, raises a bullet between his eyes and the light on a hook, How did you get in here?, he asks without turning at me. It's my room, I mumble. Your room, he chuckles. I'm going to have to kill you. Why? Do you know what I'm doing here? Not really. Do you think I am a figment of your imagination? Do you think this is the tunnel to the afterlife? This is *not* the tunnel to the afterlife, this is *my* garage! Ha!

Iris pulls me back roughly. He heard us, she whispers. Let's go, Tim, what's wrong with you?

Nothing, he's in my room.

What are you talking about? It's his garage. Let's get out of here.

We run across the street, while Gregoire drops a toolbox on the floor and swears in French. We don't look back. There was nothing to see. Iris's calm face tells me that he is not following us.

Chapter 18
Until the owl reigns over our hearts

Never so dark were the night sky's stars covered with tar and soot. Grasshoppers bump into each other like drunk coalminers after a day's work and a night's soak in cheap rum and noisy drums in the local decrepit bars, a car illuminates the path in front of us, we follow the trail of fresh air to the gardens down the road, we don't look back, there is nothing to be seen, we ride together, nighthawks estranged from their nests.

Let's stop for a while, she says. She is gasping, she needs air. We sit on the grass and watch the fat yellow moon. She turns on the radio. Bach's Cello Suite No. 1 is playing.

What is he building in there?, she asks.

I don't know, but I'm sure it's not a playhouse for the children.

We remain quiet until an owl takes courage and launches a midnight love call.

Chapter 19
The descent of authority into a field of alacrity

The Mayor woke up early the next day. On his way to the office, he called his secretary from the car to tell her he was stopping on the way, because people were blocking the road.

At the other side of the large group, The Lawyer crushed a cigar stub on the asphalt under the sole of his shoe and collected the excess saliva in a navy cotton napkin. From the back seat of his car, The Quiet Boy saw a vein in his father's temple, pulsating. The Lawyer got in the car, opened the glove compartment, took out his practice revolver, laid it on the seat next to him, then searched for the cigar case. He opened the case with his right hand while rolling his left thumb on the flint wheel. He saw his son in the rear mirror and exhaled a prolonged *oh*, he put out the fire, inhaled smoke thirstily and delivered a whole sentence: I'm sorry son, the camels have gone the wrong way.

On the other side of the mob, The Mayor would not use the term *camels* to describe the Muslim citizens who brandished signs ranging from We love our town to What is ours is ours. Nor he would use the term *yids* to define their Jewish counterparts, who occupied the other half of the road. Nor he would utter the word *toad* to refer to the unknown hand that launched an egg against his windshield, perhaps not knowing who was in the car, despite the tumult around him. The Mayor kept an undisturbed demeanor, lowered the window and called Father Frank by name, who has been watching the scene bewildered, and asked him what was happening, although he already had a pretty darn good idea of what was going on.

They stopped in front of the Mosque, inflamed and determined, Father Frank said.

Has there been violence?

No.

Who organized this?

Apparently Imam and Rabbi are having talks about it.

Good, good.

God help us.

The Mayor stopped the engine and asked Father Frank to watch the car. Who knew what impulsive teenagers might do when swept by waves of electrified crowds? He made his way through the demonstrators, some said, Mayor!, and, Make room!, some didn't, some yelled, Justice!, some yelled, Go home! Finally he met the leaders in the center, in the shade of a mobile crane that was holding the stray pillar from the Mosque at a low angle. The two leaders said, Mayor, and the Mayor said, Gentlemen, but they did not shake hands. The Mayor told them that it was not necessary for the mobs to block the road and that he was sure that these minor divergences can be defused at the table of open and honest negotiations. Imam immediately retorted that the time of talks has passed and that his community will not tolerate injustice and impunity. Rabbi raised his hand and fluttered documents. The law is with us, history has spoken, he uttered with pride. The mob echoed his brief declamation with cheers, a few clenched fists and many pointed fingers. The Mayor tried to hide his discomfort, and made a gesture of friendliness by laying one palm on each of the leaders' backs. He was refused with defensive body language.

Very well, he said, let us carry on the talks in my office.

We have talked about this, Imam said. It is time for action.

Rabbi agreed with this statement and retorted, Imam, your community will have to stop the insults.

While both crowds hailed their leaders' utterances, The Mayor stepped between the two and suggested a truce: This uproar will not benefit Town, tourists will choose other destinations. Gentlemen, we have just opened a new wing at the Golf Club, and, let's face it, both your communities invested in it.

Under the pressure of this revelation or, better said, the reaffirmation of an economic reality that, behind the conspicuous divergences, unifies opposing parties in a common interest of self-preservation, both leaders agreed with The Mayor's suggestion. They turned to their respective supporters. Soon the mobs dispersed and the street traffic calmly resumed.

Chapter 20
Remember the time of the tossed dime

Breaststrokes cleave the water. I count them methodically as I advance in the middle lane of the pool, a soft sensation of wool reminds me of the days when Grandma used to let me play with the cats, tie plastic mice to their tails or hold them in my lap while we watched the rain dripping on the window, while she soaked laundry in chlorine, chlorine that fills my nostrils in the pool, twelve laps to go, Dad blows his whistle each time I touch the wall, Keep it strong, Tim, you can do it, you're five seconds under, come on, come on, My thighs burn, my cheeks burn, Dad, Come on, Tim, you're a sprinter, focus, focus, Father, I have a cramp, I can't, I can't go on, I need to stop, Tim, son, are you okay?, I can't move, Dad, Lie on your back, son, use your arms, I can't, Hold on, son, No dad, don't jump into the water, you'll drown, Dad, Nooo!

Breakfast's ready, mom announces calmly.

I don't open my eyes, but I can see omelettes floating in my room, I can taste my own dormant alpha waves, they're like my Dad's aftershave, I can hear him by my bed, talking about his favorite artist, Salvador Dali, and the elephants with elongated thin bony legs. Why are the clocks melting, Tim?, Because time is an illusion, Precisely, son, precisely.

Tim, are you up?, mom asks.

Yes son, are you up?, I don't know, Dad. My brain is playing tricks with my self-awareness. Son, your brain is your consciousness, but your consciousness is not your brain. Now, get up, Mom is waiting.

I'm coming, Mom.

Chapter 21
Immersion into the birth of a political necessity

What stays still will turn into movement. It's only a matter of energy, Mr. Popp taught us. What moves will become inert, when energy sucked from the matter will seep into another dimension. What would reality be or look like if we had ten-dimensional optical nerves? Would we see the sparks of electricity between approaching fingertips, the surge of chemicals in a kiss, the pull of gravity on each cell, or our invisible fathers watching over us?

We jump on the bikes. Iris turns the radio to the max.

On the road, we pass a few cars, all moving in the same direction, in a silent procession, drawn by a loudspeaker that was delivering a passionate speech in a hoarse voice. We cannot make out the words. I exchange a glance with her. I think it's him, she says.

We stop where the crowd thickens. There were about fifty people present, all facing the fountain. On the narrow rim, the speaker stands and gestures imperiously.

His veins are pulsating, his eyes are oversaturated with blood.

Chapter 22
He spoke to the crowd

The Lawyer's veins were pulsating, his eyes were oversaturated with blood. From a makeshift podium he spoke to the crowd gathered in the square.

We want to see Town Hall shake itself out of complacency and move forward. We want to see The Mayor begin his work and not stop at the first confrontation. We want our streets free from any attempt at usurpation. We want our freedom unaltered, not sundered by petty material interests or wrapped in religious exclamations.

My good citizens, I declare before you, today is the birth of change. Change for the unification of our souls, our desires, our scope. Change for the reaffirmation of our grand past, and our grand future. It is time to end conflict and alleviate the pain of the quiet and the marginalized.

We need to govern our Town as one body. We feel that we have the right and the obligation to do so. Our Town is a constant point of friction between certain communities. It is one of the places where the principles upholding the right of small groups to self-preservation are put to the test, day by day, minute by minute.

The whole problem of coexistence among our peoples boils down to the wrongful appropriation of other peoples' wealth. A great man once said, End the philosophy of plunder and the philosophy of war will be ended as well.

Change, my friends, will free eyes and open them to new horizons.

The time of the hyenas, jackals and cowardly wolves is gone. The challenges we face are real. We must choose hope over fear, and unity of purpose over conflict and discord.

Our communities of Christians and Muslims, Jews and the few Hindus in East Town, and certainly, last but not least, the many quiet nonbelievers, many of whom are gathered here, will move together to bring prosperity and happiness back to our lives.

My good citizens, join me! For change!

The crowd burst out into a delirious ovation. From nowhere, a platoon of volunteers mingled with the people and distributed flags and pins with the words Change on them. Is The Lawyer running for mayor?, some asked. But most didn't even care. They always liked the strong presence of the most successful lawyer in town and they believed he can be a good leader. He doesn't want to be a leader, a mother argued, he wants us all to get involved to stop the partisan interests.

That mother might be right.

Iris took Tim to the old oak tree, whose thick trunk can easily conceal their presence. They saw Gregoire, orange sunglasses that keep a reddish toupee combed back, as he too mingled with the crowd. He approached The Lawyer and shook hands with him.

Gregoire left the throng. They follow him at a safe distance. The ice cream truck was parked a few blocks away. He hushed a pack of kids lined up to get ice cream. I ran out of cream, he said bluntly and nudged his way through the disappointed sweets lovers. He turned the engine on and within seconds was out of sight.

Chapter 23
War and peace and it looks like this

Mrs. Tolstoy, your son suffers from an unusual form of delusional disorder, he has frequent disconnections from reality, although he might seem normal to everybody else for certain periods of time of different random lengths, caused by sudden chemical imbalances in the thalamus, he is transposed to different worlds, with different rules, where even the physical environment appears altered to his perceptions, yet do not cause him any harm, unless there is a strong emotional connotation to the ongoing delusion, which may happen sometimes if the stimulus has reference to a trauma in the past. And, while all this lasts, Tim might present symptoms of psychosis to the observers, as you, I am confident, have noticed in your home.

Yes, he thinks that reality around him is melting, Mrs. Tolstoy said.

Precisely underlining my diagnosis, this so-called *melting* is indubitably a fabrication of his imagination, and I have yet to determine if it causes any psychological damage, but for that I shall require the boy's presence here for a thorough examination for possible physical transformations his body might endure. Moreover, I have been told that he is frequently in the company, a girl, right? How old is she?

His age.

The companionship he has with her, from what we have discussed here, in our sessions, Mrs. Tolstoy, seems and is, as matter of fact, beneficial. He might have a special bond with the girl, Iris, that even at this early stage can bring some balance to his tumultuous inner experience. We need to keep an eye, though, on the developments of this relationship, because we do not know much about the girl's maturity level and need a deeper understanding of your son's condition.

They are good friends.

Precisely, which enforces my thoughts and my keen interest in finding a good and speedy amelioration of Tim's ailment, under careful and precise scrutiny, also considering the recent developments and agitation in our Town that do not help him at all, not that they might aggravate the circumstances, but they might increase the chances of seizures and, god forbid, even the incipiency of more grave illnesses, such as autism or — the list is long, mind you.

I understand, doctor, Mrs. Tolstoy said.

Mrs. Tolstoy, my action plan is to see Tim at his and your earliest convenience before the stress level around him rises.

Thank you, doctor.

My pleasure.

Chapter 24
Gasification of the instincts of preservation of life

Weeds growing rampantly on a neglected roadside exhale a rancid odor, violently deep into our nostrils, squeezed into an anvil of curiosity that pushes towards the mines and a twilight fear that pulls us back. What if he's a serial killer?, we think, pedaling on the trail of Gregoire's ice cream truck. The mines are maybe a mile away. I smell hay mixed with vinegar and a trace of pulverized vanilla. The sun casts a purplish light over The Valley, my pulse is throbbing in my belly, an ant is crawling on my fingers. The road is steep, the climb is hard, what is an ice cream man doing in this derelict landscape, and what was he building in his garage? Crows in rows cross the forest then over our heads launch raids on squirrels down in The Valley. We are almost there, and it seems that somebody is signaling us with a flashlight. He's seen us! No he hasn't, it's the truck, Iris says. Stuck in mud near a pile of petrified timber, headlights on low beam facing the entrance to the mines.

The Mountain roars like a beast in pain, bangs and drilling noise echoes from the depths, though the mines have been deserted for decades, after the big accident when many perished, few have returned to dig up the last diamonds. Legend has it they were buried alive in a pouch of sulfur.

Chapter 25
Blood dripping from his palms

Tim's hand is marble-white. He's shivering.

We advance through the bushes, towards the big hole in the rock.

He's burying corpses, I say.

No, he's not. Turn off the radio, Tim tells me.

Tim is watching my mouth closely, checking my earlobes in quick glances when he thinks that I cannot see, but I can. His nose is bleeding. I wipe the blood off his snowy lips. Are you okay?, I ask him.

The thin air, the steep climb, the thrill of danger.

We've gone too far, he says.

No we haven't, I say.

How do you know?

There is blood dripping from his palms. We stop near a bundle of prickly cocklebur shrubs.

Are you hurt?, I ask.

No, I'm fine, he says.

There's blood on your hand.

It's from the cockleburs. It's just dirt, see.

Jesus.

Tim, there's a wound under the patch of blood.

I'm fine.

You're sweating, Tim.

I'm freezing.

The mines spit waves of warmth in clouds of dust with stench of chemicals and burnt organic material. What is he doing in there?

Chapter 26
Diamonds pierce the plot sharply

I wind the crank of my combo radio and the flashlight comes to life. I put it down and help Tim clean himself. Wounds that look like they were made by the blade of a dagger squeezed in clenched fists.

We enter the mine.

The wooden beams are rotten and charred. The narrow rail tracks are covered in a thick layer of dust and rust. If it hadn't been for Gregoire's footsteps, we wouldn't even have noticed them.

He used a wagon. Footstep marks. We can hear ourselves breathing. Tim is relaxed. He is holding my hand.

We are past the range of the truck's headlights. For a moment, tomb silence settles in. Then a gush of ascending air current sweeps coal dust into our faces. Seconds later, there is a thud, like the implosion of a submarine. Tim squeezes my hand.

The mines were a working colony, he says, wiping the soot off his face. They were abandoned when the engineers realized that the soil was becoming softer and water was seeping from the ceiling. They went back to the maps and soon they figured out they were digging under The Lake. Fearing that the tunnels might collapse, they ordered everybody to come out immediately, but the order could not be carried to the farthest corners of the mines. The tunnels collapsed that morning. Many men were trapped inside. Some returned weeks later, allegedly to find survivors. Everybody knew they were all dead. They came back for something else.

What?, I ask.

Diamonds, he says.

Chapter 27
The light at the other end of the quiet telescope

The Quiet Boy knew that, when the door of the office was cracked open, his father was not at home. The mother would not hear him tiptoeing in the hallway. She is concentrated on a huge pile of documents in the kitchen. His sister might hear his steps, but she won't understand why her brother is tiptoeing. The Quiet Boy was drawn by the grandeur of the office. Large room, paneled in massive oak, with meticulously sculpted bookshelves, a Bösendorfer piano, a large bucolic painting by some Rubens imitator, the globe fluorescent in the dark, the enormous desk loaded with papers, monochrome legal encyclopedias and, finally, the corner cabinet, heavy as a bull, unbreakable for those who don't know that the key is under the gargantuan leather chair, in a velvet pocket stapled into the pattern of the fabric. The Quiet Boy hasn't opened the cabinet before, but he has seen his father in the hallway mirror, many times, arranging the precious possessions on the shelves, on hooks, in expensive glossy boxes with expensive locks. The cabinet doors opened slowly. The spotlights turned on automatically. The brass hooks held two shotguns, one sniper gun and one automatic, that The Lawyer has never brought outside the office, as far as The Quiet Boy can remember. He touched the oversized gun sight with the tip of his left finger and traces the shape. He decided to look through it. To do that, he hoisted the gun off the hook and leaned it against the desk. He turned off the spotlights and slid a curtain aside to let the few rays of twilight bathe the room.

There were no moving objects on the street. The Quiet Boy leveled the gun. The telescope magnified the nervures of a leaf on the hood of a parked car. Then he panned across a newspaper, dropped, perhaps unintentionally, on the sidewalk. It was the *Town Chronicle*, with big block letters on the first page: THE BEGINNING OF AN END. The breeze turned the page, and the mundane article that was not grave enough for the frontispiece of public attention, became illegible to the magnifying power of the telescope. The *Town Chronicle* was swept by the breeze into four walking legs, two on high red heels, two in a black cowboy boots. The Quiet Boy tried to lock in the faces, but they swiftly disappeared into a poorly lit alley. He found instead a squirrel, crossing between two houses on a wire with a nut in its mouth. The Quiet Boy pulled the trigger.

Chapter 28
Ocular cavity filled with lead

The air is getting thicker very quickly. We cover our faces with the shirts. We are definitely not alone. Somewhere, farther down in the gut of the mines, somebody is shoveling and whistling a marching song, taking a break for couple of seconds, then the thud, then whistling again. Iris winds the crank of her radio. It creaks too loudly. The shoveling and whistling stop.

I close my eyes.

I think of bright enormous supernovae, transparent and incredibly hot, scrupulously cut and polished by a galactic jeweler, they turn into gigantic nails that pierce my palms, my feet, my temples, and space becomes a neuronal claustrophobic concept, metal leeches in a spongy void, where the predicament of fury lingers. It betrays the matter, its shivers make the transition of forces into arks, and Noahs into Joans of Arc. It is cyclical, it returns into space, back into the future that does not exist because time is an illusion, yet we are full of hope because it is our sole refuge, our second neuronal concept where the conscience takes a vacation, depriving us of the unity of reason with matter. And we realize in the end that it cannot get less emotional, less chemical than this.

Chapter 29
First drop of blood of hope

Thursday, July 27th

Diary, today I had the first drops of blood. It was warm and I didn't feel any pain. Mom said it came a bit late but it is still within normal parameters. I have to check the tampon every hour for leaks. My breasts itch and my belly is filled with thousands of tiny volcanoes. When Tim grabs my hand, he blushes, but he doesn't know that my whole body shivers in anticipation of an eruption of magma.

I must say one thing about Tim. Sometimes when he is near me, I feel that he's really absent, caught in one of the black holes in his universe. But sometimes when I'm alone in bed, listening to the radio, I feel his fingers walking on my belly and around my navel, like thirsty travelers in a desert, around a well, then I feel his palm covering my flower and a soft finger exploring the petals and that magic spot and everything seems to turn into an ocean of fires. He glances at me, disguised in the heart of the eye of my heart, looking at his heart that smiles at me and follows the contour of my heart with the whole thousand fingers of his heart and he kisses me with the mouth of his heart on the mouth of my heart, and the whole bodies of our hearts unite in a singular flow of low pulsations and a pulsar between our bellies make babies and blood awaken.

I need to check the tampon. Hold on.

There is a slow thin thread. I don't feel pain.

Tomorrow we are going to the mines. Tim thinks the ice cream man buries human bodies there.

Chapter 30
A big gush of fresh air fills our lungs and empties our hearts

At the end of the tunnel, from behind a big pile of stones, light comes at us in flickers. Gregoire is there. Thuds have stopped and are replaced by scrapes. He is heaving heavy objects when the whistling stops and is replaced by sighs of effort. His body casts an elongated shadow on the walls, like a hunchback. He is coming out.

I tell Iris to turn off the light. I can feel her hands sweating. We hide in the dark, our backs against the wall, our faces made of coal, our lungs and hearts made of soot. We close our eyes, so he cannot see the whites. All cats are the same in the guts of the dark. He emerges from the pile of stone with a corpse on his shoulders. She wants to shriek, I cover her mouth with my hand.

My wounds are healed, I say.

What?, she whispers through tears.

My wounds are healed, I tell her again.

She covers my mouth with her hand. Gregoire dumps the body in the wagon with a thud. We realize there are other bodies piled in the wagon. He stops and turns the light towards us, pans the walls, over our heads, then scrutinizes the far end of the tunnel. Then he throws tarpaulin over the bodies, props his heels against a rock and shifts the wagon. He climbs into it and pushes a lever. An engine roars, and the wagon starts moving. We pull our feet off the tracks just before the smelly load passes by. A dead hand, sticking out of the pile, with no nails, mummified, dehydrated, moves in front of our faces. The stench reminds me of Gregoire's garage, the tools he uses, the rotor saw, the workbench, his collection of blades, his smirk as he looked into my face, the rotten teeth, scruffy hair and lumberjack hands. I can see on Iris's face the same question, Where is he taking those bodies. We don't utter a word.

We advance, the ground becomes muddy, and the walls seem to cry. Bent by the weight of The Mountain, they let streams of water gush out. The rocky beast is awakening and bleeding. Pieces of rock break off and fall on the tracks, spraying dirt. A loud implosion signals the collapse of a gallery. The vibration spreads through the granite, dislodges more material and sends a wave of black water rushing below our knees.

What is happening?, she yells.

He's blowing up the mines, I say. There is no exit in sight. We stop for few seconds and wait for Iris to wind the crank. The water is dirty and viscous. It barely flows, and doesn't have enough strength to hamper us. We fight for air with every step and soon we smell a hint of the night forest and hear a lonely nighthawk circling The Valley. We come out of the mine under a pitch-dark sky.

There are no stars, and the moon is on the other side of The Mountain. The ice cream truck is gone. The water comes out of the mouth of the mines in a steady flow, a rivulet of black sap of soot and coal and pieces of wooden beams, wiping away the tire tracks. We rush to catch them before they are completely gone, and follow them to the place where we left the bikes.

The bikes are gone.

Chapter 31
The light will be bent at MacGuffin's tavern by the gravity of an inconsistent prism

The Lawyer pulled the car on the gravel in the Golf Club parking, turned off the engine and lit a cigar. He turned up the volume on the radio. He liked particularly this fragment of Bach's Brandenburg Concerto No. 4. The first puff of Cuban smoke touching the windshield coincided with the sound of another car pulling into the next parking spot. A maroon Golf, with one fender in gray paint. The driver wore a red cardigan with a stylized Che

Guevara portrait on it. His hair was combed, his face shaved, nails cut and clean. It was Gregoire.

The two men nodded at each other. Gregoire walked into the Golf Club and took a seat in a booth. The Lawyer followed a minute later, after he dropped the cigar near the gutter and crushed it with the sole of his shoe.

What do you have for me, Gregoire?

I have removed the last artifacts from the mines.

What is the production?

I haven't opened them. There has been an unforeseen delay.

Gregoire stopped talking as the waitress put the two whiskey glasses in front of them. He pulled out of the jacket a purple box and positioned it between them in the middle of the table. He covered it with his big hand and took a sip.

I found two bicycles on The Mountain. They followed me.

Who followed you, Gregoire?

The kids.

What kids?

Those kids from school.

The Lawyer emptied the glass of whiskey and put down the glass slowly. He weighed his words carefully.

Gregoire, I do not want an unfortunate series of events to jeopardize my endeavors. There is no need to remind you of your legal status in this country and the means by which you can carry on your life and business in Town. You will have the share of profits, as we discussed. Do not let me down. What is in the box?

I need an advance!

A bead of sweat rolled down Gregoire's temple.

What is in the box?

The Lawyer grabbed the box from the inert hand.

It's empty, Gregoire. Three days. I want to see this full in three days.

Gregoire bottomed-up the whiskey and wiped the sweat off his face.

Three days, Gregoire.

The Lawyer unfolded a bill and put it under the glass. He pushed the box to Gregoire's chest, showed him three fingers, then exited the Golf Club very slowly.

Chapter 32
The interpretation of a flying submarine

The Psychiatrist lowered his voice and looked at Tim's face intensely.

Tim, close your eyes, breathe deeply, slowly, thoroughly, feel the weight on your eyelids, go to your little imaginary place, sit down, stretch your arms, engage your soul, relax, you are entering a profound, unfathomed trance, deep dance of images, relax, relax. Where are you?

Father is loading the boat with fishing gear. I'm standing by the car and loading film into the camera. Come on, Tim, let's rock and roll. I'm coming, Father. I jump into the boat and he pushes off and jumps in after me. Grab a paddle, boy, you're a big man now. Wasn't I a big man already, when I caught that big fish?, A man must prove himself at all times, he says. We paddle in the milky mist that hovers over the waters like peeling skin after a sunburn. The Lake is packed with trout. They swim in dense groups underneath the boat, hit it nonchalantly and come recklessly close to the surface. Stop, son. A heart-wrenching silence. The mist clears, just enough so we can see the trees on the shore. Father, why did we stop? We pass the fish bank. Father doesn't say anything. His face is sober like on the day of my first violin lesson. Chin up, straighten your spine, posture, posture. Give me your hand. He takes my hand and puts it on his heart, over his brown leather jacket. This is your future, Tim, he says. Then I see his last smile. Then the blood on his hand, gushing from the exit hole. The, water, is, cold, is crushing my skull. I slip, needles, thousands pierce my skin, Tim!, he shouts. My thighs burn, my cheeks burn, Father, Come on, Tim, you're a sprinter, focus, focus. Father, I have a cramp, I can't, I can't go on, I need to stop, Tim, are you okay?, I can't move, Father, Lie on your back, son, use your arms! The second bullet enters Father's left temple and exits through the right. The impact throws him in the water. I'm trying to swim.

Yes Tim, you swim. How do you swim?, The Psychiatrist asked.

I—

Breathe, Tim. Slowly. Tell me how you swim.

I swim around the boat. When I get there, he's gone. I can't move. I dive as fast as I can. He's gone. I could've, I could've—

Tim, who shot your father?

I could have dived earlier!

Who shot your father, Tim?

A gush of wind sneaked into The Psychiatrist's office through the cracked window, but it is not a random gush of wind. Somebody with an acute sense of atmospheric pressure would know that the sweaty pressurized air comes from the marching crowds that advance on the street, led by The Lawyer, who forms a chain of bodies across the pavement. His voice is powerful enough to draw the doctor's attention. He walked back to Tim from the open window.

I will snap my fingers and you will wake up, The Psychiatrist said.

Chapter 33
The clash of civilizations and the martyrdom of the metaphor

Rabbi's group was occupying the whole width of the southern stretch of the road. The local police have closed the traffic along their route and officers are watching closely, as the chief instructed. They were standing passively at crossroads with their fists clenched on rubber batons. The marching groups thickened with every dozen steps they take. People joined from the sidewalks, walked out from buildings after they waited patiently behind curtains for the right moment to come out with fresh painted banners, Justice for All, Today Is Our Day and some more daring, such as Death to Terrorists, Ban the Turban or even Mosque Grotesque in gothic script over a picture of the Mosque with the broken pillar morphed into the unicorn of a mephistophelian creature.

The group was made of few hundred solid adherents. Within minutes they entered Town Hall Square. Rabbi sent a boy named Simon to take a shortcut through the back alleys and check things out on the other side. Simon took a path only known to him and only suitable for his slim body. Through the crack in Ms. Kaczynski's plywood fence, then behind the garden house, up to its roof, then swinging on a branch and a leap on Mr. Strauss's garage, tiptoeing so the bulldog Levi doesn't hear him, crossing the unkempt garden of the neighbor whose name and appearance is a mystery to the community because he never comes out of the house and if it weren't for the TV light at night, everybody would think he'd died, Maybe he's dead, thought Simon and imagined a scene where two police officers break down the door and find a skeleton in front of an analogue TV with a static image and power cord plugged into a programmable outlet, buried in a pile of bills and flyers and cobwebs and putrefied cat food. Simon closed his eyes for a second and shook his head, trying to get rid of this macabre scene. He almost smacked his head against the rusty marquee. He cut his way through the lilac bushes and wound up in the middle of the Muslim crowd.

Imam's nephews did not recognize Simon, although they should have, because they used to play hide-and-seek every afternoon, until the little Muslims reached an age when excuses for forgetting about the mandatory prayer time were no longer accepted. So they lost contact and forgot each other's faces. Simon needed to keep his mouth shut. He knew that he has something in his voice that would draw the crowd's attention. He elbowed his way to the first lines of the march and then adjusted the pace to that of the others near him. He glimpsed a few banners, Our land is sacred, Insidious Jews back off, We fight, Day of justice, and one in Arabic that could mean Allah is great, judging by what the women who are carrying it yell in the language Simon can understand. He also caught a few sardonic remarks vis-à-vis the Jewish institution to reclaim the land on which the Mosque was built. You will all be judged!, yells a student behind Simon. He felt his heart soaring through his throat and seeking refuge on another planet.

The police improvised a human chain on the sidewalks, between the curious onlookers and the marching crowds. When a hesitant spectator conquered his or her fear, they let him or her join the crowd without asking questions. They have not received any instructions from the chief of police, nor from The Mayor, on how to react if there is a violent outburst. Probably that will not happen, they thought, and the senior officers reviewed in their mind their life experience when they had to confront similar situations. It is not in Town's interest, they thought, to have a civil confrontation. The number of tourists has decreased significantly. They'd better get back to their senses!

The sun cast a penetrating light over Town. Only now, Simon saw the reflection of the sky in the tips of the concealed knives under the white shirts. He also saw some arm-thick clubs, and broomsticks that contributed to the shadows on the asphalt, like heavy lions that lurk in the shadows of the savanna. The mob was two streetlights away from Town Hall. Simon slowed his pace and detached from the group, broke through the line of police officers. He nudged a few reporters without looking back, he did not mean that, he just wanted to bring the news to Rabbi.

The Jewish crowd and their many supporters made the turn on Town Hall Road. Gasping and wiping sweat off his forehead, Simon delivered the information. They have knives and arm-thick clubs, he said. Rabbi didn't look at him. His men came prepared too, Preventively, they would say. If ever asked.

The two crowds stopped in front of Town Hall, facing each other like two massive frowning cowboys with the veins on their necks ready to snap. Cave silence infected the air.

Chapter 34
Psychoanalytical revenge of the digital switchboard

The Psychiatrist pushed the lime-green button on his phone and told his secretary to connect him to the police, because there was somebody with a Molotov cocktail outside. The secretary wondered how a cocktail, regardless of its name, can be a matter for the police, yet she complied, Right away doctor, but she kept other thoughts to herself, while The Psychiatrist continued to tap with a sharp pencil on his mahogany desk, waiting on the phone, doodling on his notepad. Tim got up from the couch, shook off a few chills, wiped his forehead with the back of his hand and walked outside quietly.

Chapter 35
He moonwalks on boiling ice

I walk on you, Antarctic of my melted blood, the veins of iron of my great white polar Ant nesting in my icy dormant humanity, skin peels off my body and reveals an empty shell and a frozen hell, eels send electric signals from across the reality, frugality of hope, banality of the composition of life, decomposition of music into air and strings, No, Father, I have not practiced today, I am sorry, I am sorry, this illusory impulse of saving the cruelties of the past, this guilt of the future through a well-footnoted and documented relativism of time, toss a dime and decide faster which side of the sinking boat you are on, we march but we don't walk, astute and mute we elbow our way through the crowds, we can escape the heavy capes with our own biographies engraved on them, bestowed upon us by the ferocious wizards of the west, and the rest is an empty chest, left behind ajar, in greed, in ignorance, or in pure discontent, by the last tsar with the best intentions for his seed, for the proliferation of his sperm into every single soul that will accept it, because it's guaranteed, because it gives sense to our lives, because it's fail-proof, I can see perfectly the Discobol from my roof, Father, the world is spinning in his hand and we fall into the sun and we'll drown in hydrogen, the Greeks were right, we'll choke on our pride and abnegation and voracious ambition, to build what, to be what, to whet your fedora, sharply and ingeniously looking at the crowds waving, in waves spitting, Father, I have not practiced today, how can I escape the ambitus of causality, Father, why do I want to escape it, my cape is heavy, heaved from a transient awareness, the my room that has no dimensions, no time, no echo. Father, are the knees that I kneel on truly mine?, Are the mines that we crawl into truly hurting the earth, no worries, it's like an indigestion, we dig out diamonds like we pluck kidney stones, like cavemen roll the stones and tame fire, or divinize desire while devouring bears in Stone Age lairs. Father, free me from you so I can learn who I am.

Chapter 36
Realization of the octopus's escape

Where did he go?
I don't know, doctor.
Get me The Mayor on the phone!
Right away, doctor.

Chapter 37
The juvenile front of questionable auspiciousness

The alley where Iris met Tim separated two buildings and had a dead end. It was a brick wall without much purpose, since on the other side it just served as support for billboards or graffiti sneaked at midnight under the feeble streetlight, created in a hurry and left half-done, interrupted by Town Police Patrol or by the presence of a rival graffiti gang. *Paint should not be confused for blood*, it read on the wall, but the crowds that marched on the road could see it, since it was covered with a poster for a renowned alcoholic beverage.

Iris cranked up the radio and heard the same roar that came from behind the brick wall on the alley, while a reporter is explaining with a pompous emphasis on strong adjectives the unfolding of the events.

The opposing crowds have finally met in Town Hall Square. Imam, Rabbi and The Mayor, with their adjutants, lieutenants, counselors and The Mayor were exchanging inaudible dialogue to the rest of the crowd, right on the steps of Town Hall. The Lawyer's supporters were not far away from the scene, as they were making the last steps of their march. In the square, banners and voices were soaring, one higher than the other, contusive sharp objects are brandished, from both sides, juicy vegetables are flying over the leader's heads, some missing their targets, some extremely accurate, vigilance was on everybody's mind, a sense of immediacy seized the hearts, obstructed minds and instructed muscles to contract, to react, to grind the lowest corners of the subconscious, to root out all repressions, to make mouths yell out, Time to act!

Turn down the volume, Tim said.

Okay.

They spotted Gregoire's ice cream truck parked under a poplar with the man at the wheel, the beard, a baseball cap, pair of vigilant eyes, carefully trimmed nails, he was fixing them with a smirk, raised two fingers, preparing to demonstrate a victory sign, but it was not a victory sign, he brought the two fingers to his eyeballs, slowly, then pointed at them, as if to say, I am watching you. He took off down the road, away from them, displaying the two bikes, chained to a bike rack, in the back of the truck.

Let's go, Iris said. She was firm, and so self-confident that Tim felt a natural impulse to obey. They overlooked the possibility of danger, the certitude that Gregoire knew about their presence at the mines, the fishiness of the whole deal with him meeting The Lawyer, the mummified human bodies, the rotor saw and everything else. What the hell, they thought, those are our bikes, we are the rightful owners. They lost sight of Gregoire at an intersection with a sign that was completely eaten away by rust, making its name impossible to read.

People started rushing to Town Hall Square, a group of teenagers agitated spray-paint cans and while they got ready to produce graffiti, they were caught red-handed by a police officer on a motorcycle, leaves being lifted by the pulsation of the streets, crows on light poles, fliers erratically landing on rooftops and balconies and an out-of-service school bus. Tim and Iris made the next turn on the road and walked against the current of people, which became thinner and thinner, owners of convenience stores and tobacco shops turned the door signs over to show the word Closed. They stopped in front of a crying little girl. Where is your mommy, Tim asked and leaned towards her, and her mother appeared from nowhere, grabbed her child, told her, It's okay, baby, and ran away. Iris yelled with a glass-breaking high pitch. Tim turned and saw Gregoire standing behind Iris, his hand on her shoulder.

I believe these are yours, he smirked and threw two bike bells at their feet. Tim kept his composure and his unmoved face and thought that Gregoire's forehead wrinkles looked like a purple canyon seen from the moon through a telescope. Tim unfroze and yelled, Leave her alone!

Iris freed herself and they ran away leaving Gregoire behind growling.

The Synagogue was the closest refuge that they found. They closed the iron gate behind them, rushed inside the building, slammed the heavy oak door, then rushed to the next door and slammed it closed, locked it with a heavy iron key, looked at each other and caught their breaths.

We need to get out of here, Iris said. He knows we're here.

He might. But he did not follow us, Tim said.

How do you know?

Tim didn't know and didn't have time to answer, because the loud, firm knock on the door provided an alternative answer. It might be one that they do not like, or an answer that ransacked their fears and primitive instincts of preservation. Or it might be an answer with no question or no beginning or no end, just like the universe, just like heaven or hell. Another knock, and another, and a bang with the fist.

I'm opening, she said.

She unlocked the door, while the robotic voice on a speech synthesizer on the other side was struggling to utter, Who's in there?

See, it's — Luc, she said.

Luc was Rabbi's aide, the Synagogue's factotum, the best boy of Judaism, as he was praised in a sermon not long ago. Luc wore the speech synthesizer all the time, and he has even forgotten the days before the glass splinters were removed from his larynx. He wore a tag with his name.

Luc closed the Synagogue and ensured them that nobody was inside and that they can use the back door if they wanted to go somewhere else. Luc also ensured them of his hospitality and offered them some Jewish bread. They refused politely and choose to exit through the back door, while Luc wished them in a monotone, Peace-be-with-you, as they smiled back, opened the door and inhaled a strong scent of grass.

Chapter 38
He lies down by the wall that has never been touched

Iris and Tim laid on the grass behind the Synagogue, close to the wall, so nobody on the street can see them. She cranked up the radio. Then she snapped her fingers in front of Tim's eyes, genuinely worried about his lack of focus, or maybe just to tease him. Tim moved his index finger, like a paintbrush, over the elliptical shadow of a satellite antenna on the wall of the Synagogue.

We'd better go, she said, then changed the frequency on the radio.

Chapter 39
The wall must come down

This is not the wall we expect to be demolished by a licensed demolition company or by the circumstances of an armed conflict, at the laser point of a rocket launcher, with a margin of error of such and such distance, depending on the calibration, this is a wall full of nonsense, it blocks an alley, forms a dead end between two imposing buildings, creates unnecessary detours, generates piles of non-recyclable trash and not to mention on one side serves as a meeting ground for subversive human elements and on this side serves as support for the proliferation of consumerism!

The crowd yelled, Yeah!

The speaker was encouraged by this exclamation and continued.

For we cannot linger in an ebb and flow of expeditious happiness and numbness of soul, for we cannot continue to watch through a glass of stone, darkly, as we wrinkle our conscience and crook our backs and diminish ourselves to silence, while divergences splinter our community and petty grievances promote conflict.

We must Change! Change! Change!

Crowbars, claw hammers, mattocks, some light pickaxes emerged from the crowd, and were passed from hand to hand to the front. The perfect synchronicity of movements, the articulation of muscles, cheers and hurrahs in tandem reduced the wall to rubble in a matter of minutes.

Let us rejoice and join and meet our brothers before it is too late.

Swept by words and determination, the crowd continued their march towards Town Hall Square.

Left behind, as an echo in a cave, the speaker stepped down from the bench. The Lawyer, from across the street, made him a sign that many might interpret as a death threat, slicing the throat with four fingers, but looking closer, the speaker realized that it means something completely different.

Chapter 40
A little old lady in a shoe transposes the timeline

Gregoire mumbled, Fuckers, at the direction where the punks have disappeared, and returned to the truck before somebody else could spot him. It is too late for him as well. The Quiet Boy pulled the black sunglasses over his eyes and came out from the hideout with a dose of adrenaline in his blood that made him lose grasp of the passing of time. It has been only a dozen seconds since Gregoire spun on his heels and spat on this very spot. He has seen worse. He has read about the despicable nature of human expectorations and other products of the body. He ignored

Gregoire's odor, which still tarries in the air, picked up the bike bells and stashed them in his knapsack.

The Quiet Boy returned to the hideout and closed his eyes for a second, blew air into his palms and whistled the first notes from Beethoven's Fifth Symphony. This morning he listened to a rendition with the Berliner Philharmoniker while he tapped on his desk with a pen and thought of an old lady, dressed in black, knocking on his door.

He undressed, stepped into the shower and opened his mouth to a stream of hot water. He leaned his palms against the wall and watched his turgid erection with an admonishing look. He poured a whole bottle of liquid soap over his genitals and let the water wash it off without any intervention. The horns invaded his ears, his spine, throughout the scherzo and he released the semen on the bridge of the attacca at the opening of the triumphant fourth movement.

His father had left the house about half an hour ago. There was some agitation on the streets. He knew he had to go too. All major events have a secret observer behind an eyeglass of vigilance or ignorance or coincidence. Neither is more relevant than the other under the cold scrutiny of a systematic analysis of the intertwining of causality and randomness. While reasoning all these statutes of fate, The Quite Boy got dressed quickly and stormed out of the house with three items in his knapsack: the black revolver, the black silencer and the gun-sight telescope.

Chapter 41
The great opening of the uterus with an artificial insemination of consensus

By the time the people reached the schoolyard, the news that the Synagogue has been attacked has reached their ears. What do you mean it cracked?, It cracked open, I'm telling you!, You mean like a contraction when a fetus is ready to pop out?, Yes, it is in the neighborhood of your metaphor, Can you be more descriptive?, Listen, my friend, I know as much as the newscast has conveyed, and I'm surprised they conveyed it that fast, since according to them it only happened just a few minutes ago, The guy, that robo-clerk must have called the reporter, Yeah, might be him, Do you think it's the same people that attacked the other two churches?, What do I know?, I bet some subversive groups are trying to undermine the order in Town, Listen to you, you are now a defense analyst, Do you think a Synagogue clerk with a speech synthesizer can communicate the urgency of such an event with the necessary tone inflections?, True, he must have had an aide, Or the criminals themselves draw the attention of the media, This is also a possibility, Shouldn't we speculate less and check the facts ourselves?, Yes we should, yes we should.

Despite their sympathy for The Lawyer's ideas of change, the two citizens broke free from the group and accelerate towards the Synagogue. On their way, they suddenly had an impulse to go back and let The Lawyer know about what happened, due to his affiliation to that respective ethnicity. But they did not go back, because the subsequent thought is that, He knows already, anyways.

By the time the two citizens reached the Synagogue, a police patrol car, an ambulance and a fire truck already occupied the street, transversely, and a few passersby gathered by the yellow DO NOT CROSS tape. The female reporter was pushed back with firm orders, Please ma'am, it's police BUSINESS, she stepped back, talking incessantly into the microphone because her TV station focused all their resources and attention on her story. Even though she was in a medium shot, the viewers could easily notice her CLEAVAGE, generous as usual, yet this visual aspect did not interest anybody, on the contrary, one could tell from the officer's look that he totally declined the innuendoes, if there are any, or the appeal to his basic instincts, which he could control without any effort at all. The orders were clear, ignoring the few radio static interferences. Nobody crosses until we figure out what the hell happened, as per his boss, the chief of police. The gravity of his boss's voice was an efficient inhibitor for the officer, and he raised the law enforcement baton as a barrier between him and the voluptuous reporter.

The police are determined in securing the area, she said into the microphone. Soon after, another wave of orders flowed through the two-way radios fastened on the muscular shoulders of the police force.

The two citizens managed to find a good vantage point with sufficient elevation opposite the Synagogue. It was not long until a newly arrived sergeant directed the loudspeaker towards them and addressed them with an authoritarian, Hey you!, though not soon enough to prevent them from seeing the damage of the Synagogue: the rear wall reduced to rubble, shingles in disarray, like a battalion without a leader, cracks fanning out onto the lateral walls like cobwebs stretching out as large pieces of concrete continue to fall.

Is it an earthquake?, Nah, I doubt it, See the houses nearby, not a single scratch, the collapse is coordinated, the material was drawn to a single point, see, it doesn't look like demolition, it's more a submission of matter to a greater will.

Chapter 42
Post-relativistic clash of absolutes

The great will, sheer will, the transposition of one's psyche into a class of disembodied pure principles, subsumed to the universal intelligent entity, assumed it is unique, was definitely not a matter of concern for the opposing classes of citizens gathered in the belly button of Town.

Nor did they consider what would constitute the definition of Good, as that something that determines the persistency of life into its autonomous scope, because moral order exists only in the realm of the self-conscious, and if one wishes to impose one's will over another, one must not have a legitimacy of superior power, nor a legitimacy of self-determination or proliferation, but a shared and mutually accepted vision of the continuance of Good, unaltered by the perception of the flow of time.

Suffice it to say that the situation at Town Hall Square was on the fringe of an inevitable clash of human bodies. Seconds dropped into the hungry past like iron balls into an hourglass: heavy, implacable, dense. Imam, Rabbi, Mayor, their lieutenants and Father Frank, who had joined them, were exchanging fierce words and gestures in the hallway of Town Hall. They started the negotiations on the steps outside. As a new argument was brought into the conversation, a step was climbed by the speaker, utilized to emphasize his point. Soon after, the other parties followed, to keep abreast in pace, in stance, eye-to-eye, eye-for-eye, forehead to forehead, at the same elevation from the ground level. So talks have escalated, bounced up by a ballet of passionately crafted phrases, exclamations and gymnastic-diplomatic body-language assertions.

One fist from the dozen present rose suddenly higher than the others. Gentlemen!, The Mayor exclaimed. The fist did not reach its target, but ricocheted into Father Frank's chest and put him on the floor. The Mayor rushed to pick him up, while the lieutenants struggled to hold back their leaders from jumping at each other's throats.

At the same time, Simon managed to break through the feeble line of police officers and snuck inside Town Hall. The lieutenants recognized him immediately and conceded nonverbally to his access to their boss. Simon delivered the message, which petrified his boss's face. After Rabbi's brain revisited all the implications of such news, he blurted out, What the fuck?, which, coming from him, generated the same intensity of terror, if not higher, on everybody else's face, including Simon's. Rabbi added a quick, I'm sorry son. Simon knew what Rabbi meant. He heard this particular statement from his real father on many more occasions than this isolated one, and always lacking the explanatory excuse.

The group broke into pieces like a shoal of fish invaded by a ravenous shark. They did not need to explain much to their respective crowds, the people knew what happened. The people have an instinct of the course of history.

The Jews, infuriated and pushed forward by the loudspeakers, engaged the Muslims through the line of overwhelmed police officers that ended up mashed in the middle.

Chapter 43
Discovery of the impetuous Achilles' heel of the tortoise

What are you waiting for? Do you want your bike back or not?, she asked.

Gregoire's house lies in an apparent air of abandonment. At the edges of the covered windows, a pulse of agonizing light seeps out in tortured waves. He may be home. He may not be home. We hear squeaks, but it might be just the house itself grinding its teeth. And there is this smell of black waters, of rancid soil, of chemicals used to beautify the imminence of decomposition. We glue ourselves to the wall, cloaked in a lilac bush, and peek inside the garage. He is not there.

The lilac bush is growing around us, a giant tortoise around two confused Noahs, reality is pushed into us violently, we crawl into the garage through a small window at the feet of the wall, an old remodeled cat door, the odors morph into the white scent of my childhood, my white room.

Chapter 44
The great escape of the two magi from their invisible capes

What is this escape into another world, contemporaneous and alive in a superimposed space, are we seeking refuge into myths or familiar chambers of the past and bright chambers of the future, what is the white if not the full absorption of light into our souls, the full absorption of owls into the night's bowl of equitable distributed nourishments, to each according to his needs, from each according to his capacity, a reinterpretation of Marx for the sake of the Third World's voice, white ants swarming on our plates, convinced that their world is flat.

I'm thinking out loud, my books are in order, the bed is made, the violin is in its case.

Iris puts a hand on my shoulders and her lips say, What is this?, she repeats it several times, until the words come alive in sound.

She grabs my chin and turns it to a big block of white stone in the middle of the room.

On top of it is a human body under a white sheet of linen.

I put my fist in my mouth, she screams. We spot the bikes, thrown in a corner, and we dash at them. Very soon fear penetrates our spines, like a syringe, we muffle our lungs into a tense brittle silence while a loud bang thunders on the door.

Then silence.

Then a thud on the door with a heavy boot.

A rusty chuckle on the other side of the door.

No words.

Silence.

Mom's voice from the other side, Dinner's ready, Tim, open the door.

Iris's whisper, Don't open the door.

A mummified hand emerging from under the linen and hanging like a pendulum.

Iris's scream.

The pure white walls of my room and their fulgurant light.

A gelatinous membrane between our bubble of air and the depth of a freezing ocean. The membrane opens and we see The Mountain, the sky, flocks of swallows soaring.

We dash out of the room, pedaling ferociously to the mines upwards.

Chapter 45
Noah the Avenger and God the Avenger both claiming the undoing of the Ark into the wood that it was made of

Great floods come with dark skies and great winds.

At first, the mines started to pour out dark waters from The Lake, thickened with soil and remnants of ground coal and rotten wood. During the escalation of the conflict in the little town, the stream grew wider and turned into a dark green molasses, unnoticed, impassive.

Anticipation of fear has a stronger drive than fear itself. It gives the blood a certain tension and enhances the probability of clearer foresight. Anticipation is the last step before the mind crosses the border into the realm of the subconscious. It is the threshold where the range of possible outcomes is the widest, where the uncertainty principle has the most variables in equation, where entropy is at a level where it disgraces all heresies of the order of nature, where volition dissolves in the lentor of the passivity of the intellect and ruptures occur between the willingness to preserve life and the temptation of the warmth of the oblivion in the quietness of a painless, lowly existence.

Iris and Tim took a little-used trail towards the mines, driven by an urge to unveil a mystery, to set things right, to bring the lawless Gregoire to justice. They forced their feet into the pedals like spears into mindless fish that swim into rivulets too close to the shore, branches slapped their wrists, weeds and cockleburs whipped their thighs and tangled in the spokes. They crossed the last meadow, they climbed the last hillock, they stopped on a height that overlooked the entrance into the mines, where Gregoire's truck once stood. The mine spat a gruesome, rapacious stream of water, it shot into the air a scent of soil, of burnt oil and coal, and it roared like The Mountain was regurgitating a whole history of indigestion, of unwanted dreams.

They left the bikes under a big rock.

The old entrance into the mines was compromised. They looked for another one and found it, not far away, almost completely camouflaged under the roots of a once-majestic oak tree, now leaning towards its demise.

You are my hero, Iris said. I don't understand why, Tim said, Do I look like a guerrilla fighter, awoken by an unexpected military insurgency in the middle of the night?, she wiped the fleck of mud off his face and smiled briefly.

They walked into a ventilation shaft, kept their heads low. No wagon rail tracks. Wooden resistance beams, here and there, made the contour of a narrow tunnel used for air circulation and quick escapes for the miners if ever needed, though there are no signs it has been used for the latter purpose. They slogged across the muddy ground, the awareness of their own breaths growing as the air thickened and the rumble of The Mountain grew. They heard a violent thud of an implosion. The Mountain was collapsing. They stopped and tried to catch the vibrations in the air, perhaps somebody's voice, perhaps a cry for help, or the shrill of the spirit of the rocks. Another thud and the ceiling cracked open and water started seeping through, thin as a superficial wound, then a little wider, then rocks started to fall and with them a few objects, hammers, chisels, ripped gloves and a leather jacket.

A blow pushed Tim to the ground.

He felt Iris's mouth next to his face. She asked him if he was okay.

I guess, he said.

They rushed out of the mine as The Mountain was spitting jets of water, furiously. The mine was spewing water in powerful waves, untamed armies of liquid earth. The meadows, the forest, the cockleburs, the solitary boulders were being consumed in the voracity of the flood. The water poured down towards The Valley, leveling the scenery into a uniform palette of flowing deadly shapes that covered everything.

Chapter 46
The descent of man into the dead valley

Their mouths frozen and their bodies liberated from fear, magnetized by the determination to get to Town. They avoided the stream, but didn't have a lot of alternative trails. The Mountain was steep, the sharp edges of the rocks above frowned at them in contempt. They were mere steps above doom. They continued their descent in silence.

The trail ended at a massive monolithic rock, impassible and cold. There was no way around it. Going back felt like a knife into their hearts. They looked at each other, then they looked at the tumultuous newborn river, which was calmer, but still reigned over The Valley, undisputable ruler of the faiths and lives of the helpless.

We go with the flow, Tim said with a flat voice.

They spotted the trunk of a fallen tree, floating a tad askew on the river, close to them. Its very shape, like an enormous slingshot, gave them confidence that if they rode it, it won't turn over. They took a position close to it, adjusting for the pace, wetting their ankles. Iris slipped and her leg got stuck in the mud, waist-deep in water. She screamed. Tim jumped on the log and tried to pull her out. He failed. Their hands, connected, stopped the heavy log in place and changed its course for a moment. He jumped into the water, closed his eyes and dipped his head. Blindly, he searched for her foot. He found it, but could not release it, not like that, not with his eyes closed, not with his lungs almost empty, not with his father's voice in his ears, Chin up Tim, straighten your spine, posture, posture. Tim straightened his spine. He let his hand follow the voice and grabbed a shoelace in the darkness and pulled it vigorously. She was free. They jumped on the stump and spat out water and leaves.

The river carried them placidly towards Town.

Chapter 47
Tubular encapsulation of fatalism, randomness and well-tempered eagerness of the acknowledgement of the fetus

Two hours before the great regurgitation of the waters of The Lake, the aquarium at the Golf Club had fewer visitors than usual, but it was still open, despite the fact that turmoil was engulfing Town. Before it all started, Gregoire was instructed by The Lawyer to go to his job and to look normal, casual, distant.

Listen Gregoire, the time has come, The Lawyer said. I can't wait any longer. Whatever they do, there will be blood. I want you to lie low until all this clears. I want my diamonds. Diamonds, Gregoire!

Gregoire swore in his mind, and sniffed profusely.

You hear me? Go to the aquarium, make yourself an alibi, do you know what that is? Good. Then you find those kids and find out what they know, you hear me? And if they know, you take care of the problem graciously, quietly, permanently. Good? Good.

Then you go back to the mines and extract everything. I will not spell it out again. Then you will be showing the merchandise to me, tomorrow.

Gregoire had swallowed his pride some time ago, when he came to Town, by means of acquaintances, in conjunction with dubious business relations which led to meeting The Lawyer. He had traded his knowledge about the mines in exchange for the laundering of his dark past. Today he needed to swallow his anger. He punched the mirror in the garage with his bare fist when he gets home. He did not mind the blood. In fact, he watched the blood gushing from his hand and clenched his teeth. Ten seconds later he threw a hammer at the door when he realized that the two bikes have disappeared.

The Lawyer told Gregoire on many occasions that he didn't have vision, he didn't see that far into the future. Gregoire could follow a conversation with his intuition and gauge the direction in which it is going in the next few seconds, but he could not foresee the unwrapping of future events hours in advance. Fuck vision, Gregoire thought. He left a pile of coins on the table and threw in another one when The Lawyer frowned at him and asks rhetorically, You don't tip?

Later in the day, Gregoire dived in the big pool to entertain the guests at the aquarium.

Inside the transparent tunnel, a girl tapped on the thick glass with her doll, imitating a bee that did not understand the concept of transparent solid matter. Gregoire smiled at her and shook his head and his finger, and the girl's mother voiced the instruction, Honey, it's not allowed to tap on the glass. The girl stopped, lowered her chin to her chest and felt ashamed. The neon tubes in the glass floor turned on to compensate for the lack of natural light that the imminence of the sunset was causing. The tour guides turned on their walkie-talkies and seemed to grow more agitated by the second. Following orders from above, the aquarium doors closed immediately. The open enormous pool, which has the glass tunnel through its belly, was covered in less than a minute by the hydraulic retractable lid that protected it from unfortunate precipitations.

The first moments were of sheer confusion. Nobody seemed to know what was happening. The guides passed on conflicting orders. There was a storm coming, some speculated, or, We are closing early. A supervisor with more tact tried to calm them down, knowing this is not a plausible and satisfactory explanation.

The speakers throughout the aquarium and Golf Club blurted.

Attention, attention, attention. We have received an urgent announcement. It is an order to seal our facilities and let no person get in or out.

Mothers pulled their infants closer to them, lovers squeezed hands, lone visitors sought immediate refuge in the nearest group. Everybody fixed their eyes on the speakers, as though a voice from the skies was talking to them.

Attention, attention, attention. There is a grave flood approaching Town.

The silence has never been so deep, so brusque, so smashing.

Chapter 48
Interregnum of objective causality into a manifestation of social monstrosity

The Lawyer returned to his flock to begin the march towards Town Hall Square, a march planned in such detail that at the moment when the Jewish and Muslim crowds will collide, he would intervene with such fortitude and deliver his message of reconciliation with such persuasiveness that the conflict will be instantly defused, all citizens will be enraptured by his presence on the spot, which will allow him to use their undistributed attention to channel their minds to his principles, direction and will.

Sure, he thought is a modern Gandhi, a citizen commented out loud.

The Lawyer dismissed these comments with exercised smiles, impeccable rhetoric and self-sufficient logic. He replied, Fellow citizens, I do not consider myself a Gandhi, or a prophetic pacifier or a messenger of any transcendent authority. Like many of you, I realize the intrinsic human need for peaceful cohabitation and natural right to exercise one's will in the pursuit of happiness and freedom. I never accepted and I shall never accept violent manifestations of oppression nor any other expressions of superiority of one group onto another. My task, our task, is to defuse this counterproductive conflict that emerged from the Jewish and Muslim communities and bring Change to our Town, which will serve a prosperous and peaceful future. Sure, many of you think that I, as a generator of opinion and catalyst of social principles, might be predisposed into assuming a certain political power to channel the realization of such an ambitious project. For the need of efficiency and preservation of the human ways of life, I affirm the necessity of political systematization. Hierarchies, institutions, plans, rules of law are absolutely necessary elements of keeping civilization on top of nature's tendencies towards disorder, anarchy. We march together, we march for change!

Cheers from the crowd, brandishing of flags and bouquets of white roses reinforced the attachment to their leader.

News of the movement of Rabbi's group and Imam's group have reached everybody's ears this morning. They were all prepared, no lingering with unnecessary, pompous words, lack of action, exaggerated introspection of the psyche of the characters is neither needed nor enjoyed at this point by anybody.

Dozens of supporters followed The Lawyer to the center of Town in rhythmic pace and choreographed moves. Their silent advancement raised few eyebrows on the way and few passersby joined the group on the way. They marched by Greogoire's ice cream truck. Somebody saw the two bikes on the rack and told to his friend, I didn't know he had children. The friend shrugged and said nothing.

In front of the crowd, The Lawyer looked impassibly at the road ahead of him. He answered his cell phone a few times and exchanged a glance and a salute with The Psychiatrist, who had interrupted his session with a client to see what was going on the streets.

The streets are veins, souls are blood, the flow of them gives life to Town.

Simon managed to break through the feeble line of police officers and sneaked inside Town Hall. The lieutenants recognized him immediately and conceded nonverbally to his access to their boss. Simon delivered the message, which petrified the boss's face. After Rabbi's brain revisited all the implications of the news, he blurted out, What the fuck?, which, coming from him, generated the same intensity of terror, if not higher, on everybody else's face, including Simon's, to which Rabbi adds a quick, I'm sorry son.

The group broke into pieces like a school of fish invaded by a ravenous shark. They did not need to explain much to their respective crowds, the people know what happened. The people have an instinct of the course of history.

The Jews, infuriated and pushed forward by the loudspeakers, engaged with the Muslims through the line of overwhelmed police officers that ended up mashed in the middle.

Rabbi is pulled outside of the crash by one of the lieutenants. What is it?, Call for you. Who is it?, A very high authority, What?, I think you should take the call, sir, Very well.

Hello, this is Rabbi. Who is this?

Your highest authority, Rabbi. You must listen. Disengage your folk. A tragedy is upon you. Furious waters will hit Town. The big monster will devour the small monster.

Simultaneously, Imam is grabbed by his keffiyeh and advised to go to a quiet place where he could and should take a phone call from a significant authority.

Yes?

Imam, you do recognize my voice?

Imam cleared his throat and gulped a full load of shock.

I do.

Imam, you will stop the fight now. You will take measures for your folk, as nature has reversed her furies upon your Town. The flood is coming, you will all be shattered by the force of destiny.

The fight lasted less than ninety seconds.

Loudspeakers, abrupt orders, adrenaline and instinct cut the crowd into groups that scattered to all possible directions, driven by imminent of death.

The flood stroked a few minutes later.

The wave swept Town Hall Square like a gargantuan broom. Cars, benches, trees thrown at each other with brute force, windows reduced to smithereens, birds forced to soar into the sky with no chance of finding a place to rest soon, humans sought refuge on rooftops, in rooms with no cracks in walls, some managed to climb tall thick trees and even flagpoles.

Water infiltrated basements, underground garages, small shops on main roads, on side roads, filled potholes and drainpipes and gutters, burst into illegal businesses in backyards, leased warehouses or mobile homes used as offices for god knows what cosmetics distribution network, broke into accounting offices and law offices and consulting practices and obliterated thousands of paper records, hundreds of computer hard-drives that were not backed up. It seeped into the nightclub, and cleared shelves of beverages, tables of ashtrays, but did not enter the soundproof private rooms. The owner of the club took special care in creating a perfectly sealed door, for customer convenience and privacy. He installed an efficient air-conditioning system that fed air from the top of the building, not from the polluted street level. It makes a difference, he said, in a commercial scripted interview.

The fury of nature pounced upon the deserted schoolyard, devoured doors and hallways, filled up the empty classrooms at the first floor in seconds with mud, mulch and fish.

Nobody was there.

The bell engulfed in the waters kept hollering the alarm until a vagrant spare tire from an old car smashed it to total underwater silence.

Chapter 49
Preservation of life and passion behind unbreakable steel

The Manager of the Community Bank started the meeting on time. He was the first to take a seat, facing the window. He laid his notebook with the topics of the day on the table. He smiled briefly at the employees, cleared his throat and frowned at the numbers in the report in front of him. He did not say anything. The clerks looked at each other. Some thought this was their last day at work, some thought of The Manager's tie, which was a tad askew, some thought of the sexual encounter that they will have that night with their wife or husband or common-law partner or a stranger in a bar, respectively. The blonde divorced girl from the reception thought of the sexual encounter she will have with The Manager tonight. Their faces did not betray any of these thoughts. They just looked at each other and fiddled impatiently.

The Manager raised his face from the numbers and looked out the window. The unmoved horizon, buildings and trees, was suddenly melted by a fluid motion. He quickly realized what it was, a huge tidal wave.

A second later, he took a deep breath. He dismissed the meeting instantly and ordered, without blinking, Everybody in the vault, right now! The clerks looked at his transfixed eyes, then out the window. They obeyed instantly.

The wave pushed through the windows of the Community Bank, spat the heavy executive chair into the vault's door. The waters destroyed the bank in few seconds. The thuds were heard by the clerks and The Manager inside the vault. The bank was filled with water. Were there any customers?, the divorced girl asked with her ear on the steel cold door.

Today, there were no customers.

Chapter 50
View of naked Aphrodite, as she lies on her back with her womb wide open

The clouds clash with the dust that soars from Town, the flood has swept the dry fields and derelict construction yards and jettisoned dormant pulverized matter into the sky.

Do we need to say our names to affirm our existence?

Iris's hand is attached to my hand, the tandem of our steps.

I am tired, she says. We can still hear The Lake turned into an apocalyptic river, it calmed down, it flows quietly, probably by now The Valley is already covered, Town is drowned, a few lights can still be seen in the distance.

I am tired, she says and puts her head on my shoulder and her hand on my chest, like she needs to use my heart as a pillow.

A small meadow opens in front of us. The hollow tree in the middle of it is perfect for a good night's rest. We think it contains more heat than the open space under the naked sky. The silent sky. Clouds run over your body fast, expose stars, freckles of a godly bust, we enter, we sit, we sigh, she mumbles, Good night Tim, she curls like a spoon on the moss.

The Valley opens in the shadow of the moon. No traces of clouds, winds have rushed to catch the end of the civilization and quench their zealousness into faraway oceans. A giant boat approaches me.

Father!

He smiles, his echo dissipates words, Are you cold, son? Take my jacket, smile, there are stars in your pocket.

Waters at my feet, I see Town twinkling in water, reflections of rich skies.

Aphrodite comes down from the stars, naked, translucent, gigantic.

Town is a miniature at her feet.

She kneels in The Valley, one knee on one road, one knee on another, her body catches color, I see her golden skin, her thighs, her navel, the pinkish breasts and fine thin lips, her big eyes, like two suns of the night.

She grabs water in her palms and pours it on her hair.

She sees me and blows a kiss in the air, then blows air in her palms and stardust rains on me.

I fall asleep and dream of birds in a white cage.

Chapter 51
The rebirth of hope through the discovery of the delicatessen

We are going to starve to death!, the teller cried.

No, we are not. The security system sends a signal to the dispatcher once people are trapped inside. The vault is designed to keep robbers alive for hours. See. Fresh air.

The Manager climbed onto the table and tapped the ventilation grids.

It's working. It'll be fine, he said.

But what are we going to eat, to drink?, the teller continued to cry.

We will figure out a way.

From the back, a feeble voice said, I need to go.

Though weak, the voice was heard. The Manager turned his head towards the source. What do you mean?

After he asked his question, The Manager realized whose voice it was. He saw the blonde divorced girl with her hand on her belly.

I need to go, she repeated.

I see, The Manager replied in a low voice, suddenly feeling not that attracted to her. Now, this is a problem, he added.

He knew that the closest toilet is already sunken under water, god knows how deep. He must find a solution. He knew that it is part of his job description to find solutions, to give answers, to be responsible for the wellbeing of the employees at the work place, including their bladders.

How about the drawers?, the divorced girl said.

The Manager explored the intricacies of that question. The drawers, to which his mistress is referring to, were in fact the safe deposit boxes that the Community Bank offered to its clients. The Manager was the only person who had the back-up key for all of them and he must keep it on him, at all times.

Reluctantly he said, Fine, what the hell. He opened a drawer in the corner, at the back of the vault, removed a copy of Brancusi's Mademoiselle Pogany and told the divorced girl that she could go there.

I can't.

Why not?

Not with all of you here.

The Manager and the loan officer decided to turn the table on its side, as a shield.

So be it, he said. Don't worry.

The divorced girl lowered her head behind the table, and her underwear to her heels, and shed tears in silence while she quickly relieved herself. Then she shut the drawer, rapidly and without saying a word.

These few moments of general embarrassment were used by The Manager to tacitly look through the other safe deposit boxes, both to distract the group from the divorced girl and out of sheer curiosity and the hope to encounter or provoke a miracle that might lead to their salvation.

He plunged his hand into stacks of cash, jewelry boxes, life insurance policies and various collectibles with sentimental values to their owners. Nothing of value there. In other boxes he found several wooden cases with old French inscriptions on them and the label of an international auction case.

How about that, Château Margaux!, he said.

The Manager knew that one of those bottles is valued at a few times his monthly salary, and if he decided to pursue his train of intentions he will unequivocally lose extremely valuable customers.

Boss, we're thirsty!

Everybody in the vault huddled around The Manager with their pupils dilated, awaiting a decision.

What the hell, he said. He ripped the seal from a box, unscrewed the cork and passed the bottle to the first in line. Be considerate with each other!

The first bottle was emptied in less than minute. Mouth to mouth, wiping the bottle with the sleeves or the palm.

Chapter 52
Regression into the timeline to save the metaphor from decay

On the day of the great flood, The Quiet Boy woke up early, from a dream so intense that he mistook it for reality.

He was in a tree house, just like the one up the hill from the school, and he was shooting people he didn't like with a sniper gun. Until a sparrow landed on the gun barrel and would not go away. No matter how hard he shook the gun, up and down, left and right, the sparrow would not go away. He was afraid to touch the bird. He was afraid, because he thought that if he did he would not be able to have an erection anymore. He didn't like to touch himself. When he did it, he did it out of necessity, because his body told him to release that sticky liquid. So he did not touch the bird and hoped it will go away.

Somebody pulled his sleeve. He put the gun down and looked behind him.

It's his little sister.

He woke up now, sweating, still thinking that the gun was next to him, in bed.

I can't sleep, she said. I'm afraid of T Rex.

The Quiet Boy told her to stay here and wait in his bed, while he went downstairs to get water.

He tiptoed downstairs. The stairs didn't squeak as they did when his father walked on them with his heavy step. He knew his father has woken up before him, because he had told his wife last night, I'm gonna wake up early. I'm going to the rally. I don't need breakfast.

As usual, his father was in his office. He was thumbing through some papers. The door was cracked open. The Quiet Boy saw the big pistol on the desk. The Lawyer made some notes on scrap papers and put them in the safe and locked it. He then concealed the pistol under his shirt, looked at the watch, then at the cracked door. The Quiet Boy was in the darkness of the hallway.

The Lawyer stormed out of the house.

The ticking of the big pendulum marked the passing of a few minutes until The Quiet Boy came out from under the stairs and walked into his father's office.

He found the map of Town on the desk, full of circles and arrows and abbreviations underlined with a bright red marker, then a dotted line around the mountains, an X on the mines and few other Xs and checkmarks on other places. He rolled the map, put an elastic band around it, opened the mahogany cabinet, fetched the sniper gun in his case and a box of ammo and rushed out of the office carrying everything under his arm.

He went to his room and packed a blanket, a raincoat, crackers and juice boxes, flashlight and matches in his knapsack. He kissed his little sister on the forehead, tucked her in and climbed in the attic.

He opened the roof window and watched the horizon of The Valley with the binoculars.

The breaking dawn was purplish and steamed with an air of implacability.

People formed groups at the outskirts and marched slowly towards Town Hall Plaza.

A few hours later, sirens pulsated here and there, police cruisers and fire trucks built a perimeter around the center of Town.

I want a cookie.

The little sister has woken up and climbed into the attic.

The Quiet Boy put a sweater on her and gave her a cookie. Their mother has been on the phone the whole morning, trying to find her husband. She kept the news on TV on minimum volume, so as not to wake up the children.

In the afternoon, the sky changed. Clouds stampeded The Valley and dusty wind gushed over the houses.

The crotch of The Mountain exploded. A huge tidal wave emerged and razed everything to the ground. It came towards Town, violently.

The Quiet Boy passed the binoculars to his sister. She crawled to the attic door and yelled, Mommy!

Their mother rushed to the attic, grabbed the binoculars, threw them on the floor, told the kids, Stay here, in a firm voice and ran downstairs.

She came back two minutes later with a big bag full of things.

Chapter 53
Aphrodite and the tyranny of a perpetual mask

She was standing in front of the mirror and saw the reflection of the face of The Psychiatrist as he entered the room, in silence. The Psychiatrist approached his wife, slowly, put his hands on her shoulders and leaned forward. His lips hovered above her head.

Don't, she said.

The Psychiatrist was used to this answer. He backed off gently.

She wiped her blistery face with a cotton pad, tapped a lost tear on her cheek and absorbed it, then put on the mask, today an embroidered Venetian mask, with a neutral expression.

Her condition has worsened.

The Psychiatrist was the first to deduce the diagnosis, although his dermatologic knowledge was minimal. The cutaneous porphyria was a crude disease. He saw how her skin was swelling under exposure to the sun, how her face was itching so badly that he had to tie her hands behind her back, for her protection. A few months later, he wrote in his diary, First symptoms of hallucinations, depression, anxiety, paranoia, She feels that her face is constantly on fire and she is blinded by the light, The mask is compulsory.

He bought her the first mask on her birthday. He ordered one with a Raphaelesque smile, discreet and wise. He administered her painkillers, then tied the mask behind her head. She accepted it immediately as a second nature, a second self. Her smile became too painful to endure so she started to rely on the expressions of her mask collection.

On the shelves, the white gloves and the vials were arranged methodically. The Psychiatrist watched the neckline of his wife with interest and longing and well-tempered sadness.

It's getting darker outside, he said, clouds were gathering, everybody rushed to the Plaza. Let's go out. Let's go to the cabin, honey.

I don't think it's a good idea.

She wiped the mirror with the cotton pad.

The mirror was reflecting a gargantuan tidal wave rushing from The Mountain.

Chapter 54
Squid pro quo

The day after came with clear skies and great silence over the flooded Town. Here and there, on roofs, in trees, on floating doors or fishing boats, people moaned and dogs licked their wounds.

There were no reports of deaths.

Houses and buildings have been flooded, all the cars have been swept away, trees have been reduced to stumps and electric poles to an underwater conglomeration of tangled wires. People found refuge in attics, some in waterproof basements, because that is where they had all the supplies, and that is where they could save their lives, within seconds after the realization of the catastrophe. Those that sought salvation in higher elevations are blessed with more air at their disposal, yet soon they will realize that those locked in the depths of the waters are more fortunate to have more food for immediate consumption.

News traveled slowly. Strangers started to talk to each other. Hey you, a man on a tree yelled to a man in the boat, wait for me. The man in the boat turned towards the man that jumped into the still water and approached him.

The rower collected a few more people on his way to stable ground.

They climbed on a rooftop, helped each other and collapsed on their backs after hours of long strenuous effort to survive, clinging to whatever object would float. They took off coats, turtlenecks, shirts. Men remained naked to the waist, women kept their bras on and spread out the articles of clothing to expose them to the sun.

A few hours later, after their clothes were dry, they started to talk, shook hands, I know you from the doctor's office, Your son goes to school with my daughter, I always liked the color of your dresses as you walked by my window.

In late afternoon, hunger set in. No one mentioned it. Some decided to share the apples they had in their pockets, or the crackers, or the bottled homemade natural juice with no preservatives. The modest sharing of nourishment lured the minds of the group on the roof into dormant vegetation, with parsimonious usage of words and body movements and irregular moaning.

What will happen to us?, a woman asked with her eyes closed.

Five minutes later nobody has answered her.

Chapter 55
Archimedean trajectory from a dreamy state to a concrete meaningful purpose

Bend one's will like molten steel under a pressure hammer, thwart the linearity of causes and effects, magnify the importance of a second, the meaning of a moment of awkward silence and awe, and you will get to the core of reality, to the essentiality of the being, to the full extent of control. You will patrol through dark waters teeming with devouring carnivores, and you will be immune to destruction.

Father Frank told the people that the net upward buoyancy force is equal to the weight of fluid displaced by the body. The raft hit the Church with implacable inertia. Father Frank's hands were covered in a thick layer of dried mud like the skin of a rhinoceros. It will fall off if you squeeze it hard or chisel it with a sharp blade, he said. He pulled Iris, Tim and the others on the roof of the Church.

Faces rose from their hiding places, from under the armpits of mothers, from under the folds of a raincoat or a soaked cardigan or simply from a pair of big palms that were holding an exhausted body and a blank mind. Trees and chunks of barns and beauty shops straddling the stream in unison, the sun is red and cold, people breathe a scent of mold, It's from the rotten wooden beams, Father Frank explained, part of the roof has collapsed, everybody crowded on a flat area and clung to each other to stay warm, those whose clothes have not dried, those whose bodies shivered and whose tears gave a salty taste to their lips.

They have not seen a body afloat, they did not smell decay. Tim grabbed Iris's hand and felt an urgency to foray deeper into Town, to go home.

Chapter 56
Consciousness and lividness at the maximum amplitude of the pendulum of immediacy

Grains of soil and slivers have trickled through the rims of the mask onto her face. The itch was excruciating. The Psychiatrist helped her undo the knot at the back of her head and took off the mask. Their attic was dark and clean. The water has settled at the bottom of the stairs. Their socks were wet but are not given much attention now. He realized that eventually he would have to take them off, to avoid pneumonia or some other ailment.

He put the mask on the couch where she used to read the thick novels and sleep through the long and quiet Sunday afternoons. He blew the slivers off her face, she sobbed and shed a few tears. She screamed when he plucked a larger shard from her cheekbone. She hit him in the chest with her fists. He budged a little, but his face remained unmoved. He executed an incision into the hollow depths of a ruined body. He knew how she felt. Her nails stung his chest with desperation and pain and furious anger, which no hypnotic metronomes can numb.

Leave me! Go!

Her scream was deafening, but his brain refused to accept its damaging effect on his eardrums. From outside, no one can hear.

We are trapped in our soundproof recording studio of pain, he thought, while removing the last dirty pieces from her face.

She fainted when he applied disinfectant.

He laid her on the couch and wiped the sweat off his forehead and threw the handkerchief into a dark corner.

He cracked open the slanted attic window and gazed at the boulevards of water, the islands of roofs, the remnants of the recent furies descended over a collection of heterogeneous destinies.

He reached for his pocket and took the first bite from his vegetarian sandwich.

Chapter 57
The strange loop

The mother looked at The Quiet Boy with an inner conviction that what he wanted to do was dangerous and extremely uncomfortable for her maternal instincts, yet she showed no signs of disapproval. She told her son to, Be careful, be back by sunset. She wanted to add, Call me every hour, but realized instantly that all the phones were inoperable.

The Quiet Boy plunged through the window into the inflatable rubber boat and the mother tossed him the knapsack. She did not think about the unusual weight, nor about the items crowded inside.

The Quiet Boy paddled between rooftops, among floating pieces of old furniture. He split the muddy waters with a nervous prow, pushed a wooden chest aside with the paddle, and imagined a dead face being pushed to the surface by an upward current or some wizardry of the darkness, but none emerged. He did not find this odd, death is as probable as it is improbable, depending on the relativistic circumstances of the life-threatening cause, yes, a flood is one of them, especially when there was no warning, Why was there no warning, is it important, where is father?, he thought, and dodged a cat that jumped from nowhere to her salvation. She landed in his boat and they stared at each other for a good minute.

He resumed rowing between rooftops, floating pieces of furniture and streetlights.

They waved at him from a distance. We're here!

He didn't see them. He was not ready to see anybody. He imagined his father in his office, drowned, his body suspended in liquid just under the ceiling, contracts and thick folders in disarray, the safe box tossed on the floor, in a sea of irrelevance, irreverence and futility.

None of these thoughts matched reality. The Lawyer was alive. He was in the Council Room, on the third floor of Town Hall. He watched calmly as the water level rose slowly through under the massive door. He discarded the cigar in an ashtray and walked to the window.

Son. Over here.

The Quiet Boy climbed through the window into the room.

Did you bring it?, his father asked.

Yes.

A door was cloaked in the bookshelves of the Council Room. For not being a member of Town Council, The Lawyer knew much about the unrevealed architecture of the building. He spent many nights with The Mayor and The Club, puffing cigars, drawing on maps with red markers, exchanging pleasantries or cards at bridge nights. Now there was no time for pleasantries. He took his son to another room, above the waters.

There are times when we entangle ourselves into self-referential logic, he explained to his son as they climbed a poorly lit spiral stairway with no echoes and no windows. It seems to us that our brain mirrors the reality, son, we follow patterns of thinking like branches unfold from a trunk, like twigs unfold from branches, we give ourselves the illusion of systematization but it's merely a descent into chaos, the farther we step away from the trunk. You see, son, we are a hand that draws itself on a piece of paper. We eschew the possibility of genuineness by luring ourselves into a closed circle. Finite mutation. Mute finality of scope. We are simply to be. Tell me, is there more to this clogged reality? Is it as good as it gets? Action, reaction and that's it? I know, you don't have to say anything. Give me the knapsack.

The Quiet Boy gave the khaki knapsack to his father. The Lawyer looked inside, said, Very good, then put it on his son's back.

Causality is merely a product of logic, he continued. Alter the logic with religion, with brochure morality, with advertisements and mindless consumerism and you can fabricate a whole system of consciousness.

Consciousness.

The word funneled through the ventilation shaft in swirling echoes.

The Lawyer pushed a brick, a secret door opened. They entered another room.

The others were there.

Chapter 58
When the pawn has had enough with the chessboard and shoved off

The sun doused the clouds and died in the wet purple horizon of the first day of the flood. The woman with the red sweater has lost her glasses. She has been crying for the past hour. Nobody had enough strength to object or to interject with a wise and soothing saying, not even Father Frank, who has kept himself busy trying to find a shelter.

The woman with the red sweater found the slant of the roof unbearable. She grabbed the shingles with the ferocity of a lioness and did not close an eye the whole day. Not that the angle of the roof made standing impossible, on the contrary, one could easily sleep with one's head pointed towards the sky, but the proximity of the waters made her nauseated and, Very troubled, as she kept saying to herself.

Miss, it is God's will, Father Frank patted her shoulder. She pushed his hand away.

The woman took a deep breath, as if she tried to suck in all the air in the universe. She hid her head in her palms and didn't make a sound. Father Frank turned to Tim.

Help me open the roof, Father Frank said.

They removed a load of shingles and stale air gushed out. They entered the attic, which proved to be a good shelter for the night. A miracle of God, Father Frank said, and invited everyone inside, There is plenty of room, he said.

One by one, the roof survivors climbed down. Some helped each other, some said, I can manage by myself, to which the helping hand retorted with a simple, Okay. They moved quietly, enthusiasm mingled in soaked bodies and exhaustion. Hopes flickered in the back of minds and could only be pushed forward by a force not present, by an indelible necessity.

The woman in the red sweater remained behind. No one really paid attention, no one utters a word. She must have her own painful thoughts. Father Frank helped Iris climb down.

No, wait! Father Frank shouted.

Running feet on the roof. One pair chasing another, then stopping. Don't do it, Father Frank pleaded. Then silence, then the liquid thud of an object in contact with water. A last cry, Stop, don't go, then splashes and more cries from afar.

The woman in the red sweater has left.

Father Frank surrendered to the unbearable reality. The woman with the red sweater jumped in a boat and departed from the imminence of perdition, to find a safe place, I need a safe place, she cried, I can't stay, I'll come after you, I'm sorry, I'm sorry, and a minute later the echo of the dawn brought one last, I'm sorry.

The lair warmed up with the presence of people. They looked thorough the opening in the roof towards a darkening sky that seemed to have no dreams except for a pair of eyes that can never close.

Chapter 59
The I of the beholder

Where were we? White symbolizes peace, no, no, white symbolizes purity, no, no, white is milk spilled by the cat on the couch next to me, right before Dad enters the house, after a hard workday, tense, torqued in thoughts, and he looks at me with an accusing face, and is too tired to verbalize anything with transitive verbs, I did this and it caused that, and just drops his enormous suitcase on the floor. He makes me a sign to help him with his coat, then tells me to Clean that milk stain, and sends me to my room to, Practice that violin.

Let's see—

The capricious number 6 – tiptoeing? Maybe the pastoral naked-by-the-river number 9? Definitely the fire-spitting number 10! Devil's laughter, teasing, nudging number 13? The jumpy 14? Or the revolutionary damn-the-inequality-of-classes-what-is-to-be-done-comrades number 24? Or play them all, methodically, textbookishly, score after score, chin up, spine elevated like an ambitious skyscraper to the rooftop of meritocracy, autocracy, idiosyncrasy, auto-sufficiency. Paganini madness!

My father arching his back when explaining certain passages from a score with the large gestures of a Greek philosopher. Levitate through music to a spaceless-timeless state. Music is awakening.

Never resting, the notes move me, they push me into a stream of continuing change of perceptions, realities, sensations at the verge of estranging myself from I. Comfortable alienation between four white, withered walls. The I, through which I see the whiteness of my room, my white insomniac attic, the people snoring next to my spongy white ears, the moon melting in dark shades of blue on their foreheads or in stripes on the wooden beds.

The sense, the structure, the nonsense, the logic, the rhyme with not much echo into our brains, the breaths we take, the enumerations we utter or think about, the causes and effects we do not understand, they roam around us like implacable invisible gravity waves, the bow on the string, the emotion and the sound thereafter. Recycled cycle of time into the I of the beholder.

Hold me, Iris.

Chapter 60
The defiant [cat] and the frustration of the owl

The dreams that the rooftop survivors had the night before evaporated simultaneously with the dew that condensed on their eyelids. A cat meowed in the corner of the attic at a girl who wanted to grab it, because she liked the way cats purred in her lap. She flanked the cat with her palms, like two big brackets and talked to her softly, Hey kitty, where were you hiding?, and the cat meowed briefly and surrendered to her new master, licked the girl's thumbs and normalized the blood flow in her pawns.

We're hungry, padre, a single man in his fifties broke the silence.

Then he thought ironically that, Father Frank is a saint with stashed manna in his coat, for dire needs and cataclysmic circumstances!, but kept the thought to himself.

The survivors thought of the inevitable rescue. The news must have reached the ears of the central authorities by now, news helicopters should be heard swirling soon, rescue boats, with crates with food and water, Band-Aids for bruises and broken bones, Has anyone broken anything?, No, a voice here, No, others added, everyone is fine, a few stitches might be needed here and there, but we are essentially fine, and specifically starving.

What is with that cat, anyways?, the single man asked.

It's mine, the girl answered.

It'd better be.

Father Frank looked outside, more like in a mute prayer when he raised the two hands to the ceiling of the Church, he did not seem to look for a ladder from the skies, that would lift them into a military helicopter, he was praying or simply circumventing the pressure of his emotions and trying to reach a rational solution for salvation.

The sky sent a response to the prayers in the form of an unlikely presence. One devout believer interpreted the sign as powerfully symbolic, as guidance to redemption or to whatever may benefit that believer's immediate needs, others less devout looked at the presence as merely a random occurrence of nature whose pitiful trajectory happen to intersect their pitiful lives in an inspiring or helpful way, as prey would fall easily into the hands of a hungry hunter. The least of the believers, or how they liked to call themselves both in public as in private, the observationalist agnostics, defined the presence as a total meaningless interaction of owl and man.

The owl fluttered its wings nervously, erratically, could not find a place to land, settled for the ruins of a barrel, until the ruins disintegrated under its weight, then soared again into the sky croaking a damp sound of frustration and angst.

The cat jumped from the girl's hands, sprang onto a beam and then onto the roof in a blink. Gracefully she flattened her body and waited for the owl's acceptance of inevitability. The acceptance came shortly.

The owl descended in a spiral towards the Church scouting for the least dangerous spot. Its landing was brusque and rapid. The cat sprang into an arch, faster than many eyes can follow.

No, kitty!

The girl followed kitty's path and tried to reach for the opening in the roof. She sliped on the beam and fell over it, onto a thin section of the attic's floor. The plank of wood cracked and, at the moment the cat jumped at the owl's throat, the girl fell in the water and shouted, Mummy!

The mother pushed Father Frank aside, and reached her hand down.

Emma!, the mother cried.

The crack proliferated through the skeleton of the Church, and the chain reaction shattered the roof and destabilized the few remaining sustaining structural elements from the bell tower. The tower roared and catapulted shingles in all directions. The old brass bell lost support and surrendered to gravity, smashing everything on its way down.

Emma!

The bell stopped a meter above Emma, caught in the ropes. Father Frank and a few other men tried to reach for the other end of the rope. The rope failed, and the bell covered Emma peacefully, like the hand of god tucking her into a liquid crib.

They sank together, bell and being, in a big bubble of air, at the mercy and implacability of the buoyant force.

Chapter 61
Bawls in an ironic setting of usefulness or uselessness

Luckily, the air in the vault has retained its freshness due to the good quality of the ventilation system and, Mind you, the fact that we have not rushed to pick the first offer, but waited to find room in our budget for a high-quality system, The Manager explained. He tried to boost the morale of the employees, after one night of claustrophobic sleep and anxiety over what was behind the heavy, watertight steel doors.

One by one, the tellers, the accountant, the personal bankers, the loan officer had taken turns at the special safe deposit box, revealed to them by the divorced girl the day before. The Manager, has held onto this unspoken right to the very bitter end of today, when he accepted the necessity of what was to follow.

He walked with dignity to the back of the vault, opened the box, told the accountant, Hold the table and look away, and performed the necessary duties with eyes straight ahead, like a man, like he would teach his son, like he would preside a roundtable or a seminar on the relations between unemployment and the dynamics of the cash flow. While he performed the function he concocted an association between finance and biology. He grabbed a bill of high denomination with his thumb and index finger from a thick pack at his feet closed his eyes and used it.

Nobody made a reference to this utterly embarrassing moment. Nobody thought of inflation, return on investment ratios or the devaluation of the national currency. The stacks of bills around them did not widen their pupils anymore, did not have an effect on their blood pressure, did not rouse in their brains dark thoughts and wild scenarios of material comfort. Last night they did not dream how to break into the vault and then disappear on an island in the Atlantic. Last night, they were cold. Men sacrificed their coats so women could wrap them around Mademoiselle Pogany and use her as a pillow. They punched the bags full of money to level them into mattresses, they lined up the boxes of Château Margaux on the floor, to use as seats. The women sobbed occasionally. We're going to die, they whispered. No we are not, the men replied, help is on the way.

Many of those present felt that shame loses strength if shared in a group to which one has a significant level of affection or sense of attachment. Many thought that the exteriorization of shame is a burden heavier than shame itself. So they thought of the future. Because the future was open to any possible paths, of which one will reach a favorable hand to them. They hoped that help will arrive soon.

But help was not on the way. The alarm in the vault did perform its duty, but the signal was not received by the responsible parties. At the other end there is utter silence.

Chapter 62
Gauss's bell and its practical applications

The bell sank with Emma to the altar's floor and it pulled the rope down, but the men managed to grab the other end. It's a miracle, ma'am, she's alive, Father Frank soothed the grieving mother, We'll rescue her, Who is going to rescue us?, the single man interjected but nobody really paid attention to him.

The men debated the likelihood of Emma's survival. The bell fell perfectly vertically, There is enough air for her, We just have to pull it up, That won't work, Why not?, If she is not attached to the bell, she'll drown, I don't understand, It's physics, the buoyant force, The what?, Gentlemen, no need to argue, it is obvious that there is a possibility that the girl is alive and has air to breathe, under the bell, What do we do, then?

I will dive to her, Tim said. You lift the bell, I will go under it, and then you pull us up.

Simple as that, the logic stood for itself, it canceled out all other alternatives and the groups agreed with it, after a few moments of murmurs, mumbling and scratching of heads.

Father Frank was the first to bring coherence to the overlapping dialogues.

Chapter 63
The unexpected appearance of the pawn at the secret tea party

Gentlemen, we have gathered here at this crucial hour to affirm our bond and dedication to The Plan. As we all know, the events have ironically precipitated recently in Town, to no hindrance to us until now. However, our sources have kept us abreast up until yesterday morning, when the communication lines were disconnected on all channels. The last update I have from The Capital is that—

The man's speech was interrupted by a new body that entered the visual cone of their attention. The light was scarce. Yellow flickers of candlelight bathed the faces of the men. Gentlemen, our esteemed friend, Mr. Lawyer, has kindly decided to participate in our meeting.

The men cleared their throats.

The four men at the round table wore black cardigans, embroidered with golden threads. From left to right they are: The Neurosurgeon, The Politician, The Banker and The Advisor. The four men bowed their heads gently as The Lawyer approached from the dark corner where he was hiding, so he could put his black cardigan on. Before he walked forward, he whispered to his son, Stay here, do not say anything, put on what's in the bag.

The Lawyer found his place at the table. He said, Gentlemen, and put both hands on the table.

Things have not worked out as we hoped, The Advisor said. The Capital gave us the new coordinates of The Plan the day before the flood. The crowds have moved faster than we expected and the sources within have reported that elements alien to our partnership have caused disturbances. It is too late to allow or disallow the social unrest to interfere with The Plan. Damn it, gentlemen, for the time being we are merely pawns in the hands of nature.

Agreed, Agreed, Agreed, Agreed.

However, I have managed to secure the papers and their security is certain. He produced a black suitcase from under the table and puts it on the table.

I believe The Lawyer has something to say, The Advisor concluded.

Indeed. Gentlemen of The Club, my own affairs have been gravely perturbed by the recent events in Town. My associate—

The Frenchman?

Yes, The Frenchman, has failed to complete the mission and his whereabouts are unknown to me at this time. I am guessing he perished along with the merchandise.

How unfortunate.

Yet another addition to the story is a fact, also not negligible, that Dr. Tolstoy's son, the boy named Tim, and his friend have followed The Frenchman to his house and to other places. They might have some knowledge about my affairs. I do not know the extent of them.

We all agree that the termination of Dr. Tolstoy was indeed beneficial to The Plan. Do we believe that his son is seeking revenge? The Politician asked semi-rhetorically. The men nod their heads.

Indeed, The Lawyer continues. However—

An unlikely interruption came not from the dark corners of the room where The Quiet Boy was standing in silence, but from above it, from the roof, whose structural integrity was failing at this very moment under the weight of a live creature. The shingles cracked and the creature fell inside, onto the floor, with a thud. The five men jumped to their feet, quickly reached for the guns under their cardigans, but soon realized that the intrusion was merely an accident, judging by the looks of the creature. They inserted the guns back in the holsters, under the cardigans.

The creature was the woman with the red sweater.

Forgive me, she muttered.

Rise, woman, The Neurosurgeon told her. She got to her feet and shook her hair to clean off the dust. Who are you?, he asked.

I know who she is, The Banker intervened. She is no danger.

Very well, The Politician said. Mr. Lawyer, you can bring your son forward.

Chapter 64
Claustrophobic underwater unrest and the nervousness of the rest

When Tim reached the bell the men pulled the rope twice swiftly and lifted the bell about twenty centimeters. Tim will crawled under the bell.

He whispered, Hi, Emma, and she said, Hi, without raising her eyes. Are you afraid?, he asked, she shook her head, Me neither.

The men above lowered the bell to the floor and waited.

Some nights ago, Tim had dreamt about demons. They were not dark, hideous or had bodies engulfed in flames and exfoliating skin, or horns and thorns on their heads, or beady big bulging eyes with no pupils, or pointed razor-sharp teeth that could cut through bone as if through rancid butter. None of that. They were humanoid shapes made of a dark fog that lured him on a dusty road by a dense forest. He remembered clearly the still air, the dim light of that afternoon and a sweet smell of vanilla in the air. He was a light, humble, cold creature of Europa, moon of Jupiter, waving at alien space probes and being mistaken for craters. The demons took him deep in the forest.

He felt the soft moss under his bare soles, stings from cockleburs and blind insects that flew into his skin, he turned into a white glow, a foamy, snowy body into the vast darkness, How can you tell how deep the darkness is?, he thought. He felt the breath of the trees as they walked by him, as he walked by them, as they sniffed each other's presence following the traces of vanilla and the gravity pull of an inescapable attraction. The demons mumbled an echo, You must come, he looked at his milky hands, he touched his mouth. He could not speak. Words died in the larynx, like interrupted fetuses. The dark trail opened into a glade, with demons in a ritual circle on its border, all pointing to the center, shedding light on a massive wooden cube with an entrance cut open at its bottom.

The gate to yourself, the demons said, and stretched out their arms and wings of fog and suddenly it felt so hot in the glade, suddenly the air became unbearable and heavy. The soothing gate to your consciousness, the demons said. You must enter, and they blew a wind that pushed Tim inside.

The path was lit by the glow of his body.

It was a labyrinth.

Stairs ascending, descending, corners that ran nowhere, walls blending into sinuous shapes, illusory geometries, spirals turning onto each other, defying gravity, mystifying logic, You look at us and you think we do not exist, the walls spoke to him, I look at you and I think you don't exist.

Then Tim thought that there was something sexual about all this and felt ashamed.

We are born from the movement of your steps, you walk on us and we immediately become matter on the flesh of your soles. You return us to the physics of your consciousness.

Who are you?, Tim shouted.

Follow the path ahead of you, they said.

At the end of the spiral, Tim saw the archway to the tower. A small chamber with walls of fog. In the middle a pedestal. On the pedestal a small cube, with the lid open. It was filled with sand.

You must touch the sand, the cube said.

It burns!

The sand is you, the cube said.

He dipped his vaporous white hand into the sand. The tips of the fingers first. It burnt and cut into his flesh.

Deeper, the demons shouted in chorus.

I can't!

The cube echoed and shuddered, bent its walls, its floors, curved its rooms into enormous eggs, gelatinous spaces and wombs, Tim's hand plunged deeper, to the elbow, It burns!, to the shoulder, the bottomless sandpit locked him in its excruciating girth.

From the sand, white ants emerged and started marching on his neck, spiraling, spreading, descending over his body, covering it all, until he became one with them, one with the sand, and all that remained was the echo of his thoughts, I am a grain of sand inside my own cubic consciousness.

He opened his eyes.

He walked again on the dusty road.

The demons are made of fog and lure them into the impenetrable unknown.

Emma shook his shoulders.

Are you okay?, she asked.

His heart and thoughts were throbbing. We have to go, he said, Hold on tight to the clapper, I'll put my arms around you.

The men in the attic have counted thirty long seconds.

They pulled the rope with hefty jerks and long breaths. The bell started to rise, holding a bubble of air for the two angels of the depths.

Chapter 65
Death and the maiden

The mother knew that when the kicks in her belly stopped the fetus was asleep. It was an interlude of peace for her.

The old woman to her right was tired and did not say much, probably thinking of her own death. They have been trapped in the underwater tunnel at the aquarium for more than thirty hours. The bubble of hope is shrinking.

The girl with the nametag was the most relaxed of them all. At least she was certain that the glass cannot crack. Her death will be by suffocation, not drowning. When the batteries of her walkie-talkie died, she hurled the device into the door and cried for an hour. Now she was resting, like the other two women who were too slow to respond to the emergency call. Their backs against the cold glass.

At one point they were holding their hands together, the pregnant woman in the middle and the other two at her sides. They thought that rescue was imminent when a loud object smacked into the door, but it was just a bench, swirled by the water. The fish have disappeared.

The girl with the nametag wiped her forehead and swallowed the last drop of moisture from her mouth. The pregnant woman was asleep, too. Her head fell on the old woman's shoulder and her hands held her belly like a magic orb that could foresee the future if one knew how to touch and how to talk to it. It could be night or day. Eyes did not tell the difference between the neon light that stayed on and the scarce sunlight that penetrated through the few meters of water above them.

The girl with the nametag raised her head and rubbed her eyes gently. The waters were moving. It may be a new wave. They do not come alone. The waters never come alone. They brought a tow truck floating upside down, with the crane hook stuck in a big empty gas tank that pulled the whole mechanical beast to the surface. In seconds, the metal wreck would hit the tunnel.

The girl woke up the two women and showed them what lied in front of their eyes. They embraced each other and kept their eyes fixed on the tow truck. It stroked violently, not far from them, and sent a shockwave in all directions. The tunnel was big enough to stop the tow truck from advancing but not strong enough to resist the impact.

The thick glass moaned under the pressure. The crack spread quickly, while the beast settled on the floor of the aquarium and tumbled next to the three women, with the steel cable poised to cut its way through the tunnel, like a chainsaw through a hollow tree.

The glass broke and water invaded the tunnel through a small opening. The women screamed. The girl stopped crying and looked closely at the steel cable as the water level increased and sent chills down their spines.

The force of the current ripped the crane off the truck and pushed the cable down onto the tunnel.

I have an idea, the girl yelled through the thunders of the screaming waters. Grab the cable, it will pull us out! The other two women did not understand what the girl with the nametag meant, but they obeyed instantly. They reached for the steel cable. They held tight and thought of death. They frowned in agony when the water reached their necks.

When more glass broke the old woman thought that God was watching. She felt a warm touch along her spine. Her face relaxed and she tightened her grip on the braided metal cord. The steel cable broke apart from the crane. The hole in the tunnel widened.

The current, the tank and the cable obeyed the laws of nature: they pulled the women out of the tunnel while the tow truck died on the bottom of the river. The tank emerged in full force above the water and took a rapid turn along the current. The women reached the surface in seconds. It took them a minute to regain their senses. Then the girl with the nametag broke the silence with a scream of Help!

Chapter 66
Might makes right

The girl screamed, Mom!, and the mother screamed, Emma!, when the bell emerged from the water. Father Frank and two men were waiting on the beam that traversed the Church from one side of the attic to the other. They told the other men on the platform below to swing the bell a bit so they could reach the boy and the girl. They told the girl to let go. Then they told Tim to let himself fall into their arms.

The people in the attic watched the scene in silence, holding each other in pairs, or clinging to each other in small groups. Alone, in the corner, the single man puffed on a cigarette that he had managed to rescue from this moisture and disgusting mud. He leaned his elbow on a ledge and tapped with one heel into the wall behind him. The hollow sound that the wall made did not draw his attention. When the mother calmed down from crying and hugged Emma enough to convince herself that her daughter is unharmed, the single man heared the hollow sound. The others were congratulating and hugging Tim.

I could just set this Church on fire. After thinking this, the single man turned towards the wall and found a door handle concealed among the beams. He pushed the door with his boot and stuck his head into a small niche. He lit his lighter and stepped in. A few seconds later, he came out of the niche with a raffia sack in his arms. He dropped the sack on the floor in front of everybody. The thud scattered a cloud of dust at their feet.

Well, padre, what is this?, he said.

All eyes were fixed on Father Frank.

Well, mister—, Father Frank says.

The single man puffed a smoke ring and said, Whatever.

—what lies on the floor, Father Frank continued, is indeed what some unfortunate people may call manna. If you go deeper in that room, you would find more sacks with grain, various vegetable seeds, some boxes with canned meat, soup, bags with salt and sugar, and a few with garden fertilizer. Yes folks, there is food there and yes, it will be rationed, and yes, I would have mentioned it if this unfortunate event had not happened. These supplies would have been taken to the villages uphill, sometime next week. A small helping hand for those affected by the severe drought of the past summer.

You heard the padre, there is food, folks, anyone interested?, the single man asked.

I don't want him in charge, a woman said and pointed at the single man, Me neither, Let's form a committee in charge of the food, Agreed, Then we can rotate the people on the committee.

You're not serious, folks, the single man said. Screw bureaucracy, he added in his mind.

He squashed the cigarette butt on the floor.

Father, we trust you, Iris said.

Thank you, my dear. Your name is Iris, right?

Yes.

Very well, come with me. You too, ma'am.

The single man said, Whatever, and disappeared through the hole on the roof.

Chapter 67
The zygote possesses intentionality and has semantics

He spent the night on the roof, gazing at the bright stars, remembering his childhood when he used to catalogue constellations, rushed to atlases to see if they had been discovered already. A few years later, his father persuaded him that, The good course in life is in the spirit and the letter of the law. One day he will have to have the same talk with his quiet son.

At the break of dawn, he felt a nudge, to which he mumbles, What the f— He stops the f-word there because the nudger whispered, Keep it quiet.

We have a situation, The Banker said.

What is it?, The Lawyer responded.

We are low on — on resources.

What do you mean?

You know what I mean.

Well, in that case, we have a situation.

And here's another question. What the hell is wrong with your son?

Listen, his hands grabbed The Banker by the collar, My son is not of your concern.

He would not let go of that bag.

He is not supposed to!

Easy, keep your voice down, Mr. Lawyer, you know our rules. If I remember correctly, you drafted them.

The knapsack is none of your business. My son may be silent but he can fire a gun.

The Banker released his collar from The Lawyer's hands and retorted in a normal voice that there is no need to escalate a counterproductive dialogue.

The situation is, Mr. Lawyer, that we are running out of food.

Oh yes, that.

The two men, in their black cardigans, descended from the roof back to join the other members of The Club, where they stumbled upon an odd sight. Everybody except the Lawyer's son was crowded into one corner. His son was in the opposite corner, holding the barrel of the sniper gun in the dusty sunrays. The Lawyer ran at him, snapped the gun out of his hands and slapped him on the back of his head, shouting, What are you doing?

He gets scared when he's cornered, he told the others.

From the look in his son's eyes, he knew that somebody has tried to snatch the knapsack, or simply tried to take a look at it. Gentlemen, he said, there is no need to subjugate our scope to the frailties of our bodies. I assure you, there is no food in this bag, no content pertinent to The Plan. We have to find alternatives.

I am sure Mr. Lawyer has suggestions to bring forward, The Banker said.

Mr. Banker, I would rather let The Advisor speak, The Politician said.

Very well, gentlemen, The Advisor began, let us remember the story of the zygote that possessed an unlikely amount of intentionality and strong ambition. The zygote was a young man, knew nobody, had no material means, no special qualifications, but had a restless determination to pursue his scope. So what did he do? He entered a political association, made himself indispensable to those who had the power, through carefully choosing the social context in which benefits could be reaped, under different coats, such as fundraising galas, seminars, dinners planned three months in advance, services rendered at the exact time and with the exact words. The zygote was not at the mercy of probability, or what common mediocre people call chance or luck. He was always one step ahead in the social causal link. Only in this way was he able to elbow and nudge his way through the hierarchy of power. What lesson do we learn from this, gentlemen? We learn that we have to have one palm on the helm stern and the other on our foreheads, scouting the horizon.

Aye, Aye, Aye.

We know what we have to do now, The Advisor continued. The woman with the red sweater is asleep. It is time to wake her up.

Chapter 68
Guitar gently weeps and the device annoyingly beeps

Gregoire woke up after having been passed out for at least twenty hours. He was running out of air. He raised his head swiftly and hit the door from inside. What the hell is this?, he groaned. It was dark and his thoughts were scattered. His face was bleeding. He had bruises all over his hands. His left thumb was cut deeply, the blood coagulated in a thick black swelling. It will infect. He needed to get out of here. He pushed the door open with his foot. He has lost strength. The door was heavy and he had to push it with his back. He felt he was in a coffin. The door opened and fell to the outside with a sharp noise. He heard a splash and cringed as the sun bathed his face.

He remembered what had happened. He was in the garage when the wave came. He was cutting open a body to get the stuff from inside. He passed out. When he woke up, he swam to a floating wardrobe of solid oak and crawled inside. He closed the door and passed out again. Now he was born again. From another womb into another life. He swore briefly and tried to straighten his back. He combed his hair with his fingers and threw the mud overboard in disgust.

Nothing was moving around him. The waters were still, no sign of life. Few houses were left uncovered. He saw a plain of roofs and a grove of electric poles sticking out here and there. Town's center was in the distance. The tallest buildings were there. Probably that's where everybody was. He should try to paddle his way there. He looked at his left palm and saw the cut. He swore again. He pulled a scalpel blade from his arm. The numbness turned into throbbing pain. His guts were coming to life too. He felt a burning in his stomach and his throat was collapsing into itself from dehydration. Ironic, he thought.

He tried to detach a piece of wood from the floating coffin and use it as a paddle. He didn't succeed. The wound opened and blood dripped slowly on his boots.

A girl's voice yelled, Hey mister!

He instinctively hid the wound behind his back.

He turned to the voice, which came from a roof, behind the crown of a tree.

Mister, over here, the voice said.

He saw three women on a roof, two sitting and one waving a scarf at him.

He dipped the healthy, unspoiled palm into the water and pushed himself forward. In minutes, he reached the eaves, docked the wardrobe parallel to the roof and pulled himself out. The roof was almost flat, like most of the roofs in Town. It's the tradition.

The women have found a spot near an opening in the house. He said hello, but didn't look them in the eyes. He saw the round belly of a woman, the grey hair of an old woman and the bosom of a young girl. A nicely shaped vibrant chest. The women said, Hello, too, and asked him if he was alone.

I am. I don't feel good. You have food?, he asked.

The women shook their heads.

You pregnant?

The pregnant woman nodded.

You checked the house?

There are only toys in the room below us, the girl with the nametag answered.

You tried to make a fire?, he asked.

We couldn't get it started, the old woman said.

Help must be on the way.

You are the only person we've seen.

Hmm, he said.

The old woman looked him in the eyes, then looked at his wound. Let me look at that, she said. She cleaned the wound, and Gregoire nodded his thanks. He told the women that he wanted to check things out. He would go into the room below and see for himself what this house has to offer.

Not what he had hoped. A dozen plastic boxes with toys, discarded clothes in a coffer, many dolls, What the hell?, a gargoyle, an electric keyboard. He didn't care about the rest. He tripped on a guitar case, swore, and opened it with the metal tip of his boot. That'll do, he mumbled. He climbed back on the roof and told the women, I got it. He dropped the guitar case at their feet. He told the girl with the nametag that he needed her help. What are we doing?, she asked, We're making a fire, I'm gonna go back in and throw you pieces of wood. He produced a pocketknife, and bit on the blade like a pirate. The women thought that that was not necessary. He jumped back in and, seconds later, pieces of plank popped out. The pregnant woman said, Thank you, it's enough.

He came back onto the roof.

The pregnant woman put her hand on his shoulder. He said nothing. He hasn't been touched in years. His spine shuddered from an electric charge, synapses snapped in a fast line of falling dominoes from the back of his head to the tips of his fingers, the hairs on his chest, serpents swirling in his crotch. Minuscule diamonds fueled his veins. He was a mute shadow crooked over the guitar case.

What are you doing?, the girl with the nametag asked again.

I'm making a fire, he said.

With the guitar?

It's wood.

You do NOT touch the guitar.

Fine, he said and closed the case in silence. He swallowed a ball of anger.

The fire grew quickly. The women reached for each other's hands.

At that moment, they heard the annoying sound from the room below.

Chapter 69
Always look at the bride side of wife

The knife entered the loaf of bread with little resistance. The Psychiatrist and his wife liked crisp bread with butter and thick slices of goat cheese. They took small bites, sized to the mouth opening in the wife's mask. She swallowed slowly. Every movement of her face was prana exercise, exorcizing pain through flow of air into lungs, through poignant thoughts of splendid sunsets by a well-chosen ocean or enrapturing vistas of the Alps. Her husband knew how to distract her mind, most of the time, when her mind is malleable, for her own good. They swallowed together, and he followed the pace of her breathing. One more, he said, and put another piece in her mouth. Are you okay?, he asked. She nodded and chewed in silence while he prepared another piece of bread and cheese and brought it towards her, with two fingers, gliding lightly. She squeezed her lips together.

I want to tell you about the dream I had, she said.

She expanded her chest, her breasts morphing into big lungs and absorbing all the air between them. His heart shot comets of blood through his body.

I dreamt about living with you in the mountains and you were laughing and rubbing my belly and kissing it and whispering stories to our unborn child and I had no idea what you are saying. I begged you to tell me and you just laughed, and wouldn't tell me.

I dreamt about travelling to the magic cities of the Old Continent and us running around like kids and having fantastic dinners and making love in all the castles.

I dreamt about seeing your hometown and your grandmother's barn.

I dreamt about telling you, remember when we pulled the car over and couldn't help ourselves? Well, baby number two is on the way. As I cried and you jumped around like a crazy man.

I dreamt about you dedicating your books to us.

I dreamt about me constantly telling you, if you don't put that camera down I swear I will —

I dreamt about all the showers we would take together, the kisses, the presents, the hugs, the tears, the trips, the pictures, the family we would build, the stories, the friends, all of it.

Then I opened a letter covered with dust and saw your handwriting. You were writing about the dream I'd just had.

The Psychiatrist grabbed her head in his palms and kissed her forehead.

She cringed and he removed her mask.

He kissed the swan on her shoulder, tattooed in white ink, intact under the chisel of the decade of shadow over it — it had been raining when he'd painted it deep in the epidermis.

At the light of the candle, she endured in silence, tried to bite her lips during the first penetration, but could not move, the sheer numbness of her whole body, the whip stretched along the nerves and veins, it smells like rain, she thought, it's only water dripping from the eaves. She left everything to the moment, the darkness or the memory of long past light, contorting the linearity of space into a dense dot of discolored dreams, she thought her body screamed, senses dim in anticipation, lionesses flat and tense on the ground, for they cry on the insides of their round eyes, for they are ready to release tension and accumulation in muscles and the liquidity of their bones, the moment that divides the flow of perception traverses into the air, evaporates the small space between mouth and mouth, chest and chest, from body into body and return to the nocturne oasis, this is catharsis, he thought and left the cerebral fetus into the agony of the imminence of birth, cap the cerebral womb with a steel plate, it was not too late to make the owl shut up, I am my brain and because of that my body moves, and he cried and moved, arched his back to reach the other end of possibility, the other end of the other womb, the real womb, in which he dreams, in which he rests his fin, energizes his skin and deposits his milligrams of masculinity and unquestionable undeniable unbearable proclivity, to which ETERNITY is an irrelevant concept that purely describes time, to no use now, to no meaning and transcendence, because we do not exist outside conscience, and the unity of ME and YOU is a unity of the immaterial fluids, it happens because we desire it, it happens because of absence of thought, of surrendered will or incredible victorious will, the extremities of the string that binds us and cages us and frees us simultaneously from the eggshell that, once broken, reveals another crude eggshell, it happens because LOVE is another line of causality that seeps through our organs, like massive armies, invades us, and conquers us and makes us her emperor and goddess, to us she surrenders, we puppeteers, she puppeteered, and as we glide our fingers down the string we find the crowns of our heads, we look up at ourselves, we pleasure ourselves with the recursivity of love, I am inside you, You are inside me, come again, I come again, from the top of the flight of the hummingbird we are—

Chapter 70
Nothing but[t]

—a long, very long, obtuse shaft that pushes the air from the top of the building right into this room, then right into our hungry lungs. The loan officer's concise and flowery description brought no excitement to his coworkers. He climbed onto the desk, reached for the grid and tore it down with his strong fingers. The gush of air from above slapped his face and discharged an unpleasant amount of dust. The shaft fed air to the vault that was usually filtered and cooled to a constant temperature for the priceless works of art stored there.

It may be our only salvation, The Manager decreed in a prissy voice. He added that it was unlikely that their presence has been noticed by any authorities whatsoever. The last bottle of Château Margaux was emptied a few hours ago. The men were hungry. The tellers wiped the sweat off their foreheads with money, then discarded the notes like toilet paper. They stopped using the drawer in the corner when their intestines were emptied of the last traces of digested food and assimilated wine.

The men exchanged a few phrases about how steep and long the ventilation shaft was, where it ended, whether it lead outside the building or whether their bodies can fit through it. Some thought they will die of asphyxiation if they try to escape through the shaft, some did not care, Anywhere but here, Isn't it ironic, don't you think, Stuck in a vault with all this money and all you care about is your claustrophobia?, I don't care, man, I want to get out of here, Boss, what do you think?, Screw the money, the chief teller said, I'm out of here. He grabbed a big sack of money, tossed it on the table and climbed on top of it to reach the shaft, then realized that his increased stature won't help him much. He looked at the others. No answer came for a few good seconds. Perhaps their brains were stuck in a loop, fears were being sorted, priorities classified, instincts assigned to different probabilities. Screw this, the loan officer said and grabbed another sack of money, piled it on top of the first and climbed onto the little mountain. He reached for the shaft and pulled himself up.

Anyone care to join me?, he said.

Without waiting for an answer, he crawled up and away, obstructing the flow of air but making good progress. The mumbles turned into an echo, then diminished into utter silence.

The group in the vault looked at the ceiling as if the skies were ready to talk to them. They waited one minute, until the chief loan officer broke their numbness and followed his coworker into the shaft. He returned sooner than they had expected.

I need the sculpture, he said. Mademoiselle Pogany. The ventilator is at the end of the shaft. It blocks the way.

The Manager said, Fine, take it, which sounded like an order and this time he helped the employee climb the stack of money and shove himself into the narrow tunnel. The bangs followed a couple minutes later, the cheers followed another thirty seconds later. Come on up, we're on the roof!, the men screamed from the other end.

One by one, the tellers and the personal bankers, women first, climbed into the shaft. Don't look, the women in skirts said to the men helping them. Some replied, I'm gonna close my eyes when I push you up, others said, You have nothing I haven't seen before. Some were more elaborate, Forgive me if I have a claustrophobic attack with your panties above my head. The Manager interjected with a brief observation that there was no time for sarcasm, Some of us are indeed suffering from anxiety over closed, poorly ventilated spaces.

The divorced girl was last.

I don't want to go.

She looked at The Manager and fixed his pupils like laser-guided missiles.

I'll help her, he said to the others. Your turn, gentlemen.

The men disappeared one by one into the ceiling.

The Manager remained behind alone with the divorced girl. It's your turn, he said.

They climbed onto the pile of money and he made a lattice of his fingers. The girl stepped onto newly built ladder and tried to pull herself up.

I'm too small. I can't reach it.

The Manager put his hand, by chance, between her legs, held her in the air, at the level of his eyes. He felt the thinness of her panties, the pores of the well-crafted embroidery and the softness of her flesh. She froze and closed her eyes. He froze too and sweat sprang from his palms. She bit her upper lip, took a breath of stale air and pulled herself up, using the last drop of strength in her upper body. Help me, she said. He spread out his fingers and grabbed her butt, tightened his muscles and pushed her completely into the shaft.

Chapter 71
Surgical incision of Morse Code into the divisional resonance

Everything happened very fast.

After the clash of the crowds, The Voice warned Imam over the phone of the imminence of the disaster and he directed his followers to the safest place he could think of in those nerve-wracking moments. Take them to the hospital, Imam! Nobody remembered the hallways they dashed through, pushing, elbowing each other, the corners they turned, or stairways they climbed up or down, how many wheelchairs they pushed aside, with or without immobile patients in them, stunned by the sight of a mad throng dashing through the hallways. Some stopped and helped the ill and the helpless. They took refuge in the nearest ward. We'll be fine here, Where is your family? The catatonic patients were addressed last, poked and yelled at, Hey you!, Wake up, man!

When the wave hit the hospital, the first floors had been cleared, and everybody was somewhere behind waterproof doors. Cabinets had been leaned against doors to offset the water pressure, windows were barricaded with whatever objects they thought would be fit for the job. Imam led his group into one of the operating rooms, behind the strong doors, strong enough to hold off the fury of the flood. They locked themselves in. Probably not necessary, a devout Muslim friend dared to say, We are not fugitives and water does not have the intelligence to pick locks.

In the first days, they drank water from the sink, ate whatever pita they had stored in their large linen pockets and, when they ran out of it, they prayed for a day, then two, then three, then turned to the large stock of dextrose perfusion bags. Imam advised precaution and moderation, We don't know when rescue will come. They took a mouthful each.

The days passed and a new improvised self-sufficient circle of life took shape.

They took turns on the operation table to rest. Every four hours, somebody would tap the sleeper on the shoulder or shake him strongly, Hey brother, time to wake up, my turn. The table was better than the ceramic floors. It kept the spine orthopedically straight, with enough comfort for decent relaxation. The surgical instruments were stashed, at Imam's order, in a basket, To avoid any accidents. Artificial light was used sparingly, although the rays breaking through the tiny window at the edge of the ceiling were enough to provide illumination on the Quran and to give them an idea of the time of the day. Not that they did not trust their wristwatches, the few that had them, but it gave them a sense of the natural flow of time, according to the refraction of the sunlight through the water under which they were buried.

The light was flickering, it was coming in punctured stripes, it was orange in the morning, grey in the afternoon and purple in the evening, as mud rose and various objects passed by the window, a school bus, tree limbs, shopping carts, a displaced ATM, in an oblique trajectory from a nearby bank towards its resting place on a sidewalk, and from time to time humanoid shapes, or at least that's what they thought. This made them think of death, more often, more intense, I heard your lungs explode when you drowned, one said in Arabic. His neighbor invited him to shut up and pray.

On the sixth day, unusual symptoms of fatigue appeared. Imam opened his eyes and walked over the sleeping bodies and leaned with his back against the wall.

He heard taps in the wall, from the adjacent room. He immediately thought that it was a rescue team, but resisted the impulse to alert the others. The taps had a precise cadence, short, short, short, long, long, long, short, short, short, then a pause, then the whole sequence again. It is Morse Code, Imam thought and quickly refreshed in his mind the alphabet of dots and lines. He grabbed a scalpel from the basket and tapped on the wall his response.

h-e-l-l-o

Chapter 72
Impromptu genesis, few objections, no faith

The entire line of the horizon, the mountains that girdled The Valley of Town remained unmoved for a week. Nothing happened. Nobody came. The Lake moved over Town, under the eaves of the tall buildings. Low houses were engulfed completely, trees, if they remained standing, shyly showed only the upper parts of their crowns.

The food committee managed to ration the food with efficiency and, as long as nobody's stomach was growling, the small population on the roof of the Church had no objections that could have disrupted the flow of this impromptu social gathering. The last elected committee, with Tim as its chosen leader, was the first to see the bottom of the crates that a few days ago had been filled with Spam cans.

Father Frank, we are running out of food, a mother said.

Father Frank considered the consequences, the possible violent outburst of the single man, who always had his eyes fixed on him, whether he was puffing the cigarette or not, always mumbling something and scratching his beard, he considered the general hysteria that might infect the men, he remembered his prayer from last night when he masterfully composed this sentence in his mind and delivered it with a subtle articulation of lips, Pater noster, qui es in caelis, sanctificetur Nomen Tuum, intensify our care for each other with your love, give us the strength to reason at the dawn of senses and the rise of ultimate necessities, et ne nos inducas in tentationem, sed libera nos a malo. Et cetera, et cetera, padre, so you're praying, ha, give me a break and tell Him to bring me a boat. He ignored the single man's remark and spent the rest of that night in complete wakefulness.

Father Frank.

Yes, yes, Tim, I'm sorry, I was thinking.

I thought of something. Father?

Sorry, didn't I say what?

No.

What?

We can plant the seeds.

The seeds—

Yes, there are tomato seeds, beans, all sorts of vegetables. We can grow them.

What are you saying?

Rescue is not coming. Town is too isolated. Nobody knows we're here. We can build a greenhouse.

A greenhouse. But soil, water—

We'll collect the soil from the eaves, it's composted.

The plan was shared with the others and, as expected, no instant consensus was found. Let's be realistic, nothing will grow here, It will take weeks to grow something, Rescue must be on its way, We will never find enough soil, There's at least a dozen of us, that won't be enough, We ran out of food already, Folks, please, have faith, Do we have other options?, I guess we'll all starve to death eventually, No, we won't, What makes you so sure?, Or we could simply get out of here now, why stay?, He's right, And how do we do that, mind you, do you think you can swim as far as The Mountain, walk a week or two to the next town and call for help, it's impossible, She's right, Or we can build a raft, And how do we do that, we have no tools, But we have brains and muscles, Faith, my friends, faith, You have faith for all of us, and don't call me friend and don't touch me, it makes me feel dirty, I'm sorry, Whatever, So what do we do, then, I guess Father Frank and the boy are right, Everybody, what do you say?, Fine, Fine, Fine, You?, Whatever.

Father Frank received the nodding heads and the willingness of a few men to volunteer with a lot of quiet satisfaction. He found joy in his heart and thanked his God in a quick mute prayer. Soil was collected from the eaves in whatever containers they could find or improvise, crates were emptied and lined up, according the ad hoc architectural plans agreed upon and to the orientation of the sun. After the eaves were cleaned, they realized that the material was not enough and debated briefly another wild idea to collect soil from the Church's backyard. A bucket at the end of the rope would serve as a scoop. How ironic, the single man said, We wind up digging for soil in the depths of the water. Some of the men found this observation quite interesting, but kept the thought to themselves and all they said to the single man was, What if you talk less and help us more?

By the end of the day, the greenhouse was built and the people were exhausted.

They slept deeply under the starry sky and dreamt of nothing.

Chapter 73
Communication with the poignant otherness through the irrelevant thickness of the division

The answer came soon.

h-e-l-l-o

Imam said, Allāhu akbar, in his mind and answered.

w-h-o a-r-e y-o-u

w-e a-r-e s-u-r-v-i-v-o-r-s w-h-o a-r-e y-o-u

s-u-r-v-i-v-o-r-s d-o y-o-u h-a-v-e f-o-o-d

n-o d-o y-o-u

n-o

The sons of Allah were awake and their ears were glued onto the wall. They launched into a spirited whispered debate over what the next question should be. Ask them whether they know a way out of here, They wouldn't be here if they knew, Imam cuts short the dispute, Ask him, brother.

d-o y-o-u k-n-o-w a w-a-y o-u-t

w-e a-r-e n-o-t s-u-r-e d-o y-o-u k-n-o-w a w-a-y o-u-t

n-o

What does he mean they're not sure?

How would I know? Maybe they're thinking of the ventilation shaft as we did. We just don't know where it leads to. Imam, brother, ask him how many they are.

h-o-w m-a-n-y a-r-e y-o-u

t-w-e-l-v-e y-o-u

t-w-e-l-v-e

How about that. What's his name?

w-h-a-t i-s y-o-u-r n-a-m-e

The answer did not come soon. Perhaps the man or woman in the other room thought of the shortest way to explain who he or she was. Perhaps the name was very long. Finally, the answer arrived.

i a-m r-a-b-b-i m

The sons of Allah did not hear Imam when he translated the letter m, the first letter of the interlocutor's name. They released the lions inside them and made serious efforts to rephrase the words of awe and disgust before they were uttered. Those infidels!, what the hell are they doing there? Say it, brother, we're a wall away from hell, allāhu akbar and save the fury in us!

Brothers! Brothers, calm down. They're asking something.

w-h-a-t i-s y-o-u-r n-a-m-e

Tell them, tell them! Dogs are lucky in their cage!

i a-m i-m-a-m

The rest was silence.

Chapter 74
Frenetic succession of apparently incongruous pulses

Frozen sound dripped down from the purplish night sky. I find my name written in the membrane of the water. I remember my past lives from the vast Russia, the idiot, the demons, the long bow and the stubborn violin, then melted under my fingers, curved by my father I played Tchaikovsky, relax, Tim, relax, phoenix bird, Dad, phoenix, we are what we want to become, truly son, no bullshit, isn't that a bit self-referential?, It has to be, Tim, we always have to come back to ourselves.

My dad spoke too philosophically, I never quite understood what he was saying, because he spoke little and thought he was saying a lot, but what does it mean, Dad, really? You'll realize when the time comes. I unsuccessfully tried to convince him that the time had come.

He praised me for my good ear. You have the talent, Tim, but you must tame your fingers. He used a stick to punish the finger that was out of place. Legato! Pizzicato! Now you must practice alone. Now you must concentrate.

I was letting the partitas, the romances, the gypsy dances pass through me. I was a dune in the middle of a sandstorm. I became the little prince.

From my corner I have a view of the hole in the roof, the clear round fat white milky impassible impossible moon and the flickers of the waters in the distance. The attic resonance with low-key vibrations. Millions of cell-sized ants rush through my senses. They are humming and splitting in two, tirelessly, ceaselessly multiplying.

I feel a warm hand on my neck. Shh, she says, they're all asleep. My sweat suddenly feels cold. I recognize her voice. I am dreaming. You are not dreaming, she says.

Iris.

She sneaks under the improvised blanket, next to me.

Her breasts are warm and soft.

The sound of the growing greenhouse, the seeds exploding, the feeble roots thickening and spreading through the body of the soil, hummingbirds and bees on the prowl, the microscopic nature.

I can hear it all.

Chapter 75
Locked-in syndrome and the irregularity of the division

A day later, the taps started again, or, better said, they were heard again.

short, short, short, long, long, long, short, short, short

From both sides of the wall they started simultaneously.

Is that an echo, Imam?

No, I think they're tapping SOS too.

Three seconds.

short, short, short, long, long, long, short, short, short

What do they want?, How would I know what they want?, They must be desperate, too, Really, you think?, I do not appreciate irony right now, brother, It wasn't ironic, I was just making sure you know that is a SOS message, I know at least that, Maybe you should ask them what they want. Why don't they ask us first, we're the ones who need water.

w-h-a-t d-o y-o-u w-a-n-t

Simultaneously, a second delayed from the other side of the wall.

w-h-a-t d-o y-o-u w-a-n-t

Are they mocking us?, Why are they saying the same thing?, I think it's just the echo of what we're saying, No man, it clearly comes from the other room, It's them, What do we do now?, We should keep our tempers and discuss it, What's to discuss, that is clearly contempt, But they started with the SOS message, I thought we tapped that first, brother, Whatever, What do we do now?, Tell them what we want, see if they answer and if they don't, that's it, We'll die here, we ran out of water yesterday, brother, We have these D5NS bags left, That's not enough, Ask them.

w-e n-e-e-d w-a-t-e-r

The seconds passed implacably in silence. A minute. Two minutes.

w-e n-e-e-d f-o-o-d w-e h-a-v-e w-a-t-e-r

Bloody Jews, They are willing to trade, I guess that's what they're good at, Don't be so judgmental, tell me you wouldn't trade with them in this dire situation, We have to think about it, they screwed us before, What's to lose?, We give, they give, I guess, I prefer to die than negotiate with *them*, Brothers, pride is never more valuable than one's life, Imam is right, We should talk to the Jews, Whatever, Fine, I agree, Ask them.

w-h-a-t d-o y-o-u s-u-g-g-e-s-t

w-e e-x-c-h-a-n-g-e

h-o-w

v-e-n-t-i-l-a-t-i-o-n s-h-a-f-t o-n-e h-o-u-r o-n-e p-e-r-s-o-n

w-h-a-t

o-n-e p-e-r-s-o-n

r-o-g-e-r

w-h-o

w-e a-g-r-e-e

The preparations did not take more than ten minutes. The Muslims prepared the D5NS bags in piles, and used the boxes to improvise a ladder to the ventilation grid in the ceiling. Then they waited.

Do you hear anything, brother?, No, nothing yet.

They waited another forty-five minutes, they bit their lips in anticipation of the end of dehydration.

Imam was chosen to perform the exchange. As a matter of fact, there was no question of one being *chosen* for the task, but the unspoken consensus and force of habit pointed to their leader. Imam asked no questions and nobody asked him anything. The brothers felt tired. They have given up on the reading of the Quran. Their eyes were heavy and their stomachs were growling.

Surprisingly, those who had the largest share of D5NS were the least lively. The thinner ones have given up their ratios, and some even took just a few drops per day. For the benefit of the needy brothers, they thought. This explained the large number of bags left that they hoped it would give them an advantage in the exchange.

The grid was pulled down and Imam climbed inside.

A thud was heard a few meters away. Somebody from the other room has climbed inside. The two men crawled towards each other in sheer darkness. The bags were pulled up with a string, like grapes in a bunch.

The thuds approached each other, somewhere above. The men gazed at the ceiling. The two most stoic brothers, the ones that have saved their energy, chat in a corner, leaning against a big steel cabinet, painted white. As the thuds moved above their heads and they looked up, they noticed a crack in the wall, behind the cabinet. They did not think of an earthquake or that Imam's weight caused the crack. They pushed the cabinet with their shoulders. The large metal box made an ear-torturing screech. Shhh, the brothers said. Behind the metal box, a door emerged, perfectly flush with the wall.

The brothers instantly forgot about their admonishing. Jaws dropped at the surprise behind the metal cabinet. A door that connected the two rooms.

A goddamn locked sliding door.

The brothers tried to budge it.

On the other side, symmetric movements and sounds suggested that their counterparts were trying to do the same thing.

Hands jiggled the door from both sides, but it didn't budge. It's locked, brothers, Well, break it, what are you waiting for?, Wait, why do we want to open it in the first place?, You stupid, Imam is crawling in the shaft right now, You know what, why don't you shut up and help me?

Their efforts were remarkable enough to send a good number of decibels to Imam's ears.

What's happening?, Imam shouted from inside the ceiling.

Not only they did not hear Imam yelling, but their efforts intensified.

Imam's nervous question was heard, though, by the other person crawling in the shaft and dragging a bunch of bags after him.

Imam?

Rabbi?

Rabbi yelled at his group, What the hell is happening?, but they did not respond. The noisy chaos came from both rooms. Imam asked his group the same thing, in the common language that Rabbi could understand. He didn't want to jeopardize what seemed to be a good deal, by faltering or not showing leadership or speaking defiantly in another language that might create doubt, reticence, an impulse of some ad hoc retaliation just for the sake of equilibrium, or just a plain thought of retreat in Rabbi's brain.

While the twenty-two men crowded into the corners of the two rooms, like the final of a crucial soccer game, all trying to get a grip of the door, or make at least a small contribution to the opening of the division, Imam and Rabbi exchanged few pleasantries, whispered, fumbleed, tried to brush off acute itching, wiped the sweat off their mouths. They dragged the bags with D5NS and water respectively, passed them to each other, before counting them in the confined space.

The negotiation is brief, Two bags of water for one bag of dextrose, Come on, the water goes much faster, One bag of dextrose for one bag of water, Fine, Fine.

The two men squeezed in the ceiling soon realized there will be no need for an unusual trade operation in a claustrophobic space, with a lot of inconvenience and hurdles for proper communication. The door was opened with a lot of physical determination from both sides, the hinges broke out of the wall, like a loaf of bread ripped apart by many hungry hands, each reaching for a crumb of hope, desperation, anger, habit, ignorance, coincidence or sheer circumstantial determinism. My crumb is mine, because it is mine. Simple circular logic.

These were not thoughts on the mind of the two groups that looked at each other through the frame of the door. They suddenly stopped and froze in silence. They thought, Now what?, as if the Ten Commandments have appeared on a stone hovering in front of their faces. Or perhaps this is the perception of the Jewish side. The Muslim side saw a luminous Quran, defying gravity and shooting out incomprehensible symbols into all directions. Like a tiny spectacle of miniature flames and embers jetted into space.

The two groups stared at each other, paralyzed and mute. The sound that followed did not come from the twenty-two men. It came from the ceiling, which has suffered much structural interference from the crawling men in the shaft. Combined with the jiggling of the doorframe, the ceiling lost integrity and the Imam and Rabbi fell prey to gravity. The thin plastered ceiling cracked like the membrane of an uterus and the leaders fell into their respective rooms, with all the bags on top of them.

Their fall was instinctively absorbed by the men on the ground, who were watching the ceiling in anticipation of a revelation. Arms were spread out, muscles tensed to soften a landing that could have been, if not fatal, at least bone-breaking. The bags of water and D5NS were also rescued.

Gentlemen, I think we can work this out somehow, one of the leaders declared after regaining balance on his feet.

We have no choice but to agree with this point of view, the other leader agreed immediately.

Imam and Rabbi cleared their tunics, shirts, pants and head coverings of dust, and diffused a sense of well-tempered calmness. They used the embarrassment that climbed up their spines to defuse the tension in the room. Their faces relaxed. Suddenly, everything seemed much simpler.

The Muslim brothers devoured the water and the Jewish brothers devoured the D5NS bags with breathless gulps. Twenty-two patients changed roles with perfectly balanced choreography. The doses from the first trade soon proved to be insufficient, and a new trade was rapidly improvised. Bags flowed from one room to the other quickly and precisely. Hands reached out and grabbed them with hefty determination.

After the operation was completed, the men patted each other's backs and gestured thank-you's in the common language to everybody else in the two operating rooms.

Seven hours later, the weakest of the twenty-four men started to regurgitate a yellowish puree. Soon the first signs of paralysis appeared in the Muslim room.

Chapter 76
Growth of life matches the speed of hope

From the moment when the seeds were planted in various pots, crates, improvised receptacles, until the head of the first bud broke out to face the light of day, only twelve hours passed.

The single man looked at the bud and mumbled, Bloody hell, out of one corner of his mouth. He plucked the cigarette butt from the other corner of his mouth and crushed it with the boot. He yelled, Wake up folks, time to enjoy a freaking miracle!

The freaking miracle he was referring to is an uncanny, unexpected, unlikely event that befell onto the souls that were not hoping for a fortunate turn of events for the benefit of their stomach or life in general. In a corner a citizen commented that, The expectancy for a favorable resolution to an extreme matter of life and death is rarely matched with immediate satisfaction, which may cause even more stress to the subjects, to wait is a way of dying. To which he got a brisk reply, Give me a break, you cannot psychoanalyze suffering, suffering is reality, it simply exists, it does not have an intrinsic contingency. To which the first citizen snorted with derision and took a puff from his pipe.

The survivors touched the little green creatures, bodies of chlorophyll that emerged with unnatural speed from their seeds, some can be seen growing with the naked eye, millimeter added to millimeter of life, the bulging of a new leaf, expanding, morphing its contours, filling the little spaces around it.

Don't touch them, Emma told the single man. Why not?, he said and touched the baby tomato and smelled his fingers like he tasted cocaine.

Those who have risen to their feet approached the miracle, gazed with awe, wiped their tears or the morning dew off their shriveled cheeks, uttered the words, Miracle, and, Thank you,

Father, or started a debate on the very topic of the possibility of such forcefulness of life.

Fancy words we use this morning, do we?, the single man spat out the rhetorical question and resumed puffing on his cigarette.

The realists assumed that the seeds were genetically engineered. Probably Father Frank didn't even know. Oh, but I think he knows very well and uses churchy subterfuges to promote religious theses, What the hell are you talking about?, Keep your voice down, Don't tell me how to speak, don't you see, the mercy of god through our prayers has brought us salvation, ha!

The last speaker used air quotes, not just to express a certain sarcasm, which he found very subtle and intellectual and made him feel good about himself, or to follow a fashion of the days, as employed by the urban youth, or to mock the sign of the cross, as employed by the Christian believers, he simply tried to catch the attention of the woman in the group who kept quiet for the whole morning, deep buried in thoughts. The speaker believed that his large gestures and raised voice, the flushing of pectorals major muscle and the biceps branhii will enter the visual cone of the woman and will attract her attention. He hoped that the woman will smile at him, while her glands would secrete a special dose of estrogen, targeted at him. Just thinking of this word, estrogen, how humorous and ticklish it sounds, was enough to give the last speaker a sudden rush of blood to his penis.

The woman noticed the protuberance, but did not release the dose of estrogen. She prefered to think that she missed her period, not that she expected it, not that she was completely surprised, because all the prerequisites were met, her husband was drunk, she was tired and didn't want or care to resist, it was about two weeks ago, then the husband disappeared and she didn't even know if he survived the flood. She touched and rubbed her breast discreetly and instinctively, it itched and she felt that it's growing and hardening. Or perhaps it's all in her mind. She felt sorry, because the last speaker interpreted this gesture as a sign of positive reaction. Far from the truth. She took a step back and looked to the ground. She felt ashamed and sad.

Under their eyes, the plants were growing fast. Within a day, they had grown tomatoes, bean pods, even potatoes. The believers were exploring the roof. Maybe we should turn the roof into a garden, What do you mean?, You know, we spread soil all over, then we plant the seeds, It's slanted, So what, the angle is acceptable, we can walk on it, can't we?, True, So, if we can walk, a garden can grow, True.

The believers and a few converted realists, even a nihilist, who thought, What the hell, I am bored anyways, started the excavation process with sudden enthusiasm. Buckets were passed from hand to hand, lowered into the water, soil ransacked, ropes pulled, soil spread out on the roof meticulously, to cover every surface, women leveled and tilled the soil with a responsible distribution of resources, and meanwhile a song was improvised, with clumsy rhymes, nobody cared, they repeated it in chorus and a few assumed the role of a polyphonic echo.

On the other side of the roof, Father Frank kept his thoughts to himself for the rest of the day.

Chapter 77
The resurrection of the pons dissolves the division

The water was consumed fast to the last drop. The brothers turned to the D5N5 bags in excess and emptied them to the last one. When the pains in the stomach appeared and regurgitation started, they collected the yellowish puree, Whatever it is, into a bucket and covered it with a sealed lid. The collectors did not say, This is disgusting, brother, yet briefly thought that, This was the works of those devils in the other room. The thought lasts a second. Moments later, the collectors themselves felt a rush of nausea into their heads, an electric discharge down their spines, a convulsion in their stomachs, a contraction of the digestive tubes and subsequently a production of yellowish puree into the same buckets they were holding for their brothers.

The demons emerged from the walls. They were shapeless at first, lines floating in the air, interrupted deformed contours, They walk through our bodies, They walk through their bodies, They have knives, They don't have knives, What the hell are you talking about?, They want to kill us, Nobody wants to kill you, Relax, Give me water, Brother, you drank too much, Rest, Pray, No, the demons are around us, You're hallucinating, I'm telling you, shush, lower your voice, see, they're all around, they look like them, the demons are coming out of them, Relax brother, Don't tell me to relax, They'll kill us, We shouldn't have opened the door, We shouldn't have drunk the water, it's poisoned, They are drinking it too, brother, They kept the good one for themselves, Hey you, stop rambling, We are drinking the same water, See, here, I take a sip from your bag, see, who is poisoning you now?, He's right, our brother is right, He is not, I see them too, the demons, their keffiyeh, they are laughing and throwing rocks at me, Nobody is throwing rocks at you, They're coming, *olam habah* is near, heaven is near, Nothing is near, take off your kippah, You're sweating, I take it off when the demons take off the keffiyeh, I won't take anything off, The demons have been sent to us, it is Allah's will, Insha'Allah, Whatever my friend, point your dagger elsewhere, Look at my hands, do you see a dagger?, No, Do you?, my hands are bare, You are seeing things, The wings are spreading out, They're coming at us, Who's coming at you?, The demons.

Imam and Rabbi had listened to this absurd dialogue without intervention and both thought that the sleep of reason produces monsters. They felt weak and nauseated, but did not believe that there was something subversive about each other. One could not survive forever with water and dextrose in saline solution.

What do you think of all this?, Rabbi asked. Imam looks at him with a mild face and eyes half-open, or half-closed. I think we are lucky that we found the door and that our chances of survival have increased, what do you think?, I agree, but I don't understand what's happening with them, I thought I was a good shepherd, It's not you, you are a good shepherd, Rabbi, I think it's from what we put into our bodies, Look at them, many look paralyzed, They're hallucinating. They are seeing demons, And daggers, It's insane, Yeah, it is, What's happening?, It appears to be a locked-in syndrome, A what?, A locked-in syndrome is when a patient is aware and awake, but cannot move or communicate due to complete paralysis of nearly all voluntary muscles in the body except for the eyes, basically the pons is damaged, The what?, A part of the brain, it's like being buried alive, more or less, I see, what is it to be done? Are you quoting from Lenin?, What? I did not, Yes, you did, Did not, Yes, you did, Did not!, Whatever, Okay.

Chapter 78
Anger, eager, dagger

I can't take it anymore!

Gregoire manifested his anger in a peculiar way, which the three women found very distressing. He knelt on the floor above the spot where the annoying sounds were coming from. He laid his palms down in a pose like an agonizing prostration, a desperate plea to make the sound stop. Then he stroke the floor with his forehead. Three times, hard, until a speck of blood emerged. The sound stopped immediately. As if a supreme being had snapped his or her fingers.

Gregoire sat up and paid attention to what was happening below him. He sensed an abnormality and an urge to unveil what is covered. He thrust the knife down into the plank of wood in front of him. He was a master at opening cavities. He felt the veins, the texture of the material, knew where the weak points were and how to detach piece from piece, how to toss them aside, dug deeper and then ransacked the entrails of a space that could deliver his redemption.

He opened a hole in the floor. It brought to light the middle of a dark, secluded room. He didn't understand these people. How can they have rooms with no windows? Gregoire wiped his palms on the floor and stuck his head inside. A man appeared, timid and shielding his eyes.

I'll be darned. Who's there?, Gregoire asked.

The man in the light pointed at his own neck. He meant that he could not speak. He turned on the speech synthesizer on his neck and began to speak. Gregoire thought it was a joke because the man sounded like an untuned radio.

You the one who was making that awful noise? You an android or something?

The man was not an android. He noticed that The Frenchman didn't use verbs in the second question.

My name is Luc. I have a speech impediment.

Luc had found refuge in that dark secluded room. He was able to keep himself alive for so many days with tantric meditation and careful planning of resources. When he ran out of water and his throat became very dry, his speech synthesizer started to wail like a dying piglet. Gregoire spat on his palm and reached towards Luc. Then, realizing that his gesture was not well received, he wiped his palm and repeated it with a clean hand. He pulled Luc out.

The old woman, the pregnant woman and the girl with the nametag received Luc with smiles and soft hellos and invited him to sit next to them. He told them how he had heard noises outside the Synagogue, saw the wave coming and climbed up the stairs. He locked himself in that room and lost consciousness. So we're on top of the Synagogue?, the pregnant woman asked. Yes, I thought you already knew, Luc told them.

They didn't know and this revelation didn't make them feel better or worse. Gregoire scoffed and looked the other way. Something is not right about this, he thought. Then he scouted the horizon for a solution to his frustration. His stomach was growling. We need to move, he said.

Why?, Luc asked.

Listen pal, I don't care. I need food.

The man is right, Luc, we need to find another place, said the old woman. We are hungry too.

The old woman sounded wise and Luc knew she was right. Coming from her the suggestion seemed reasonable, coming from The Frenchman it seemed suspect.

I cannot leave, Luc said.

Why not, pal?

My place is here.

This ain't right. I'm going. Who's coming?

What's your plan, sir?, the pregnant woman asked.

We take the wardrobe and that door.

He pointed to a floating door not far from them.

Luc and Gregoire exchanged a look of profound mistrust. Luc's hesitation confronted The Frenchman's roughness. This ain't right, the two men thought at the same time, arching their lips in fake smiles. Gregoire jumped into the wardrobe and paddled towards the floating door. He tied the improvised raft to the coffin. The women were ready.

Give me your belt, pal. We need it.

Reluctantly, Luc obeyed the plea. Wait for me, he said. I'll be right back.

He disappeared into the secluded room. The synthesizer made that awful noise again, then it stopped.

He forgot his batteries, Gregoire scoffed.

Maybe we can spare your wisecracks, the girl with the nametag answered.

He looks at her and calms his face. Maybe we can, he said.

Luc came out of the secluded room with surprising agility.

Gregoire, the old woman and Luc took the wardrobe after a quick evaluation of their weights vis-à-vis the buoyancy of the wood. The pregnant woman and the girl took the raft.

The men started paddling with two wood planks.

Chapter 79
The breasts under the red sweater and the eyes in the golden faces

The woman with the red sweater was asked to take off her clothes. We must make sure you are not jeopardizing The Plan, The Advisor explained. She knew that was a lame excuse, yet she obeyed the order. It is not an order, ma'am, it's just, you know, to build and maintain confidence, The Politician added. The Banker raised a finger to make a point, Remember, ma'am, that you dropped into this room without notice. The woman removed the red sweater, exposing a red bra, large, firm, full, young breasts, milky white skin, athletic belly, small navel, waist like a cello. The men held their breaths and made a circle around her. She knew what was going through their minds and their pants. She hoped that it will not lead to rape, but she also knew that if you resist men, it might get worse. It usually does. The men did not care much about the red sweater that lied at her feet. They walked around her, slowly, looking at her body as if it is a wonder of antiquity, a perfect marble statue.

Now please remove the pants, ma'am, The Neurosurgeon said in a very low voice. I'm sorry, the woman asked. The Neurosurgeon cleared his throat and clumsily attempted to speak up. Please remove the pants, ma'am. The woman unbuttoned the pants slowly. The men thought that the gesture had a profound erotic connotation. The tips of her fingers rubbed the buttons gently before being pushed into their hole to widen the crotch of the pants. She is toying with us, they thought. I'm gonna play with them, she thought. Men respond to positive stimulus, they might change their approach if they do not perceive resistance. They might even give up, if their hunter instinct is not satisfied. It's all a question of power being exercised and recognized, she thought, while letting the pants slide down slowly along her thighs. She bent over to help the pants pass by her knees and travel down the calves. She straightened her back and stepped out of the pants, then pushed them next to the sweater, slowly, with her bare foot. She stood straight and crossed her palms over her navel. She could have covered her intimate parts, the men thought, and finished another turn around her. But no, she has left her lingerie exposed, to feed the hungry eyes and the voracious brains. They can see, through the fine embroidery, the lines, the shapes, the contours, the carefully trimmed hair, the delicacy of her flower. She felt their watery eyes and the rapid pulses buried under the black cardigans.

The lingerie, ma'am, The Lawyer suddenly broke the silence. Is it really necessary, umm, Mr. Lawyer?, the woman asked with a confident voice. She subtly inserted a tone of provocation, an affirmation of her refusal to cooperate until the end, yet an acceptance of the necessity of the fact, whether this really meant her salvation. I'm afraid it is necessary, ma'am, take your time, The Lawyer responded. I will take my time, she thought. She closed her eyes and walked her palms from her navel up, following the lines of her body and stopping at the back. She released the tiny hooks. The bra snapped, freed the breasts from an unnecessary pressure. The Banker happened to be right in front of her at this very moment. The bra dropped on the floor and exposed her nipples, in their full glory. To her surprise, the men did not stop their march. All five took turns in front of her, did not necessarily stare at her but took their time to view her from all angles. The pointed nipples, coral reef in the middle of a white wide sea, the volume that exudes vibrant life, the symmetry and the boldness, the youth and the restlessness, or perhaps none of these, because beauty and sense are in the eyes of the beholder, perhaps naked breasts do not mean anything to them, and it's all a circus, it's all just a game of puppetry, in fact the world is full of freaks.

Your panties, ma'am, The Banker interrupted her train of thought. She inserted her thumbs under the elastic and hesitated. The men kept walking in circles and she understood there is no need for them to repeat the order. She played her game, they played theirs. She fumbled over the border between skin and fabric and slowly started pushing down the panties. She decided not to bend over this time. The lingerie stopped at her knees. She stood erect and didn't move a muscle. She cannot crumble now, she must not shake. She felt humiliated but not fragile. She accepted the reality but allowed herself to think of revenge. She dismissed this thought immediately and let fear enter her heart when one of the men suddenly stopped and kneeled in front of her. The man completed the movement of the lingerie down to the ankles and gestured to the woman to lift her feet one by one. He tossed the last piece of clothing on the pile.

Open yourself, the man told her in a flat voice. What?, she felt tears surfacing. Do what he asks, The Neurosurgeon added with the same flat voice. I don't understand, the naked woman said and started shaking. Use your fingers and open yourself, the kneeling man replied. She moved her right hand over her pudenda and slowly placed two adjacent fingers inside. Open, the man insisted. She spread out the fingers slowly as the first tear rolled down her cheek and dropped on the man's head. The man didn't budge. He stared at the woman's crotch impassively, with no sign of an intention to touch her. He just watched and watched and watched, then suddenly told her to open wider. When she reached the full extent the man told her to stop and mumbled a thank you. Gentlemen, anyone else care to check? The other four men shook their heads, they trusted the inspector's satisfaction with the observation. Ma'am, for the time being we are satisfied, The Advisor said. The Neurosurgeon was the first to give her a minimal relief. In his low voice he said something like, We apologize for the inconvenience. The Lawyer bolstered her feeling of relief when he told her that she could get dressed. She wiped the tears off her face and kneeled next to the pile of clothes. She sobbed and turned her head towards the men. I know where to find food, she said. The five men turned to her and she knew that now she has really got their attention.

Chapter 80
The ox, the moron, the charisma and the schism

The Mayor was one of the most ignored important characters in Town. He was the quintessence of the oxymoronic relevance of a public figure mingled with the necessity of exercising a function of power under the selective scrutiny of the media, the selective indifference of the voters, the passion of certain social groups that philosophize about social constructs like, Let's bring health and prosperity to all our neighborhoods, or, Zero homeless people, or, Stop child hunger, what do they know of how hard it is to pacify politics and society, the vociferous interest of the few and the voiceless interests of the many.

He daydreamed, I sit at my desk all day I think of sunny vacations, or how to get a fatter commission from a fake public acquisition, or how to run my reelection, the thought of eternal recurrence, the will to power, I am the joker, the invisible hand is the charcoal, my face is the smoke, they yell but I am not allowed to choke, because it is all perception, because it is all a happy deception, I smile, on the headline they print VILE, still I am here, this is *my reality*, my thoughts are *mine*, their thoughts are *mine*, the implacability save us from the misfortunes of the appearances of equality, we are *so* different from each other that between me and my reflection in this dirty window is a space of infinite others, infinite causalities, not just thick dusty air, but infinite possibilities of the evolution of conscience, I can be saved or I cannot be saved, I can light a cigar now or I can eat it, I can ignore the growling of my stomach or climb onto the roof and wave a shirt on fire to draw attention, or I can watch the paintings of my predecessors in this office and wipe the dust off the frame of an early portrait of mine. I can duck and let the stone fly through the window, over my head. I will crush the pieces of glass under my thick sole and open the window.

You almost hit me!, The Mayor screamed.

Uhoh, I'm sorry, dude. Just checking if there was somebody inside. Are you flooded?

The man behind the question wore an almost disintegrated trucker driver's shirt, which was the color of his rugged beard. He was one of those pitiful creatures who spat his discontent wherever he felt like.

The man with the torn shirt was paddling on the back of a full-size wooden replica of the Charging Bull. Do I want to know where that comes from?, The Mayor asked himself, or what its absurd appearance means? He gave the answer himself. He didn't want to know where the truck driver and his bull were coming from. He cared more about where they were going.

The Mayor quickly adopted an electoral tone and did not make a reference to the Charging Bull or to its flotation qualities. My friend, do you have any food or do you know the whereabouts of food? The man exploded into a robust guffaw and imploded immediately into an ad hoc flash of awe and unmitigated epiphany. You are The Mayor, pardon, damn, crapper-cracker, you're alive, man, I almost killed ya, sorry 'bout that, sure, I have food, hop in, I got her stocked up, Her?, Yeah, Mr. Mayor, my bully. Your bully?, She named her Aunt Bully, after my wife, Who named it?, My niece, she made this, it's a replica, she wants to go to art school or something, Your niece is very talented, what's your niece's name, my friend?, Iris, Mr. Mayor, Iris, hop on.

Chapter 81
Puddles and the appearance of the poodle

The Manager was the first to try to make his way to the highest point on the roof of the bank by hopping over the large puddles and cursing every time he landed knee-deep into the, Damn crap water. His frustration was not shared by the divorced girl. She thought her lover was gracious, courageous and a good leader. She shut off all senses. In her mind she mixed the visuals of her lover's jumps with the sound of Schubert's Military March. She thought this mental film editing is cute and smiled with the corner of her lips. The tellers who noticed her reaction had no idea that she also imagined the nights when her boss was dressed as a ballerina and she was dressed like a lion tamer, when she applied the whip on his back a few times until he asked her to stop because it was inflaming his arthritis. The tellers also had no idea that when the divorced girl jumped over the puddles she thought of the same nights when he applied the beating on her thighs with a pink flamingo feather bouquet while she moaned and asked for more. He was wearing suspenders over a Heidi outfit and she was covered in fluorescent paper garlands that took her ten hours to chip out from a thick origami do-it-yourself atlas and stick all over her body before he came home a bit tired because, We lost a big account, yet jovial enough to change the outfit in like ninety seconds, No wait!, he jumped in the shower first while the champagne bottle popped in the bedroom, then he changed and tiptoed behind her with teeth clenched on the feather bouquet. He bit her earlobe and pushed her onto the bed. She liked it.

The last puddle was too wide for the divorced girl's agility and she landed right in the middle of it. The splash was a magnificent contrast to her silhouette. Generous and lavish as a party of fireworks that the people of Lilliput might throw to celebrate a gargantuan joy. The splash fell on The Manager as he froze before being able to catch the woman. She disappeared in the puddle and for a moment it seemed that an ocean has engulfed her and enormous white sharks will devour her within seconds but no, It's a goddamn puddle, and he jumped in for her, to realize that it is only half a meter deep, that she has not been devoured by sharks, that she hit her head against a protuberance of concrete, that she bruised her arms and tore her shirt, that her tears could not be distinguished from the muddy water on her face. He could not tell if she was sobbing in pain or trying to catch her breath, but he hugged her while the employees applauded the heroism, and the relief that they will not have to suffer the same humility, lesson learned, tactics redefined, Why do we have to go there anyways? Because I can see a boat, people, The Manager said. They soon realized that the boat could carry them to a source of food, or simply to a better place, where they could rest and eat and hope to get their lives back, but, What can be a better place now, in the vast derelict Town, inundated, forgotten, Goddamn it's been days and no sign of rescue.

The boat did not come alone. It came with a baby poodle in it, which had once been white and well-fed, but was reduced to a brownish shivering fur-ball that could induce only pity and awws and an inexplicable desire for patting, He's so cute, and he was immediately washed, not that the water used was cleaner but at least it gives the sensation that something has been done for the benefit of the little helpless creature, Where's your mommy? the employees gathered next to the boat that was pulled closer to the eaves with a broom, nobody questioned what a broom was doing on the roof, so much for the better, the counting is quickly done, We have to make several trips, and the prioritization was established with no debate, as usual women first, then older men, I'll go last, The Manager said, to which the divorced girl instinctively added, I'll stay with you.

They could not help to think that a poodle was also meat, in limited quantity, though, what a dreadful thought, even considering it's possibility was despicable, Man, that is sick, the dozen or so consciousness of bankers struggled with themselves before allowing the intervention of the brain and a chain of synapses that could eventually lead to a movement of lips, tongue, vocal cords. The poodle remained, for now, an adorable being and a benefit to their mood, the perfect distraction and companion until they could find a place to go to.

In the distance, smoke thickened by the minute. Sign for hope and reason to cheer.

Chapter 82
Reflections on love, the dove, the absurd context

After they made love, The Psychiatrist and his wife laid on the floor naked, for hours, without saying a word. The silence was necessary and comforting.

The days of the beginning. The days of her clean face and incessant smile, her liveliness when she mocked him for being too serious after a day spent dissecting depression, hypnotizing addicts into dealing with the roots of the problems or dehypnotizing back into reality lunatics who kept living into an illusion of satisfaction or happiness, extracting mothers and fathers from childhood psychosis and explaining to the patient that, You can be more than your past, consciousness is flowing, is ever-changing, jump on the raft and live your life. Ironically without knowing that this therapeutic metaphor might mirror a real-life situation, such as the one that they live in now. The days of the long walks hand-in-hand under the torpor of the hot sun, and the vitality of her skin, full of desire, perpetual tactile desire quenched wherever whenever they had the privacy and occasion, in waiting halls of the countryside train station, in the middle of the night, chuckling and moaning in the company of neon lights, in Grandma's barn on the stack of hay, Hey, don't pull my hair, she giggled, and he replied, I'm not, it was a bumblebee, maybe there was maybe there wasn't, the years have passed but memories remain, swarming under her mask and in the attic of his mind. They have changed and love has transformed itself as has everything else. The masks have become a necessary extension of her body and an extension of his well-tempered detachment. They went to yoga classes, they read extensively about the Four Noble Truths, they took a trip to Dharamsala and almost got an audience with the Dalai Lama. Months later, she got pregnant and then lost the fetus, but that turned out not to be related to her soon-to-be-discovered condition.

The fetus was the first rupture. The love after that would not be the same. It would come in inconsistent incisions into each other's psyche, from calm attempts to consider compassion as the foundation of their marriage, to outbursts of anger and shouts of despair, I want you to leave the house, one day it was said and the glass of wine was shattered against the opposite wall. Life after the miscarriage became a race of suffering, her aggravating condition, his dedication to her and the nights of solitude with a torn soul and the temptation of escape. The love was countless hours of meditation, forgive yourself, forget the pain, no, the pain did not have to be forgotten, the pain had to be understood and accepted.

The fetus became a book forgotten on a shelf under layers of dust. Never opened, never talked about. A book that, if removed, would leave a much deeper scar than if left alone, in oblivion. It was hidden in their smiles at social gatherings, at parties, in the small talk they made with their friends over cocktails, in his work, in her paintings, in the letters they wrote each other when he went to such and such a conference and she stayed home, her naked body wrapped in oil paint, I am giving birth to art with my own body, she wrote in her journal, but he never knew, it was hidden in their voices when they talked to their parents. You look unhappy, sweetie, their mothers told them in private. I am okay, Mom, they answered separately, often at the same time, he at his office, she in her workshop. And it was writhing in their loins like a ball of needles when they talked to their in-laws. They hated their in-laws, but never talked about it.

The fetus returned to them years later in another shape. It was an invisible mask that they pulled over their bodies. They no longer saw each other naked. It was ritual, it was consciousness, it was guilt, it was inertia, it was their skin of numbness.

After they made love, The Psychiatrist and his wife felt nothing.

Chapter 83
Riding Aunt Bully

The Mayor was amazed at the truck driver's ability to maneuver the floating bull. He kept this observation to himself. The truck driver showed him the trapdoor, built at the root of the tail. Watch your head, he said without looking. The Mayor was surprised to notice how spacious Aunt Bully was on the inside. He found himself waist-deep in a heap of supplies, all within the edibility period, or else he would have smelled rancidity, he would have seen maggots and the air would have been impossible to breathe. He dipped his fingers into a jar of prune jam and pushed them down his throat, then addressed his stomach half-admonishingly, half-ecstatically, Are you happy now? Yes, his stomach was happy. The Mayor didn't think the truck driver was a brute, in fact it was the truck driver who invited him on the bull and indulged him with all these goodies, who cares how they got here as long as they are here. The Mayor asked the man with the torn shirt if he was hungry. Nah, my belly is good, the truck driver answered, and continued to splash dauntlessly, pushing Aunt Bully forward, towards places where no bull has been before.

While chewing on whole-grain crackers, The Mayor quickly enumerated in his head possible diagnostics for his sailor friend, ranging from brain damage to insufficient mental development. The crackers, with the homemade jam, were delicious, they silenced all other senses, including the sense of equilibrium and the force of gravity that suddenly turned upside-down, tossing everything in all directions, causing The Mayor to spill the tuna oil, What the hell, Aunt Bully was turning legs-up, the trapdoor is shut in a blink of an eye, a loud splash followed shortly after and a scream of excitement more than dread, That is odd, then suddenly silence as the bull seemed to have stopped. The Mayor dug his way out of the pile of food and realized what has just happened. The Charging Bull has turned one hundred eighty degrees, submerging the trapdoor.

Let me out of here! The Mayor screamed, and pounded the wall. No response. The truck driver drowned, he thought.

The truck driver has not drowned, he was struggling to climb back on the bull. Damn politicians, he thought. They feast, and think they rule the bull. The bull ate him. Ha! Soon, the man with the torn shirt realized it's no biggie, retrieved the paddle and knocked on Aunt Bully's belly while asking Mr. Mayor from the bottom of his lungs if he was okay. Yes, I'm fine, you don't have to scream, now get me out of here, I can't, there's no door, What do you mean?, The door is in the water now!, I know that!, I can't open Aunt Bully, I'm gonna asphyxiate in here, Umm, I'm running out of air!, Uh-oh.

Pondering the implications of having a dead mayor stimulated the truck driver to quickly find a solution, the only solution, but one which will break his heart. He stared at Aunt Bully's balls for a few minutes, before grabbing them with his big, strong hands. He jiggled them with tears in his eyes but with full deployment of muscular resources. What are you doing?, The Mayor screamed? The truck driver did not answer this question and carried on with the removal of the balls, because he knows very well how the balls were attached, with hinges on the inside, then nailed from the outside, his niece's little secret, which he found out about on a Saturday night after he had sent her to bed early so he could check on what she was working on. He interpreted his niece's artistic precociousness with a simple philosophy, The girl needs to know balls. The nails loosened and surrendered, he pulled them out with his teeth, he opened the testicular door and stuck his head inside. Mr. Mayor, over here!, Thank God.

Chapter 84
Careworn, canned worms and a bit of futility

Sagging faces, symptoms of sore throats, sputter tainted with crimson nuances, the ritual of rotating the food committee without uttering a word, You just have to stand up and the president of the committee would know that his or her time is up, Father Frank praying when nobody was paying attention, he didn't want to agitate the spirits, although the believers knew what he was doing when he suddenly disappeared in a corner, behind a stack of crates, making the sign of the cross with his tongue, just like the others, for a reason that nobody knew.

The single man and his frequent scowls, What is that?, It's a gourd, Never heard of it, can you eat it?, Yes. Then the late afternoon run-ins between those with big appetites, the stoics and those in the middle.

The pangs, the indigestion, the newly discovered allergies, the withered hands of the sophisticated ladies bereft of their moisturizing creams and body lotions, the neglected and now diminished awe vis-à-vis the miracle of the garden, Folks we are self-sufficient in food, an optimist's remarks from time to time to cheer up those around him, or at least to shake the lethargy a bit, Or we'll all go insane, no worries, rescue will come, Annoying freaking optimist, the single man remarked, while crushing another butt of an improvised cigarette under the sole of the boot. You're smoking actual grass now?, a lethargic man asked him, Are you crazy?, the single man replied. It's ground-up tomato seeds.

A few hours later, the single man kneeled on the edge of the roof and spent the evening spewing a yellowish puree in the water. He was heard bawling and holding his spleen as though he had been stabbed. In the morning he trudged along the perimeter of the room, looking down.

The garden was churning out vegetables at a rate that the survivors could not keep up with. People were seen throwing tomatoes at floating pots, using cucumbers as darts and crows as targets. They calmed down after Father Frank admonished them to be responsible. They winced at the break of dawn, the chilling morning winds, the waning moon. The smoke was seen after the dew evaporated and the sun dried the fog. In the distance, on some unseen roof, somebody was signaling, or simply warming up, but definitely making sure that the thick black smoke is in contrast with the washed-out horizon.

We have to answer, many said out loud, there are survivors out there. The problem became how to reply with the same visual efficiency, so the two groups could notice each other and build a bridge of communication. We have excess food, the Church survivors thought, and since the others are signaling with smoke it can be only a cry for help. While some of the believers searched for flammable material that could also produce smoke, others started a debate on, Whether this is a good idea or not, If they come here, there won't be room for everyone, We are packed like sardines already, But how do you know how many they are?, There might be women and children, True.

A small pyre was conceived and a patch of the garden was sacrificed. A realist overheard the word sardines and connected it instantly to the word oil and the word oil to the word smoke. Why not?, it can make smoke, she explained. The few sardine cans were brought forward and opened with the attached key, Thank god for that, to reveal a not-so-pleasant image that erased the morning lethargy or the spasmodic enthusiasm vis-à-vis the smoke signals and brought everybody's attention to a disgusting reality. The cans were swarming with larvae, as if the sardines decided to have an afterlife of perpetual metamorphosis, from one state of existence to the other, the permanence of life, and the impermanence of form, Who cares how they got in there, they're there, fish is no more, We can still try to use the oil, Fry the damn maggots! The battle cry in chorus, Fry the maggots, boosts the spirits and the fire was lit. The smoke was meager and, despite the quantity of earthly invertebrates and oil that was poured on the pyre, remained meager and eventually turned white.

Tim had kept to himself for the past few days. After the death of the fire and the general collapse into a new session of lethargy, he decided to pat Father Frank on the back and suggested an idea that immediately crossed through all the ears and brought instant consent. A good idea, Tim, you can take the raft and go to those people and try to bring them here.

The raft Father Frank was referring to has not been built yet, but it was obvious that it will have a structure of wooden crates, rope, torn shirts and raffia sacks.

Chapter 85
The raft, the coffin, the time to treat the wood with respect

The closest to the dark smoke was Gregoire. He chopped the door of the wardrobe with precision. The glossy varnish burned darkly and slowly. This should get somebody's attention. With every blow of the knife he was closer to the hinges. He felt it is time to slow down or even stop, not because he might blunt the steel blade, but because there was somebody approaching, judging by the tiny waves that broke against the eaves at his feet. He followed the source of the waves and saw an improvised raft made of wooden crates, tied together with rope, torn shirts and threads undone from raffia sacks. He squinted, wiped the sweat off his forehead, and spat in the water, to his left. The three women behind him, used to his expectorations, kept their eyes focused on the incoming raft. Luc watched the fire and the fire watched him.

Gregoire prepared his throat for another expectoration, but choked on a swallowed scream, It can't be!. He squinted again, focusing on the paddler. It's that boy, the kids with the bikes, yeah, yeah, I'll be damned.

In his mind he composed different scenarios that involve illegal activities, perhaps murder, lost diamonds, the taste of freedom, the taste of French red wine, the taste of sulfur, the taste of blackmail, if blackmail can have a taste. Not being gifted with perfect eyesight like The Frenchman, Tim continued paddling, excited to notice waving hands on the roof of the house and the dying fire producing the black smoke.

The pairs of eyes meet and it was Tim's turn to conceive a spectrum of causality, alternative future, alternative pasts, in which he was stumbled upon in Gregoire's garage, plucking diamonds from mummified autopsied corpses, then being teleported instantly into his white room and his father would have asked him, Did you practice the violin today Tim, and since he hadn't he would have rushed shamefully through the door and bumped into Gregoire's chest who was waiting for him outside, guffawing, Did you find the bike, he would have hollered, Where is your friend?, He can't bring

The Frenchman with him to the Church, but they were not alone over there and The Frenchman is a crook, he'll find a way to dispose of them, he can't with so many people around, plus The Frenchman himself is not alone, he has company, I see an old woman, quiet, aristocratic, I can read a life and adventures on her face, I see a pregnant woman, in the sixth or seventh month, she is haggard and in pain, her face is livid and sunken from hunger, I see a girl with a nametag, she works at the aquarium, our eyes have met once, I see the man from the Synagogue, watching the fire, the man with the robot.

Tim did not start paddling in reverse to offset inertia or to give course to certain impulses, because Gregoire and the others acknowledged his presence by voicing repeated hellos and over heres and the loud question, Do you have food? Tim replied that, yes, he had food. He moored the raft to the roof and handed over to The Frenchman a big pot of vegetarian stew, Anything is good now, the women thought, the old woman was vegetarian anyways, so she felt blessed and waited her turn, while everybody else dipped their hands into the pot and swallowed without chewing. What, no meat?, The Frenchman mumbled through a mouthful, but nobody really cared what he was saying.

The pot was emptied in less than a minute and the blood rushed to help the digestion, so for the next half hour or so, lethargy settled over the roof of the small house and no thoughts of murder crossed Gregoire's mind nor any thoughts of miscarriage in the pregnant woman's mind, or thoughts of death in the old woman's heart or thoughts of her period being due in the girl's mind or thoughts of the battery dying in the voice synthesizer. Just a few glances between The Frenchman and Tim. Glance jagged, You don't have the gall to say a word, boy. Glance opposite, This man is frozen hell.

Chapter 86
Crossroads and what lies beneath the water

Gregoire was concentrated on the strokes of the paddle, on steering the raft, on using the appropriate muscle for every move, on sensing the blade of his knife close to his body, in its place, on planning something, the something that has to happen, it is only a matter of how and when. He suddenly got a taste of vanilla on his tongue and spat it in the water, Can you stop doing that?, the pregnant woman asked. Yeah, he said, and looked away. Where to now?, Tim pointed to the next turn, Judging from the tips of the trees, we are over Town Hall Square, Tim said.

The flotilla, the wardrobe, the thick door, the raft, meandered through the waterways, following Tim's outstretched hand, eventually entering a narrow alley, where opposing rooftops are too close to each other, almost kissing the tips of their noses.

The next stroke hit something hard in the water. The splash was absorbed into a solid object beneath the skin of water.

The women looked overboard and screamed, Oh my God!

Tim and Luc looked into the water and saw the horror that emerged. Tim turned white and Luc's face petrified. The muscles of the passengers paralyzed. Except for Gregoire's. He alone realized what the horror was.

The human body barely kept the resemblance of what it was before it was opened. It is not grotesque, The Frenchman thought, What is wrong with these people?, it's a clean corpse, no parts drooling, hanging out or brutally eviscerated. Some archeologists might describe it as a peaceful corpse, yet the hollow inside it, the gore from the incision, the obvious traces that the entrails have been ransacked shook the women's stomachs brutally and the yellowish puree came out in the next seconds, while the old woman embraced the pregnant woman around her belly to prevent her from falling into the dirty water. She slapped her on both cheeks too late, because the woman fainted.

Gregoire had no words of consolation for the girl with the nametag, who cried erratically, choking and panicking. His repeated like a scratched disk, What the hell, what the hell, over and over, foaming, and swallowing from the shock, he fabricated an explanation for the fact, the waters swept his garage, scattered the bodies as he left them in a rush, they were coming back at him, Like I'm their mother, what the hell, he closed one fist and the nails pierced the flesh, and with the other pushed the paddle into the corpse and the corpse floated away.

New sounds came to life, from nowhere, HALLELUJAH, the chorus, the trumpets, the bass, What is this noise?, Gregoire unclenched the fist, It's music, Tim whispered and the girl with the nametag stopped crying, FOR THE LORD GOD OMNIPOTENT REIGNETH, I got that, it's music, but where it's coming from?, From the Church, Really?, HALLELUJAH, HALLELUJAH, Is it where we are going?, the old woman asked, almost smiling, remembering her days in the Church choir, Yes, THE KINGDOM OF THIS WORLD IS BECOME, Why are you taking us there?, the girl asked, That is where everybody is, What everybody?, The Frenchman raised an eyebrow and his eyes flickered like diamonds, AND HE SHALL REIGN FOREVER AND EVER, That is where a miracle happened, Tim replied over the echo of the chorus that became stronger as the sound bounced off the walls around them, the end of the alley was near, KING OF KINGS AND LORD OF LORDS, those on the rafts paddled faster, for comforting of souls may lie ahead, for where we are many, we feel strength growing in our souls!

The convoy passed through the narrow end of the alley with crude determination.

The Church was near, but there was no next turn.

From their left, in the same moment, with the same forceful impact, another floating convoy loaded with survivors rushed toward the sound of music, not paying attention to their surroundings.

The flotillas collided with sound of crushed wood, the wardrobe travelers yelled, What the hell?, and the front paddler from the boat yelled, Watch out!, but the eye was faster than the body and inertia pushed the unbalanced bodies into the water, What the hell?, What are you waiting for?, Jump after them, the old woman frowned at Gregoire and almost pushed him into the water, not that there was danger of drowning, come on, they are close, Gregoire saw Tim's body plunging with precision into the water, like a needle into a blister, he followed the boy, legs first and whoever was unfortunate in this superficial accident was restored to their place in the final notes of Handel's Hallelujah chorus.

Chapter 87
Agglomeration of vegetarian lambs of God

The first introductions were made, Hello, I am such and such, I am Gregoire, Oh, I know, the ice cream man, Yeah, and you are?, We're from the bank, we survived in the vault, one of the tellers explained quickly, then made a few remarks about the heroism of his manager, the ludicrous amounts of money left behind, the claustrophobic ventilation shaft, which was their way to salvation, By the way, and let me say this, I had no idea there was so much money there, Dude, what are you saying?, Gregoire adopted a conspiratorial lower voice, I'm saying, man, we slept on money, Goddam.

The old woman interrupted this whispered dialogue, while watching the pregnant woman's face as she opened her eyes, on her lap, she didn't fall in the water, she was away, in her world, and she has returned, You'd better grab those paddles and find the Church, this woman needs rest and food, the old woman said.

The sight of the garden on top of the Church brought cheers to the rowers and milked out more muscular activity, so they could get there faster. The response from the gardeners on the roof was no less enthusiastic, even though the nihilists and the realists, who have clustered around the single man, were rather quiet and expressionless. Father Frank opened his arms widely and did not cease to repeat, Welcome, welcome, and asked for help from those around him. The women disembarked first and formed a line in front of the pots filled with vegetable stew. They dug their hands into the food and walked away slowly, swallowing with minimal chewing. There was plenty for everybody, everybody being a term that raises eyebrows in the single man's group and isolated frowning when the number of faces rapidly increases, I am not giving up my sleeping space, the single man said, because soon the question of where these people would rest their bodies would become the topic of the rest of the day.

You can stay here, You can stay there, the attic is big enough for at least half of us here, the rest can sleep in the garden, Is not very cold outside, it is still summer, Folks, just be careful with the garden, it is what God gave us and we should not spoil miracles. At least that was widely accepted by everybody, even the nihilists accepted the necessity of the garden, maybe not in the terms presented by Father Frank, but still, respect was the word of the day, no matter how you put it, We have to work together, whether we like it or not.

Then there were the questions of fire, hygiene, ablutions, intimacy, wearing the same clothes day after day, drinkable water.

Then there were the answers. Matches, rainwater, a large linen sheet used as screen for those in the hygiene corner, the food committee, which will have enlarged responsibilities.

Then there were the questions, What about the others?, What others?, The boss, the colleagues from the bank, Oh, yes, them, I guess Tim will get them here, Shouldn't we go now?, it's kind of late, Well, I guess it is.

Chapter 88
Dream sequence with dark knights

Aunt Bully has lost some weight since the two men have gratified their digestive system and discarded overboard the wrappings and the cans. So you think you know where we're going?, Sure, Mr. Mayor, I saw the smoke over the roofs, smoke ain't growing without people around, to which The Mayor choose not to object, although there were a few scenarios under which smoke may appear without the presence of men.

The dream sequence that was about to begin, to which The Mayor left himself easy prey, was incited by the following factors. The purplish glints of the sun's electromagnetic radiation though the pellucid layer of clouds, the sinuous dark waves of the waters, the silence of the neighborhood, the cadence of the truck driver's paddle strokes, the faint echoes of what seemed to be music coming from a radio, the sudden rush of blood away from his brain to help the production of gastric acid, the serene gliding of Aunt Bully and her slight rocking from left to right, her legs sticking out erect like—

—our canopy bed, made of cherry wood from your grandpa's orchard, remember honey, you could stretch your legs and touch both pillars with your toes, you were very bendy, honey, and then you stretched out your arms and reached for the pillows, You just love to watch me, you say, Well, I say, you are beautiful, I adore the pinkish hue of your belly, and you were lying on the bed, stretched out like a big X, adorably stripped off your puffy nightgown, and you would just let me wait, or I think I waited on my own, I had to remember you, the last letter of my alphabet, then it was the Y then you were dead, I'm sorry, Mayor, the doctor said, and then he crossed a Z on the chart and told me that your heart was tired and that your blood was thicker and didn't flow. Hold my hand, you said and you talked slowly. Then I whispered something in your ear, I don't remember what, perhaps it was just warm air, it tickled you but you loved it, then you fell asleep. The room at the hospital had no doors and it smelled like a cold moon. The five doctors entered from nowhere, dressed in black, unusual policy. I don't know who approved that, and what's with the masks?, I'm sorry, Mayor, we're afraid that the transplant is out of the question, it's just a matter of days, at the most. What are you talking about? I asked them, and what's with those masks on your face, take them off, I want to read the truth off your face. There is no other truth. Then you died. So be it.

[This is where a sleeper confuses dreams with reality.]

Oh, it's you, The Mayor said. I was sleeping.

Mr. Mayor, we have company. The truck driver has stopped Aunt Bully when it encountered another floating vehicle that was transporting a group of men, Spooky folks, Mr. Mayor, they all wear black cardigans, and there is a woman with a red sweater and a boy who looks kind of shy, Why are you whispering?, They are here.

The Mayor made himself visible to the sailing club and their company, all surprised to recognize the familiar face. He made up a name for the truck driver, a fairly decent one, out of the need to put a name on a face and further the dialogue, and he was slightly surprised to notice that the truck driver did not protest the naming and in fact seemed to like it.

Mr. Mayor, you survived, one of the five men observed.

No time for truisms, sir. I would rather ask you what is with the outfit. I might have lost track of time, but I do not believe that we celebrate the annual costume holiday yet.

Mr. Mayor, we all know you are a keen observer of reality and a wry orator. The cardigans are simply part of a ritual we have subscribed to, and, as you may well know, our country has legislated the free expression of association and religion as long as it does not infringe on the social order, which I believe we do not do by simply wearing articles of clothing that for some may not look ordinary, which I agree that they may not be, pulled out of the context, yet in our case we simply manifest our fellowship for a certain cause, not relevant to anybody in particular, therefore there is no need to persevere with prying curiosity, justified and understandable to a point, which brings me to the position of asking you, in return, if you do not mind, what are you doing here?

The Mayor did not answer right away, because the man with the black cardigan did not stress properly the word *what*, and it sounded more like a statement, although many statements were indubitably by nature implied as questions, and by this fact leaving more ground in the conversation for the elaboration of each party's position. Instead, The Mayor addressed the woman with the red sweater, who had noticed him and fixed her eyes on him from the beginning. Her face seemed to convey its own message, yet there was something that stopped her from speaking.

Good afternoon, madam.

Mr. Mayor.

I reckon you know who I am.

Indeed, sir.

Nice to meet you, madam.

Thrilled to meet you, Mr. Mayor.

Please, please, too many formalities, you can call me by my first name. While saying this, The Mayor noticed how the woman stressed the word thrilled as if she was trying to convey a subliminal message.

The woman simply replied, I couldn't do that sir. It wouldn't be appropriate.

The Mayor and the man in the black cardigan continued the conversation in a more casual tone, establishing that they have a common goal, which was the source of food the woman had mentioned to the group earlier.

I have food, Mr. Bull said.

He could not finish what he wanted to say, because The Mayor embraced him collegially and forcefully, a gesture that silenced Mr. Bull immediately.

Chapter 89
The divorce or the boat is not big enough

The Psychiatrist turned to his wife and tried to wipe the sweat off her forehead, but she pushed him away slowly and firmly. It's over, she said.

His first impulse was to engage in analysis, leafing mentally through hundreds of cases where the word over has been used, putting things into context, or extracting meaning out of context, the system may have deviations, the uncertainty principle, you cannot know both the motivation and the direction in the same time, because if you do, you interfere into the subject's deterministic cycle, and the subject will never be the same. He replied after a few moments of silence with a short, What do you mean, and while she prepared her answers he thought about what he felt, about the glacialness of her tone, about unhappiness and suffering.

I am not happy, she said. It's not the mask, it's not the pain. I am just not happy. It's the years when you touched my face and your hand was cold, the nights when you undressed me with no words, the nights when you did not undress me at all, when your body was away, when your mind was away, when you looked at my mask just to wipe off crumbs and dust, the lust that was like a therapy session, the long silent hours.

I want you out of my life, she said.

Chapter 90
Panis angelicus

It was the first night that some survivors had to sleep under the bare sky because the attic was filled with tired bodies, in all the corners, all the niches, in improvised hammocks hung from the solid beams, on and under raised beds made of wooden crates, over one another, children on the bellies of their mothers and fathers, the few stronger ones and the stoics attempting the lotus position against the walls, to save space for the benefit of the others. The rest, because they have drawn the shorter sticks, stretched their bodies in the garden, on the roof, counted stars out loud to make their presence and discomfort felt, until they were silenced by the shivering cold or the shadow of Father Frank, who was praying in his spot, at the border of the tomato patch.

The new arrivals came from the dense fog of the next day.

First, there was a woman wearing a white Venetian mask, ornate with fine gold and purple embroidery. She seemed to be made of porcelain. Immovable like a marble statue, fixing a point on the horizon and never looking left or right. Maybe she was blind, hence the mask, or maybe she was dead and was kept erect by a hidden mechanism behind her. There was a man with her. The intellectuals recognized him. The Psychiatrist, whom many call *my therapist*, was paddling, his eyes also fixed on the horizon.

Next, there was an odd-looking man maneuvering a wooden bull that was floating upside-down. And there was another man with him, sitting on the groin of bull and watching closely the paddle strokes of his companion. When the wooden bull approached the Church, the girl named Iris yelled, Uncle!, but no one really heard her.

Soon after, the womb of the white fog gave birth to a group of five men, a teenage boy and woman with a red sweater. The men were wearing black cardigans and all looked in the same direction, over the shoulder of the woman with the red sweater, who was wiping tears and dew off her face. She fixed her hair and reached for the hand of The Quiet Boy next to her and whispered something like, It's going to be fine. But one of the men pulled the boy back and held him tightly.

The single man, who spent the night on the roof, scratched his chin. What is this, a goddam costume party? No one really heard him. The fog slowly evaporated, carried away by a breeze.

The next to appear was the rugged face of The Frenchman. The children immediately recognized the ice cream man, but their mothers tempered their enthusiasm at the sight of an untrimmed and mean looking beard. On the same raft, there was Tim, three women and the guy from the Synagogue. The girl named Iris yelled, Tim! In the convoy that followed, they could see a bunch of people, in business-like attire, or what was once the formal attire of the bank employees. Nobody really knew their names. Even if they still had their nametags on their chests, nobody would care to look. The nametags were lost in the flood. Some even had pieces of cobwebs on their shirts, for god's sake.

This is just great, the single man muttered, to express his frustration with, All these people around, we're too crowded, we'll never have enough food for everyone.

That is why it is time for prayer, my friends. Father Frank's intervention was welcomed by the whole population with different degrees of enthusiasm. He told people to, Stand here, and here, you all will face this way, we are going to sing a beautiful song and we will watch the red sun and we will hold hands.

The group was assembled quickly into a number of rows and the choir of the red sun was born. The chattering diminished, then turned into mumbles, then expectant silence.

Father Frank delivered a brief speech in which he mentioned the fortuitous and joyful salvation of our brothers in faith, then he said something about the hand of God that stretched out and surrounded The Valley, When it may seem that he takes away, he actually gives, he explained the necessity of altruism and selflessness in this dire context, because, They can only survive if they work together. He referred as well to the miracle of the garden and its bottomless resources, still inexplicable. Isn't this another sign of divine generosity?, he said and he elaborated a long phrase that seemed to have no punctuation and no breathing, referring to the, Preciousness of life and all that comes with it, and finally concluded with the words from the song, known to many from the sermons. Panis angelicus.

The song began with the male voices in the back, those who knew the lyrics starting first, *Panis angelicus*, others following a beat later, *panis angelicus*, emanating an unrehearsed polyphonic fugue, syllables chasing each other in a sublime unfolding, it was perfection. Father Frank raised his arms to lead the next singers into the chant, *fit panis hominum*, the pigeons soared above their heads and dropped the seeds on the intro of tutti into *figures terminum*, the bass voices, the tenors, the tone later, the reciting of the previous line when Father Frank lift his index fingers and pointed to them, Now the women filled the air, *O res mirabilis*, the wind caught up with them, the leaves caught up with the pigeons, circling the roof in a spiral, in an immense imaginary cathedral that holds them all, *manducat dominum*, the men, *pauper, pauper, servus et humilis*. Father Frank pointed to the sky for them all to sing da capo *Panis angelicus*, and again, the octave higher for the youngsters, or the key of their own choosing for the few who have just found their voice and learned the lyrics on the go, and again, while the many closed their eyes and let their bodies do the singing, and their mind do the praying, as they felt fit to their beliefs, to the momentary effusions, to the birth of a moment of grace.

Chapter 91
Penis impossibilis

Grace, for one of the men, came in the form of an outstanding ERECTION. The man was Gregoire. He sang the ode of the angelic bread with a sweet scent of vanilla invading his nostrils from over his shoulders, and it had a taste of a woman's skin, and the taste of a wet womb, and he felt the woman's breathing full force right into his nape, it was warm, it drove him insane. After the last verse, Gregoire spun on his heels. The woman had her arms crossed on her belly, though she didn't look pregnant, and The Frenchman had the glance of a woman who was defending something that she didn't know what it is yet. Instinctively, she hid her navel under the double dome of her palms, without paying much attention to her chest, which was pushed forward. Her breasts became full moons, big moons larger than the sky.

Gregoire stretched out the corners of his lips and displayed one row of teeth, the conventional way of smiling, then said, Madame, and lift an imaginary fedora. The woman bowed her head to avoid eye contact and clutched her elbows with opposite hands. She didn't realize that this gesture didn't help her defense much. The involuntary flushing of her chest, a trick that women use to emphasize their femininity or sexual availability by manipulating the size of their breasts, had a natural effect on The Frenchman's groin, fueled by an additional supply of blood. His pulse accelerated and his synapses focused on a certain subject, yet the subject remained beyond reach, because when The Frenchman extended his arm, the subject pulled away and took a step back.

Now the woman realized the unwanted exposure of her cleavage and the swelling of her breasts above their natural relaxed position. She felt sorry that her bra had lost its elasticity and felt a jet of nausea from her stomach.

Monsieur, I'm sorry. I do not feel well.

Gregoire was not the man to accept a rejection with ease. Sure, he can hear a no behind various enunciations, diplomatic or frank, depending on the speaker's style, but he simply cannot accept them. His first reaction was to intensify his efforts. Only in a shrinking room with no doors or windows would he accept reality. It is what it is, he would think.

However it was not what it is now. His groin made a step forward and then his legs followed.

Monsieur, I am pregnant, I need to lie down.

Let me help you, he said.

While the choir dispersed and people sat down or started eating vegetables, nobody really paid attention to anything. The prayer was in a way an energy drainer, a day-dreaming stimulator and hope infuser, senses tended to be fooled easier by a good disposition rather than a malevolent disposition. Some psychiatrists said that a slight tendency to depression actually increases awareness, not that this was fully applicable to Gregoire and the pregnant woman. Both had a weakness that called to an instinct, for the man, the call of the manhood, the beast, the zest, for the woman, the incipiency of maternal instincts, the cells that split in her uterus and the storm of hormones that messes with her head.

She tripped on unearthed roots. Gregoire caught her before she touched the ground. She closed her eyes and didn't think of anything.

Chapter 92
The sword's edge cannot cut the sword

Gregoire's mossy hands carried the pregnant woman into a secluded corner of the attic, where light was scarce and the air was old, where no one would consider looking, not until sunset when they will need a place to lay their heads. Gregoire's erection retreated into a sudden state of anxiety when a man grabbed his elbow and whispered into his ear, We need to talk. There was something about the abruptness of the tone and the grip on his elbow that gave Gregoire a hint of what that man wanted to talk about.

Put her down, the man said.

What the hell do you want?

Tone, my friend, tone!

What the fu—

I have a gun with a silencer pointed at your heart, fucker, lower your voice!

The man pushed the gun into Gregoire's flesh to make his point.

What the—

Do you get it, dumbshack, you understand now the exceptionality of our situation, do you?

Oui!

Whisper! Fuck. Good. Listen. Where is the stuff?

The stuff.

Fucking rhetorical! The stuff!

What the hell are you talking about?

Où est la marchandise?

La merchandise. You The Lawyer?

The zipper, dumbshack! What did I say about lowering your voice? Good. I will not repeat the question, because it will be freaking predictable, wouldn't it?

I lost it.

Fucking lost it? What do you mean?

I was in the garage and the flood came.

Don't stop. Enunciate. Make sense!

I had it in that box. It's gone. The water came and swept everything away.

Fucking!

The silencer remained pushed into The Frenchman's flesh while The Lawyer took a few moments to reflect on the newly acquired information. The dumbshack might be telling the truth, but he might also be trying to distort it.

The chorus, turned into a gregarious flock, moved around, looking for a place to sit down, for some privacy for biological functions, to chatter with the person in the vicinity, to willingly ignore the masked man's conversation with The Frenchman, They must be acquainted. In the sea of eyes, there was always one pair that watches, but didn't want to be watched. That pair of eyes was attached to a body whose hands reached for its neck to check on the status of a voice synthesizer that provided not only the tool of speech but another secret, that for now only silence can protect. That body, not wanting to be seen by The Frenchman, hid in the crowd and crouched, pretending to pluck a tomato that will be inserted in the mouth and chewed slowly.

A hand landed on the Luc's shoulder. Luc, son, are you okay? The voice was Father Frank's. They showed each other mutual respect and a sort of calculated coolness, in the spirit of civilized brotherhood, or simply an emanation of the above-mentioned respect. Father Frank knew Luc well enough to sense his distress. Luc has never covered the synthesizer with his palm for such a long time. I am fine, the answer came, faded because the palm filtered the sound. Luc stood up and merged with the crowd, again changing direction, away from The Frenchman. His eyes met The Frenchman's. Many tiny invisible daggers flew between them.

Luc found the pregnant woman. She was asleep. He hid in the shadow next to her, sat down and put his cheeks on his knees. He was a ghost. Nobody could see ghosts. He detached the collar from his neck and opened the battery compartment. He had tucked a tiny velvet bag inside. It was hard to take it out. He feared that the contents would spill. He was careful. He opened the bag in his palm. The diamonds were there. He smelled them, like fresh buds. There were not many places where he could hide them. The Frenchman would want to see his synthesizer. He packed the stones into the tiny bag once more, and looked at the pregnant woman. She was sobbing in her sleep. His eyes followed the line of her body and stopped at the sight of a few pubic hairs. He thought that the fashion of wearing underwear really low was very inappropriate. His imagination ran wild, but he quickly settled on a solution. He tied a string to the tiny bag. He pat the woman's crotch. He inserted the bag into the woman's underwear. She moaned but didn't wake up. Luc was sweating. He quickly finished the operation.

Gregoire pointed at him. That's him, he said.

The Lawyer fixed Luc in his gaze and whispered to The Frenchman to fetch him.

It took Gregoire ten seconds to elbow his way through the crowd.

There is no way to go, you prick, he said.

Luc stood up and adjusted the synthesizer.

The Frenchman was in front of him and grabbed him swiftly by the sleeve.

You're coming with me.

When you hope that no one is watching, there is always somebody watching. It was a quiet observer, nicknamed by many The Quiet Boy. He was standing at some distance from the scene, but he saw the Synagogue guy doing some business with that woman's genitalia. He found that peculiar. His actions had not been violent, and the man seemed panicked, rather than swarming with erotic desire. The woman was still asleep. The Frenchman took the Synagogue guy away, and no one really paid attention to the woman. The Quiet Boy approached her. She smelled nice. Her breasts were firm. She was dreaming. Her navel was exposed, as well as a few pubic hairs. And the end of a string knotted into a hole of her panties. He pulled the string. A tiny velvet bag emerged. He looked around him. He was hoping that no one was watching. He opened the bag. Diamonds. The woman moaned.

She may be dreaming of an egg splitting into many cells.

He put the velvet bag in his pocket and stood up calmly. His knapsack was where he left it. His father told him never to lose sight of it. One of the kids was trying right now to open it. In seconds The Quiet Boy was next to the knapsack and pushed the kids away. There were other kids watching. They giggled then they ran away. The little curious brat who fumbled with his knapsack started crying. The Quiet Boy frowned at him. The brat stopped crying and displayed a devilish smile. Then he ran away.

The Quiet Boy immediately checked the contents of the knapsack and exhaled with relief.

The brat had his reasons to smile. His accomplices had approached The Quiet Boy, tiptoeing from behind, and extracted the velvet bag from the pocket. Those tiny hands have a surreptitious modus operandi. They were not wondering if they were being watched, but there was always somebody watching. The brats giggled and blended into the crowd.

The carrier of the velvet bag bumped into a massive body dressed in a black cardigan. I believe you have something for me, the man in the black cardigan said. The brat lost the smile and handed the velvet bag to the masked man. You tell anyone, we kill all of you, the man said. The brats looked down and said they will forever keep their mouths shut.

The man made a sign, and the other men approached him. They whispered something and one showed to the other the sleeping pregnant woman. They quickly checked the contents of the velvet bag and seemed satisfied. The Banker asked The Lawyer, How do you explain this?, The Lawyer responded that this is not the circumstance for explanations, We must see the woman, he said.

Four men in cardigans surrounded the pregnant woman and feigned a conversation. The fifth man leaned over the woman, checked her pulse, made a judgment about the profoundness of her sleep, waved a vial with chloroform over her nose, then stripped the woman's underwear just enough to expose what was covered. He produced a latex glove and a tiny flashlight. He clenched his teeth on the flashlight. With two fingers he spread out the woman's labia and looked inside. Nothing. It just took a few seconds. Gloves, flashlight, underwear, pants back on.

She's clean, the man said.

I guess that's all there is, The Advisor said.

Where is the rest? The Politician asked.

Patience gentlemen, we'll find it, The Lawyer answered.

We cannot stay longer with the cardigans on, The Neurosurgeon intervened.

Where are the other stones, Mr. Lawyer?

I have already answered, Mr. Banker.

The brats returned. They were playing catch. They bumped into the men in cardigans. The Banker dropped the tiny velvet bag.

A heady stampede burst out. The forest of feet was dense and the velvet bag was at the mercy of unruly kicks from all sides, until it landed in the shadow of a heavy shoe that hovered above the ground. The brain at the other end of this body with the heavy shoe collected the information from the peripheral sensors, put them together and ordered the hands to pick up that strange object.

I'll be damned, The Manager mumbled when he looked inside the bag.

The divorced girl, as the most faithful shadow, echoed the words and added a rhetorical note to them, What are they?

Her lover built a cone with his palm and puts the cone on her ear. You know what they are, he said.

He inserted the stones furtively into the divorced girl's cleavage, a natural and logical hiding place, proximate and secure, accessible only to four hands. We will deal with this later, he concluded. Don't you think that someone might be looking for them?, Well, too bad, they got kicked in the water, Uh, I don't know, Relax dear, I'm in control, Yeah, over my cleavage, Shh.

Boss, what do I do with this?

The Manager turned to the teller. The baby poodle was shivering in the teller's arms. Its eyes were creamy with pus.

This will be taken care of. I'll take it. We're all children of—

He didn't finish the sentence.

The poodle was transferred immediately to the divorced girl, with arms outstretched so no mud dripped from the tangled fur onto the executive shoes. The girl embraced the animal with unrestrained joy and pushed it affectionately against her chest, where her warm heart was. The poodle didn't feel the beating heart though. The poodle felt a bulging between the girl's breasts and grabbed it in its tiny fangs.

Come back!, the girl cried, but the cry was ineffective. The poodle disappeared into the crowd with the velvet bag in its mouth.

Chapter 93
The Centurion

The Charging Bull is well upholstered with something on the inside, because the world outside is immediately silenced when she closed the trapdoor behind us.

Iris smells enthralling today. It makes me think of my grandfather's garden. I think I have been there twice, maybe thrice. I remember pulling Dad's beard when he was showing me tulip buds. They grow from the inside, he said.

What grows from the inside, Tim?

Um, nothing, I was just thinking of my dad.

Her candid eyes want to ask me why I am thinking of my dad again, but she doesn't say anything. Instead she whispers, I want to show you something.

She opens a secret compartment in the bull's skin and produces a crank, then inserts it into an interior appendage of the bull's tail.

Do you know her name? Ha, you don't? Aunt Bully.

What a name!

She cranks up the tail.

Propelled by the tail of Aunt Bully, we sail into the sea of light.

She says she wanted to show me something. How do you steer a wooden bull?, I ask. She says that I should not worry, that it's her baby and it will listen to her, we are not far anyways.

She stops.

We have to turn, she says.

We crawl like mice in a spinning wheel.

Cans of marmalade and tuna roll over our heads.

It all feels white inside the bull.

We can go out now.

If she opens the trap door, we will drown in less than a minute.

Heroically, like Russians in a submarine.

She opens the trapdoor.

No water runs in.

In fact, more light floods Aunt Bully from the outside.

She opens the trapdoor and goes out first, through the bull's balls. I follow.

It's summer in City.

There is no one around.

The benches in Bowling Green Park are empty, stores are closed, streets are clean, no cars to be seen.

There is no one around.

A yellow taxicab speeds down Broadway and stops abruptly by the park. A man in a black cardigan comes out and rushes into the nearest building. The taxicab disappears in a cloud of smoke.

He didn't see us.

We cross the street and put our backs against the wall of the building.

The man in the black cardigan enters a café at 11 Broadway, a few steps below street level. We follow him and raise our foreheads above the ledge of the window.

It's dark inside.

There is nobody inside except the man with the black cardigan.

He is talking over the counter with another man.

He opens a wooden box and spreads the contents on the bar.

Diamonds.

In the dark, they glow like nebulae.

The bartender shows satisfaction and shakes the hand of the man.

Then they both look at the window.

A split second before they see us, we lower our heads.

The man with the black cardigan storms out.

He doesn't see us.

He walks fast down on Broadway.

He walks through the intersection with Battery Place.

The lights turn red and green and red really fast.

There is no one around. No cars, no people.

He stops on State Street, as if he has forgotten something.

He hesitates. He wants to look back. We hide behind the corner of the Museum.

Under the lion and the spear.

I can see steam coming out of her mouth. She is a warm summer day.

He looks back and doesn't see us.

He turns and keeps walking fast in the middle of the empty road.

His heels echo against the building.

Like in an empty theatre during rehearsals.

He walks past Bridge Street.

He stops at the mailbox at the intersection with Pearl Street.

He takes a suitcase from inside.

Across the street an old man sitting on the bench looks at him.

The old man points at something. Then he becomes air and disappears.

The man runs down on State.

The lampposts melt like willows as we run by them.

City is melting.

He takes the road by the park.

We run behind him and take refuge behind trees.

He turns his face at us.

It's Gregoire.

He doesn't see us. He looks away.

He stops behind a shrub, takes the cardigan off, doesn't care if anyone is watching. He unpacks the suitcase. He installs the gunsight and waits. We come closer and crowd into each another behind another shrub. We can't really see his face. It's sunk behind the butt of the gun. He points to a boat with two people in it: a man and a boy, his son. The father says to his son, This is your future. The father smiles. Then we see BLOOD on the father's hand gushing from the exit hole of the bullet. He pushes his son into the cold water and calls his son's name. The second bullet enters his left temple and exits through the right. The impact throws the body in the river.

Chapter 94
Cellular epiphany

Did you hear that?

Hear what?

It was like the sound of a gun.

Imam's hesitancy in making a definite statement was justified by the excess amount of earwax he possessed. He inserted an improvised toothpick into his ears and stirred vigorously while Rabbi flipped one of his side curls to expose the auricle to a maximum collection of sounds. The sound of the gun's discharge was faint and was not repeated, so this concentration on auditory stimuli did not help. Seconds later, however, both Imam and Rabbi felt similar vibrations next to their chests, in the inside pockets that were holding the cellular communication devices. At first, they exchanged a defensive glance. They each made note of the other's similar facial expression and only then considered that the vibration of the devices might be related to the sound of the gun. The next thought dismissed this idea, Nonsense. The devices kept vibrating. The next thought in their minds is, How come after so many days it is still working?, but they left the question unanswered. The devices kept vibrating. They both said, Excuse me, and retreated to opposite corners of the operating room and answered.

Imam speaking.

Imam, you do recognize my voice?

Yes.

Imam?

Yes!

You must speak up, Imam.

Yes.

Imam?

Yes. Sir.

The purpose of my call, Imam, is not to answer your question about how come your cellular device is functioning under such improbable circumstances, but to remind you to detach yourself from the illusion of time.

I beg your pardon. I'm not following, sir.

You will look now at the other corner and will notice that you are being watched.

Hello, this is Rabbi. Who is this?

I am the authority.

Yes, sir.

Probably you are wondering why your cellular device is functioning after days without recharging and you must be thinking of various logical and mystical explanations.

I, I—

I assure you none of those are correct, but this is no time for explanations. The time will come. Do not attach yourself too much to this concept.

What concept, sir?

Are you listening? Time. Let us not make this too absurd. You will look now at the other corner and will notice that you are being watched.

Imam and Rabbi looked at each other, diagonally, bishops across a chess table, one on black, one on white, in the same dimension, observing each other, but never having the chance to meet, unless forced by the fangs of the queen to sacrifice for the benefit of a comrade-at-arms, to ameliorate a position, to simulate a sacrifice, or to do it for real, intuiting a future advantageous position. Nothing seemed odd for the observers of the bishops and nothing blocked their view. Unbeknown to the otherness is the symmetry of the gesture and the similarity of the surprise. Eyes met with surprise, with concern for obedience, with consideration for faith, revelation and the wisdom of the ancients, of the saints, Muhammad, Moses, the smell of white prickly roses.

<table>
<tr><td>He's looking at me.
Good, good, wave at him.</td><td>He's looking at me.
Good, good, wave at him.</td></tr>
</table>

They waved at each other.

<table>
<tr><td>See, it is not that hard.
We realized that the habitation in that space is causing extreme discomfort for the brothers. You must lead your men to light, to the surface, and follow the WHITE smoke and join the others.</td><td>See, it is not that hard.
You must lead your men to light, to the surface, and follow the BLACK smoke and join the others. We realized that the habitation in that space is causing extreme discomfort for the brothers.</td></tr>
</table>

As The Voice was narrating the instructions for both parties, the brothers were trying to catch another glimpse of the gunshot. I heard it again, No it was just the echo, We are underwater, how can you really hear?

<table>
<tr><td>It will be a long night. At sunrise you will all join forces and build the bridges of your survival.</td><td>At sunrise you will all join forces and build the bridges of your survival. It will be a long night.</td></tr>
</table>

Some of the brothers noticed the peculiarity of what Imam and Rabbi were doing, verging on the absurd. Despite their awareness of the situation, they did not bother to ask themselves if their leaders are actually talking on the cellular devices or not, in fact the symptoms of the effects of the dextrose overdose and the dehydration were ubiquitous in the operating rooms. What the brothers did know for sure is that they could not spend much time there, they need alternate means of existence.

The instructions came very shortly. In one hand the two leaders held the cellular devices and with the other hand they pointed at things.

We must break the window in that room. We all move in this room. The wa—

The water will fill the room, we rise to the ceiling and we exit through the window. The surface is not far.

From the surface we find a flotation object and we sail towards the—

—black smoke—

—white smoke.

Rabbi, but we will drown, Rest assured we will not, have faith, Imam, why don't we break the door and escape through the hallway, The door to the hallway might be watertight, but the hallway is completely flooded to the ceiling, We are at the first floor, remember, Yes, but, Rest assured, this is the best option, have faith, brothers, Yes, listen to your leader, Rabbi added, while the brothers retreated to into the left corner. Imam and Rabbi retreated to the right corner.

I don't feel good about this, one of the brothers said, Why not?, We'll drown before we get out, at least here we're safe, Yeah, but how long do you think we can last on the bloody dextrose?, And limited water, Why do you say limited?, I don't think anybody knows about us, the pipes will break, They won't break, The supply of drinkable water is not unlimited, I say we have to go, I hear you, brother, I say we break the window, we swim out, I can't swim, We swim out and we follow the white smoke, Black smoke.

He called you too?

Not sure, did He?

Is this what I think it is?

Maybe, what do you think this is?

I haven't really thought about it, what do you think?

I think we do it and we follow the white smoke.

Black smoke.

I'm sure He said white.

And I'm sure He said black.

We need to get out of here.

Chapter 95
White smoke black smoke

Father Frank thought that, It's ironic that one fire produces white smoke and the other fire produces black smoke.

Chapter 96
From migraine to migration

The single man was sullen, stolid, pensive, haggard and unflappable. Sleeping on the bare wood didn't do his back much good, but what can he do, it was his turn. When nights were colder, he could not use the excess of clothing to soften his place of rest. He thought about his dream from last night. The dream was rapidly fading away and he was trying not to lose it. It was about the woman with the red sweater, recently returned to their group.

She was sleeping on her back, her head facing him, so from the low angle of his eyes he watched the horizon of Town between her hilly breasts, it made him think of a red Bactrian camel, and when she shuddered and jerked her body to one side, pushed by the poignant force of a dream, she exposed to the single man's eyes the plethora of rooftops. On the ebb of the reflections, he felt a flow of inspiration.

He blurted out to all those who could hear him, We must populate more rooftops! There is not enough room here!

Immediately many joined him, Yeah, Yeah, he's right, my back hurts, I can't sleep any longer crowded like this, I might have pneumonia from the cold dew, We need meat, I've had enough with these vegetables, Et cetera, the frustrations piling up like pigeons on a few crumbs in the public square, not necessarily related to the originator. Who knows when rescue will come?, Yeah, why has nobody bothered to even check us out?, No helicopters, no news crews, no governor to assess the situation, It's like we don't exist, Folks, folks, please, we all know the remoteness of Town, even if the communication lines go down, it will be a matter of days until someone in City finds out, plus, fortunately or not, we are, or should I say were, self-sufficient in energy and the other means of subsistence, a reason why there is no apparent concern from the higher authorities.

The Mayor was correct, in principle. The higher authorities from City indeed did not give a damn about their situation, or have any knowledge of their misfortune, because if they had, it would have been mentioned in this book, somebody must have talked about it in private, Hey, come here, shh, I have a scoop, I saw a helicopter yesterday, Are you sure?, Shh, yeah, I'm sure. But this dialogue did not take place.

The sun thrust spears of light and warmth into his eyes.

Yeah, I think it's a good idea, someone added, and a committee was formed to establish the next steps.

The concept of hydroponics was brought forward. We grow plants with mineral nutrients, in water, without soil, explains the old woman, There is no need, ma'am, we have access to soil with these buckets, When the soil is beyond reach, we will have to use other means, Like what?, We will turn wool into earth. With the voice and self-assuredness of an old shaman, the old woman radiated calmness into people's hearts and from those hearts the people themselves pushed thoughts into their cerebra, from where consensus and agreement emerge. Soon after, the consensus of principle has found a uniform pace, and labor started.

The nearest rooftops were populated first. Carefully carried, seedlings wrapped in soil wads, buckets and bundles with wool from the filling of coats, nails removed from walls, held in the mouth, hammered to form small crates for the new gardens.

Chapter 97
Metronomes of hopes and illusions

We take separate ways, we are on different lists, I know, I know, it's a scientific distribution, X number of men, X number of women, X number of children, categories, sets, subsets, this amount of blankets, sweaters, bags with seeds, buckets, boats, we can wave at each other from rooftop to rooftop, I'm afraid we can't, See my rooftop is over there, yours is there, Those trees are blocking the view, We'll manage.

They have longing in their eyes and their lips move in anticipation of loneliness, their lips are dehydrated, she bites the cracks on her lower lip, he bites the cracks on his lower lips, he says, You are beautiful today, she blushes, then she says, Your beard is adorable, and combs his beard with the tips of her fingers.

Anonymous survivors.

Iris cranks up the handle of her radio.

She tells me that, Maybe we can catch a broadcast or something, maybe they know about us.

The static sounds like tiny rain droplets on tin foil.

Maybe we are made of tin foil.

I tell her that listening to the sound of static on her radio makes me think of deserts and long caravans.

How ironic, she says. We are in the middle of a flood and you think of deserts.

I tell her that after water, drought comes.

The five men in cardigans retreat inside the attic until the first round of boats departs. The list of those who will remain in the Church is in Father Frank's hand. We are on the list. Father Frank knows that we need to stay together.

What are you thinking? she asks me.

I don't know what to tell her.

I'm thinking of what will become of us. I'm thinking of my father. The killer is here. I saw him. We were in City, you and me. We both saw him.

She is cranking up the radio.

I think hope is worth a chance.

Hope is the dead end of logic, I say.

You may be right, she says.

People start coming out of the attic as some room has been cleared after the departure of the convoy of boats. There are five new faces in the crowd. I look at her. She looks at me. We both know.

The song starts. Static mingles with sound of an acoustic guitar.

Father do you think they'll bomb the park?

Some look over their shoulders. What is this oddity? The five new faces mingle with the others. They are quiet. They only exchange glances with the others. One of them has a son. Their faces are a bit pale, like they have not exposed themselves to the sun in a long time.

Father do you think they'll take this long?

The pregnant woman asks if that is Pink Floyd. Yes, it is, Iris responds. How is your baby? she asks. It's kicking, the woman says. She hasn't heard this song in years.

Father do you think they'll try to break my walls?

Gregoire looks at me. Then he sees the five men. One draws his attention and he changes his face. It's his tic. He rubs his moustache. Nervously.

Oo-ah, Father should I build a doll?

Somebody asks what radio station that is.

I don't know, Iris responds. Then she turns the volume to the maximum. A very bearable maximum. She continues to crank the radio, slowly.

You found the dog? The Manager asks the blonde divorced girl. She puts a finger on his lips. Keep it down, please. Yes I did. And where are the … stones?

Father should I apply for resident?

Father Frank checks the list again, looks at us, smiles, You'll stay here with me, we know that, then checks a few details with the relocation committee. How many seeds do we have left? he asks them.

Father should I trust this wonderland?

I'm thinking of my mother.

She's fine, Tim, she's a survivor, Iris tells me.

I hope she climbed into my room.

Father will they put me in the hiring line?

The Quiet Boy looks at me. He's holding tightly to his knapsack. His father, too, acknowledges our presence.

Oo-ah, is it just a waste of lime.

Can you check if there's anything else on the radio? The single man has been fidgeting his fingers the whole day. The woman with the red sweater had left in the first boat. She is trying to get away from something. She does not look back.

Iris finds a faint voice on the radio. Sounds like a newscaster. It comes in bits.

Town, inaccessible, national emergency prevented the access, governor, no reports, air fleet stand-down, survivors questionable.

Then static.

Keep cranking, the single man says.

It's not that. The reception is bad. They know about us.

If they do, where are they?

Nobody knows.

There is a whisper around us. Where are those five folks with black cardigans? I don't know, don't ask me. They're gone. Many left with the boats, my friend.

On the other roofs, fires are started. People wave at us. They seem relieved and joyful. The boats are brought back.

The new candidates for relocation are forming queues.

How many of us are here, anyways?

The pregnant woman doesn't want to go. She says that something bad is going to happen. Do not worry, child, says Father Frank.

Chapter 98
The last rain, comfortably numb, uncomfortably soaked

The rain started violently, as if the clouds were shattered by explosives. It was not nighttime, but the skies became darker, a burden they carried with them from god knows where, and come to a final clash above The Valley.

The long convoy, Iman and Rabbi, and their lieutenants in the first boat looked everywhere, at the clouds, the boats behind them, ahead, to visualize the trajectory to the white smoke black smoke, Do you hear what I hear?, There are people there, Where is the smoke?, Forget the smoke, I know they're there, I do not recognize these places, many houses have drowned, I know where we are going. Rabbi's last sentence sounded prophetic to his comrades, like Moses's voice might have sounded to his compatriots, Moses knew where he was going, the geopositioning flame was in his head.

The rain was thick and noisy. Droplets bounced off water, like bullets.

The pathways were lit by light stored in shattered mirrors, crooked trees, cracked walls. It smelled like wailing ghosts, lingering in inexistence, silenced by the pattering of persistent water ellipsoids. The brothers paddled, they followed the voices, or the echoes, there was water seeping into their mouths, they closed their eyes and let it in, the salt of the sky, it was welcomingly sweet, their hairs blackened, dense and neat, no thoughts of covers or the fear of loss of lovers, they followed the lights from the fires, and the dim calling of imminent desire, who thought of boiling alveoli, thine eyes glittering in the night are my blind flashlight, my eyes hear music, your eyes hear voices, somewhere in an attic, round the corner a scratchy gramophone plays a sad song, *And that was called dove for the workers in throng, probably still flies for those who are wrong*, You know the song, it makes you think of reincarnation, of timelessness,

Nonsense, we die and that's it, Then how do you explain where all the new souls come from?, This question has been asked before, how do *you* explain?, Life consumes life to perpetuate itself. These questions have been asked before, many times. The brothers followed the song, *I feed you, I don't feed you, I feed you, I don't feed you and all of that horsing around*, Yeah, it's spiritual, but it makes me knit my veins into a bowtie and decorate the neck of my heart.

They stopped because they were told to. They passed along the message that came from the oarsman in front. Someone yelled at the house, Is anyone there? A man stuck his head out a window and yells back, We're coming out.

They came out, a man and a woman wearing a mask. They hopped into the first boat and exchanged greetings with the leaders. They thought there was something odd about those two people, they did not seem very close to each other, they avoided touching themselves. Are you two related? Imam asked, This is my wife, the man said, I am the Rabbi, Yes I know, I am The Psychiatrist, Your wife, My wife has a skin condition, she can't be exposed to light, don't mind the mask.

The gramophone kept playing the Leonard Cohen song, *Well never blind, we are bloody and we have the bruises.*

Sorry about that, The Psychiatrist said. I forgot to turn it off. It will die out eventually. Battery only runs for two hours at night, then recharges with sunlight.

Ah but you went astray, didn't you ape, you just burned your bridge to the cloud.

Where are you going?, Imam asked.

We saw smoke, so we thought there were survivors with supplies or rescue heading our way.

We heard a gunshot, The Psychiatrist said.

We heard it too.

Chapter 99
Quail, food chain made of soft aluminum, inflatable side dish

The Lawyer shot three rounds before he hit the bird. He hadn't expected the silencer to fail on the third shot, but it did. Fuck, he said, then put the gun down and paddled quietly towards the drop zone.

The caliber was too big for the soaring quail, and had left the creature headless.

He wrapped it in a shirt.

His son awaited him at the rendezvous point.

Do you have the pot?

The Quiet Boy nodded and showed him the matches, the firewood, the knife.

Not that the boy did not realize where they are, he is vaguely familiar with the place from his father's stories, not that he realizes the void below, the oddity of the tiny white island they were standing on, it looked like Solzhenitsyn's big white forehead, surrounded by water to the rim, Do you know what this is?, his father asked. The Quiet Boy didn't have to say, I don't know, because his father delivered the explanation quickly by himself, just to ease his son's apprehension of what is to come next, not that The Lawyer had a precise idea of where the consumption of the bird will take place, out of sight, voracious unrepressed delight, the rendezvous of man and meat. The knapsack can fit the quail, we need some brushwood, yeah, that'll do it, you got the matches, good.

The Lawyer opened the hatch, the tip of the white dome, It looks like a submarine, doesn't it?, he said it more to himself and stuck his head inside the white dome. Just like I expected, we're fine, son, follow me.

The golf dome at the Golf Club, windless, absolutely waterproof. It had a bar in the shape of a sailing boat inside, for convenience, for relaxing times, for quick deals during breaks, while the caddy swept the grass off balls and hoped for at least a five percent tip.

The descent from the top was slow.

While holding onto the metal elliptical beams, The Lawyer's son recited, *Then they took Jonah and threw him overboard, and the raging sea grew calm.*

He liked the Book of Jonah. It was his favorite, because it was short and has an easy plot.

But the lord provided a great fish to swallow Jonah, and Jonah was inside the fish three days and three nights.

So Jonah did not enter the great fish by his own will, like we do. It was laid out for him. It was his destiny.

And the lord commanded the fish, and it vomited Jonah onto dry land.

What is destiny anyways? Who knows? God may yet relent and with compassion turn from his fierce anger so that we will not perish. God is cool!

When God saw what they did and how they turned from their evil ways, he had compassion and did not bring upon them the destruction he had threatened.

Wicked god! He has to see, he awards and punishes post factum. Show me, then I give you.

The grass was surprisingly soft and had a very natural feel.

It's artificial, his father said.

The Quiet Boy had not thought otherwise.

They camped on the deck of the sailing boat. The Lawyer started the fire, then told his son, Go see what's in that fridge, check the cupboards, is there running water?, good, bring me the bucket, give me the knife, have you ever removed feathers and boned a quail?, has your mother taught you this?, never mind, hold this.

It was canned caviar. His son found it in the mini-fridge. They will eat it later, they wanted fresh meat now, they had enough of vegetable stew and all that miracle garden crap, Goddammit, if they only knew where we were, somebody must have heard the gunshot, we were far anyways, the sound could have been mistaken with a burst pipe, goddammit, they won't notice our absence.

The Club had its ways of knowing. He was, in the end, the one responsible for the diamonds, procurement and distribution, collection of funds, use of connections, he was the main piece in

The Plan, The damn Frenchman lost the stones, damn, he chewed on a bone, it needs more boiling, Do we have some salt?, go check if there is salt there, great, bring it here, damn this is good, eat, son, eat.

Eat, as this is my body.

The tiny pile of bones was tossed overboard, into the fake green plastic sea.

The opening into the white sky of the golf dome coned the moonlight into a private limelight over father and son, as they were looking for the perfect spot to lay their heads, their bodies, for the night, the cold night outside, the warm night by the fire.

Tomorrow we're gonna play some golf, son, Don't worry, the dome is strong, and sealed like a woman's womb!, he laughed loudly and the echo reverberated into the darkness.

Chapter 100
Adrenaline fills the zeppelin

What is the sense of youth, for it fades into oblivion and is washed out by a sniff of gravity raving my mind into this corner of wood in the Church of deliverance. The moss tingles my toes, the mental foes haunt at night when the floors creak. I am documenting the spread of civilization, first we populated the nearby roofs, then we made fire, collected rain in buckets, cleaned the corners of maggots. I am an animal caught in a snare. Iris asks me, What are you doing there?, I am writing in my journal, Really?, she asks, what are you writing about?, I am writing about the Siberia in my heart, Wow, that is very sentimental and philosophical, she says, Thanks, I say, What else are you writing about?, I am documenting our ordeal, because many of us will not remember, Why is it important to remember?, she asks, Because if we don't remember we don't exist, Why do we need the past?, she asks, Because it is our cause and the effect cannot exist without the cause, Yes, but time has also no beginning, she says, True, I say, but we cannot ask these questions outside time, awareness is time, Who did you write about so far?, she asks, as if she is trying to change the subject, or simply acknowledging that you cannot answer truism with truism, I am writing about our conversation and before that I started with a short introspection, So you are one of those self-referential authors, she chuckles. I create and, saying it, it becomes creation, I say. She chuckles, I don't know, I say. Now you're trying to extract yourself from the loop, she says.

It is a sunny day, the first in many days. We have the following with us, A, Father Frank, observant and vocal with the sheep that need direction, the weak listen, the strong argue, infer and agree sometimes, B, the group of women who sing ditties at night, they are the old woman, quiet like a canyon, the pregnant woman, who guards her belly like it's a boulder of gold, she is the first to wake up in the morning to watch the spectacular sunset, C, the girl with the worn-out nametag, she has befriended Iris, D, four men with black cardigans, they did not share the beginning with us, they appeared from nowhere, they were not among the first immigrants, they whisper to each other nobody knows what, I overheard once they were talking about a plan, if it were something to the benefit of all of us, it would have been said in a louder voice, or maybe they know something and do not want to alarm us, or maybe it is one of those ingenious plans that need to be fleshed out in detail before it is shared, like the invasion of a country for such and such reason, or the solution to a major economic crisis caused by widespread greed in the system, whatever system means.

I would like to insert a quote here, *My vault is not full with hallucinations I have but with my lack of control of them*, end quote. It's from Jack Cerouak. Maybe these men are aristocratic descendants of blue blood, maybe they are very high up and have powerful fists that, unlike those of martial arts gurus, can break through a Mount Everest of laws. Maybe they are members of a secret society, if secret is defined as purposely concealing information about the origin, motivation, scope and structure of the group from the rest, because if disclosed to the rest, they, being ignorant, will want to disrupt the wellbeing of the secret society, will want a share of that magnanimous grandiose scope, reap the benefits of the juxtaposition of power next to the plethora of resources that comes with it. Would not this diminish the exceptionality of such exclusive endeavor? Of course it would, and because it is diminished, it will lose its potency. And where there is no potency, my god!, or their god respectively, we will not be able to assure the proliferation of the group values beyond the borders of this fleeting life because death, yes death, is one thing an exclusive group would not deny, because if they did, they would contradict the legitimacy of their scope. They say, Our scope has to pervade the time, the age, the changing fashions. Like the moral code of the age of enlightenment, it has to be timeless. Yet time is real and space is the illusion. Time births space.

Iris puts her hand in front of my face, interrupting my contact with the paper. So, she says, are you writing that I interrupted your contact with the paper?, Well, I say. I look up at her. As a matter of fact, As a matter of fact what?, she says, Are you repeating what I am saying?, I say, Are you repeating what I am saying?, she says. I like her, but she can be so annoying. She smiles. Tell me about your journal, she says, See those men there, what do you think of them?, I whisper, The Frenchman is associated with one of them, she says, He came with us, there is something odd about him, he's nervous, he's fidgety, he smells like juniper, he sneaks behind my back and smells my hair, then scratches his beard and mumbles that he was thinking about something and those men around him always frowning always murmuring, there is something ghastly about them, Where did they come from? I shrug, What will become of us? she asks, I don't know, some rescue operation must be on the way, No one has heard of us, she says. If they had, we would have seen something by now, Miracles are not forever, I say, Why do you say that? she asks, Look around you, this garden cannot last forever, Did you just write that?, she asks, Write what?, That miracles are not forever, Yes, I did, Are you gonna write what I am about to tell you now?, Probably, I say. Let me ask you this, she says, did you write about the others?, she leans towards me. I can smell her skin, her breasts touch my shoulder, the warmth of her breath flutters into my lungs, like the smell of freshly baked bread. There are many others with us but I don't know who they are, I answer.

Chapter 101
Where water recedes and euphoria proceeds

What was odd is that it hadn't rained in four days. The sun was stiff and the sky was flat and indifferent like a spotless military uniform. The souls were resting, the sweat evaporated quickly.

On the evening of the fourth day, when the sun shed reddish stripes on the moss in the eaves, the old woman noticed that the level of the water has decreased. It was a subtle change, but she saw the lines where the water had deposited a layer of brick-eating bacteria.

The old woman thought of the end of days, of the end of time and the reversal of everything into primordial causes.

Then she lied down on her stomach at the edge of the roof and tried to reach the water. She couldn't reach it anymore.

The waters are receding, she thought.

She did not feel the impulse to share this with the others.

Everyone was busy with something, plucking the garden, tilling the soil, making transports to other roofs, admonishing the kids, having a private confession with Father Frank or puffing smoke rings into the air, out of boredom, then making some inappropriate remark, Wash that poodle one more time, lady, and you'll turn it into diamonds. The single man didn't know how ironic his comment was in the general context, because diamonds had been very close to the poodle at one point. By early next day, the waters have retreated by the length of Gregoire's arm. I'm telling you, Gregoire said, the water was at least this much more, and he showed the people around him the length of his arm. They all rushed to the eaves and looked down to check for themselves.

Can you imagine?, We're saved, Praise God, Folks, our prayers have been listened to, If you want to view it that way, I don't, What happens now?, We have to wait until the waters are gone completely, Where is all the water going?, The Valley is like a cauldron, Maybe the earth is drinking all the water, Thank you for this satisfactory explanation, You're welcome, Still, I don't see any rescue, We can still swim to the mountains, Are you crazy?, it's pointless now, you can't carry that much food, the next town is too far, Then we wait until the water recedes, I've had enough with this veggie stew, Friends, we should be happy and thankful that nature is turning our way, Yeah, Father is right.

Father Frank was right. Over the next few hours, all the inhabitants of the roof and attic of the Church, joined by the other roofers, lied down on their stomachs and watched the water levels go down, slowly but visibly. In a day they'll be completely gone, the girl with the nametag said to herself, but the person next to her heard her and said, Yeah, I guess they will, What do we do next?

Chapter 102
The Plan revealed over Coriolan

The Club did not appreciate the general enthusiasm of the populace. Of course they noticed the waters receding, of course they thought about consequences, the probability of rescue and of life going back to normality, of course they were considering that they had to carry out The Plan in a timely fashion or they will lose momentum, Or maybe we lost it already, Where are those bloody diamonds, Mr. Lawyer?, I wish I knew, This is not a satisfactory answer, What do you want me to do? The Lawyer asked with clenched teeth.

The Politician tried to cool his temper and could not think of anything to answer.

Gentleman, we cannot talk here. I have an idea.

The Advisor's idea was simple. He went to Iris, had a quick talk with her and displayed a smile. She smiled in return, then handed him the radio.

There you go.

What's this?, The Banker asked.

The others knew that The Banker did not possess a lot of imagination.

This is a radio with a crank, The Advisor explained. We go over there, and we use it.

They caught the faint sounds of the classical station, then, as The Advisor rotated the crank faster, the noise turned into music with sense, then the sense turned into an audible orchestration.

It's the *Coriolan Overture*, The Lawyer explained.

The decibels of the mighty *Coriolan* built a shield around The Club so they talked beyond the reach of unwelcomed ears. They did not raise their voices, they articulated the words clearly, with arched lips and precise diction.

We must act quickly or we'll lose the diamonds that are already in escrow, The Politician started, When is the election?, The Banker asked, Soon, very soon, We need the last shipment to secure the favorable decision before the election, If it wasn't for the flood, Too late for that consideration, When did you make contact with The Client last time?, The Neurosurgeon asked, The day before the flood, The Lawyer responded, Was he impatient?, I couldn't say impatient, but he was certainly waiting for the completion of the deal, Are you saying that The Plan relies now on The Frenchman's ability to complete his tasks?, The Politician asked, Gentlemen, I assure you that he is very determined to complete it, He values life and freedom too much, Don't you think we were too hasty with Tolstoy's elimination?, It was necessary for The Plan, The Lawyer said, then took a minute to reminisce about the day of the execution, he was there, he saw everything, he wished he had pulled the trigger so Gregoire didn't have to ask, What about the boy?, Forget the boy, The Lawyer told The Frenchman when he returned to the car, in the woods. Mr. Lawyer, The Advisor said and had to repeat it again to interrupt The Lawyer's daydreaming, What, Mr. Advisor?, If we do not get the stones soon The Client will revoke the deal and will not guarantee the security of the escrow, Leave that to me, The Lawyer said, We heard that before, I said leave it to me, Mr. Lawyer, we need to make sure The Plan goes through, we are not talking about a few petty billions, this is not business at the golf course, or on board a yacht, or with some board of directors, this is THE PLAN, I know, I know, Mr. Advisor, Don't raise your voice, Mr. Lawyer, please, please, gentlemen, no need to escalate, The Politician intervened, Where is The Frenchman?, The Banker asked, I've sent him for the stones, he says he knows where they are, he says the stock is in three places, Why did he put them in three places?, Because he's superstitious, always divides things in three, Where is he getting them from?, The Politician asked, I told you it is my business with The Frenchman, At this point, Mr. Lawyer, I think we need to know, This was not our agreement, those stones are my share, it's my responsibility, It is ours now, Mr. Lawyer, The Neurosurgeon intervened, from now on I propose that The Frenchman reports to The Club, what say you, gentlemen?, Yes, Yes, Yes, And I say yes, Mr. Lawyer, The Neurosurgeon concluded, Very well, gentlemen, so be it, when he returns I'll have him report to us, Under no circumstances does he need to know the magnitude of The Plan and his role in the endeavor, Yes, Mr. Neurosurgeon, I understand, The Lawyer bowed his head, not necessarily in submission, but simply because a sunbeam struck his retina and inconvenienced him. The Lawyer looked at the wide clear sky and refreshed his eyes.

An eagle was circling Town, slowly.

Having said this, we need to prepare for the aftermath, what do you make of this retreat of the waters?, The Politician asked, Maybe the waters found another channel, water follows gravity, Mr. Politician, Thank you, Mr. Banker, I guess you are right, What about the woman with the red sweater?, Yes, right, we must not neglect her, I think she is bound to silence, she didn't see us, Maybe we overreacted, She had all the attributes for being the carrier, Yes, perhaps, we had to search her, Has anyone seen her recently?, Yes, she's around, Good, we must keep an eye on her, We must also not stay together too much, people are slowly coming back to their senses, someone will notice soon the disappearance of the masked men and the appearance of five new faces, I don't think they will notice, there are too many, they barely remember themselves, They did not even recognize the garden miracle, You too, Mr. Advisor, you too believe in this miracle nonsense, It was a figure of speech, Mr. Banker, but I give you credit, bankers do not have a good sense of irony, That is humorous, Mr. Advisor, Thank you, Gentlemen, there is also something I need to share with you, Yes, Mr. Lawyer, On the first day of the flood I was contacted by The Client and he conveyed that certain circles in City are interested in our political ideas, What does this have to do with us?, The Politician interjected, tour ideas are a diversion, it's local politics, it's irrelevant, it's just a means to feel ourselves present, it's a distraction for the population, Mayor knows, he's with us, he spoke to City, did he not?, Good, so I don't see your point, Gentlemen, this is what The Client told me, I thought The Client is just the link, He is the link, but he is also involved with the circles in City, and he is the only one that the really important person trusts, You mean The Inventor?, Yes, The Inventor.

The men remained quiet for a solid minute while The Advisor kept cranking the radio. The first to compute the ramifications of this news is The Neurosurgeon. Are you saying that The Client might be leaking intelligence?, he asked. The Lawyer did something that was not in his nature. He scoffed. He didn't have the answer. The other men knew this. And he knew they knew. Gentlemen, The Lawyer said, after putting his thoughts together, what I am saying is that there is a possibility. The Client is not aware of the details of The Plan, he is a facilitator for The Inventor, and, as we all know, The Inventor is not a person who will make direct contact, especially knowing the colossal impact of The Plan on the whole planet, if I may say this, and I don't think I'm exaggerating, You are not, Mr. Lawyer, we are all aware of the magnitude and the necessity of absolute control over the dissemination of this information, we do not want chaos, society may collapse, governments may lose control, It's all hanging on a fucking thread, The Banker said, Mr. Banker, we have not arrived to a resolution yet, The Neurosurgeon tried to appease him, We will make contact with The Client, we will assure him that the merchandise will give him satisfaction and he will deliver The Plan to us, if not The Inventor himself. Do you really think he will give us The Inventor, it's absurd, you know that, The Politician said. Ten seconds of silence. We will use persuasion, The Lawyer unfroze the group's thoughts, Impossible, We have to consider this course of action, he continued, the flood has delayed us, he will want more, and more can be blinding, can be numbing for one's sense of gratification, What are you proposing?, The Politician asked with interest, We offer him more, we make him come here and we ask him to deliver The Inventor, That will not happen, We shall see, we shall see.

Chapter 103
Nothing less of seamen in her wet dreams

Iris lied on her back on a bed made of raffia sacks filled with other raffia sacks and watched the night sky. It was dark and vibrant, luminous and packed with stars. It was so bright she could see the lines in her palms when she covers the constellation Ursa Major with her fingers spread out.

She lowered her hand and covered her navel, slowly, like she was touching a very fragile and thin canvas.

She fell asleep.

In her dream, she was standing on a beach looking out at a calm ocean.

The sand was becoming her skin. She became an extension of the earth.

The ship emerged from the contour of the big orange moon that enshrouded the horizon.

The ship was old and was packed with seamen.

And it's approaching very fast.

She rose to her feet and exfoliated a skin of sand.

She stretched out her arm and believed strongly that she can actually touch the ship.

She realized this was absurd.

As the ship advanced towards the beach it shrunk in size.

She realized this was absurd.

The seamen jumped overboard when they realized this chronochoric oddity.

They swam along the ship towards her until they could walk on the sea floor.

The ship was as thick as a man's arm.

The seamen clumped and tramped until their hips were above the water.

The ship was as long as a breadknife.

She tried to take a step back. Her feet were rooted in the sand.

Their knees were breaking the water with determination. They were advancing.

The ship was as big as a green plantain. The prow was erect and majestic.

The men took the ship in their arms and surrounded her, on the beach.

I'm crying for things that I tell others to do without crying, she told the seamen.

Tears are salt and water, the seamen said. They squeezed the circle around her.

What do you want?, she asked.

We want you to bear this ship for us. They point to her womb.

They took a step closer.

I can't, she said. I don't want to.

You have no choice, the seamen said.

They were prolife.

The circle was so tight that she looked up to reach for air.

She was prochoice.

Chapter 104
Return to innocence

When the poodle returned to the blonde divorced girl, recognizing her as his new mother, he did not bring the velvet bag with the diamonds in it. The girl noticed that and thought it would be stupid to ask a dog what happened to that object, knowing that the object has no significance whatsoever for the animal. She ignored her disappointment and assumed protection and care for the dog for a reason that she has not shared yet. Her lover has not shown her attention since the big rain. She felt lonely and dirty and invested a lot of feeling into her new small friend.

She sat down in a corner of the attic and watched The Frenchman talk to those five men, and how the five men gave him some instructions. The Frenchman changed his face to express an intriguing combination of frustration, fear, determination, violence and perhaps tiredness. Someone yelled, Look, the water, then she heard loud chatter on the roof, most likely about how surprisingly low the water level is. Where did the water go?, the woman with the red sweater asked. There was no answer.

The blonde girl saw The Frenchman hastening towards the edge of the roof and she heard a splash. It's okay, he yelled from the water, it's not that deep. Then he paddled away. Probably he took that odd bull-shaped sculpture, the blonde girl thought. Immediately after, one of the five men went back to Iris and gave her back the radio.

Iris grabbed Tim's hand. They raised their voices, but the dialogue was incomprehensible.

Then there was Father Frank, who tried to quench the thirst of a kid, I know, I know, my boy, we are running out of water, we have to be careful with our supply, Father, the kid's mother asked, how long is this going to take, I don't know ma'am, I don't know, it seems that God is putting us at trial in various ways.

The air was dry. The water was becoming a faint memory. Even the flooded streets looked appealing now. The mud dried on the walls of houses and fell in flakes. Like the earth was sucking in all the water, awakened from hibernation.

The blonde divorced girl caressed the dog and he fell asleep on her lap.

Chapter 105
The fangs made of surprises

Iris lured the poodle with a sugar cube that she saved from the last food distribution.

What do you have there, sweetie?, she asked. The poodle dropped the velvet bag at her feet and swallowed the sugar cube in a split second.

Oh my god, she said. Tim, look at this.

Tim looked at the wad of diamonds in Iris's palm.

Look, there are more in the bag.

Keep it quiet, they can hear.

They lowered their voices and after a short deliberation decided that the best hiding place for the stones was in Iris's radio.

It has a hidden compartment, she said. For storage or an additional battery.

They hid the stones inside and disposed of the bag in the water, making sure no one was watching. They resumed eating their stew. It was almost dark, the moon spiced their food with twinkles of stars, and made it look dark blue, like a still lake.

The next day, one of the five men came to them and asked Iris to lend him the radio. We want to hear some music over there. I'll bring it back, the man said.

At that moment, Iris felt a very strong sense of property and of justice and almost wanted to shout, You don't mess with me!, But Tim gently grabbed her elbow and told her, It's okay, we can listen to music later. His eyes are telling her that, They will not look inside, don't worry. She conceded and gave the radio to the man with a forced smile. Don't break the crank, she said. The man replied, Don't worry, my dear, you'll get it back exactly as it is now.

Until she got back her radio, Iris kept her eyes on the five men and tried to read their lips. She used to be good at that. What are they saying?, Tim asked her at one point. But she wasn't sure. Maybe it's something that we don't want to know, she said a few minutes later, when she said the same men coming back with the radio.

See, as I promised, thank you. We all like Beethoven, the man said.

We sure do, she answered.

Would it be possible to ask for another big favor, Iris? Iris, right?

She nodded.

You see, our friend Monsieur Gregoire needs to check a few things out for us. He'll also try to find a source of drinkable water, for all of us. So the favor you could do, not just for us, but for the whole group here, is to lend us your wooden bull, so he can move faster. I heard you made it. My congratulations, miss, it's a very ingenious art, demiurgic I might add, exemplary and revelatory, and very powerful and poetic in that sense, you know I am a huge art buff and I had no idea that Town sheltered such a talent.

Thank you.

Miss Iris, I had a brief conversation with your uncle, I saw him around here, is he gone?

I think he's on other roofs helping people to set up gardens.

I see. He mentioned briefly that the Charging Bull was your creation and that you have other work in your garage.

I'm preparing for art school.

After all this is over I'd like to see it. You know, I know people. I can make connections.

That's very considerate.

So what do you think? *L'art pour son beauté et utilité?* Art for its beauty and utility?

Iris fixed the man's eyes and tried to rip them out with an invisible force. The man was discomfited by this visual connection and lost his train of thought for a moment. He interrupted the eye contact and pretended to clear his throat.

Iris eventually gave her consent.

Tell him to bring it unspoiled, she said.

The man agreed and returned to his group. Immediately after, Gregoire was dispatched, but not before he exchanged icy glances with Iris and barred his teeth.

Chapter 106
Serenity, trinity, possibility

Gregoire has split the diamonds into three packets.

The first he deposited in the vault at the Community Bank under a Dutch name, the bank didn't ask for ID, a name and password were sufficient. That's why we have so many clients, they trust us, we work on Swiss principles, privacy, confidentiality, secrecy, we don't ask questions, The Manager told him when he rented the place in the vault. How would you like to pay? Cash, Gregoire answered without blinking.

The second he stashed inside a wooden Jesus statue, as big and thick as a whiskey bottle, and he stuffed the rest with gypsum so if a curious eye peered inside Jesus, it would think that Jesus was solid plaster. But Jesus could float, even with that big load inside. The flood came. It swept the statue off the kitchen counter and tossed it against the wall. The statue exited the house through a tiny window, then smashed against a tree, where it got stuck for the next few days, in a hollow. The tree roared under the pressure of the stream and split in two, freeing Jesus to a new course, under a bridge, where it saved the life of a cat, fortunately for the nameless cat when she lost her equilibrium and fell from the narrow edge of a steel beam right onto Jesus, on her paws, as nature dictates. They floated, cat and wood, until sunset, when she found the closeness of a roof more secure and jumped off. The statue continued its course through the window of a school bus that had landed vertically on its tail and leaned against a wall, and exited through the other window, then almost entered a collision course with an open mail box when it hit another object, flipped on one side, swallowed water and sank, then continued through the desolate streets night and day. One morning it heard a human voice saying, I think I hit something, but that human did not care to investigate further and carried on with the rowing, then later the statue cruised in the vicinity of a chimney, but the chimney soon collapsed just below water level and the void sucked in everything around, including Jesus. Soon after, the statue returned to the surface, and continued unhindered through back alleys, above parking lots, over smaller churches that were completely submerged underwater, over the school, the post office, the police station that had one storey, by the windows of Town Hall, or at night just beyond the light of a flashlight that was opening the way of a stray citizen, and finally, late one evening, it stopped in the hands of a Synagogue worker who was looking for apples and food floating around the building. The man lifted Jesus from the water, turned off his speech synthesizer and thought that the best place to spend the night was inside the building.

Gregoire dropped the third packet inside the corpse he was working on when he saw the huge tidal wave coming. He thought fast, and his hands moved before he finished the inference. He zipped up the body bag, then covered his face, because the wave was about to hit the house, the garage, and glass splinters would be thrown in all directions. That's all he can remember.

Chapter 107
The Voice in a gamma ray flawed scanner

Why are they so quiet?	They haven't said a word in hours.
What are they thinking?	Who knows what they are thinking.
Who did Imam talk to on the phone in the hospital?, How was that possible?	For sure Rabbi talked to Him on the phone, it's the only logical explanation.

These were thoughts that the brothers on both sides have been grinding in silence for hours, if not days. Now that the waters have retreated, leaving behind Town like a swamp reeking of self-pity and numbness, the twenty-four brothers were slowly eating vegetables and scratching their beards, while considering alternative scenarios for what is to come and about what the others are thinking. They were trying to explain how their leaders, Imam and Rabbi respectively, devised a bipartisan and efficient plan to salvage their souls from the hospital operating rooms where they would have definitely have found their doom, after all. They all failed to find a reasonable explanation. It just happened.

Then they sat in line on the edge of the roof and watched people trudging through the mud on the street.

Is The Voice real? Did those conversations actually take place? Of course they did, Imam and Rabbi moved their lips, produced sounds with meaning, the phenomenon called language, they were having a conversation, sure, they could have filled in the other party with their mute imagination, giving the appearance of a real person, ha, if The Voice can be actually called a person, with all His impersonal and behind-the-scenes deeds, why does it have to be that way, so imperceptible, so questionable, so outside the realm of the mind, is the mind so weak that it cannot handle the truth, is the mind a door with no handle that needs to be smashed open with a heavy boot, so truth can flow in and out, mostly in, not that we should stop asking if anyone knows the answers to these questions but we should ask. Why do we crave these answers?

The cellular devices rang again.

Yes Sir. Imam, why do you always sound surprised to hear me?, It's more of an unwavering joy to hear you Sir, That doesn't sound very convincing, Imam, Sir I have never doubted my faith, Yes Imam, I know, Sir while my devotion to you is unquestionable my heart is filled with uncertainty, You creatures always want to be certain, if only nature was built like that or if you were more evolved say more like me, I don't understand Sir, Forget it, Yes Sir, It is time for change Imam, Indeed it is Sir.

Hello, Hello, Sir, How are you?, I'm good, It is time, Rabbi, It is time for a change.

Nobody on the streets paid attention to the men talking on the roof, perhaps they did not hear or perhaps they considered it normal that the communication signal has been restored in the area.

Soon the brothers knew, because their leaders came to them and shared the instructions learned from The Voice.

The brothers descended to the streets and greeted the citizens of Town.

They shared their food and whatever rainwater they had collected so far.

Food was not what the townsfolk need exactly.

They were thirsty. It hasn't rained for a long time.

Water supplies were depleted.

The people were talking to each other, What are we doing now?

Imam and Rabbi assured them that it will be fine.

How do you know?, people asked.

We have been told.

Who told you?

We had conversations on the phone.

To which the people sighed with relief. Maybe Imam and Rabbi were right.

Everyone was looking towards the sky.

Where are the helicopters?, Where are the army trucks with blankets and water tanks?

They don't know. But Rabbi and Imam assure them it will be fine.

We don't know how many died.

Do you know how many died?

I haven't seen any dead.

This is strange. Do you know anyone who is missing?

Not to my knowledge.

Where is your family?

Oh, they went ahead to our house to check for whatever is left.

Then they will go their ways. Then the brothers will mingle with the people.

The brothers thought about going back to their families. Yes, but their families were taken care of, no one was left behind on the day of the uproar in the Town Hall Square. The brothers offered food for water. They would not be very successful. They would give up the food for nothing. At least they can do that. Imam and Rabbi would help until nightfall.

When the moon rose at night, one of the brothers told everyone around him that they have to dig a well.

Chapter 108
First contact of ill-perceived appearances

They're coming.

Who's coming?

The Client. He said he's bringing someone.

What are you saying? Someone who?

The Someone.

The Inventor?

The Banker could not continue his question in awe with, What the hell, because The Advisor covered his mouth with his palm. There were people watching, and some might be able to read lips, who knows, one must always consider even the slightest probabilities.

How do you know?

The Lawyer told me.

The Banker did not continue the line of questioning because he used his intuition to fill in the blanks, which didn't have to be verbalized for the time being. Town was waking up under the hot sun, the flood was gone, the mud turned into petrified soil, what was relatively abundant from the rainwater has become scarce. The five men and The Quiet Boy did not invoke gods in their minds and ask for mercy or ask for water, they went to their secret chamber and drank the water deposited there. They also knew that in order to keep this competitive advantage in the race for survival, their new endeavor must be of resolute secrecy. The attic of the annex at Town Hall may have been broken into through the roof by the woman with the red sweater, but the secret chamber behind the secret chamber did not suffer fortuitous accidents of trespassing.

The Client will arrive soon, The Lawyer said. Act casual.

They walk down on the road.

A group of men was taking turns at two shovels. They were digging a well in a park. They did not show an intention to stop or to rest. There were women and children at the shelter of trees.

The day was hot.

Have you heard from The Frenchman?, The Politician asked.

I have not seen him today, The Lawyer responded. He did not realize that Gregoire had in fact been in his line of sight earlier, but at a distance.

When The Lawyer looked in his direction, Gregoire was on the roof of a building, searching for something. It was a tin box hidden behind a brick, in the wall. Gregoire tossed the brick over his shoulder and opened the box. Inside, cigars aligned like guerrilla fighters at dusk, all facing el comandante, wearing proudly the stars on the beret and the scarves of camaraderie. There was also a matchbox.

He shook the matchbox, then pulled out a match and lit a cigar.

Gregoire thought that no one had the right over his life. No one can bend his will. No one can tell him what to do. Things have to be put into context. It may seem that he takes orders. But it's on a quid pro quo basis. He gives, they give. Fuck diamonds. He can get countless more for himself later. He knows other places. Greed is ubiquitous. Other miners have swallowed diamonds and remained buried. It is a matter of time. This cigar is an extension of his freedom. He looks down at Town. He is a King. In his own way. They don't know what he is capable of. The cigar is an extension of his masculinity. After he finishes, he will crush the butt under the sole of his boot. Then he will light another cigar. It is an extension of the strength of his arm.

He looked at the scars on his hands. They were almost healed. Then he had a flashback. He had fallen on sharp objects when the wave caught him in the garage.

He must go back.

At least one packet should be there.

He crushed the cigar butt under the sole of his boot and climbed down into the street. There was mud everywhere.

All the faces were grey and sunken from dehydration.

Maybe his was as well.

He walked for five minutes. He felt he was being followed. Two clean faces were taking the same turns. They were wearing fedoras with large wide brims. The eyes were concealed in shadow.

He knows who they were.

He did not know their names.

Names are irrelevant. They falsify reality. Names are fleeting. Names can be changed.

He decided to stop. He was his own master.

The two men stopped behind him. He could hear them.

One of the them said, We have arrived. Gregoire replied that he knew.

The man that talked first approached and put his hand on Gregoire's shoulder.

Aren't you going to greet your partners, Monsieur Gregoire?

Gregoire turned to face the men and looked them in the eyes.

Certainement, he said, then wiped his hand on his shirt and stretched it for a good shake.

Chapter 109
Water breaks into sins and slivers

The line for water was five minutes long starting from the well and walking slowly toward the end, at the end of the park. Father Frank distributed potatoes and bean sprouts to mothers with children. He whispered words of comfort as he pat the children on their backs. It will be fine, ma'am, the flood is gone, We are dying of thirst, the woman said, I know ma'am, God has peculiar ways.

A group of men was digging a pit with sticks and bare hands. One had a shovel. It was short and hard to maneuver, One of the men says, I got it!, and the others rushed to him and accelerated the digging. They unearthed the water main and tried to pierce it with whatever sharp objects they had. Then they thought to dig further and find a joint. The pipe was supposed to be weaker there. They dug under the joint, prop it up on a boulder and with a metal rod jiggled the pipe. The joint loosened and a creamy thread oozed out. It's all infected!, a man sobbed and collapsed on his knees.

Father Frank did not ask himself why these men were trying to break the water main when taps all over Town produced nothing but mildew and rotten liquid. The men stopped and looked at Father Frank and he saw in their eyes many questions. The Earth has many gifts, he told them. He drew the sign of the cross in the air above the pit and walked on.

At the end of the line, he found a mother with her daughter, pale and weak, barely able to move as the line advanced. At this rate, they will not make it to the well. The girl's name was Emma. Her face was dirty and had two vermilion spots. Father Frank noticed this sign of liveliness and found it very exciting. It made him remember the prayers to Archangel Gabriel. Emma's lips were poised in such a stance that a broad smile and even an innocent giggle seemed imminent.

Oh, the candor, the purity, the divine vibrancy!, he thought.

He took Emma and her mother to the Church.

Follow me, I'll show you to the guestroom.

He cleared the desk with the edge of a thick hardcover book.

The guestroom had not been affected by the furies of nature. The doors were watertight.

Wait here, he told them.

He walked into his office, the adjacent room.

He walked straight to the cupboard. It was massive, made of wood and had a large brass lock. Compliments of the bishop.

The key was where it was supposed to be, fitted into two tiny hooks, under the unit, where only two fingers can reach. His hands were shaking. He opens the cupboard.

He took two glasses, put them on the desk, then wiped them with his shirt and rinsed them with some brandy.

He filled the glasses with mineral water. There were no sparkles. He opened the drawer and took out a brown envelope with the bishop's seal on it.

He opened the envelope with a small stiletto designed for this purpose.

He looked at Jesus's portrait, soiled and imbued with damp air.

He looked down at the floor.

He looked up at Jesus again. Jesus had a calm look. It was like he's saying, It's okay son, go ahead.

He distributed the contents of the envelope into the glasses. The white powder dissolved in seconds.

It will be like a dream.

Emma's mother called his name. Father Frank!

He took the glasses into the guestroom.

Here, it will quench your thirst and help you sleep well.

Thank you, Father.

Emma finished first. Her mother gulped her water in one shot. I'm tired, Father, she said. Can I lie here? Emma, honey, are you okay?

Father Frank didn't say anything. He covered the mother with a blanket. It's not immaculate, but at least it's dry. The mother fell asleep instantly. The name of her daughter remained half-uttered and her lips half-pursed.

Mommy is sleeping, Emma said.

Yes, Emma, she is. Let's let her rest awhile. Do you like stories?

Yes.

Let me read you a story.

He took her hand and they walked into his office. He closed the door behind them.

Do you like stories with princes and princesses?

Yes.

Do you want to dress like a princess?

Yes.

But you can't tell Mummy. It has to be a secret.

Okay.

The droplet of sweat emerged at the top of his forehead. At first, it was imperceptible, but as it grew in size and advanced down the forehead, it sent an uncanny feeling to the spine, and from the spine into the groin. The blood was collected rapidly and pumped vigorously into the manhood.

He darted to his closet and pulled out a folded piece of linen. It was white and beautiful.

Look, Emma. This is what angels and princesses wear. You have to change now.

Okay.

He unbuttoned her dress.

Are you cold?

No.

He removed her clothes.

She did not feel shame.

His heart stopped and dropped heavily into his lower body.

He looked at Emma and sucked in the droplet of sweat with the corners of his mouth. He thought the girl was very beautiful. Her skin was so smooth and clear. It reminded him of his childhood, when he played with lambs.

He covered her bellybutton with his hand.

She giggled and shuddered.

The room was spinning with her. The powder has reached her brain.

She lost strength in her legs.

He caught her before she touched the floor.

He laid her on the couch.

He watched her body for a minute. He clothed her in the white cassock. It fit her perfectly.

One day, perhaps, she will join the choir with the other children, Father Frank thought.

Chapter 110
Heart unloaded, helicopter takes it away

I had an affair, she said.

The Psychiatrist suddenly felt that the loaf of bread tasted like dust.

Why are you telling me now?, he asked.

She did not answer, and continued to clean the kitchen table, then the countertop, then the fridge. It was all a mess after waters disappeared in a hurry. Dry mud peeled off things, like molting snakes, to emerge in a new suit, shinier, clearer, cruder, appearing fragile but stronger than ever. She picked up the smithereens of a vase and tried to put them together.

It happened one summer, she began. You were away. It was before the first porphyria crisis. I was at the art gallery. He was kind and educated. He took pictures of me. Very beautiful pictures. I told him I was growing apart from my husband. I told him your work was more important. That you were not happy with me. That you might have an affair. That you didn't know what my dreams are. And you didn't care. You didn't want to travel with me. You didn't want children. You were fundamentally a dissolved, joyless man. It went on for a year. You were away most of the time. But then I started to have the crisis. You saw the blood, you saw the scars. And then you changed. You bought the masks. You bathed me, you washed my hair. You made breakfasts and lunches and dinners. You gave up the conferences. You took fewer patients. The more pain I felt, the more caring you became. When we made love you were there.

But I became estranged from myself. The *me* that loved you died behind this mask. The *me* that longed for you before the disease and the darkness has turned to vapors. I am nothing but inertia of memories. I'm trying to put my heart together from ashes, but I can't.

The Psychiatrist saw a tear rolling from under her mask. His eyes were wet.

He unbuttoned her dress.

Are you cold?, he asked.

No.

He removed her mask.

She did not feel shame.

Then they heard a helicopter gliding hastily above the neighborhood and disappearing into the horizon.

Chapter 111
Ghosts visiting

The Citizens Guard entered Town from the south, in force, with precision and discipline. First, truckloads of water bottles. Sergeants with loudspeakers called the crowd to come closer. We have supplies, You will be subjected to physical inspection and sampling, Please approach in an orderly fashion.

They didn't bother to explain why they were so late, why they brought such assertiveness, why it all seems planned out carefully on a large map by High Command, why all the guards wore white chemsuits, why they were organized in teams that collected samples of mud, leaves and various stray objects, why they asked people, Open your mouth, say Ahh, Thanks, here's your water, or looked deep into their eyes, with thin flashlights, then checked their hands, chests and backs for skin irregularities, Did you lose hair?, No, I didn't, Where did you get that scar from?, I don't know, can I have water now, please?, Yeah, sure, there you go.

In a tobacco shop, two sergeants evaluated the situation.

What do you make of this?, It is premature to assess, we must remain vigilant, Did you recognize the symptoms?, Not yet, but something is out of place here, How many dead so far?, Four, All in the same condition?, Yes, the bodies had been processed before the flood, How did they survive so long?, We don't know, that is the question, We must pull out quickly, I have my orders, Me too.

The sergeants both looked at their wrists, where instructions from the High Command were being listed on mini displays. They conveyed the instructions to their teams.

We are out in five minutes!

Water has not been fully unloaded, sir.

Drop them on the ground, let them deal with it.

Roger.

Bring the other trucks.

Roger.

Move! Move!

Yes, sir.

The guards jumped into the trucks and unloaded the boxes with bottled water in seconds. All was thrown on the ground. The dehydrated crowd swooped upon the supplies like vultures. There is plenty for everyone, a man yelled. The sleep of reason produces monsters.

The trucks were pulled out of Town.

A dozen new trucks replaced them and the operation was repeated.

Crates with food were unloaded. Guards didn't even climb down from the trucks.

Move! Move!

It took exactly two minutes.

A hand from the crowd snatched a suited guard by the sleeve, What is happening?, What are all these? Why are you suited up? What took you so long?

The guard pulled the sleeve back. He didn't care much about these questions. The grip became tighter.

Answer me!, the man demanded.

The guard smacked the man's hand with his Geiger counter. The man blurted out, What the hell?, and tried to reach for the apparatus. The guard hit again and again, with a result contrary to his intentions. The man was infuriated and screamed, Help me! Two pairs of hands grasped him by the waist and gave him more elevation so he could enforce the grip on the guard. The man clawed the chemsuit with all his force. The guard was pulled down from the truck. What the hell is this?, he yelled as he landed on the concrete, You surprised, buddy?, the man yelled back, I suggest you imagine my discontent when the government sends aid so freaking late, in chemsuits, sticks flashlights down our throats and gives no explaNATION!, the man uttered the last word with a thrust of his boot in the guard's ribs. The guard crouched and sobbed in pain.

The sergeants gave the last, Pull out!, order. Trucks followed the one-way road around The Park, slowly at first, the guards threw out the last crates of food. They didn't look back. The guard with the Geiger counter was left behind, partly because he has already disappeared in the sea of people, partly because it all happened so fast and the other guards could not react and were not expecting that reaction from the crowd, Such lack of consideration for the government efforts, they thought to themselves as a cloud of dust soared behind the galloping trucks.

It happened so fast that by nightfall people thought they had seen ghosts, if it weren't for the loads of food and water, a sign that something had happened and someone was there.

Chapter 112
The Middle Way of the spyglass

Reality is bent in our eyes. Nor is everything permanent and self-sufficient, nor is everything illusory, but all is interdependent, entwined, impermanent.

The Neurosurgeon lowered the spyglass to hip level and remained pensive, looking out at the park from the headquarters of The Club. The others remained seated around a map of Town. What do you see?, The Politician asked.

The Neurosurgeon put the spyglass to his right eye once more.

I see that we are severely attached to the permanence of things. That we believe that things really *are* nothing but themselves, intrinsic, independent and eternal. In order to loosen this grip, we need a flow of continuous critical reasoning. Even if it can cast a doubt in our minds, a mere suspicion about things not being permanent in itself may impact our minds, will be sufficient to untie our grip on reality, may release us from the slavery of illusions. This is not enough, though. We need further reinforcement of critical reasoning to point us more towards the realization of impermanence. This is also not enough. We need further convictions. We need to shift to what is called the inferential understanding of impermanence. This again is not enough. If we want this process to influence our behavior, we need to gain direct insight or intuitive experience of impermanence of things. This again is not enough. It needs to be further perfected. The grasping of permanence is deeply embedded in our consciousness. One insight cannot dispel it. It is a long process of deepening our insight that will eventually dismiss even the slightest tendency towards grasping at permanence of things.

What are you saying?, The Politician asked without lifting his head.

That we are severely attached to the permanence of things.

I got that.

Contact has been made, The Neurosurgeon changed the tone. He moved the spyglass as the objects of his attention changed location. It seemed that The Frenchman has contacted The Client, he continued. There was a third party with them. Is it him? What are the odds? What are the reasons? Yes, it may be him.

The other four men raised their heads and looked at The Neurosurgeon, patiently waiting the unraveling of the observations.

What is he doing here?, The Banker addressed the question to the group, but he fixed his eyes on The Lawyer, implying a subtextual dialogue where he would say, This was not the plan, this is not what we agreed, there are too many uncontrolled variables. To which The Lawyer would say, What is important is that The Client is here, that we made contact, What happens if the source is jeopardized?, The Banker would ask, The Plan itself will be endangered. To which The Lawyer would retort curtly, We have the alligator by the tail.

This dialogue was whispered. It did not distract The Neurosurgeon, it did not make him blink, rub his left eye, flinch, fidget his fingers or alter the tone of his voice to exhibit nervousness or insecurity.

The authorities are pulling out, he continued, unruffled. They've sent the Citizens Guard in chemsuits, a strange reaction, I should say, on their part. There is one guard left behind, he is still wearing the suit, the crowd is angry, there is an impetus to lynch him. There is a young man, no, three young men, no, two young men and a young woman around him, they are defending the guard with their bodies, they are trying to calm the crowd, the mob is giving up, they realize what the departing transportation vehicles have bequeathed. There are crates scattered around, and people rip them apart with their bare hands. Water bottles are being emptied into mouths and discarded. The wells are abandoned in favor of the newly discovered facile nourishments. Amazing. The mob moves from one place to another in a pattern described by the alignment of iron filings at the pole of a magnet.

Where is The Client?, The Banker intervened.

The Client, The Frenchman and the source are moving away from the scene. Apparently they do not show interest in the new developments, which proves that they are driven by a more powerful force on one hand and more than likely that their appetite has been recently satisfied. Odd.

What is it?

The two younglings and the suited guard are following them. They are feigning a casual walk, however, it is obvious that they are going in the very same direction.

Who are the teenagers?

They resemble those two friends we have acquainted. The boy is Tim, the girl is—

Iris.

Thank you.

Where are they going?

I don't know. I lost them behind a building.

The five men took a moment of reflection. Before moving forward with The Plan, it was time to open the door to the secret chamber at the back and access the plentiful food and beverages stocked there for their benefit.

Chapter 113
The white guard appears in bright spectral light

They stopped in front of the gable. The sign carved in stone read *Nihil Sine Deo.*

Nothing without god, the guard said. Why did you bring me here?

We thought it'd be better if you stayed with Father Frank for a while until Town calms down, Tim said.

The guard, Tim and Iris entered the Church. Tim called Father Frank's name and Father Frank emerged from his office a minute later. His walk was wobbly and his hands were shaking. He hid these signs of internal turmoil as he approached the new group. When asked if he felt okay, he responded that he felt a little tired but generally he was fine. He already had two guests, but he was happy to receive more.

I am from the Citizens Guard, the guard explained. The others had to leave.

Father Frank did not show any signs of inquisitiveness, not that there aren't many questions to be raised, like, why is there only one guard left behind, why is he still wearing a chemsuit, why doesn't he take the mask off, why did they come *here*, why *now*, what is that device he carries, is there an epidemic breakout, are we doomed, is it a sign that after a miracle we awake to suffering, is he an angel sent by fate to judge me, God you see everything, forgive me for I have succumbed to sin.

Come please, come to my office, you can quench your thirst, he said.

Father, we must go, Tim replied.

Tim, you don't have to, Iris said.

I have to.

Iris turned to Father Frank and told him that she has decided to stay with the guard and the other guests. After Father Frank told her who the guests were, Iris showed a quick smile and felt a bustle of enthusiasm as she remembered the nights she spent with Emma in the attic talking about dolls and princesses.

Tim took the first steps backwards, as one departs from loved ones. Having a mute fear of permanent separation, one tries to record as many visual memories of the other as possible.

The guard rested on the couch.

Opposite him, Iris laid down next to sleeping Emma.

Emma's mother turned from one side to the other, while mumbling in her sleep.

Opposite her, Father Frank sat at his desk with the rosary in his hand.

He prayed for everyone's souls, including his.

Fringed light through the stained glass enshrouded their faces.

Chapter 114
The white guard's dream

~~He thought he was someone else. He, the conscious mind that was dreaming, was looking at himself from outside his body. He immediately dismissed this thought and stroke through it with a line and it kept it visible to his inner eye should he later have the disposition for self-analysis.~~

You ~~think~~ know you are dreaming.

You are someone else. You are outside my body.

You see the moment of your birth. First your head comes out. You don't scream. Then your shoulders emerge. The umbilical cord is wrapped three times around your neck. The doctor tells you that if you were five minutes late you would be dead. You don't cry and you try to open your eyes but your face is covered with amniotic fluid. The doctor decides to cut the cord right now. If he hesitates, you'll die. From the chest down you are still in the womb. He inserts the beak of the scissors under the first wrapping of the cord. You see his hand shaking. Then you realize it is not his hand but the whole room that is shaking. He cuts the cord. Then he puts a tiny oxygen mask on your face. He pulls you out. You don't scream.

The room fills with amniotic fluid. You think it's absurd. Mothers don't carry that much amniotic fluid. Things and people start to float around you. The room fills up to the ceiling. You think you are having a panic attack. You watch your newborn body and your mind fears death. Your newborn mouth smiles. Then you remember that being born underwater may be a good thing.

The roof opens and you plunge into the ocean.

The fishermen think you are an abandoned child and fish you out, into their boat. Who drops a child in the water? they ask.

You tell them you are not a child and you feel ashamed because of your nakedness.

You grow to the size of a boy under their eyes. They do not seem surprised. Fishermen see odd happenings all the time. They can even hear the voice of the ocean.

They pull the boat ashore and gather the fishnets.

You step onto the sandy beach and thank them.

You know you are dreaming and you find this numb awareness rather comforting. You think that because you know you are dreaming you can do whatever you want in this tiny universe.

The fishermen depart into the ocean, singing and roaring in unison.

A wall of glass appears around you.

You are in a gigantic hourglass.

You panic when you realize that it is not the hourglass that is gigantic but everything outside it. In a stream of sand, you fall into the lower room. You tap the glass and cry for help. The hourglass is on the kitchen table. Your mother is using it. It gives her the precise baking time for your favorite cake.

Again, you think this is absurd. You forget that you are dreaming. All this is very real to you. You think you don't deserve to die asphyxiated in an hourglass.

Your mother leaves the kitchen. She doesn't hear you.

The cat nudges the hourglass off the table. It breaks and sets you free. You are back on the beach, by the ocean. You ~~think~~ know again you are dreaming. You are calm and you feel very light, almost weightless, like a hallucination.

Chapter 115
Monochromatic chase and the reappearance of red

Pale white sky, black asphalt, Town is washed in shades of gray. The gray faces of people, gray trees, gray buildings, ashy sky.

I am colorblind.

It happens from time to time. The Psychiatrist told me it has to do with some sort of separation anxiety.

They are there. I know they are there. The blinds of the coffee shop have been pulled down in haste. The sign has been flipped over to show the word Closed.

The back alley is empty. I stop by the back door.

It's all shades of gray around, the washed white fur of a stray cat that jumps out of a garbage container, the weak stained black of the brick wall.

The door is open.

I enter. The kitchen repels us with a fetid stench. I walk slowly, my feet raising dust off the floor, my head nudging the brassware hung from the ceiling. The sound of clinking metal flashes through our spines. Billions of ants flock on the tips of my fingers.

They are there. Voices of a faint dialogue. They are arguing about something.

Then the clean click of the loading of a gun. Sudden silence. They must have heard me.

Their dialogue resumes.

I'm safe.

The kitchen opens into the main hall next to the bar.

It's dark. A few shreds of light pass through the blinds and slice the air in oblique layers. Dust is propelled in all directions by faint air currents generated by their movement.

Three men. One is Gregoire. Opposite him are two men with fedoras. One is arguing with Gregoire, the other is utterly silent. There is a suitcase on the table between them. The quiet man has his hands crossed over it and keeps it beyond Gregoire's reach.

Their irises are black like soot. Their faces are white like flour.

Light is particle and wave. Light has no color. Color is in the eye of the beholder. There is only the black and the white.

Gregoire addresses the talking man with the word, Client.

The Client addresses Gregoire with the word, Monsieur.

The subject of the conversation is the suitcase. They both point at it and throw furtive glances. Gregoire clenches his fists. The skin on his knuckles is ready to snap. The Client frowns. The wrinkles dislodge microscopic particles of dust and sweat. Disagreement is boiling in the crushed air between the two men.

The Plan must be delivered immediately, Gregoire says.

We want guarantees, The Client responds.

You have exposed us to risk. You brought him here.

Gregoire glances towards the silent man to make his point. His right hand covers a pistol with a silencer. It's on the table in plain sight, between them.

The presence of a gun always changes the behavior of the heart of man.

The scarcity of light always influences the mind of man.

Sometimes it gives birth to beasts.

The Inventor has decided to accompany me for reassurance, The Client explains. He wants to meet *them*. He, too, clenches his fists.

You know this is *impossible*.

You don't understand, Monsieur. I am the link in this business! I do *not* appreciate intimidation! And condescension. And delays. And divergences.

He delivers the word *I* with a heavy respiration. The Client's voice is raw and metallic.

The man called The Inventor makes a first movement.

He blows his nose. He calmly inserts the embroidered handkerchief back into the breast-pocket. He clears his throat. He cracks his knuckles.

He remains silent.

You understand what is at stake here, Monsieur?

I don't like your tone, Mr. Client.

Gregoire decides to stop talking. His composure has reached a critical point. His eyeballs are shrinking. He drums his fingers on the pistol a few times. By that he means his is ready to take action and is not afraid to show his intentions. He is in control. No one tells him what to do.

On fait quoi maintenant? The Client asks with an expiration of hot air from his mouth. What is it to be done? In the shadow, the contour of his face looks like a steam locomotive climbing a vertical wall.

The ceiling fan creaks and budges. Probably a last drop of electricity running through its veins. The boost unclogs the fan into a languid rotation.

On the floor, in a blot of weak light, RED liquid drips from the dark.

In the back of The Client there is an exit bullet wound.

The cartridge from Gregoire's gun is rolling towards me. Gregoire has not lifted the pistol from the table. He pulled the trigger while drumming his fingers. Like the bullet had snapped out of his hand.

The Client doesn't realize what happened. He doesn't feel pain. His face shows shock and anger. He is rendered speechless. His lungs are pierced. He leans forward and thuds his forehead against the table. He's dead.

Then Gregoire's chest opens and blood pours out from a tiny hole. There is no sound. He drops his chin and spits into his palm. He tries to rub the blood off his shirt.

He looks up.

You stained my shirt, he says.

I had to do it, The Inventor says calmly.

You had to do it. Gregoire continues the rubbing. He stops after a minute, his head sunken into his chest, in silence.

The Inventor stands from the table. The suitcase was hiding in its shadow a pistol.

He walks out of the bar through the back door, where I came from.

Chapter 116
When the wolf had no ears
and the lambs had no information

What do you see? The Banker asked.

I see the townsfolk flocking around with their backs bent under the weight of the food they carry. Interesting pattern. Like particles after collision at enormous speeds and energy in an accelerator. They depart from the collision points in straight lines, then curl up onto themselves. They don't know where to go. They spin on their heels. Their energy dies out rapidly.

The Advisor threw his silk handkerchief towards The Neurosurgeon. While the handkerchief is still in the air, he said, Use this.

The Neurosurgeon caught the handkerchief and wiped the lens of the telescope.

I see the boy and a man with a suitcase.

Chapter 117
He knows they were following him

I know you were following me.

The Inventor made a sudden appearance in front of Tim. He appeared from nowhere, like a self-duplicating ghost.

Tim tried to kick the man in the shinbone. His muscles were frozen. Proof that the brain controls everything. In the same flash of a second, while he was considering all the options, he even had time to insert a brief moment of self-criticism, I am weak.

Don't worry son. Come with me.

He went with the man, not knowing why, not knowing where, but just feeling that it was something necessary and logical.

They crossed a parking lot, acting like a father with a black suitcase and his son. They climbed over a short concrete wall. The man looked in all directions for witnesses. There were none. They climbed down in a ditch. A film of dust soared from their footsteps and uncovered the pale green of dormant grass. They found a place to sit down. Tim sat down in front of him.

Do you know what this is?

I have an idea, Tim answered.

Chapter 118
The opening of the suitcase

His lips are moving. He talks about five men in black cardigans. He talks about their ambitions, about the power they want. He asks me, Why do men seek so much power? Why do they want to control everything? I don't know what to say.

He says he is holding the key to a great power.

It is what all men would want to have, he says.

He discovered it. That is why he is called The Inventor.

He puts the suitcase on the grass with the opening facing me. The key is in the keyhole. He asks if I want to see what's inside. I want to see but I cannot speak. My body is frozen. My thoughts are petrified.

His palms are guarding the opposite sides of the suitcase.

He doesn't speak.

He slowly opens the suitcase until the lid is perfectly vertical.

A great bright light, blinding and powerful, comes from inside.

Chapter 119
Under the hot sun

I can stare into the sun for hours and voluntarily go blind, the loan officer said.

Why would you do that?, the teller asked him.

Because I can.

If you can, it doesn't mean it's recommended.

I can do whatever I want.

You can do whatever you want.

So what's the deal with life anyways?

What do you mean?

What is this instinct for self-preservation?

It comes from within. It's circular. Life has to continue because it exists.

That explanation doesn't satisfy me. I can still stare into the sun and go blind.

You could die.

There is that possibility. So what keeps us alive?

What keeps us alive is when we realize the limits of our power and reason and we stay within those limits.

I say we remain silent for a while.

Okay.

They remembered that talking under severe dehydration did not help the retention of water in the body, and did not help the mind. On the contrary, it might develop hallucination and shift the focus from what is important. They knew that at the Community Bank there was a big water reservoir, somewhere in the basement they thought, that connected with the fire detectors and fed the sprinklers. This was their secret. It was one thing that they have decided to keep to themselves. Their manager didn't know that. He was preoccupied with the general vision of the bank, and didn't know how the security system works, who services the fire detectors, how often, etc. Sure, The Manager knew the costs, because he signed off on the expense budgets, but that was pretty much the extent of his interest. The Manager was more concerned with the security of the vault, because he had to believe in his service when he acquired high-valued customers for his bank. He talked only with influential people. He had even convinced some of them that an economic crisis will follow, that the market will plummet and it's safer to keep paper money in the vault rather than letting them earn a petty interest. Once he told his employees that it was important to think for the customers, to anticipate their fears and annihilate them with solutions. That's what he said, Annihilate fears with solutions before the customer realizes what he actually fears. Reason is slower than fear. Fear has to be tackled with preemptive strikes. That's what he said.

The Manager was somewhere with his mistress, the blonde girl. He had other arrangements for water. That's for sure. He had no idea where the teller and loan officer were. Under the hot sun, trudging in silence. He thought his employees didn't know about his affair. He was naïve. Who cares. There was water in the bank and probably they were the only ones who knew about it because they paid attention when the new fire alarm was installed. Everybody else was preoccupied with their jobs or was looking at the clock, waiting for closing time.

There was nobody at the Community Bank. Nobody thought that the Community Bank can provide water in times of drought. Nobody thought that water can be found by breaking into the basement and opening the water tank or indirectly by setting off the fire alarm and the sprinklers will do the rest.

But they knew.

One of the few things the teller had control over was the combination of the vault and the location of the key. Follow me, he said, But we can set off the sprinklers here, the loan officer said, Why would you do that, we will waste it, Then what do you suggest?, We open the vault and bring the water there, Yeah, but wouldn't that set all the sprinklers off?, No, the system in the vault is isolated.

It was part of his job description. At the end of the shift, at five p.m. sharp, the teller took the cash from the register, put it in the steel box, opened the vault and deposited it in the designated niche. Then he inspected the safe deposit boxes, closed the vault, inserted the key in the secret compartment under his desk, greeted the security guard and walked to the parking lot at the back of the building. There he lit a cigarette and emptied his mind for five minutes, which he found very satisfying.

Help me, the teller said.

They produced some rags from their shirts and a sweater left behind by the previous inhabitants of the vault. They took turns on the table, wrapping the rags around the sprinklers to create a funnel for the water. They emptied four steel drawers of jewelry, life insurance policies, artwork, wills and letters with sentimental value. They positioned the drawers under the sprinklers. They each collected a big wad of money and stared at each other for a few seconds. We have to do this simultaneously, the teller said. The two sprinklers do not work independently, don't ask me why. He lit his wad of money, then, with the flame, he lit the loan officer's torch of cash. The torches puffed dark green smoke into the air. The smoke rose with the help of their hands to the sprinklers, and within seconds the rags produced a steady flow of water.

They killed the torches with the soles of their feet and plunged their mouths into the drawers and sucked the water like two hellbeasts.

Chapter 120
Dermatology

When Gregoire opened his eyes, he saw the dead man in front of him. He looked at his watch. He has been passed out for almost an hour. His abdomen was punctured and he was in pain, but the bleeding was minimal. He ripped his shirt and cleared the clogged blood around the wound. Death is a random event. It's like having a cup of tea. He squeezed the skin around the wound. Some thick blood gushed out. He wiped the blood and squeezed again. The tiny packet emerged. It was wrapped in plastic. It was dirty as hell. He felt the bullet stuck in the layer of fat under the skin. It was a small caliber. The bullet bit right into the diamonds he had taped on his abdomen and pushed them inside the skin. He put the packet in his pocket and spat copiously on the floor. The spittle had no signs of blood. Which is good.

He stood and shook his head rapidly to correct his dizziness. He wobbled a few steps to the bar and opened a bottle of absinthe with his teeth, spat the cork out, swallowed half of it and poured the other half over the wound. He disinfected a small cocktail fork, leaned back against the bar and ransacked the wound for the bullet. When he found it, he dropped it on the floor, poured more alcohol over the opening and wrapped an apron around his waist.

He opened another bottle with his mouth, while staring at the footsteps that lead out of the bar.

Chapter 121
Measures and measurements, part one

Excuse me, Father, may I?

Of course, Mr. Mayor, go ahead.

Dear Townsfolk, constituents, I should say friends, we live in tough times, we all want answers. Thank you all for gathering here. As hard as it may seem, I hope Town Hall can bring you some relief. I have sent a team to check the water pipes.

Chapter 122
Truth must be kept silent

I remember that the last rain had glued her shirt against her body and her breasts rose from silence with force, like a sculpture unaware of its purpose. She came running to me, under the eaves, and asked if I was still writing about everything around me. I told her yes, and kept staring at her breasts. She noticed but pretended she didn't care, but of course she did care, and she let it happen, she knew I was thinking this and I was writing it down at the same time, without looking at the paper, I got that good, I was able to write straight lines without looking, I even felt the borders of my notebook. I want to sit down next to you, she said, Please do, I said, I want you to look me in the eyes and tell me what you think, she said, You already know what I think, I said. Of course I do, but you have to say it, Thoughts change when they turn into speech, I wrote this down. I didn't say it. She looked me in the eyes. Thoughts change when you say them, she said. She combed my hair with her fingers. Don't write it down, she said, Why wouldn't I do that?, Because you need both hands to do it, she said. She has a way of finding logical loopholes. Why did I do that?, she said, I think because you know I like you and you want to fuel that feeling, That is one explanation, Also, probably, I had something in my hair, Less likely, she said, but also a reasonable explanation, You hair is wet, I said, I know, I watched the rain, You will catch a cold, I will not, and this is not a probability, I know, How do you know? I asked, Because you will stop writing everything we say and everything we do and you will give me your shirt. The truth is complete when it stands by itself without someone having to say it. I want to see her naked body, I want to cup her fresh breasts in my hands and follow their curvature with the tips of my fingers, I want her to remain silent while I do this. You see me don't you?, she asked. What can I tell her, that my hands are mute. Yet they are moving. I want her to be shy and cover her chest with *her* elbows, I want her to be shy and cover her chest with *my* elbows. I want her to be natural about this. This will make me comfortable and will make me want her more. I want her to take her time with me but never leave me, because I do not like those games. I like games, but only if they take place in the realms of certainty. I dismiss the others, they lack integrity. I think it's not healthy to write about integrity while she is waiting in front of me with her shirt and hair soaked, with her eyes pleading and her mouth hovering with expectation. What do you think?, she asked, I think you might catch a cold and I will give you my shirt. I need to ask you a favor in return, please take my pen and write while I take off my shirt, Okay, she said, then took off her shirt.

Chapter 121
Measures and measurements, part two

Friends, friends, may I have your attention, please. Thank you. I apologize for the interruption, we tried to move as quickly as we can, I know you are all thirsty, yes, yes, excuse me, may I have your attention please, Father Frank do you think you can help here?

My pleasure, Mr. Mayor. Dear friends, we have an important message. Please come closer, bring the children forward, all from the back, I know it's hard, we have a godsend, some good news that Mr. Mayor will share with us.

Thank you. Friends, we have found water! It's difficult to cheer, but it's true, we're not sure why the authorities have left so quickly, the supplies they left behind are almost running out, which is unfortunate, we haven't been in touch, I haven't been in touch with them, I wish I could give you a reasonable explanation, which is, by the way, not important. But what is important, and I will be brief here, is that, limited as it is, the water we found comes from the emergency reserves, through the water main controls that we can access here at Town Hall. Father Frank will organize a small committee, he has experience in this field, and experience, if nothing else, is the best sign of competence, don't you agree?

The murmurs started in the back of the crowd and grew like a blood stain.

He doesn't know what he's talking about, Give him credit, he's trying his best, Shush, keep your voices down, do you want water or not?, He doesn't have anything, it's just promises, You know what, I'm tired of your negativity, wait and see, what if he does?, does it cost you to wait, do you have options, I guess not, Shut your beak, Hey, watch your tone, Folks please, you dehydrate faster if you agitate, Spare me the lectures, Listen, Mr. single man, I've had enough of your sarcasm, why don't you cooperate at least for once, I was born to do things my way, Boy, aren't you a diva.

Mr. Mayor, the citizens are growing impatient.

Yes, yes, sorry, Father, yes, please take over. I will instruct the team to receive the citizens.

Ladies and gentleman, Father Frank continued, please form a line, women and children first. One line please. The corridor to downstairs is narrow. It fits one person at a time.

Chapter 123
The ivory tower looks down at its fungus-infected feet

There are reasonable chances that he's dead, The Banker said.

What makes you think that?, The Politician asked.

We haven't heard from him.

We haven't seen him, The Neurosurgeon added.

The Frenchman didn't make contact today, The Lawyer added. He lit a cigar and sucked in a big continuous draw until his cheeks collapsed. He held it in briefly, then exhaled all the contempt he was holding in his lungs.

We cannot count on The Frenchman, The Advisor said. He was a dispensable asset, important, but dispensable. Now he's a liability we cannot control.

What about The Plan?, The Banker said.

They remained silent. A few were grinding their teeth, a few were piercing their palms with their sharp nails, The Lawyer remained unmoved and fast-forwarded his reaction to this rhetorical question: Fuck this emotional response, fuck The Frenchman, fuck The Club, I am moving forward from anger and freezing my pulse, I will use *them*, get The Plan, get rid of them, get out of this mudhole.

What about the crowd?, The Politician asked.

The crowd, The Neurosurgeon added.

They are already ransacking the building for food and water.

Like dogs.

Like dogs.

They found the water downstairs.

Soon they'll be here.

Hungry beasts will smell flesh through the walls.

We must talk to The Mayor.

He can't be talked to now.

What about the priest?

The priest is with them.

Yes, but he has weaknesses.

He does. We cannot use them now.

We should.

The timing is not ideal.

What about the woman?

What woman?

The woman we looked into. The woman with the red sweater.

She is irrelevant.

That might be an incomplete judgment.

We don't care.

What about the Tolstoy boy and the girl?

Ah yes, the Tolstoy boy and the girl, The Lawyer intervened. I'll have my son find them. Fuck, what a mindjob.

Can we use his mother? The Politician asked.

His mother is unaccounted for, The Neurosurgeon responded.

Inconvenience.

It will be dealt with later.

We need to acquire more intelligence.

We can trust *him*, The Lawyer said. He pointed to his son, standing in a corner, awaiting the path laid out for him.

The Lawyer said, Son, then shot his eyebrows in the air, as if his mouth has moved to his forehead. He said, Go and find them, find out what they're about and bring them or their knowledge here. Take the knapsack and use it, if necessary. In fact, make it necessary.

The Quiet Boy arched the corner of his mouth. It was a smile. He left the room.

Chapter 124
Simon and the bears

Simon lived with his parents until he was five. Then one night his mother simply did not come home. They never heard from her again. One day he heard from an aunt that she was in Indonesia, working on a cruise ship. His father was diagnosed with liver cancer when he was seven. He told him that he has to rest for a while. He got interned in a clinic in the far north, and then they never heard of him again. The aunt told him that he had to go away for a long time because his health was not great and he needed fresh air all the time. For a long time Simon thought that his father lived in an ice-hut, because they say that in the Arctic you get the best air, despite the hole in the ozone layer.

He spent the duration of the flood in Mr. Kaczynski's house because there was plenty of food. Mr. Kaczynski had an obsession with food supplies.

He never met Mr. Kaczynski. After a week in his house, he got used to the idea that Mr. Kaczynski would never return and that he could have as much food as he wanted. As long as he remained the only one who knew about it.

The knocks on the door were firm and loud. Three of them. Like someone was using a heavy sledgehammer. Nobody has knocked on this door before. Not intentionally. He was never afraid, he always knew how to control his fear, when darkness was impenetrable, when the stench of decay was unbearable, when the nights were quiet and the moon was howling, or when the rain was dropping like bullets on the roof, when one day a helicopter flew above Town and never came back. One night, he dreamt that he was the last survivor, that he forgot the language of man. He dreamt that, years later, the light from the sun became too hot and bright, and he had to keep his head down all the time. His back became severely crooked, like a hunchback's, and one day he kneeled, propped his chin against the ground and turned to dust like an old stump.

Today he was not afraid.

He waited a minute behind the door before he opened it. He could feel the unwelcome guest on the other side of the door.

He opened the door.

They stared at each other.

It's you, Simon said. I thought you were dead.

The Quiet Boy nodded and asked, Where is Tim?, Simon said that he is not sure, Perhaps he stayed with his mother or his friends, or the flood swept him away, what's in your sack?, do you have food?

The Quiet Boy shook his head. He didn't have food, but he sure could use some.

Come inside, I have some leftovers. Not much, but I can spare some.

Simon ransacked some cardboard boxes while The Quiet Boy took a seat on the couch. He never let go of his knapsack. He puts it next to him and put one hand inside. He was holding onto something.

I must have some jam left. Do you like jam? I don't have bread, but I have some crackers. Do you like crackers?

The Quiet Boy liked jam and crackers.

The boys stared at each other over the jar of jam and the pack of crackers.

What you have there?, Simon asked.

The Quiet Boy didn't answer. He took a cracker with his free hand and dipped it in the jar. He liked it. He did it again.

Listen, Simon continued, I barely know Tim. I can't say where he is. Sorry to say, but they might not have made it. Town's a mess. We can't say anything for sure. You know what I mean. Not sure if I can help you with that.

The Quiet Boy stuffed his mouth with crackers.

Where are your parents?, Simon asked.

The Quiet Boy stopped chewing and fixed Simon like he did not understand the question. It's not a question he liked. He pulled his hand out of the sack. It was a stuffed bear.

Take it, he said.

Thanks. Did you make it?

The Quiet Boy nodded.

That's what you carry with you?

I like bears, The Quiet Boy answered, and dipped another cracker in the jar.

Chapter 125
The door opens without notice

Gregoire followed the footsteps to the end of the alley behind the bar, then lost them in the muddy street. He stopped to check the apron and saw a growing bloodstain. He climbed through the shattered window into the convenience store across the street and stopped inside to catch his breath. He looked around the devastated shelves and picked up a wooden cigar box. He ripped the latch off with his teeth and spat it out. The cigars were intact and dry. He bit off the end of one and stuck it in the corner of his mouth. He picked up a lighter that still worked and watched the flame and himself in the mirror on the wall behind the register. He clenched his teeth and hissed, Sonofabitch, then blew a big load of smoke into the mirror.

The boys were walking side by side with their heads down. The Quiet Boy with his knapsack strapped on his back, Simon with his hands in his pockets, splitting crackers and crushing the crumbs with his fingers.

They did not see the pair of eyes in the mirror behind the counter and the smoke that was blurring Gregoire's face.

The boys' deal was simple. Simon would supply crackers and jam and whatever he might find in the house, and The Quiet Boy would lead him to other survivors and to the certainty that he would be safe, on condition that Simon helped him find Tim and whoever might be with them. Sounds fair to me, buddy, said Simon and patted The Quiet Boy on his back. He lost his grin while The Quiet Boy grabbed Simon's hand and pushed it away from him. Okay, Simon said. We're cool.

They walked past the shattered window of the tobacco shop.

While they were passing in front of the door, the door opened violently, forcing them to stop.

Gregoire roared, and jumped in front of them. Isn't this ironic, boys?

Simon barely recognized the ice cream man. The Quiet Boy knew who the man was, despite the scars and The Frenchman's pale face.

You followed me, you pimple fuckfaces. Where is the man?

What man?, Simon asked.

The fucking man with the fucking stuff!

Sorry sir, I don't know what man—

Shut up, The Quiet Boy cut into Simon's mumble.

Listen to him, fuckface, you pisspants! How about you, Silent Bob, what do you know?

The Quiet Boy managed to raise his shoulder. Gregoire snaped him hard in the back of his head. The Quiet Boy fell like a sack of grain.

What did you do?, Simon yelled and turned to see what happened. Gregoire knocked him to the ground and he lost consciousness.

Chapter 126
The whale within the whale, part one

It's too dangerous and we have to leave her here, you say. She will dehydrate and will die soon, we have no choice, we must try. You know it would help us a lot if you dropped the notebook and helped us. I must keep it, I say. The pregnant woman is tired. She hasn't talked since the last rain. The old woman tells her stories at night. She goes to sleep smiling. She was in pain today. You told her to rest and to take deep, long breaths. Then she said she was thirsty and you looked at me. I thought of the last rain but I didn't tell you that. You would have thought I was insensitive. Today we need to find some water. The bottles are empty. Help me take her down, you say. Please.

Chapter 127
Cold cellar

When they woke up they found a note from Father Frank, Went to Town Hall.

Emma, what are you wearing?

It's a linen princess's dress, Mommy.

It's very beautiful.

Iris woke up early and took a walk inside the Church. She didn't want to wake the girl and her mother. Plus, the white guard was mumbling something into his mask. His face was twitching in his sleep.

There was something odd about the Church today. It was all so quiet, so still. The mud on the walls has turned into a crisp coating that has started to peel off. The crack, sealed with mud and tar from the road, was sporadically leaking rays of light inside, as the frail material moved and lost structural integrity. But it wasn't that. It was the air that reeked of a damp, mossy, heavy load. It's from the wooden benches invaded by insects or from the altar where candles are melting under the spears of heat from the sunlight that pierces the roof, or the decomposed leftovers of food discarded by the inhabitants of the attic. The smell intensified when she approached the door and the staircase to the lower level. Then she decided to tell the others.

There is something down there.

We know, Emma's mother said. She gave the note to Iris and turned back to her daughter. See Emma, you're a princess now.

Iris folded the note and put it in her pocket.

Emma's mother looked Iris in the eyes, Did you give her the dress?, she asked, It wasn't me, Iris responded, Do you think it was him?, The mother pointed to the guard with a movement of her face. Iris shrugged.

The white guard entered the room. He was holding the mask under his arm. The girls looked at him intensely befuddled.

What?, he said.

You took off your mask.

They didn't think about the metaphoric meaning of wearing a mask, as one can simply put on an improvised personality under certain social circumstances, for the sake of achieving a certain goal or position in a group, then when the group is dissolved or no longer present, one will resume a casual personality, closer to one's heart, I feel more myself, one will say, then later remember that the mask was also a deliberate choice, was not an alteration of the self, but rather was part of the self and the self cannot live without it. Change is essential in everything. It is imposed upon us by the very fact that we exist, that everything is interchangeable and impermanent, that everything transforms, energy into matter into energy, all is appearance over our senses, including ourselves.

I think we're safe, the white guard said. I don't need the mask anymore. There are no signs of radiation. I couldn't breathe. I dreamt of an apple orchard. It smelled so fresh. The trees were blooming. Then I woke up and I smelled the sweet-sour scent of decay.

We all smell that, Iris said.

The key was in Father Frank's desk. It was attached to a thick chain with a Latin inscription. *Nihil Sine Deo.* They remembered that they have read that before, but couldn't remember where. The descent was slow and quiet. The lights were out. I have to stay with Emma, her mother said, I can't take her there. Please don't forget about us. They said, Okay, don't worry, they built a torch from the leg of a century-old stool and plunged into darkness.

The room was large and frigid. The walls were buried somewhere in the dark. Their speech had a delayed echo. It felt like there was somebody else out here who talked back to them. I don't like this place, Iris said. Yeah, the guard said.

They found crates piled on shelves and on the stone tiles, patches of oil-green mould and roots crawling out through the cracks. The stench came from the big box in the back. It's a sarcophagus, Iris said, What do you know about sarcophaguses?, I'm going to art school, You're going to art school?, the white guard said, Yes.

Don't we take out the food and water first? Iris asked.

Let me think.

I want to look inside, too.

Aren't you afraid?, he asked.

I don't know.

You don't know.

I just want to look inside.

They broke the lid of a crate and the white guard disassembled it into few planks with his knee. He picked the best piece and inserted it into a crack under the lid of the sarcophagus, then pushed down on it with the weight of his body. Don't just say something, do nothing, he said. Sarcasm?, Iris asked. Maybe, he said. The lid of the sarcophagus budged a little, just enough for a gush of air to come out. He wiped his forehead with his sleeve and showed Iris how to push. They made an opening half a meter wide.

Give me the torch, the white guard said.

He moved the torch over the opening of the sarcophagus. His eyes widened and, as though they have taken over his sense of smell, he covered his nose with his sleeve.

What?, Iris said.

He let her look inside.

The sarcophagus was packed with dirty rags mixed with minced mummified flesh swarming with maggot colonies of various colors and sizes. It smells horrible, Yes, it does, What are those?, They are what I think and can't imagine they are. Iris rummaged through the pile with the head of the torch and reveals the sparkling stones. He dumped them in haste, she thought. There are hundreds of diamonds among the maggots, rags and putrefying flesh. She tried to think of what to say to the voice from across the room that suddenly broke their awe with a metallic, Hello.

Chapter 126
Within the whale, part two

I have met you in a line of words that has not been born yet. I have met you before the first Word, the first Thought, the first acceptance of reality because you were before everything, you were before the essence was defined, before necessity was captured into definitions and structures and logic, you were at the purest time, when even time itself was outside definition and perception, you were without cause and effect, you created me from an idea without beginning, without end, in a timeless sphere, in a borderless space, in a spaceless infinite space, you were my bellybutton, you were your own bellybutton, there was no reason to explain yourself because you simply were, and I was simply there, and I was born when I saw you, I was born when I felt you, I understood the meaning of to be, the reason of one-and-everything, I am you and you are me, and we are everything around us, we are the time, when time has not existed, we are the time when we knew it was all an illusion, we are beyond our thought of ourselves, impermanent and eternal together, essential and one, the you and the me.

You are asking me how I am feeling today and I don't know what to say. I do not raise my head from these words. My hand is moving on its own, my mind its moving on its own, I feel blended into you and when you speak I hear your voice coming from far away. From over the mountains, from the depths of The Lake, from the tunnels of a cave. You say, Look at me. I can't, because I see you already. You are here, in these words, inside the rotunda of the vowel i, concealed in the wittiness and the fluffiness of a comma.

Chapter 128
Caterpillar, wider, clearer

We have to function like an organism, with many legs synchronized, with one purpose, with one body, they said.

The well has provided for the twenty-four brothers, water, satisfaction, relative peace of mind and incentives to become pensive and consider unconditional unpremeditated compassion towards each other and towards the occasional travelers who came in their garden to ask for a drop of water or for a kind word.

Imam and Rabbi have found their kind words.

The Voice has been silent for days. In their heads, the echoless thoughts have settled. They took long hours of meditation together. How do you do this prayer?, I say this and this, What does it mean?, It means this and this, Your Allah is merciful, Your Adonai is kind, How do you write this verse?, Like this. And he wrote the verse with a stick on the ground and pronounced it slowly, then they recited it together. Do you think we can be saved?, I think and feel we can be saved, but I am waiting for an answer from out there, I am waiting for an answer too, What is the question?, I don't know. They went back to the brothers and gathered them in a big circle and spoke in the common language about their purpose, about the necessity of change, about compassion towards the others and all the good things. The brothers listened in silence. For a long time, nobody said anything. From time to time, strangers stopped by to ask for water and it was given to them generously.

Hours later, the two cellular devices rang at the same time. Rabbi and Iman looked at each other and decided not to answer.

Chapter 129
Pulses

Hello.

There was no response.

Hello.

There was no response.

Do you think he's still here?

The Quiet Boy did not answer. He wiggled his wrists, and tried to untie the bonds with his teeth. The knot was too tight.

Gregoire left a few hours ago. They could tell by the trail of blood where the exit was. The light was scarce in this basement. There were no windows. The place has been looted. Tools discarded on the floor, crates reduced to splinters, the smell of cold soil and organic decay.

Do you think he's gonna kill us?

The Quiet Boy didn't think Gregoire was going to kill them, Gregoire had a purpose, an affiliation with his father, he did not recognize him, Gregoire was afraid, he acted like a cornered beast, he will calm down when he realizes whom he captured and will release them, unless he has a collateral plan that they are overlooking, maybe he has one, maybe their capture had a purpose, with prolonged deliberating and planning, or not, they will know when he returns, they will know by what he will say, by what he will do, or what he will not do, why has he left them here. The Frenchman failed in his tasks, he will use them as merchandise, to save himself, yes, he has failed, he is desperate, he will use them, Simon has no idea what's going on, it's better if he doesn't know, that is why he will die first, the ignorant usually die first, it is bliss to die peacefully, the pain is the wait not the departure from life.

Gregoire howled like a beast. He trudged upstairs and smashed every object in his path. He cursed and roared and sputtered foam.

The prey retreated to the lair in pain. He evaluated the options. He thought that the future was meaningless, that it did not exist, that nothing conditioned anything, that the present was narrow.

He was running out of blood. His breath was heavier, he walked with heavy steps.

Maybe he will use them. He will come back and tape their mouths, and then he will go out and meet the men. He will take something from his prisoners to convince the men. They will negotiate. The Lawyer will make them negotiate. They will exchange guarantees and then he will release the prisoners.

He will kill one of them. He will kill the boy Simon and will show them that he is serious and mad. He is mad. He is mad because he failed. They will chase him for that. He has to confront them.

He will keep them until he finds the thieves. He will retrieve the merchandise, then he will kill them.

He will let them live. He will disappear fast. Into the mountains where he came from.

But they will find him. They will hire someone to find him. They can hire anyone. They will not stop until they have what they want. They do not have what they want. He does not have what he wants. He does not have what they want.

That's why he is mad. He hollered like a hellbeast.

The smell of decay descended upon them.

What is he building in there?, Simon asked. What's with all the small knives?

They have been through his garage. The thieves. They took everything important. They found everything.

There was stuff covered with tarpaulin in the basement. Simon and The Quiet Boy could not see clearly what it was. Motes of light scattered on a big pile in the opposite corner.

There was a chute above the pile, made for discarding stuff easily. The whole pile might have travelled through that chute.

It stunk.

The air was dry. The flood did not come inside.

He planned it. He was cautious.

The water caught him here.

Like a submarine with independent compartments, the door closed instantly.

It was made of steel. They could see reflections of metal.

What is he doing up there?, he stopped yelling but he was making a lot of noise. He was trying to turn on a machine of some sort. It was clogged with water. The generator was working. A circular saw. He let it run for one minute and turned it off. He was quiet. The machine has made him think.

The present was no longer narrow.

He will come downstairs and cut them with the circular saw.

No he won't. He needs them. No, he doesn't need them, he is a hellbeast. He was good. Any being wants to live. He wants to live. He needs them to live.

He will put down the circular saw and sit down on the bench in the garage and think. He will remember the big flood coming. He will remember when he woke up and all the stuff was still there.

For a minute he will feel safe.

He will turn on the circular saw and realize that the cord is not long enough.

He doesn't have a longer cord.

He will swear and spit on the floor.

He will come back to them and ask them if they are afraid.

They will not say anything.

He will say, Good boys, and close the steel door behind him.

Chapter 130
The heart of the bear stuffer

Welcome to my Synagogue, he said slowly.

She knows who he is. They have met before.

Hello Luc, Iris said.

You know him?, the white guard asked.

Yes, I know him.

Why is he talking like that?

She didn't answer.

Luc approached them so they could see his hands. You did not have to come here, he said. The sound of his voice was cold and wide like the blade of the knife in his hand. He was a holding a toy bear in his other hand, with the belly cut open and stuffing spilling out. He handed them a piece of paper.

Read it, he said.

Iris walked to him and took it.

She read the note, I dream of the day when the evil and the ugly will be unearthed and will see the sun. When those who are barefoot will smile and those who are clothed will feel naked and humble. Where there will be no more reason *to have* and there will be only the reason *to be*. When those who were silent will speak and will be heard and those who were speaking will know how to listen. When the purpose to understand will be higher than the purpose to survive to the detriment of the other. I dream of the day when we will understand that we have to rise from the depths and reach for the light. I dream of the day when they will find me.

Follow me, Luc said.

He stepped back into the dark. They sensed him ahead, but the light from the torch could not catch him. A wooden door opened and stepped moved forward on the stone floor. They entered a long corridor. They could tell by the closeness of the walls, the elongation of the echo, the stifled footsteps, the crown of the flame bent backwards under the drag of the air current.

They stopped when they heard the clinking key ring. Another massive door opened into bright natural light. It was Luc's room, his lookout. It was hidden under the brow of a hill and gave a view of the lower parts of Town. There were three windows carved into the soil of the hill shaped by a circular wooden enforcement concealed by moss and roots from the trees hung from above. From the outside they looked like nests of eagles.

The room was clean and organized. To the left there was an archway and a storage area. A huge pile of stuffed bears.

To the right a brass basin with clean water, sponges and a bunch of tiny brushes.

He turned around and looked at his guests.

He didn't say anything. On the floor, there was a bucket filled with rags and maggots and diamonds. He took a handful and placed it in the basin. He rinsed the rags and scraped off the diamonds with his hand. He used a brush for those that were stuck in fabric or with bits of flesh. He knew where they came from. He rinsed the diamonds and put them in a smaller basin with no water. He repeated the operation until the all the stones were separated. He put the rags with maggots and bits of flesh in a box on the floor. He dipped a tin cup into a basket of soil and spread the soil in the box until the rags were covered. He emptied the basin into a bucket and refilled it with fresh water from a canister. He poured some water into the smaller basin over the diamonds.

I see an enormous heart with three eyes. The birthplace of bears stuffed with diamonds. The most expensive toys on the planet. I dream of the day when they will SEE ME.

Chapter 131
Persuasion into the land of whatever

My grandma once told me, Simon if you can beat a goose with a stick, think twice, because the goose can jump at you and bite your finger off.

For a long time I didn't know what to make of this. Like, who was the goose? I didn't know anyone that I could beat and get away with it. Oh yeah, maybe I did. A few kids at school. But they all had cousins who cared about them and would come back after me. Yeah, I guess they were the goose.

My father would come home and beat me with a rubber stick. He made it himself, from the remnants of a tire swing that broke. I guess broke is one way to put it. He would come from behind and hit me in the calves. He knew I would collapse and would not move. He did not look when he was hitting me. It was like he was dreaming or meditating, like he was trying to remember what to do.

I guess in his own mind he was trying to make sense of the world. For each hit he would ask, Why, why, why, then at the end of the series he would complete the sentence, Why did you break Mr. Kaczynski's window, why didn't you tie the shoelaces, why did you wipe your snot on your sleeve, why the fuck do I have to pay more for your school, aren't you good enough.

One day he didn't finish the sentence. He said, Get up and bring me the bottle.

I brought him the bottle. It was half empty. He opened it with his teeth and spat the cork on the floor. He turned it upside-down over his mouth and emptied it. Some of it spilled. He didn't care.

Tell your mother, he said. I need to rest.

Then he got up and left.

Maybe the Arctic air did him good.

I heard the cold air makes you think better. With one condition. That you are not alone. That there is someone next to you to hear your congealed whispers.

My mother left a few years after him. She was tired too. Many nights she slept on the floor. She was that tired. She couldn't walk to the bed.

Do you think he's gonna kill us?

Maybe, The Quiet Boy responded.

Aren't you afraid?

No.

Your father knows him, doesn't he? Sure he does. They have some business. I bet that must be good for us. Unless he didn't screw up his part. But I guess he did, didn't he? Yeah, I thought so.

So, your knapsack, eh? Are you carrying something valuable? Something that can change our situation? I'm surprised he didn't check it. He's kind of impulsive, isn't he? Yeah, he is. You know, I always wondered why you are so quiet. They all want to know. I mean we all have lots of thoughts and imagery. Your inner world must be so vivid. You can imagine beyond what we can hope to imagine. You read a lot. I saw you reading at school all the time. You seemed very happy. Who do you like at school? What a question. Not many are likable. Maybe it's just a trait of our generation. We define ourselves through contrast with others. That's it, isn't it? We must not be like those weaker than us, like those we hate. We must be like those whom we worship.

He's coming, The Quiet Boy answered.

Chapter 132
Forces and waves

You do not talk about it, the Inventor said. He closed the suitcase slowly.

Dad, where did you go?, Is this how it ends, in a veil of fear, at the dawn of reason, where hope has perished and we succumb to our lowest needs, we despair and we grab the air with our lungs, the rare air, the quiet, heavy air, we grab the waters with our thirsty nails, the dark, oily waters, we shield our eyes from the blackhole sun.

Dad, he showed us the light. It reminded me of the early white mornings when Mom used to bring me egg yolk with sugar and milk that made me dream until noon. You practiced your violin, it sounded like a dream. With concert hall reverberations. You came to my room, opened the window and showed me the sun. The large orange disc.

Dad, are they treating you well?, Do you travel on camels and elephants?, Do you fly on eagles?

Dad, you died. You told me it's just a transition.

Why don't we see it before it happens?, Do we think it's a transition just to be less afraid?, Did we invent death?

Dad, do they have music there?, Do you still have free will?, Are you one mind?, Are you still you?, Do you blend with other dads?, Do you remember me?, Do hear my violin?, Do you remember Bach?

Dad, how do we make sense of this world?, Is it in the questions?, Is in the answers?

Chapter 133
Terms and conditions

P: I'm afraid, gentlemen, that things are getting out of hand.

A: Yes, the signals are not good.

N: Fear is not a correct approach.

P: It's a figure of speech, Mr. Neurosurgeon.

N: Perhaps it is, Mr. Politician.

B: Your son has not reported back, Mr. Lawyer.

L: He has not, we must proceed with patience.

B: The Frenchman is an unstable character now, Mr. Lawyer.

L: He is.

B: Maybe he's dead.

L: He's not. We would have known.

P: What if The Mayor talks?

N: The Mayor will not talk. He is conditioned.

A: Even if he talks, he is limited to his knowledge.

P: He can expand the knowledge into relevant conclusions.

N: He will never reach *that* conclusion.

P: It has been done before. Imagination precedes logic, Mr. Neurosurgeon.

N: Imagination is conditioned. Subject to biology, society, intellect.

A: I must advise that imagination is the primal cause of all creation.

N: Bogus.

L: Gentlemen. The Plan.

P: Can we use The Mayor to get to The Frenchman?

N: I recommend against it.

P: We can use the other connections.

A: Those that he is unaware of.

B: To leverage the risk.

L: We can't have any guarantees. We lurk in nonsense. It's all bits and pieces.

N: We must admit we have lost control.

L: I wouldn't go that far.

N: Your confidence baffles me, Mr. Lawyer.

L: My confidence precedes your logic and observation.

A: What about the contacts in the government?

P: Why are you looking at me?

A: For the obvious reason.

P: There has been no contact. The brief intrusion of the guards is inexplicable.

L: On some channels there is some communication with the exterior.

B: Are you sure?

L: I have some information.

P: Who is it?

L: Some ethnical groups have made contact. Not at their initiative.

B: How does this concern us?

L: They have appealed to the masses.

N: The masses are ignorant. Ignorance is bliss.

L: The masses can create momentum. The Frenchman is sensitive to momentum.

B: What are you saying?

L: He will find a way to use it.

N: We are not sensitive to the momentum.

B: We are not.

L: We have to be.

N: I recommend making contact with The Mayor.

P: Agreed.

A: Agreed.

B: Agreed.

L: Fine.

B: How do we proceed?

L: We must establish a channel with him.

P: An indirect channel.

A: Exactly.

B: How about the woman with the red sweater?

N: Yes, she is conditioned. I know where she is. I will bring her.

L: Good, we have the terms. One hour, gentlemen.

P: One hour.

Chapter 134
Elopement

You say one hour of love is enough to suppress the perception of time. Come to me, you say. I follow the light of your candles. You are taking me to your room. It is the right place to be, you say. Nobody will bother us. You show me your collection of dolls, those made of porcelain, precious and delicate, those you made yourself, stuffed with cotton wads and sand. For balance, you explain. You keep them in the coffer. You look at me and smile. Why do you smile?, I ask. You're writing now in your notebook without looking, you say. You're right, I say. I look at you. You are so beautiful. You look down, as if you were shy. I will write with my mind now.

You close your eyes and ask me to touch you. My hands are free. They have to be free. We sit down. It's hot and dry outside, but cozy and quiet in your room. I put my finger on your forehead. I say, Home, and you smile. The plains where the geography of love starts. Where the winds have no hurdles. Where beads of rain are big as haystacks. I run among them as they grow from the ground and they rise to the sky defying gravity. Like the earth feeds the sky with rain. I walk through the tree line, your eyebrows, the thin line between thought and light. Your eyes are closed. It's okay, you say. I kneel on your eyelid and put my ear on it. I can hear its heart. What do you mean?, you ask. I can hear your eyes beating. You chuckle. I kiss them both. I hover over your cheeks with large steps, light as a feather, almost jumping. I touch them both and move farther south. You must stay still, I say, I've arrived at your smile. How is my smile?, you ask. It's curved and the ends point upwards, I say. It tells you that you have to go back. No, it reminds me where I come from. You say I always have a way with words and always get away with it. I say that all I do is set them free so the other words that wait in line can take their place. I feel tension in your chin. Another heart rests inside. It quivers, like an earth that will give birth instantly to millions of dandelions. Then there is the slope around your neck. I climb down in a spiral, softly. I feel the heart of your neck under my soles, it's louder and bigger. At the northernmost point of your chest, I stop and look at you. You moan and you put your hands on my head. You are listening with your hands. The silent story of a journey. The two soft tulips on your chest. The hearts inside them. I talk to them. I kneel between and listen to the biggest heart of them all. The heart of your heart. From which millions of other hearts race in all directions. Your pulse is fast. You like my story. You bite your lips, your forehead trembles. I continue my journey south on the paths of your belly. You arch your back majestically like the sculptures from antiquity. At your belly button I look at you again. You are full of hearts evaporating from your body, minuscule incandescent hearts. I walk further south. You try to say my name. It comes out as a whisper.

I remember my first dream of you. We were on the roof of the church. The waters were surrounding us. The moon was bright and the night sky was clear. Are you sleeping? you asked. I am, I answered. We rose from our bodies and we flew above Town. We went to the mountains. We saw The Lake and the rivers pouring. We saw lights far away and maybe the ocean. We thought the night is short and we cannot go that far. We found a boat and rested in it. We embraced. I wrote you a story, then I read it to you. You liked it but you said we were already in a dream. We didn't need the story now. We woke up and heard somebody say that the waters are slowly retreating.

~~You say names are not important. Names falsify reality.~~ No, scratch that. That's not what you said. You said love comes before reality. We use words to realize that. When we make love we don't say anything. Because we create realities. We are before everything. We are at the beginning. We do not need words.

You whisper that you want me inside you. Yes, that's what you say. I will write it down and show it to you when we awake from this reality. I enter you and your body trembles. You try to say my name. It comes out as a whisper.

We lie on the floor among dolls. One hour of love is enough to lose the sense of time, you say. I think you are right. I look at you and try to define what makes you real. What were you before my words were born to describe you? Were you real? Were you somebody else's story?

I think we are born every time someone writes a new story about us. Like I gave birth to yours. Like you invented me, when we met.

I think you exaggerate, you are overly poetic, things don't work this way, you say. You smile. I know you are just teasing me.

I open my notebook and free the words.

Chapter 135
Of vision and scalpel

Gregoire climbed down the stairs slowly, one step at a time. He was walking the blade of a scalpel on the long band of a razor strop. He used it to make a proper incision into the new bodies. He was methodical, and he knew that was good. But sometimes not all things can be predicted. Things can be put back on track with a forceful correction. It's just karma. It's in your power to correct its shortcomings.

He found the boys where he left them. The boy Simon was horrified. The other one was just quiet. He pulled a chair in front of them and blew the filth off it. He swung the scalpel like a pendulum.

What is the difference between a man and a boy? The size of his dick? How many women he nails? The scars on his fists? The blood he takes? The freedom he has? You know what that pile is? Sure you do. Now, why did I do that? Those nameless bodies were dead already when I opened them. Does this make me a hero or what? They ain't any deader, I am not a criminal. What, because I want my freedom, you judge me, you think you can judge me. Why are you sweating, boy? Your dad should have known better. You are not that brave. He took it easily. It bounced against him. Too bad. He was just tad off the track of history. It happens to all men with good intentions. Now you look at me like you don't know what I'm talking about. It's just insulting. Don't do that. Look at your friend here. At least he has his dignity. He's quiet about it. I like that. He doesn't sweat. Maybe he has better sweat glands, fuck knows. But you can learn from him, fuckface. And you know why I'm saying this so calmly? Because I can, fuckface, I know what I want. You don't know what you want. You fuckers all you think about is how to get laid, your crap generation, idiots. You don't have vision. See, that's the difference between a man and a boy. Vision. A man sees the other side of the blade. Look, look in this blade. It's shiny, yes. You can see your faces, fuckfaces. But you can't see the other side. Why can't you see the other side? That's a good question. Because the other side faces me. And because I am holding the scalpel. I am holding it. I am the man because I can see the other side of the scalpel and your faces at the same time. What does this mean? I have an advantage, I have vision. What do you have? A fuckface, yes. What do you do with it? You talk shit every day and you put it in the girl's crotch. You don't get it. The fuck is nothing. The dick is nothing. The man with the blade is everything. The man with the blade decides. The man with the swinging dick, what does he do? He listens and hopes he can keep his dick so he can get another fuck tomorrow, if he's lucky. You do understand you are *not* lucky today. I *am* lucky today. Why am I lucky today? Because of some mirror, because of some fortunate series of events, maybe, fuck cares, I am here and lucky today because I have enforced my vision and you have not. Because I create momentum and you do not. Men create momentum. Boys, if they are lucky, which you are not, follow momentum. You get it? Create. Follow. So, what momentum do we have now? Do we know why we are here? Yes, we do. Do we understand our purpose? Maybe, some of us. Is about power? Sure, if you want to put it that way. Is it about the scalpel? Exactly. The scalpel is the element that defines the momentum. The scalpel is the guillotine on Louis XVI, the scalpel is the bullet in the president's brain, the scalpel is the button to the nuclear bomb. The scalpel is the quintessential decider. Sure, you can say, it's a metaphor. The scalpel cannot decide, it's a metal object. I am the decider, am I not? I am the facilitator of freefuckingwill. And when there is interference with my freefuckingwill it brings me, you know, discomfort. That gives me feelings. Not good feelings. I do not like to talk about that, because, I'm sure, you don't want to talk about your bad feelings. We'll skip that part. We will focus on the fact that good feelings are desirable and bad feelings must be eliminated. And we have to work on the cause of those feelings, because, you see, the feelings are not like a scalpel that you hold in your hand and sharpen with this razor strop, no, the feelings are like, like, umm, like air, you know, they're just there, you go through them, you inhale them, they fill your lungs, they give you cancer, they keep you alive, they change your voice, they make you cough, they pollute the air, they feed the trees. They are very unstable. I don't like unstable things. I just don't. You see, these thieves have hurt my feelings and interests. This brings consequences, doesn't it? They don't have vision, they were boys, like you, that fuck and leave a mess behind them. What else does a fuckface leave behind him? Good questions. A fuckface leaves traces. And a man finds the traces and builds a reality out of it. A reality that will be somebody else's history. See my point? My point is, I need to know where the thieves are and their names. Then we'll decide.

We don't know anything, sir.

That is one damn truth. Your quiet partner here has the decency to shut the fuck up. Which is good to a point. But we are beyond that point. Who wants to answer first?

He stood up and pointed the scalpel at the boys. You? You? They didn't answer. He made an incision in Simon's pants and exposed the skin without yet entering it.

Please, no!, Simon screamed.

That is a normal reaction for a boy. But we are on the right track. I want to hear results. NOW!

Leave him alone, The Quiet Boy said.

The Quiet Boy freed himself from the rudimentary knot Gregoire had tied behind his back. He reached in his knapsack and grabbed the pistol. He loaded it behind his back. He knew how to do that without looking. His father showed him at the shooting range.

He stood and pointed the gun at Gregoire.

Well, well, what do we have here? A boy about to become a man. How is that not surprising, coming from a little dick like you? I knew you had some vision, I knew you had something.

The Quiet Boy pointed the pistol at Gregoire's calf and shot.

The Frenchman collapsed on his back like a defeated beast, with a roar of frustration. Fuck!, he screamed.

The Quiet Boy untied Simon.

They stopped in front of the beast to watch.

Wait, I want to see it. Simon walked to the pile and lifted a corner of the tarpaulin. Mummified bodies with their guts removed surgically.

Like you didn't know, fuckface!, Gregoire roared.

The Quiet Boy told Simon it's time to go. Gregoire threw the scalpel at them and hit the knapsack.

The boys left the house without looking back.

Chapter 136
Ambiguous acceptance of the ambiguous

What will happen to us?

The Psychiatrist realized his wife was telling the truth. It has been a long time since he saw the expression of her mask changing as she was speaking. It must be the light, the shadows, the refraction of invisible particles of dust in the air or the material wearing out. Or perhaps the mask has become her new skin.

He didn't know what will happen to them, because all the past came to him as a river, ironically in the midst of terrible days of dehydration, the day when he left and did not call her for a month, when he thought over and over, I don't want you in my life, during breakfasts, during lunches, during the long swims in The Lake by himself, the letters she sent him, that he didn't open, the effort of removing her image from his brain, the collection of masks, the few times when he washed her hair and she was crying, the nights when he slept with other women, like he hoped the serotonin would numb his cognitive functions and that he would remember nothing, from the past and from the present and from the future, the nausea of the morning after, the joy of discovering possible alter egos over a cup of coffee with a muffin at a bar in the mountains, then the disappointing result when all those alter egos would dissolve like the sugar crystals when the nameless woman would wrap her arms around his neck, are you still thinking about your wife?, I don't know, he would say, they would order a martini and talk about opera and charitable events, how much beauty there is in the world, we are too small to take it all in and we have to be satisfied with the bits we get, the days when he would sit down with his wife and talk seriously about, The distance between us, about how, We grew apart, Why?, I guess it is human nature, Then why does this make us so unhappy?, It's the seed in us, we are never ready to understand it, We were never ready, then they'd talk for hours about their youth, the first dates, the unwavering enthusiasm, the unprogrammed adventures, the unanalyzed feelings, the carpe diems, the cruises, the plays, the films, the concerts, *les nuits d'amours*, they would talk about it like they'd watch a newsreel from the '30s, a few frames per second in black and white, moving unnaturally fast, almost comedic, with poor editing and clumsy angles of armies marching, factory workers aligned and uniformed, tons of bars of soap, big radios, loud and happy families smiling at the camera, their dreams of the future, their ignorance and their subsequent happiness, the days of long-forgotten compromises, before the illness, after the treatments, the therapies, the denial, the acceptance, the apathy, the courage stemmed from nowhere, or from the morale of an easy popular film, the despair at the realization of the recurrence of the routine, the regrets unrealized, the ignominy of abandonment, the lack of synchronicity, the peaks of blames and pain, the scars and the beautiful scarves, the trip to Dharamsala, You don't have to come here to open your soul, a beggar told them, you don't need to see Him, you need to see yourselves, and she cried for days and he drank water and opium for days, the days of the appearance and the disappearance of the fetus, the long months of the acceptance of the inevitable, the return of despair and the proximity of death, for better or for worse, in sickness and in health, the fallible human mind, the fallible soul, the effort to become better, This is our glory, our beauty, to grow together, I'm tired, she said and she would leave the house for three days, then pretend that nothing happened, that all realities are mute, that happiness is numbness, that awareness is suffering, that all reality is suffering.

We can't stay here, we don't have water, the wife said.
I know.

Chapter 137
Ascension

The queue for water stretched from the basement of Town Hall to the main hall and outside. The water committee, presided over by Father Frank, The Mayor and a burly man, surrounded the overflow control faucet in the water main that spewed convulsively whatever reserves were at the bottom of underground reservoirs around Town.

Thank you, Father, Thank you, Mayor, You're welcome, I'm glad I can help. Then they stopped for a few minutes while the burly man checked why the faucet was stuck, Water stopped coming, Jiggle the bloody pipe, the single man yelled from the back, Give me a minute pal, will ya?

Out of earshot of the crowd, The Mayor asked Father Frank how long he thought they can survive since the water was running out. I don't know, Mr. Mayor, the Lord is the governor of our soul, What about our bodies, Father, who governs them?, The soul governs the body, Mr. Mayor, not the other way around, Do you see any solutions, Father?, Perhaps we should tend to our souls now, Perhaps we should, Father, if you wish you can use my office for a moment of meditation, your clear insight will help us, Father,

Thank you, Mayor, I see for the moment my services are not needed, I shall retreat to your office.

He left the crowded room and climbed back up through the narrow corridor, Bless us Father, Bless you, brother, bless you, sister, Is there water for us all?, They're working on it, Are you leaving us?, I just need a moment with the Lord.

The Mayor's office was closed. He inserted the key in the lock and took a deep breath. He turned the key and pushed the heavy door forward. The door screeched like a sinking ship.

The woman with the red sweater was standing by the large mahogany desk. She had her arms crossed over her belly and was looking down.

I was waiting for you, she said without looking.

You were?

Yes, I wasn't expecting you to come that fast.

The contact person told her to be at The Mayor's office at this precise time or something bad will happen to her, He'll meet you there, you know who, the somebody you cannot say no to, you've met him before, you've met them before. To which she said, Fine, but how did you know where to find me?, They know how to find everyone.

She saw Father Frank and thought that the group was more powerful than the appearances. She could not contain her surprise to find that Father was also a member, she hoped she will not have to suffer the humiliation again, she came forward to Father Frank, in silence, like a gazelle, and unbuttons her pants, the lingerie became visible, not a sight Father Frank was expecting when he was preparing the *magnificat anima mea dominum et exultavit spiritus meus* recitation. So she welcomed him in the spiritual exercise, Do you want to see it?, It? he asked, Yes, she says, and unbuttoned the last button.

He saw a white unicorn galloping on a green field fast towards a red brick wall that was just there in the middle of the field, its muscles tense, veins prominent, the wall was near but the unicorn didn't stop, the unicorn smashed into the brick wall in the field headfirst with its horn.

I don't understand, Father Frank said.

The woman with the red sweater slid two fingers into her panties.

Didn't you want to meet me?, she asked.

The unicorn felt dizzy. He thought there is no good answer or bad answer, that chance is also part of life, that there is free will, that one can jump over a wall or go around it, that suffering can be overcome, that the body must be respected because the body is also a work of God.

The unicorn hesitated. Blood was pumping in his veins. The woman in the red sweater had totally exposed her panties.

Silence.

Then voices in the hallway. Then the voices walked away. Then silence again.

Father Frank thought this was a moment of grace. He stopped imagining the unicorn. He considered the moment as it was. Like when angels hold their breaths, when wolves gaze at the moon and howl, when condors glide majestically over torpid canyons, when lions yawn in the shadows of the savannah and all other creatures return to a momentary innocence.

Father, you need a moment?

Umm, no, no, I was just, umm, thinking. Thinking.

We can begin now if you want.

Umm, begin. Oh, no, that won't be necessary. Maybe you can wait outside.

I can wait outside, she said.

The woman with the red sweater buttoned herself up again and stepped outside, keeping her head down, thinking that people are strange and that if someone can understand life they must be tragically misinformed.

Chapter 138
Father Frank's moment of prayer, introspection, chafing, admission of guilt, thoughts of compassion, revelations, eternal life and the apocalypse

He loosened his belt, stuck his hand inside and liberated the seed quickly.

Chapter 139
The trace of blood

It started on the floor where The Client was shot. The Lawyer looked at the sole of his boot with disgust. The blood was thick and sticky. He looked at The Client's dead face. He saw a combination of discontent, surprise and confidence. It was an odd combination, which on many occasions can bring death. It is where the trace of blood started.

He saw the blots of blood by the bar. The empty bottle, the cork, an apron. He saw a rectangular contour of an object that had been placed on the floor recklessly. Probably a suitcase. Steps of a large shoe size walking out the back door at a calm pace and another set of smaller footprints.

It was hot and bright today. Not a good day to stare into the sun, no hope that a cloud would walk by. He wiped a bead of sweat off his forehead.

Not a soul on the street.

The shattered windows of the convenience store. Signs of a struggle. A stainless steel lighter on the sidewalk with markings that he could never forget. He stowed it in his pocket and followed the trail of blood to the corner of the street.

Bloody tire marks. It was from the maroon Golf, he reckoned. The Lawyer had a precise nose for details. He could memorize hundreds of random images, especially those that don't have any emotional load, fingerprints, tire marks, the seals of notaries, the imperfections of letters in wills typed on a typewriter decades ago and the shades of amber across the folding lines of the paper, he could remember all these, he could remember all the words of the conversation at the Golf Club before all this began, he could remember Gregoire's forehead, the signs of distress on his face, the ruggedness and the chafing of his skin.

The tire marks disappeared down the road where dust and crumbled dry mud was scattered all over the concrete.

He didn't need to know where the tire marks went. There's only one place where he could be.

Chapter 140
I see trees of green, red roses too, I see them bloom

Rabbi, we will get to the bottom of this well, they will keep coming, we will run out of water, we can't satisfy them all, We need to have faith, Imam, Faith has nothing to do with it, water is water, it can only be replaced with water, We need to pray more, We've prayed enough, the brothers are losing their patience, there are too many people, There is never enough prayer, Imam, We should tell them now that the well is running out of water, We cry when we pray, tears are water, What are you saying?, We should teach them how to pray, We tried that, it doesn't work, It's psychological, Imam, it keeps the mind focused.

Gentlemen, if I may interject.

By all means. Oh, wait a minute, I know you.

We have met before, yes.

Your wife wears a mask, yeah, yeah, she does, she has a Venetian mask and some, pardon me, must clear my throat. Some dermatological situation.

That is a correct observation, Imam.

It was raining when we met.

Yes, it was.

We live in odd times, doctor. First we met in a torrential downpour, and now we meet again under the hottest sun on earth. How's your wife, by the way?

She's fine, Rabbi. She's over there by that tree.

Why isn't she in line for water?

We had some at our house. The last drops.

That might be enough for two days and that's it, doctor.

Yeah, I know that.

Why did you come here?

Why did I come here?

The Psychiatrist chose to end the conversion with this rhetorical statement. He raised his eyes and watched an eagle examining the crowd gathered at the well. The brothers distributed water with slow movements while the crowd trudged forward passively. The Psychiatrist was severely thirsty. He thought that the people ahead of him looked like ants magnified under a telescope. They will catch fire under the hellish heat and will turn to ashes. No bones, no nothing, just ashes like fine dust. Then he will walk on the ashes and approach the well, collect a bucketful of water and dunk his head in it. He will hold his breath for three minutes in that cold water. It will feel so good.

We came for water, The Psychiatrist said.

You came for water.

Yes, Rabbi.

Okay.

Can you, umm, facilitate an access.

Facilitate your access?

Yes.

The Psychiatrist pursed his dried lips while flocks of black crows circled The Valley in search of corpses or safe places to rest.

What would this facilitation mean, doctor?

It's facilitation to, the water, you know, we need, to, my wife, she's, water.

Think about a smart answer, an answer that will knock your freaking brains out, and you won't even notice when it disappears, except for the millisecond when you hear the hollowness inside your skull and it feels like somebody else's skull and you will wonder where you are and how come you can feel yourself from outside yourself and you will try to rub your eyes and they will feel like a vapor, like smoke, and your mouth will feel like a cave that spits out carbon monoxide and will inhale birds and bears and torches, and then you will stop for a moment, the hollowness that you are, and will realize what's around you, another bigger hollowness, full of things like trees and planes and rivers and the dark universe where you float like an iron ball, a mind by itself with a body left somewhere behind.

The Psychiatrist collapsed on the ground. Rabbi and Imam ordered two brothers to carry him to a shadowy place and to sprinkle his face with water.

A thread of blood purled from his temple.

Chapter 141
The boots are made for walkin'

We meet again, Monsieur.

He recognized the man's voice. The man was standing in front of him. He couldn't lift his chin to see the man's face. The pain was too strong. He saw the man's boots, the thick rubber soles. The man was swinging an axe. He found it in the garage. He was surprised that the man found him so fast. The man was very well connected.

We meet again, Gregoire. Speak!

His mouth was filled with blood. Maybe his lungs were infected. He was unconscious for few hours. The boys escaped. He will get to his feet and he will find them. He will do it. He just needs some time to pull himself together. The man was still standing in front of him. What does he want? He knows what the man wants. The man cannot kill him because the information is inside his brain.

So what do we have here, Gregoire?

The man calls him Gregoire. Few people call him Gregoire. His mother was one, then an uncle. His father didn't call him anything. He just called him boy, or whatever. His father's name was Sir. Everybody called him that. It was a long time ago. Then, when he was eighteen, he joined the army and they sent him to a very dry country. It was like a big desert or something. They did not fight much, but some buddies of his died of dehydration and he had to carry them back to the garrison. He ate cactuses to stay alive and chew bones of camels and coyotes. He watched the stars at night. They looked like diamonds. Then they told him he could go. The war had ended. There's no future for you here, they said. No truck came to pick him up. They said he had to walk through the desert, it's part of the exit training. What the hell is exit training? He packed and left. The long days came after. The sun, the winds, the mirages, the thirst. He caught snakes during the day and ate them during the night. The blood kept him warm.

So what's gonna be Gregoire?

The man was swinging the axe.

One day, he got into a fight with some men in a village, far in the south, over a hooker. They were all drunk. He split a bottle in half and cut a man's face. Then they ordered another shot like nothing happened. The man with the cut face didn't die, didn't even bleed. He hadn't meant to cut deep. He realized then that he had some skills in surgery. They had a few more drinks, he paid for the broken furniture and they hired a woman for the rest of the day. Then they left.

Where are they? Where is the stuff?

For twenty-some years he walked the earth. He met people, he made deals, he had a few women but he always left them with this abrupt announcement, I'm gonna leave tomorrow. The women got used to not asking questions.

I'm asking a bloody question!

He'll be fine. Yeah, it looks bad now but he'll manage. He has been through hell before. Spitting blood and breathing needles.

Are you listening, fuckface? Yeah, that's your word isn't it?

The boots are made for walkin'. He met a man with dark eyes and rotten teeth. The man told him about the mine and what they were doing there. The man with the dark eyes said he had never heard of so many stones in one place. I'm telling you this because I'm gonna die soon. My body is decomposing from the inside, the man with the dark eyes said. The man died a month later, reduced to a skeleton of ragged clothes. He dug the hole and left the shovel at the head of the grave.

Are you dying, Gregoire?

In the mines he met a man with a hunched back. The man told him that nobody paid attention to him but he knew everything that was going on there. The man told him that the stones were not necessarily coming from inside. They put them there, you know, it's a plan, some big Plan. The hunchback didn't make much sense, but he had something strange about him. Like he had eyes behind his back. There was one thing he didn't see. His final moment. They shoved him in a niche in a dead tunnel with a pack of TNT. They did not consider the ripple effect after the explosion. The Mountain groaned and it all started. Galleries collapsing and burying all the men inside. The planners pulled out and washed their hands of the business. They thought they had cleaned everything but they hadn't. The large stock of diamonds was left behind in the stomachs of thieves.

He got arrested for arson. The man with the swinging axe came to him and offered him a deal. He was a Planner. He knew a lot about the situation, about the stones, the nameless dead. He accepted the man's deal.

Fuckface, are you dying on me?

It sounds like an echo, are you dying on me, maybe the man with the swinging axe does not exist, it's just the wind rattling through the house, maybe I don't even exist, Gregoire, maybe I'm just in your head, like the pain, the pain does not exist, the mind makes it real, do you think I'm real, Gregoire, what do you know, where are they, do you see this axe, DO YOU?

He looks up into the man's eyes. The man swings the axe with force. The rest is silence.

Chapter 142
Connection and condition

We meet again, ma'am.

He waited outside The Mayor's office. He saw Father Frank going in, and evaluated the consequences. The woman was already inside. She seems distressed now, not by his presence, but by something else. When a ghost crosses your path, you don't realize immediately what it is. Your brain will collect the information from the senses and will define your state of fear. The fear that was already created and implanted in you will be shown in a wave of adrenaline pumping into your veins.

He remembered her breasts, the red sweater, her pale face.

You look changed, he said.

You don't look changed at all, the woman said.

Change exists, whether we perceive it or not.

Perhaps.

You know why I came.

Not to save me from him.

He doesn't know anything. He's a slave of faith. I came for something else.

I have nothing to hide.

We know that. I came because you are conditioned and there are others who are not. We need your help to make them conditioned.

He took her to the others. The Club was expecting them. The Club told them they were late. The Neurosurgeon didn't give them an explanation. There was no need. They told the woman she had to take her clothes off. I have nothing to hide, she said. We know, they said. This is the ground zero of fear. Her conditioning must be verified and reinforced. What are you talking about?, We must be sure, they said, You are all out of your minds, You have no idea how close you are to the truth, The Neurosurgeon whispered in her ear, now do what we say. She took off her clothes. They came close to her. They put their hands over her body. Their big hot hands. Do you feel the connection?, The Neurosurgeon asked. Yes, she said. She didn't cry. She felt their hearts pumping in their palms. She understood that the end of fear has two doors. Slavery or freedom. The choice was hers. She had the power because she could make the choice.

I'll do it, she said.

Chapter 143
Time and life becoming

What is the meaning of this?

The man looked at Tim Tolstoy with kindness and peace in his eyes. He took his time in his answers, like his words were coming from outside time itself. They sat in the breeze of the orange afternoon, under the pointy shadows of the acacia, on the hilltop, overlooking Town. It was a dry day, but serene. The heat waves rose to the sky, bouncing off the earth, spreading swirls of distorted images, rays of light reflecting reality at tiny slanted angles that gave the impression of an atmosphere made of water and full of angels. Tim took a stance of meditation, his hands on his knees, his eyes open, his mind clear, his pulse low. He listened to the man's words as if the man was chiseling them into stone, fixing them into permanence.

This was the beginning and the end, the man said. It was the purpose. Everything thrived from it. Life, death, time, material reality, immaterial reality. It drove the eternal why. This was the reason, the source, the end, the continuity of everything, the discontinuity of everything. If we understand the purpose we can emerge from the cycle, we will be completely independent from everything, we will attain the ultimate pure deep freedom. But is this the right question? Is this the essential desire of man? To attain freedom, to be totally in control of everything? Is this why we're even asking the *whys*, is this the reason that drives us, that pushes us to struggle, to hook on to life, to fight, to survive, to suppress one another at the expense of the other, to compete, to kill, to consume, to organize, rank and grade everything, including ourselves, the creation and invention of society, the need for interconnectivity, the mutual aspirations, the individual ambitions? Isn't this all a convention? The tools we've given ourselves to deal with reality? To adapt an imperfect biological organism and an imperfect mind to the complexity of reality?

What would it be like if we were to realize this illusion? The labels we've put on knowledge and faith are incomplete and inexact. If we peel reality off everything, there is nothing permanent to hold onto. But if we peel the reality off everything we will become everything, as nothing stands apart by itself, not even us, not the air, not the water, not time, not life, not death, not energy, not matter.

Is that immortality?

What is immortality, Tim? It is life extended in reference to time. But what if there is no time? Will that make you immortal?

And what is life? What makes us so special in this universe? Is it self-awareness? Are we self-aware just because we can ask this question? Because we can manifest ourselves? Does god have to manifest himself so we can say that he is self-aware? Is a star self-aware? Is an atom self-aware? What creates this twisted loop that we call consciousness? Where does it come from? Is it put in our brain? Does it have a birth? Does it grow? Does it end? Are these questions even the right questions?

What if we could see beyond the questions? What if we could see beyond the answers? What if we could see beyond the purpose? What if we could, understand the purpose?

Are you saying you found the answer?

No Tim, the answer is not important. It's the purpose. By understanding the purpose we can realize what is outside time, before causality, after causality, beyond the beginning, after the end.

What are you saying?

I have created an instrument that allows us to see and understand beyond. The light within this suitcase can show us the path.

Nirvana?

Nirvana is a word. There are many words and many paths.

You created it?

Nothing is created, everything is transformed. We're merely discoverers.

What is it?

I cannot explain to you what it is. Everyone has to experience it for themselves.

They want this?

Yes. For them it is the ultimate power. But they do not understand. The power cannot be taken, cannot be given. The awareness is the path. They are not aware.

Aware of what?

Of the right questions that lead to the purpose. They think their purpose is to acquire power. That is what they seek. They cannot see beyond this limited purpose.

Why are you giving it away?

I am not. I am an inventor. I am weak and bound to this earth. I am not ready. My purpose is limited. I understand what is beyond but I was not ready to see it. My journey is at the beginning. I have not asked enough questions.

What questions?

The questions that help me understand what I discovered. They wanted a deal. I was weak, I wanted to accept it. The facilitator died. I harmed The Frenchman. That is not my purpose. Those are not the right questions. They will come after me. They will come after you. They will not give up. They are blind. They are trapped in their illusion, in their masks, in their rituals, in their rules.

What's going to happen?

The realm of causality starts in the womb. The suitcase with the light is in itself a womb. It's an imperfect tool. It may not give the right questions. My attachment to it ends here. I must seek my path outside the loop of awareness.

Are you leaving?

You will keep the suitcase and you will open it when you will be ready for the right questions. They must not find it.

We will guard it.

I know you will.

The man stood and took a last look at Town and The Valley. He looked at Tim and smiled. He turned and walked into the woods and disappeared forever.

Chapter 144
This little light of mine, I'm gonna let it shine

The bucket was full of diamonds of various sizes, shapes and colors. He dipped his hand in them and sifted them through his fingers. They are beautiful, aren't they?, he said. Iris and the white guard nodded their heads.

He pulled a yellow notepad from a drawer.

He explained with sign language that he cannot speak, then wrote something in the notepad. He told Iris to read it out loud.

You must help me stuff the diamonds into toy bears. They will come after us. They must not find us. They need the diamonds to buy immense power. We have to stop that. We have to rebalance life. We have to help the poor. We have to bring life where there was death and hope where there was despair.

That's fantastic, the white guard interrupted him.

We would appreciate a restraint of sarcasm, Iris looked at him while Luc continued his impromptu memo.

I just find the whole situation absurd.

Well, keep it to yourself.

Fine.

I'm sorry, Luc. Let me see.

I understand the inherent discontent in the human nature. The difficulty of compromise, we must work together, there is no turning back, they know everything.

What do they know, Luc?, Iris asked.

Who's they?, the white guard asked.

They know I took them. The Frenchman knows. He works with them.

Are you sure?

I am.

What's wrong with your voice thing?, the white guard asked.

The battery is dying.

Let him speak. Luc, what else do you know?

The Frenchman is an outlaw. He used bodies to smuggle stones. They know that. They don't care. They want the stones. There is no turning back. The stones cannot stay here.

So you're saying we need to ship them away. Isn't that a little insane?, the guard scoffed.

What's the definition of insane?

I can't let you do this, the guard said.

Iris stopped reading and waited for Luc to finish the paragraph.

What, what's he saying?

Nothing important.

Let me see.

The white guard grabs the notebook from Luc's hands and reads the last paragraph. It's all gibberish.

UY.I ELTI.AT.TA.ZL.PFF.D EW.I P.LTI.XO.XI.T.A.TH
LZZ.A EI.I.I.FX T.ZBD M.KI.TFF.ARY.AP.P.L KK.K.ZZ
NB.VL.L D.MM.I VL.TIPD.ARI.X.DA.EPL.I
FK.ITA.IF.IRR.L.AZI

What the hell is this?

By the time he finished reading the letter, which made no sense to him, Iris was behind him with the syringe from the drawer. The needle was long enough to penetrate the chemsuit, the undergarments and the skin. She pushed the syringe into the white guard's body and released all the serum.

He blurts out, What the hell?, and fell to his knees. His voice died then he hit the floor with his forehead.

Help me tie him, Luc said. They wrapped a rope over his hand and waist and another around his ankles. They stuck duct tape over his mouth and dragged him into a corner and put him into a sitting position with his chin fallen into his chest. White foam drooled from his mouth. They wiped it with a cloth and discarded the cloth in a bin.

He'll be fine, Luc said. I had to test him. He failed. I'm glad you got my message.

He took the bucket with stones from the working bench and locked it in a closet built in the rock, under the hill. He checked the guardian's pulse and wrote the time in the notepad. He checked out the room with the stuffed bears. In semi-obscurity, their plastic eyes sparkled like a sea of paired candles.

It's about your friend Tim.

What's wrong?

I know about his father.

What are you talking about, Luc?

Gregoire killed him.

Thoughts flooded her mind. She remembered the day when she first saw Tim in Mr. Popp's class. He answered a question on relativity. If it's scientific fact that time and space are relative, why can't we feel it?, Mr. Popp asked, I think our mind is too slow to sense the bullet, Tim answered.

We have to go back to Emma, is all she said.

Chapter 145
Bullet in the brain

Gregoire finally regained consciousness when the dusk was purple dark and the crows have settled down outside Town. He managed to stop the bleeding and rose to his feet. He walked outside and looked at the sky.

It was loaded with hot air, dust and improbability. He found water in a ditch, filtered it with a cloth and drank it. Then he sat down to think. Mostly about the stones, the boys and the deadly axe that The Lawyer had decided to drop on the floor next to his foot, to make a point. He's alive because he's needed or because The Lawyer took pity on him. Fuck pity! That's not it. It's that boy, whatshisname and the other one, the quiet one. He's after them. They must know something.

He waited for nightfall, then took to the road, using the shadows around corners and lampposts to hide his steps. The drought has forced the townsfolk to take refuge inside cool buildings and basements, with whatever water they could save during the day. Not a soul on the roads except ghosts. He could smell the stench of the eviscerated dead that were piled in the hospital's courtyard. It's familiar and bearable. Probably they tracked the dead back to him. Probably. He'll find whatshisname and the quiet one and break their skulls. He'll get the stones, and then he'll get the hell out of here. They can't find him. He's been through hell. They have no idea. They just know hell from maps and reports. Fuckers! It's cold tonight, as though the moon has sucked up all the air. It's the mist that descends from The Mountain. He stumbled on a drunkard who has fallen asleep in his own filth by a fence. The drunkard moaned in pain. He asked the drunkard if he had seen two scared boys with knapsacks. The drunkard said, Yeah, I've seen them. They're in old Kaczynski's house. Do you have some water?, Gregoire said he didn't have any water and told the drunkard that if he was lying, he'd break his neck. I'm telling you, they went there, what's wrong with you, man?, Gregoire left him alone but he will remember his face.

It was past midnight when he arrived at Kaczynski's house. There was a flickering light in the attic. A candle. The door's locked. He can easily break a window and get inside. He walked onto the porch and looked inside. There was a couch by the window. He broke the glass with a short blow and the shards fell onto the couch. He climbed inside the living room and stopped to listen for steps. There was no sound, no creaking floors. On the table, packs of crackers and jars of jam and two stuffed bears. Fucking kids! He heard faint radio music from upstairs. The kitchen was opposite to the living room. It's clean. Pots and plates neatly stacked on the countertop. No dust. Pots filled with water on the table. He dipped a glass into a pot and swallowed it fast. He dipped it again. He wiped his beard with his sleeve, then covered the pot with a plate. The radio from upstairs was playing an old tune. It sounded scratchy. The battery was dying. He walked back and stopped at the bottom of the staircase. It's old wood. The cracks were as wide as caterpillars, full of dust and lint. He took his boots off and left them on the floor. Twenty stairs or so. The landing was in darkness. He felt three doors. No lights under the thresholds, just a weak draft. The radio hollered from above. Another staircase to the attic. Narrow, steep and short. He looked up. Moving light in the attic. Fuckfaces, he mumbled. He climbed the stairs very slowly. The music stopped. Young fucking voices and a sound of cranking. The music resumed, louder. The last six steps. He was at the door. He pulled out the butcher knife. Shadows moving in the light under the door. He broke the door with his shoulder. He smashed it against the wall. Whatshisname was sitting on an old armchair with a crank radio on his lap. He knew that radio. He took two steps towards whatshisname and extended the butcher knife. He didn't see the other fuckface. He bailed out. One arm's length to whatshisname's skull. They have no fucking vision. The next millisecond he saw blood, red air, black air. The bullet entered the back of his head. It killed first his oldest memories, the name of his father that he did not remember but was still lingering there, the image of his mother, the childhood years, it killed the memories of the desert, the taste of snakes, the boiling water, the dirty wells, it killed all the women, all the dead, it killed the stones, the bullet killed at last the image of the night sky with stars. It exited through the temple and disappeared into the vertical stripes of the wallpaper. The Quiet Boy was behind him. He yelled, Fuckface!, Gregoire dropped dead at Simon's feet with a loud thud. Simon yelled, Jesus!, and climbed into the armchair and tried to wipe the blood off his face like a madman. The Quiet Boy walked to Gregoire's side and shot him again in the back three times. He yelled, Fuckface!, Stop that, he's dead!, Simon yelled, The Quiet Boy kicked the dead man in the ribs, He is now, he said.

Chapter 146
Whys and wherefores

The Mayor asked if he can smoke a cigarette before he went to meet the others. He was told, No, it's not a good idea. He was shown the way, the woman with the red sweater walking in front of him.

They were all waiting for him. Four men.

Mr. Mayor, you know why you're here, The Politician began.

I have an idea. I'm sure the authorities have something to do with this. I know that you, in particular, are connected with the people in City.

The authorities have nothing to do with this, The Advisor picked up the phrase and continued in a flat voice. It is our own project. We came to you because there was no other way. We lost control of certain element.

A collaborator?

No. A facilitator. He became, unstable.

Gregoire?

Yes, The Banker continued. He's responsible for the explosions at the mines, the dead, the epidemic.

What epidemic?

He implanted a chemical agent in the water mains, The Neurosurgeon continued.

What?

People will die, The Politician said.

Are you serious?

We have no sense of humor, Mr. Mayor, The Neurosurgeon said.

If he worked for you, that means you were involved, The Mayor said.

Mr. Mayor, you need to understand your position, The Banker said.

I know my position.

You don't, The Politician said. A position is defined by clarity and control. You have no clarity and no control. We do. That is our position now.

Big fucking control you have.

Knowing the variables is control even if they are adverse, The Politician scoffed. The other members of The Club retired to one corner. Exchanges of icy glances.

Why do you need me?

Our position does not allow us to capture him directly, The Politician continued. That's where you come in. Find him, fetch him for us. Hunt him if you have to.

Why didn't the Citizens Guard do that?

They did not have the information.

But you did.

We acquired it recently.

I tend not to believe it.

You underestimate your lack of position, Mr. Mayor. The Frenchman will try to blackmail us to serve his purpose. He must be stopped. Or else.

Or else?

It will get complicated. Especially for you, Mr. Mayor. You will have to explain the dead. Your reelection will be questionable.

My reelection will be questionable?

Yes.

The Mayor put two fingers to his chin and rubbed it gently in a gesture that his wife would call a momentary lapse of reason and a trial to put the thoughts in order. He imagined himself in his office, smoking a cigar, puffing the smoke rings at his portrait in acrylics, its frame made of local oak.

I'll do it. What do I have to do?

Chapter147
Searchlight of possibilities

It's very hot today. You are drinking the last sip of water. It's okay, I'm not thirsty. I don't see any sweat on your forehead, I say. You say that you never sweat, not even when you're making love. It's a function or dysfunction of my body, you say. Yes, but what about the toxins?, I ask you. Don't worry, there are other ways, you say. You know I worry about the little things, but you don't say it. You take the glass and look at the sun though it. The smoky glass changes color under the rays of light. You stare at the sun's aura for a few minutes. You say the sun is an enormous source of energy and you don't understand why mankind doesn't try harder to harness it. It's such a waste, you whisper. You say the birds are leaving Town. They can be seen in the distance, flying away. That's not a good sign. It means there's nothing left to consume here. Then you lower the glass and look at the road. Our position gives you a good overview of the neighborhood. You put the glass down and shield your eyes with your hand. This is interesting, you say. The Mayor is down there. He's talking to two police officers. He's gesticulating. Like when he was campaigning and was explaining his program to commoners on the street. He looks like he knows his position. The officers nod and take notes. The Mayor asks them if they have their guns with them. How do you know that?, I ask. You can't hear what he says. They're showing their guns to him, you say. They synchronize their watches. Why would that make a difference? I don't know, I say. I bet they're looking for looters. The waters have swept everything away. They're looking for other survivors or dead bodies. With their guns?, you ask. You're right, it doesn't make sense. It's odd there haven't been many dead people. What did you say? It's odd there haven't been many dead people. I heard they piled them in the hospital's courtyard, you say. Many had their guts taken out. Isn't that bizarre?, Yes, it is strange, I say. You keep looking out the window. Your hair smells like daffodils. Your neck is milky white. You look like an angel. Wingless angel, translucent. Weightless. Like a cloud of butterflies glued together. What are you writing?, you ask. It's about you, I say. You keep staring at the road. The policemen have left. The Mayor is checking his watch again, he seems nervous, he wipes his forehead. You should see this. I'd rather stay here in the shade. You say there's somebody else on the road. Two people. The Mayor did not see them. The Mayor disappears behind a building, where he came from. The two people are approaching the spot where The Mayor was. They're pushing a shopping cart with something big and heavy in it, covered with tarpaulin. They keep looking around them. They're afraid that someone might see them. Wait, I know one of them. It's The Lawyer's son. Yes, it's him. He doesn't talk much. He has a knapsack loaded with stuff. He's with another young guy with a pale face. Do you think they have water? you ask. Why would you transport water with a shopping cart in hot weather? Water attracts neediness. You look at me. We can't stay here, you say.

I'm gonna close my notebook and I'm gonna moisten your dry lips.

Chapter 148
The day of Bastille and the playgrounds

The past few days were totally eventless at the Community Bank. The teller and the loan officer measured the water and food supplies carefully and, according to their calculations, it would last them for a month. They moved all the food from the kitchenette into the vault, for a sense of security. The manager and the others would never think to come back here. Who knew where they are. Who cared where they are. They lost contact on the day when the Citizens Guard came. Then they all went into whatever direction, like dogs retreating to hide their chewed bones for later use.

Today, stomachs were easily satisfied. Then the rush of blood away from the brain into the digestive system. Then lethargy and somnolence. The teller slid a can of tuna across the floor to the loan officer.

We must save it for later, the officer said.

I think we plan too much. We should let it be, the teller said.

The officer smiled lethargically, whistled the famous let it be song. I could use a fuck, he said. He slid back the tuna can.

Yeah, me too, the teller said.

What do you think the whole deal is with love?

What do you mean?, the teller grabbed a wad of cash and fanned himself with it.

Well, I met this girl about two years ago, the officer said. Great fuck, I mean, she was bendy like a willow. Plus she had a tight grip on me, man. Like she grabbed onto my heart with a steel hook, deep down, man, right into my ventricle. She controlled everything that went in and went out. She was an academic. She had all these piles of books in her room, under the bed, in the dresser, on the bed while we were, you know, doing it, she was smart like a nuclear reactor, she knew great fuck, she talked about philosophy on top of me, man, Kant this, Plato that, she asked me if I loved her, my heart was racing, I heard her like an echo, I said, Yes, she said I have to read this book about human relationships, she was on top of me, man, she stretched to reach for the bookshelf above the headboard, You want me to read it now? I asked, I was panting, man, You can finish first, she said, and then the bookshelf collapsed on my head, man, I had headaches for two weeks, those books were heavy hardcovers.

Was the book good?, the teller asked.

The book?, Yeah. I remember a paragraph. I memorized it. It struck me like an invisible lighting. It was by a professor, Louis Levy. Here it is. You will notice that when we fall in love is a very strange paradox: when we fall in love we are seeking to re-find all or some of the people to whom we were attached as children. On the other hand we ask our beloved to correct all the wrongdoings that these early parents or siblings inflicted upon us. So love contains in it the contradiction to attempt to return to the past and the attempt to undo the past.

Very deep. Do you believe in this?, the teller asked.

If you think about it, it makes sense.

So you're saying that, what are you saying?

She was freaking smart. She had answers. She was a rocket. Strong like a spear. The type of woman with whom you cannot have an argument because she will demonstrate before you begin that your case has no substance, no inner logic.

Yeah.

You cannot build anything without substance. Hand me the bottle.

The handheld fan became flaccid from too much waving. He discarded it and replaced it with a fresh one. A stiff wad of brand new bills.

Louis Levy, you said?, the teller asked.

Yes.

I think I saw a movie once, or interview, yeah, it was an interview. I went out with this woman. She was a historian. I never went to her place. She used to talk about books and essays while we were, you know, making love. She had big, curly—

Red hair?, the officer asked.

The teller stopped fanning his face. In the minute it took him to answer he imagined the possibilities, all the intricacies, the consequences, the layers of truth, the contexts, the promises, the mysteries and the pieces of the puzzle, her eyes, her enrapturing, her white perfect teeth, the roundness of her breasts and her last words, You know, my level of attachment does not match yours.

Yes, red hair, the teller responded.

The two men looked at each other like they have just met. It is said that a man's brain can process one emotional impulse at a given time, in a sequence. The course of action is determined by the behavioral predispositions of the man and his reaction to the social momentum. Men believe reality is configured by action. Women believe reality is molded by their emotional projections. They read that in Louis Levy's book.

We don't need to say her name.

No, we don't.

Can I have some wine?

By all means.

Where did you find it?

Does it matter?

They emptied the Château Margaux quickly. By the time they finished, they heard voices in the Bank, which saved them from the embarrassment of pursuing the subject of the red-haired woman they shared, however not simultaneously.

People returned to the bank. The Manager, the blonde divorced girl, some of the others. They talked about solutions, about despair, they said they had no choice, this was their last chance, they knew there are some resources left in the vault, We should have never left anything behind, and how exactly did you want to take the stuff?, Through the ventilation shaft, That's crazy, we ate all that food the Citizens Guard brought too fast, we should have rationed it, That's communism, From each according to his ability, to each according to his needs, what's wrong with that?, Listen, that brings only trouble, It's common sense, When the stomach is empty and the throat is dry there is no common sense, Folks, folks, we'd better focus on why we came here.

In the vault, the teller and the loan officer had a pretty good idea about the motivation of their fellow coworkers. They will come to the vault and search for whatever food is left. They will follow the smell trail from the kitchenette. They evaluated the situation. We must lock the door, the teller said. Yes, we must, the officer says. They locked the door from inside and waited. It was not long before firm bangs were heard.

They'll never get in, the loan officer said.

I hope not.

We'll never get out, he added.

Are you serious?

Or we could wait until the food is depleted and come out and say sorry, we have no food, we thought looters were attacking the bank, so we had to protect whatever assets were left, it was our duty, or they could try to make an escape through the ventilation shaft, since it was used before.

Do you believe in romantic love?, the loan officer asked.

I think I do, the teller answered.

Romantic love is not an emotion, it's a drive. It's a flux of energy, similar to the magnetic forces that make you want to connect to another human being. Energy that transforms into reality the mental projection of the other. It's what triggers action.

The brain releases a wave of dopamine, which pushes the cognitive-emotional momentum of the individual into a state of wanting. Not lust, wanting. See the difference?

What about sex?

The bangs on the steel door became intense. This can mean only that they don't have the key, they don't have the combination, or both. Then sound of metal on metal. Open up!

Sex is a consequence or a subset of romantic love, the loan officer continued while shuffling a few brand-new unsoiled bills. It can happen independently of romantic love, too. With orgasm, you get a real rush of oxytocin and vasopressin in the brain, exciting the level of attachment to the other person. This can stimulate the growth of romantic love. See, full circle. You feel a cosmic union after you make love.

Sex.

Yeah, sex. Whatever.

The bangs were louder. The steel vibrated from the impact of objects thrust into the door. Anger and desperation boiled in the air. The teller and the loan officer took a moment to reflect on the situation. They passed another Château Margaux to each other, wiped their mouths with their sleeves and took a few healthy bites from a cheese bagel.

We can't stay here long, the teller said, munching. They'll find their way in.

Chapter 149
Division Bell

They cleaned the attic at Kaczynski's under the light of a candle. The Quiet Boy wrote a list of stuff that he needed and told Simon to bring it and leave it at the door, then waited in front of the house. The list was, garbage bags, as many as you can find, heavy-duty garden scissors, industrial duct tape, lots of towels, a can of paint thinner, a solid kitchen knife or handsaw and a shopping cart from the grocery store on the street corner.

Simon brought everything and left it on the stairs in front of the attic door. He knocked three times, that was the signal, and went outside on the porch to wait. He squinted at the stars and counted all the constellations he could recognize. When it got colder and clouds began to settle over The Valley, he started to wonder what The Quiet Boy was doing up there. He had an idea, but did not pursue it.

He was finishing a pack of crackers when The Quiet Boy opened the door with his foot so violently that it ripped the doorbell from its socket. The Quiet Boy came out, dragging a garbage bag stuffed with something big. He dropped the bundle on the porch and went back inside. Simon knew he had to drag it to the cart. It was his part of his job. He had nothing to say about it. He dragged the bag to the cart and tried to lift it. It was too heavy.

The Quiet Boy came and dropped the second bag next to the cart. How did you move so fast?, Simon asked. The Quiet Boy didn't say anything.

They worked together, lifting the bags into the cart one by one, on the count of three. The Quiet Boy covered the cart with a tarpaulin he found under the porch. They took advantage of the dark and pushed the cart towards the center of Town. They used the dark alleys and people's backyards to take breaks. What did you do to him?, Simon asked, every half hour. The Quiet Boy remained quiet. There was no smell coming from the bags. Whatever was inside, it was well insulated. Could have been a load of potatoes or flour sacks or rotten apples. Simon didn't dare to feel the bags. They looked stiff, like they were filled with sand.

When they stopped, he thought about dogs. What if they caught their trail? He discarded this thought when The Quiet Boy decided all of a sudden to take off his knapsack, take out the pistol and clean it in the moonlight. Simon immediately internalized his reaction. He found it odd that he felt secure in that moment. But he did have a second thought, that a hungry violent stray dog was preferable to The Quiet Boy who was looking into the barrel of the pistol with nonchalance.

They shared another pack of crackers and a jar of jam and a plastic bottle of water. They took turns napping for thirty minutes.

What did you do to him?, Simon asked when he woke up. He didn't get an answer. The Quiet Boy lied down and covered himself with the tarpaulin. The grass was soft and dry. He could smell the earth and feel its veins pulsating.

Simon didn't care if mysterious shadows were lurking in the backyard. It was his way of defying fear. He stopped thinking about what had happened in the attic when the lazy sun cracked the horizon. We gotta move, he said when The Quiet Boy woke up.

The Quiet Boy looked at him, cocked the pistol and pointed it at Simon's face.

What are you doing?

The Quiet Boy pushed him aside and fired the pistol at a squirrel on the fence.

You're not gonna eat that?, Simon asked.

No, The Quiet Boy answered.

They moved into a mechanical service shop and pulled down the rollup door. The stench of rancid, burned oil and a decomposed animal forced them to open the door by midday. They had to get to the hospital before anyone caught them with that stupid cart.

There was no one on the street. They looked at each other. Their faces read, Are we doing this? They pushed the cart out and kept close to the facades of the buildings, under the mud line. They stopped in front of the convenience store. The Quiet Boy entered and found on the counter a half-smoked cigar. It was Gregoire's. He knew it. He looked at it like it was a bullet, careful not to disturb the fingerprints. Then he dropped it on the floor and squashed it with his boot. Simon yelled at him from outside, Come on, let's go! There's somebody coming.

He came out and looked down the street. He saw three silhouettes approaching. He grabbed Simon and pushed him inside, then ran inside, pulling the cart after him. He rolled it all the way to the back of the store and positioned a stack of shelves in front of it. Then they sat down and waited.

The Quiet Boy cocked the pistol again. The three men stopped in front of the store. Two police officers and The Mayor.

He was last seen here, the first officer told The Mayor.

Stepping on the glass shards, they went inside.

The officer noticed the cigar butt. He picked it up and smelled it. It was recently touched, he said. He wrapped in paper and put it in his pocket.

Why is he so important Mr. Mayor?, the officer asked.

He killed people, The Mayor answered. He's planning a genocide. He must be stopped.

Is there any evidence?, the officer asked, while looking closely for footprints on the floor.

There will be evidence, officer.

You know, Mr. Mayor, we need substantiated grounds and a warrant to apprehend him. We cannot just—

Mr. Mayor, what my colleague is trying to say is that we are men of law.

The first officer nodded at what his colleague has just said and recollected the day when the captain assigned them to the same team. He didn't like that day very much. He didn't like to be partnered with an individual who doesn't recognize God, doesn't go to Church and has no respect for sacred values. But he accepted the job. Oddly enough, they were assigned the day after to provide security at the local elections. Five minutes before the closing of the polls, they were allowed to vote. He voted for the other candidate and had a pretty good idea who his new partner had voted for. The second officer did not make a big deal of showing his affection for The Mayor and his readiness to facilitate the orders coming from Town Hall not just on matters of law enforcement or security, but also on private matters, which always had something suspicious about them. On more than one occasion, The Mayor called his partner right in the middle of the shift. His partner would swerve the car and put the siren on and race to Town Hall, get out of the car and tell him to take the rest of the day off. Then he would not see his partner until the next day. It's not a big deal, the second officer would say.

We need proper documentation, Mr. Mayor, the first officer said, blowing the dust off the counter.

This time we need to set the bureaucracy aside, gentlemen.

Trust me on this, pal. The second officer patted the first officer on the back persuasively. The first officer did not like these gestures of intimacy.

We need a judge's order, he said.

In this case, it is not required, The Mayor cut him short.

I don't want division in the police force, sir. This is not quite legal.

It will be legal.

But sir—

Drop it.

The Mayor referred also to the pack of crackers the first officer found on the floor.

Even if you find half of him, if that half talks, I want it!, The Mayor shouted.

Sir, who's they?

Forget it! The Mayor stormed out of the store and stopped outside to wipe his sweaty forehead.

He told you to drop it, the second officer enforced the directive, giving his partner's back a good smack.

Simon spent all this time with a gag in his mouth. It was a corner of the tarpaulin, with The Quiet Boy's fist over it to keep it in place. He thought how ironic The Mayor's comment was and what an abrupt ending they would have encountered if the first officer had looked for the tracks of a shopping cart dragged in the muddy filth. In that moment, Simon thought about karma. Karma is intention that creates action. When fear meets coincidence, the outcome cannot be something that reason can foretell.

After The Quiet Boy released the gag, he asked again, What did you do to him?

The Quiet Boy opened his pocketknife and pierced one of the bags in the cart. He kept the blade inside without saying anything.

You don't have to, Simon said and helped him pull out the knife.

They waited in the store until dark, then pushed out the cart. They crossed the street and pushed it on the sidewalk towards the hospital.

No one was there. People were terrified by the proximity of decomposition. The boys did not find it that bad. The bodies were covered with slaked lime and rugs of different shapes and sizes. The night wind had lifted the smell and left the courtyard serene.

They parked the cart at the bottom of the pile of bodies. For the first time, Simon thought that The Quiet Boy did a good job dividing Gregoire perfectly in half.

Chapter 150
Symphony No.7, Op. 92, allegretto future-oriented

He had lost his voice due to an infection that left the recurrent laryngeal nerve largely dysfunctional. His vocal folds would simply freeze in one position and he would utter senseless sounds. He would sound like, a sinking ship when structural steel beams break, an agonized antelope in the fangs of a tiger, an untuned guitar in the hands of a tone-deaf wannabe musician.

He wrote in his notepad, I realized it was the beginning of the end when I could not create harmonics. The harmonics are produced by collisions of the vocal folds with themselves and by recirculation of some of the air back through the trachea. My folds could not close. I am not able to hold my breath.

He was a brave and dedicated Jew.

He stopped writing. I don't know if I was born into Judaism, he said. Rabbi adopted me when I was an infant. You learn a religion just like a language.

The white guard was moaning. He might be feeling some pain.

Tell me more, Iris said.

I am a little tired, he said. I've done a lot of work. You have to help me.

I will help you.

He gestured that she should stand next to him and watch what he was writing. I am tired, he wrote. My thoughts are heavy. We inherit a lot of guilt from our parents, from our histories, from what we are taught. Can we live outside our past?, I don't know, Iris said. I kept dreaming the same dream in black and white, he continued. It was about a horse jumping off a bridge. He saw a train coming. I was the train conductor. I yelled at the horse to get off the tracks. I made him jump into the river. Then for months it was all black and white, even when I was not dreaming. My life. Everything. Everybody thought I was an oaf. I thought the infection had affected my vision. Rabbi made me wear a bib until I was seven. He thought that I would drool my brains into my plate. He was a good man, though. He said that our purpose is to whittle the heathen down to size, to teach them compassion, make them understand the afflictions and the scourges they cause to themselves. Then I lost my speech. He bought me the synthesizer. Here, he said, this will thaw your character and intellect. It will keep you focused on your purpose. He said my first job is to keep the pulpit always clean and organized. Wear your garb as if it was your soul made of linen. But he became too preoccupied with little things. He didn't see the big picture. He lacked vision. He had no idea about The Frenchman. He told me one day, With little appearances you can save somebody's world. He was right about that. I started to stuff toy bears.

How did you find out about Gregoire?, Iris asked him.

I followed him. The man was ignorant. That was his bliss. A plastic bull.

The white guard was waking up from numbness. They covered his eyes with a gag. So he could focus on his situation with no distractions. His mouth was duct-taped. For the better. The stifled moans were sounds of frustration. He needed to learn his lesson, Luc wrote, I agree with that, Iris said, The mind needs to be cuffed sometimes until it finds the right path.

We need to get the bears out, Luc said.

I wonder if Tim is okay. He must be okay. I think he is.

Luc stopped writing. He looked at Iris inquisitively. He wanted to know if she was going to help him.

I'll help you carry the bears, Iris said.

He smiled. He turned the page and quickly wrote some instructions. Read this, he said.

It's the steps of his plan.

They will carry the bears into the church. They will put them in the room where Father Frank collects donations. A truck from City will come and take them to the central distribution warehouse. The Charity will take them. Each bear will be a gift for a child. When the child reaches adulthood he or she will receive a letter from The Charity. The letter will instruct the grown-up child to open the bear. Everything will be all right, the letter will say. You will not regret it. Inside the bear you will find a precious stone. You will take the stone to the following address. You will receive a great amount of money for it. You will not be cheated. The money will be yours to change the lives of those who suffered around you. The wisdom and the choices will be yours.

It's a beautiful plan, Iris said.

Chapter 151
The simultaneous arrival and departure of the owl

After having planted in The Mayor's head the false intentions of The Frenchman to sabotage Town's water supplies, because the mind of the lawman can focus easier if all the malevolent deeds are concentrated in one man, who can be easily pointed out and extracted from society, The Club decided it was time to act on such pretenses and realize the facts that were not yet realized and that might serve their declarations and accusations.

What if we have casualties?, The Neurosurgeon said.

The Neurosurgeon's brief moment of cautious thinking remained brief. I guess collateral damage might be inherent to such a plan, he said. We've been hit by a natural disaster anyways. The other three members agreed instantly. Perhaps we should wait on The Lawyer to return before we execute our plan, they thought.

They did not wait on The Lawyer to return.

They laid out the map of Town on the table.

You go there, you go there, at such and such time, we synchronize our movements, our watches, we release the chemical agent into these key areas of the water mains, such and such quantity, it will create this estimated dilution, it will reach the consumers in all corners of Town within twenty-four hours.

May I remind you that the water is already severely rationed, The Neurosurgeon said.

This works to our advantage, the dilution will be higher, the effect quicker and stronger, the others responded.

We will force City to react and send the Citizens Guard again. They will have a reason now. An explanation for everything that happened.

The reason will serve The Plan.

It will be a diversion. We need it. The situation is extremely unstable. The Lawyer has not reported back.

Gentleman, I propose to proceed without The Lawyer.

Why is that, Mr. Politician?

He is unreliable.

At the sound of this sudden proposal, all eyes met and all thoughts converged into an imminent agreement. They ran out of time. The Mayor will report back very soon. The Mayor was the quintessence of conditioned reliability. He will have results. On the other hand, there was something unusual and fishy about their colleague. He kept something to himself. That son of his was too odd, anyways. It had been more than twelve hours and there was still no sign. They had to take matters into their own hands.

It is an auspicious moment to take matters into our own hands, The Advisor broke the silence.

At that moment, on the edge of the opening in the roof, through which the woman with the red sweater had entered, an owl landed with a bleeding rat in its mouth. The catch of the day. They quickly dismissed any deus ex machina quality of this odd appearance and resumed their commitment to the realization of The Plan.

Chapter 152
The quiet goodbye with torpor and light winds

They went back to Kaczynski's house and waited for daylight.

When the sun came up, The Quiet Boy told Simon that he, Simon, had to leave Town immediately.

What do you mean?, Simon asked.

The Quiet Boy had no need to add further explanation. He did not expose the pistol or make any threatening innuendos. He had his way of showing necessity. But there's no transportation, we're isolated, Simon said.

The Quiet Boy shook his head. He took the knapsack off his back, took the pistol out and gave the knapsack to Simon. He put his hand on Simon's shoulder and nodded an *okay*. Then he left.

Simon never saw The Quiet Boy again. He opened the knapsack. Inside, a semi-automatic weapon, several clips, books, vitamin bars, water bottles, few jars of jam and a dozen packs of crackers. He added the hand-crank radio and a Jesus statue he'd found on Mr. Kaczynski's lawn. Then he walked toward the end of Town. He knew that he would never come back.

That was it.

Chapter 153
~~This is it~~

The Mayor insisted that The Frenchman be brought alive. The officers argued that in the light of the information they had it would be hard to capture him without violent opposition.

Sir, we cannot guarantee he will not shoot, the first officer said.

Well, shoot back, but bring him alive and before he does other nasty things.

Like what, sir?

I am told he wants to sabotage Town, The Mayor said.

Like a bomb or something?

It's possible.

Sir, we don't have enough resources for such a mission.

Find resources and be discreet.

Chapter 154
What is not of this world cannot be lost

They covered the guard's head with a black pillowcase. When he woke up, he asked for water and they gave him water with a straw. The guard asked, What's going on? but they did not say anything. They grabbed the guard by the arms and walked him back into the tunnel and up the stairs into the Church.

Emma and her mother were still there and they too remained quiet. Probably Luc and the girl Iris made the Shut up, we'll explain later sign. They put the white guard on the floor.

They went back into the lab. Luc wrote in his notebook that, The guard won't remember much because the substance we gave him is efficient. Then he showed the note to Iris. I don't trust him, Iris said.

They cleaned the pots, the sink, the buckets, they put all the organic debris into bags. They rinsed the handful of stones left. They planted a few in each toy bear that had an open belly and sewed them shut with strong brown thread.

They finished the work by sundown.

Iris saw the moon rising from the tired mist, and remembered that she had lost the radio and that she would do anything to see Tim at that very moment.

Chapter 155
Vials wrenched into an optionless end

The Lawyer knew that the other four members of The Club were too conditioned to act entirely alone and set The Plan back on course, The bloody freaking Plan, thought The Lawyer and spat on the sidewalk. He was sure that no one saw him, except for his son, who was there already, as they had agreed, to help his father accomplish what needed to be accomplished.

When one's determination becomes necessity, one can easily concoct a categorical imperative. Yes, he was a man of results, but he understood them not from a rigid perspective like his former colleagues from The Club, but from an angle that saw beyond cause and effect, beyond the permanence of things. It was what made a true man, vision. He taught his son this. He was not sure if his son understood, but there were signs that he did.

His son looked at him with submission, though something pulsed in his eyes.

He told his son what would happen. As usual, his words were precise, explicit and indicative. The Club had turned against him. He felt it like a boulder in his stomach. What had brought them together had set them apart, except for the confluence of interests over The Plan. He was closer to it than them.

His son knew it, too. His father didn't seem much preoccupied with The Frenchman. His father knew the job was done. His son didn't have to say it. It was just done.

The interdependencies of the members of The Club were strong enough to make them act as a group, in one synergetic corpus, because the aggregation of energies always yields more than the individual elements, however, the task at hand had a certain degree of grandiosity, like anything that tapped into the very veins of society and shook its foundations, especially when it was with a subversive connotation, like poisoning the entire population of Town, which will leave many dead, because means legitimate the end, no!, the end legitimates the means, or it's all about the means and the end is irrelevant, because the end is just a consequence, it will naturally emerge in the causal chain, as the observationalists observe, or it will emerge like a revelation, as the transcendentalists declare, but the end has no self-sufficiency, no matter how you put it.

Power is held by those who can see one step ahead of the others and who have the means to turn this quality into a position of control of expectancies. Those who know what to expect have the power. Do you get it?, The Quiet Boy nodded. He got it to a further depth than The Lawyer imagined.

He laid a map of Town on the ground and put his dirty finger on it.

They'll go here, he said. We'll wait here.

Do you have the tools? The Lawyer asked.

The Quiet Boy nodded.

They were in position a good half hour before The Club showed up, walking in pairs, at a distance from each other. Amateurs, The Lawyer thought. The water main control room was in a building in a compound, surrounded by a barbed-wire fence. There was no guard on duty. There was no need. Or he died or was let go with a phone call.

The Lawyer shared a bottle of water with his son and waited. The mountainside was covered with dense trees in the thin niche of The Valley where a one-lane road meandered. Their hideout was perfectly blended into the green scenery. The Lawyer moved the crosshairs from one head to the other, while smelling the wind, holding his breath, stretching his index finger over the trigger. The Quiet Boy watched his father with dimmed eyes, letting only the essential light into his retina. He knew it would take exactly four shots, in the head, nine or ten seconds, no misses, to take out The Club. The first shot would kill The Politician, the most agile of them all, and would draw the others' attention. The second shot would knock out The Advisor, because of his exceptional peripheral sight. He would have time to look into the direction from which the bullet sprang. The others would see The Advisor's face fixed on the hideout, right before he collapsed on the concrete. The Banker's instinct would be to cover his head with his hand, or he would pull The Neurosurgeon in front of him, so he could take the next bullet. It's in his blood, it has nothing to do with his moral principles or intensity of his compassion toward sentient beings. Or The Banker will dodge behind that rusty old truck. No, he wouldn't have time. It would take at least five or seven seconds to run there, or a minute to crawl if he was severely wounded. No, The Banker would collapse right there, he wouldn't move because the adrenaline would freeze his brain. The Neurosurgeon would reach out to catch him while he fell. It's a medical reflex. He wouldn't be able to control it. He doesn't like falling things. They break, they make a mess, they turn into splinters with sharp edges that can infect your feet. The Neurosurgeon likes perfect sanitary environments, where brains are open and anesthetized. The Neurosurgeon will be last to fall, on his side, but he will be dead before his ribs snap at the impact with the concrete. Nine seconds. The index finger must be dry and fixed on the trigger.

The four men stopped and looked around. They carried a see-through case with vials. He recognized it. Cyanide. He told his son, Stay still, don't breathe.

If they get closer to the door it will be easier. They can get away only in three directions. But if the door is open, they can slip inside.

He must shoot now.

There was a sudden change of light over The Mountain. The wind raised dust in the air like an army of knights. Birds were pushed out of the woods and leaves were scattered over The Valley. Something was coming.

It's a V-formation of helicopters. They skim over the woods and swerve towards Town.

The Lawyer's phone rang. He knew it would eventually ring. Take it, he said. The Quiet Boy answered it. We are here, a voice said. Good, The Lawyer said. He curled and closed the index finger into his fist. He kept the gun-sight over the four walking heads. The four men were confused.

The cloud of dust closed on them from both ends of the road. They sped up along the fence and ran inside the guardhouse by the gate. They closed the door and lay low. On the floor between them was the case with the poison. There were no futile arguments. The span of choices was severely limited. The next decision was the least objectionable in a man's life. Because it was an end to causality. The closure of a loop. The opening of another realm of possibilities transformed by a sip of cyanide. The stimulated collapse of awareness onto itself. They opened the box, four large vials. The Lawyer could feel the graveyard silence through the gun-sight.

The Citizens Guard will be too late.

The index finger pulled the trigger. The bullet shattered a vial and the shock tossed the four men with their backs into the walls. The bullet has made a surgical hole in the window. The Lawyer shot again and again, until all the vials are shattered and the poison was spilled on the floor. The four brains froze. He kept shooting an entire clip, just to keep them from thinking of licking the floors and ending it prematurely. Suddenly, The Lawyer saw a whole array of possibilities. The widening of the future. The widening of a womb. The conception of new notions, axioms, indestructible autonomy.

The Citizens Guard was closing in around the guardhouse. The Lawyer stopped shooting. Come out!, the guards shouted.

It is done, The Lawyer told his son. From now on, everything will be different.

Chapter 156
Interventions of the left wings of the angels into the right wings of the angels

The helicopters landed in the schoolyard, on the golf course and wherever there was flat land with no obstructions and no townsfolk gazing mindlessly at the sky, What the hell is happening, I told you they'd come, It was about time, Damn government, they couldn't care less, But they're here now, that's what matters, Whatever, Why did they leave us last time?, They say there was some sort of epidemic here with high risk, That's bullshit, I feel fine, They must have had their reasons, Why are you taking their side?, I'm not taking their side, plus, remember the government is very sensitive to the reaction of the media, Then how do you explain there was no media here during our ordeal?, Nobody knew about us, How could they not know, they know everything, That's a myth, they only know what matters, Are you saying that we did not matter?, That was your deduction, But a necessary deduction, It depends, Whatever, you people like to think that everything is relative, it's just not like that, How is it then?, Some things are absolute, Like what?, Like logic for example, logic is universal, Logic is a human construct, No, it's the construct of nature, I don't want to argue here, but I think we're talking nonsense, I agree, Why do they carry guns?, I don't know.

The platoons spread through Town within minutes, they surrounded the key objectives and the locations where the pilots saw the most people gathered on roofs, waving towels, flags and twigs in flames, Over here, over here, We're saved, This is the happiest day of my life. The pilots did not hear these words, but they could see the people running to landing places, they looked like armies of white ants, washed by the bright light of the day.

The trucks arrived shortly after, spitting jets of dust from the thick wheels. They were fully loaded with supplies, guards and volunteers, this time in regular uniforms, with nametags and stripes, but no chemsuits. That's a good sign, the people thought, We're safe, There was no epidemic, I told you, They'd better have an explanation for their long absence, There will be time for that later, you should live your moment of redemption.

The Colonel approached the people in front of Town Hall and asked them where The Mayor was. We don't know, He left with two police officers, They found the guy who did it, Did what?, The Colonel asked. The whole thing, What whole thing?, You know, the dead, the flooding and stuff. The Colonel thought that this was no time for inquiry or intelligence gathering, he will leave it for later and delegate it properly, systematically. He needed to find The Mayor now, or at least someone in charge. He gave some orders, You take a unit, go there, You come with me, You take two units and search these addresses, take those townsfolk with you, report every half hour, copy that, Aye, aye, sir.

Two platoons found people gathered outside the Community Bank. What's going on here?, the sergeant asked, There are people in the vault, Robbers?, No, not robbers, employees, What do you mean?, They locked themselves inside, they took the supplies, That's one thing you won't expect in a vault, the sergeant said ironically, I agree with you, sir, The Manager replied, Are you missing any valuables?, It's hard to say, sir, after all that happened, we lost all our hard drives, the files, You don't do backups elsewhere, We do, once a month, That's not that bad, how about the money in the vault?, Well, I guess we have to open it to see where we're standing, sir, I guess you're right.

While this conversation was taking place, three other trucks with a dozen guards pulled over briskly, at the bottom of the hill where a crowd queued in a large spiral around an improvised well, twenty-two men keeping things in order, comforting the mothers and the children who were resting in the shadows of the trees, two other men, religious leaders supervising the whole operation and raising their hands to the sky and thanking their lords respectively for the appearance of salvation, Welcome, welcome, so nice to see you, We brought supplies, We thank you, may the Lord bless you all, Thank you, I am Imam, And I am Rabbi, our brothers will help you distribute the stuff, We appreciate that, we brought water, food, blankets, It's kind of hot, sir, I know, those are the rules, nights are cold, you'll find them useful, Thank you, We came here to help you restore peace and bring the normal life back to Town.

Notwithstanding the rashness of the previous encounter with the Citizens Guard who looked more like an insurrection rather than an attempt to bring comfort to people, the hearts and minds of people welcomed the outstretched hand of the government, as it is, because what matters in the end are the people on whatever side of the barricade they may be, not that a barricade suggests opposition, but a hurdle that nature or life sets on paths of time. And after the perception of time is altered by whatever reason, when its flow is reinstated, the sense of belonging is also awakened and questions like, How much time has passed?, become less important, less poignant.

Chapter 157
The writer and the muse

I hear them coming.

It's all over, you say, there is so much relief in your breathing, the fortuitous change of events is changing the look of your eyes. Look, you say, there are trucks with food and guards all over, people are coming out of the hiding places, they look tired but happy, Who wouldn't be?, I say. From the window you see Town being reborn. It will take some time, you say, What do you want to do after all this?, I ask you, I think I'm going to a poor country to teach children, Does that make you feel good?, I ask, What makes me feel good is that I will make them laugh, What about you?, What do you want to do after all this is finished?, you ask. Your eyes are full of tears. Probably mine are, too, but I cannot feel anything. I don't know what to say. I think I'm gonna go to City and write a book there, Won't you feel alone there, like the Little Prince?, you ask, I'll try not to feel alone. I will have a rose under a glass bell. It will keep me company. You are always so protective, you say, and smile with a corner of your mouth. I will write you, I say. I will write you too, you say.

Chapter 158
Rise from disgrace into a gracious maze

Open up!, the sergeant banged on the vault's door.

On the other side, the teller and the loan officer looked at each other with mounting dismay. What do we do now?, the teller said, I don't know, the loan officer responded, Do you think we'll get arrested?, I don't think so, we just sought shelter in a case of absolute necessity, You say we plead defense of necessity, I don't know, I don't know, let me think, don't pressure me, What if we maximize our stay here?, What do you mean?, Look around, Yeah, what about it?, You don't think we can, you know, use *some*, How do you expect to extract it?, Well, we could appeal to the basic predispositions of man, So what does that mean?, We share. At this point the dismay has diminished and is replaced by a feeling of hope emerging from the pressure of fear whose intensity is suddenly transformed into the realization that there might be a gainful purpose in this dire situation, if employed with careful planning and with good intuition.

The exit through the ventilation shaft failed as a solution because it will suggest a surreptitious action which will not be perceived positively by the party on the other side of the door and will reduce the space for maneuver and negotiations. The second option was to use the benefits of physics, and specifically the laws of thermodynamics. They will turn up the heat, burn some money, make some smoke and the air pressure will rise. They will scatter bills and willingly open the door. Thermodynamics will do the rest, the air current will pull out forcefully, and the papers will flood the room outside, which was probably filled with a lot of anxious people, whose instincts will be immediately activated. They will jump like predators to grab whatever they can. They will stash their pockets, and, in this hectic disarray, the two will emerge and blend with the others, and their anonymity will be restored. No, this is not feasible, they dismissed this option as well, it's too risky, too many variables unknown, anonymity is not desirable, it's hard to maintain, so they choose the third way, sharing through open negotiation, We just open the door and talk about it, People don't like to talk when they're frustrated, They will talk, but first we need to cover ourselves with an insurance policy. The loan officer underlined the word cover because he meant it literally. He stripped to his underwear and asked his partner what he was waiting for, like it was obvious what his intentions were. Then he tied wads of bills to his ankles, calves, thighs, pelvis, hips, then turned to the teller and asked him to, Give me a hand, tie this for me in the back, will you? They used shoelaces and strips ripped from a shirt to tie the money to their bodies with solid knots. The suits of money grew to their necks, their bodies fully covered, insulated with a thick layer of freedom. They put the clothes back on, with some difficulty, to conceal their insurance policies. No one will dare to search us, they're too distressed, the officer said. They agreed that a distraction rider needed to be added, as with any policy, so they could have the upper hand. Do you think it will work?, Oh yeah. They will use physics, they will heat up the room, open the door and create the wind. Are you ready?, Yes.

They turned up the heat from the control panel until the heaviness of the air became unbearable, then waited a little so the pressure can build up. Maybe we can get some sympathy for this, they thought ironically. They turned the crank four times to the left and punch the exit code.

The door opened fast and wide, helped by the zealous hands from the other side. Drop your weapons!, the guards screamed.

What makes you think we have weapons?, the teller said.

Then the gush of warm air from the vault scattered waves of fresh bills through the Community Bank and, as expected, this drew immediate attention.

The onlookers, the other employees and even a few guards leaped frantically to catch the bills before they landed. They filled their pockets with crumpled paper, the sergeant yelling, Order, order! a few times, to no avail, everyone was hypnotized by the act of collecting, pushing and shoving each other, and as more and more bills emerged from the vault into the madhouse, the focus on the loan officer and the teller dwindled abruptly and became practically nil.

Not even the face of Mademoiselle Pogany under the armpit of the loan officer was striking enough to draw anyone's attention as the two glided through the swarming labyrinth of bodies, preoccupied with the quick acquisition of fortune. The sergeant tried unsuccessfully to calm the spirits. He yelled for about a minute, but did not dare to shoot into the ceiling as a warning. Instead, he considered the alternative, which is to take part in the collection. It's not plunder, he thought, it's a case of absolute necessity, no one can prove anything, it will be like it never happened, I just tried to maintain order, avoid casualties, do my job, they can't blame me for that.

By the time the temperature in the vault and the bank reached an equilibrium, most of the people have left in all directions, away from each other, hiding their faces and tacitly agreeing to a mutual nondisclosure of facts, I won't tell on you if you won't tell on me, We'll keep it between us, let them assume what they want, we went through a disaster anyways, No one cares, the public memory is very fragile, this will be soon forgotten, plus all those deposits are insured, Exactly. Well then, nice to meet you, I'll see you soon, Or not, Ha ha, that's right, See you, and they go to their respective houses without looking back.

Chapter 159
Paper rain and the realignment of priorities

It rained with flyers made of recycled paper for about five minutes until the pilots were given the orders, Okay, that's enough, return to your positions. At the same time, the guards glued an identical message in key places throughout Town, on the Town

Hall doors, on the trees in the park, on the walls of the school, and encouraged people to read them and to obey the recommendations. The message had been titled by the Colonel, The Government's Strategy to Revive Town and Its People. It was his idea. They printed it after he had proofread it and said, It's a go. He was very proud of that. He still is.

The single man picked up a flyer from the mud, spat on it and realized it had impermeable qualities. Town and Its People, he said. Why and? Can a town exist without its people?, Now you're picking on grammar and syntax, This is not about grammar, you don't get it, it's about hermeneutics, it's about what *they* think, You're making too much fuss, Listen, don't you get it, you make me repeat myself, for *them* people and geography are separate entities, and because of that they treat them separately, So you're saying we are as important as these buildings, the parking lots, the parks?, Isn't it obvious?, Well, I don't know, they want to help us, look it says here, The Citizens Guard will help rebuild Town and encourages everyone to participate, the Supply Centers will be established at the following locations, People of Town will have access to construction materials on a first-come, first-served basis, let's see, what else, Citizens Guard will provide extended security for the upcoming elections, Candidacies for the investigation committee will be accepted until this coming Friday, What investigation committee?, I don't know, it doesn't say.

The flyer also made reference to a detailed plan of recovery and reconstruction, which can be found at Town Hall, for those interested in reading it and leaving comments in the drop-box.

By nightfall the drop-box was full and the guards pleaded with the people to return to their homes, Mr. Mayor will read all of them with the recovery committee and the best decisions will be taken in a timely manner, I'm sorry, but where is The Mayor, we haven't seen him in days, I understand your frustration, ma'am, I'm sure he's dealing with grave cases with the chief of police, with the chief of Citizens Guard, The Colonel, Yes, We haven't seen him very much either, Mr. Colonel is very busy with the management of supplies, there's a lot of aid waiting, Waiting where?, At the central administration in City, It will take days and weeks to bring it here, Don't worry, ma'am Citizens Guard has it under control.

Control is something we can't lose, The Colonel thought, and felt immediately a spark of disgust because it was all so cliché and he had to put up with all these weasels. He opened a pack of cigarettes, then changed his mind, put it back and walked to the window of The Mayor's office to scrutinize the horizon, the activities, the general picture, to gaze at the purple sunset and feel its contemptuous weight and have no idea what the hell happened in this godforsaken Town, but he didn't care as he had a job to do, Give Town your highest attention and report on any irregularities, he was told. The only irregularities he could think of were a few looters caught red-handed and the mysterious absence of The Mayor.

Chapter 160
Farewell to naked arms

You left with the first bus at the break of moonlight, and you said it was best if we didn't spend too much time on the goodbyes, it would bring too many unpleasant sentiments, So let us look forward and hope for the best, you said the night before, then you dropped your oversized shirt and walked naked to the bathroom to brush your teeth with a green organic paste that smelled like The Lake on a hot, still day, I watched you while you combed your hair, moisturized your arms with aloe cream, then your neck, then your thighs, you sighed and you turned towards me, you were so beautiful, and I remained mute, and you lowered your timid eyes but you let me watch you, you dimmed the lights and sat down on the bed, next to me, the flickering yellow moonlight was pushing feebly through the blinds and you told me, This is not the end, there is no end, there is never an end, But what will become of us?, I wanted to ask you, We will be the meaning we choose, you said. I can't remember who closed their eyes first, but it did not lessen the light in our imagination, it was so powerful to feel you, as if you were a Greek goddess awakened inside me and I was the warrior with tensed muscles inside you, taming the beasts of uncertainty, denying the future as if it never existed, consuming the present as if it was a collection of rich endless pasts that fed our souls to the microscopic pulsation of each capillary vein, as we had been doing it since forever, with no recollection of a beginning. We were the slaves of such a marginal perception of time and we escaped from it to reach a continuum of happiness. Your breathing was ethereal, you arched your back, you curved your heart into my palms, We don't need a horizon, we don't need plans, we must remain a revelation, our togetherness is not an array of delightful consequences, we must be like a prayer, open, wide, far outreaching outside logic, if it will be, it will be, But isn't this resignation, the minimalism of desire, I asked, you combed my hair, And what about *will*, with *will* we can change reality, we can make things happen, Will is a product of reason, you said, it leaves you less room for wonder and awe. The dark-yellow moonlight was flickering on your forehead. It was great, I said, Yes, it was, you said, then you shrank like a fetus and I spooned you in my arms, you were burning like a comet, I am not afraid, you said, those without a story are alone, we are not alone, we will never be, Because we have a story, Yes. It was the truth. We said it over and over again and it remained vivid like the most vivid stories we read when we were young, they will never betray us, they will never falter, never change, they will never end. Can stories exist outside time? you asked, Time itself is a story, like everything in our mind, That is comforting, For us it is, but for many can be a source of unrest, Why?, They try to understand what they cannot and what they are not ready to understand.

We will change, you said.

It's possible. Change is a part of the story.

Good night, you said. The dreams will be the goodbye. I'll meet you soon.

When I woke up, you were gone.

Chapter 161
The first interview: The blind and the seeing are not equal

We are live and *exclusive* from Town Hall Square and proud to be the first station to be allowed to report on the recent events in this community and I am told The President has released urgent aid of at least ten million, which many citizens say is not sufficient and rather late, and frustration can still be felt deeply rooted in the souls of survivors. As you can see around me there is a lot of activity. Town is being rebuilt relatively quickly, damage is still being assessed and sadly there have been a certain number of victims. We don't have a number yet, but as reports come in I can say the number is not negligible. The victims have been centralized at the hospital, and as more bodies are found they are taken there to be identified. For details I have the pleasure to have here the chief of the operation. Colonel.

Thank you, ma'am. We, the Citizens Guard, are in a very difficult position. It's hard for me to say that we face many contradictions with certain individuals. We are still being accused that we did not do our job the last time we were here, but I remind these individuals that we had a presidential order to pull out quickly, based on the reports of serious contamination, which, in part, proved to be incorrect. The intel originated from Town, so we cannot be held responsible—

So you're saying that what was previously reported was incorrect.

In part, yes. There was no epidemic of any kind, but there were signs of criminal activity and—

Is it true that Town was under threat of biological weapons?

Ma'am, I will not go that far to speculate on this, but we had information that forced us to pull out.

People say that some of the guards were held hostage.

That's incorrect. No guard was left behind and we assured the people of Town that we would return. Which we did. Another point I'd like to make is that we are working closely with the local police and Mr. Mayor to identify the criminal sources that caused property damage, were responsible for looting and, we suspect, cases of murder. I don't want to get graphic here, for our viewers, but some bodies have obvious signs of trauma.

What about the arrests at the water main facility?

I'm sorry, ma'am, we can't, I can't elaborate on that particular information.

You're saying you don't know about them?

Ma'am, it's futile to insist, I cannot discuss our collaboration with the local police and I don't want the media to speculate. All I can say is that we are making progress with the apprehension of those responsible and we are doing our best to restore normal life in Town.

What caused the severe flooding?

We don't know yet. We cannot rule out criminal factors.

Why there was such a long delay before you decided to come back?

As I said before, Town was under the status of non-intervention until the gravity of the facts could be assessed.

Where is The Mayor?

Mr. Mayor is working with us on the field operations.

It has been said that he is using this operation for campaigning purposes, given the upcoming elections.

Ma'am, I will not make any political comments. I can assure you of Mr. Mayor's best intentions and total dedication. Now you must excuse me.

One last question, Colonel.

I'm sorry, ma'am.

Chapter 162
The second interview: Concerto for single man and orchestra

Thank you again for accepting to see us.

Yeah, yeah, it's okay, not a lot of people want to talk to you, apparently.

Yes, I find it odd, too. I'm sure they have their reasons.

You don't mind I made you come with me? I like to keep it mobile.

It's fine, I've done interviews in tour buses and on airplanes, so your truck suits me fine. Is your cameraman okay?

He's okay.

What do you want to know?

What happened in Town, Mr.—

Lady, we agreed. No names. I don't like that.

I'm sorry, cut that.

Fine.

So, what happened?

You know what, let me just tell you one thing. They don't give a damn. They speak about cohesion, synergy and bullshit. These weird stories appeared in the local press, with weird metaphoric nonsensical titles and insinuations, that don't make sense, I hope you're not gonna do that, good, why they don't just say it directly, I like straight talk, you know. They have no idea how *instrumental* I was in many decisions that helped us stay alive. Imagine, we would have starved to death if I hadn't come up with the idea to plant that garden. You know, people can be so ungrateful, they invoke such and such psalm or proverb or whatever to serve a so-called great common cause, then they lie, they distort facts, they point at you, like you are the scapegoat of their sins.

They said you were opposed to the garden.

Who said that? Why do I bother? I'm not surprised. I know you're seeking the truth, aren't we all? Ask them who sabotaged the churches in the first place. I think it all started there. Sorry, I have to make a left turn here. It all went to hell from there. There was a civil war before the flood, people died on the street, did you know that? They were clubbing each other on the streets when the big wave came, that's why you have all those dead, except for those with their guts out, but who knows what a lot of determination can do, you know what I mean? I bet there was a lot at stake, we're too insignificant to make a difference, sure you can say that every vote counts, but watch the elections. Do you mind if I stop for a smoke? Thanks, I'm just gonna pull over here. Do you smoke? Good, don't even think about it. Is he still filming? Good. Our dead were decomposing around us. Then those men came and blurted orders, Citizens Guard came, they kidnapped that man.

Who came, those arrested?

I don't know what you're talking about. Some men, we don't see them often around here. They were important, or at least they acted like they were, I think they were pulling strings, things just happened after they came. Then it was a guy, forgot his name, with a thick accent, ugly face, heavyset, I didn't like him, he violated a woman in the church, or at least I heard he did, but I think he did, he had a gun, people were avoiding him, he worked with them, with those four men.

I heard Mr. Lawyer was associated with them.

I don't think he is or was. No, he's clean. He tried to stop the fighting, but it was too late. I saw him with the French guy once, or maybe not, I don't know, but one thing is sure, I have been treated unfairly in the reports.

Are you married? Do you have children?

What does this have to do with anything? Listen, I live my life and no one tells me anything. You are asking if I resent being alone, they all are asking the same thing, curious about the abnormal, the isolated, the exception to uniformity, because that's what's interesting, that's what captivates, you have to be a political animal, or they'll hunt you down and turn you into a trophy, so what do you do to escape? Well, there are a few scenarios, all contaminated by the insufficiency of the system, the human system. Do you have a lighter, mine is kaput, I need another smoke. Thanks. We can go, I can smoke and drive. First we have the less desirable irreversible self-exclusion, you know what I'm talking about, they're afraid to say, this is the reason they invented hell, the pressure is so big, only the very courageous or the very weak can do it, the masses are trapped in the middle, in a soup of determinism of whatever-type-you-want. Second, the acceptance of reality, resignation and then what, numbness, disorientation, fanaticism, propaganda. Look at them, look at these faces, waiting at the stoplight, walking their dogs, pushing carts, connected to their realities, impervious, flat, quiet, sure they'll say they scream inside, and they do, sometimes we can hear them, but it's echoless, it has no significance, it's just a ripple in an enormous pond that fades into nothing. Third, is the way for those with vision, who do not accept the determinism of the womb, those who bring possibilities, those who create.

You're saying there's no hope for us?

Of course there is, but do we understand it, can we accept it, is it real, or is it just a motivational discourse? You see, there will be elections, things will change, perceptions will be different, they will forget, there will be agendas, many will die, more will replace them, the new cycles will recycle the old stories, the old mistakes.

I heard you saved the life of a little girl.

If I tell you, you won't believe me. The paper wrote that somebody else saved her. Do you want to hear it?

Sure.

The girl fell in the water. We were staying in the attic of the church. She fell inside the church. A beam snapped. She was too heavy for it. I jumped after her. Then the big brass bell fell and almost caught us under it. Then they pulled us out. With ropes. That's it.

I see.

Forget it. Do you really want to know who I am? Here, take this.

What is it?

Open it.

It's a picture. Are they your family?

They are no more. I am a single man now.

Chapter 163
The third interview: The holy instruction manual of the unified narrative of faith

We are at the Town Hall, in the Conference Room. My guests today are the leaders of two major communities of Town, who played and are still playing a crucial role in the revitalization process. Imam, I would like to start with you. Mr. Colonel has expressed his extreme satisfaction vis-à-vis the collaboration with you. The Muslim community is working very closely with the Citizens Guard. Can you elaborate more on this? What is your vision for what, I'm told, will be a New Town?

Thank you for having me here. As you know, we, the Muslim community, are part of the spirit of Town, and always have been. We were present from its foundation, so we feel compelled to be part of its reconstruction. I strongly believe the future is very bright, which gives us more reason to maintain our hope and motivation. I also feel compelled, on the other hand, to clarify a few things. Some allegations were made that we were on the brink of a social war, before the natural disaster occurred, that we caused victims in each other's ethnic communities. Far, far from the truth. What the press published is totally untrue, there was no fight, there were no murders, sure we were all surprised by what happened, we were totally unprepared, we were celebrating Town's anniversary, that's why you might have heard there was a big gathering in Town Hall Plaza, but it was absolutely peaceful. Some articles also suggested that the accident at our mosque was in fact caused by some criminals, that a bomb was planted somewhere outside, and its detonation severely affected the structural integrity of the mosque. Again, I can't say how untrue that is, the articles were a total lie. Plus, they were presented in a pretentious literary form that left room for interpretation. I understand the entertaining value of the metaphor but you don't play with facts for the sake of entertaining the public, it's immoral, counterproductive, it manipulates, it distorts and generates so much confusion for the public. It's totally unacceptable.

I understand your point, Imam. There are many voices that complained about what was written about the events in Town. Rabbi, what is the position of the Jewish community vis-à-vis the recent events and also your current collaboration with the Citizens Guard?

Our position is similar to that of Imam. To add to his thoughts, I would also would like to make it perfectly clear for your live audience that much of the previous correspondence about the events in Town verges on pure fiction, many letters are simple, narcissistic, florid, often rhetorical expressions of their authors, who put more emphasis on the style of their articles than on the facts themselves. Let me make a reference to just one thing. Someone claimed that we sought refuge during the flood in the

Town Hospital, that we depleted the resources there, without consideration for other survivors, that brothers from our communities actually committed murder, in the sense that patients in the hospital were physically abused and ignored and not saved when they could have been saved, that we locked ourselves in rooms protected from the fury of nature and we would not accept other survivors. A lie! In fact, we plan to bring a lawsuit against those authors and make them responsible for what they wrote about us. Here's a particular passage, and I quote, The Jews, infuriated and pushed forward by the loudspeakers, thrust into the Muslims through the line of overwhelmed police officers that ends up mashed in the middle. It's outrageous!

Do you feel your role was neglected in the reports about the events, Rabbi?

I would like to answer you with a quote from the author Joseph Conrad. Vanity plays lurid tricks with our memory. End quote. Can we recollect history through the emotional distortions of some so-called historians, journalists, no offense, or literates? Of course not. Terrible things happened here, and words are not potent enough to describe them. The recovery committee has much to do, many have to be brought to justice, order is yet to be fully restored, but to make such allegations that we wanted to kill each other, we are not beasts of the medieval ages, we are much more advanced spiritually and mentally, we can collaborate, Imam, the members of his community are our partners, in the past we had divergences of opinion, of course we did, but they were not as grave as the reports said. You know better than me, writers tend to exaggerate extensively to get attention.

What can you tell us about the facts, Imam?

We should let the committee do its job, publish the findings and then let the public decide. If we expose our version of the facts we will be considered partisan, although we suffered those things. Not that we want some strangers, experts or analysts to decide what truly happened. We have members from our communities on this committee, and everything will be known in due course.

Aren't you afraid that the public will be frustrated with the delay, Imam?

We are not afraid of the truth. The truth has its timing. It might have been revealed already, but eyes are not yet opened and ready to see it. Truth can also be blinding or deafening, and sometimes truth doesn't need the corroboration of the senses, it simply exists, but it's not perceptible. It's like the belief that we are alone in the universe.

Are we alone in the universe, Imam?

Theologically yes, practically no.

It's surprising to hear that from a man of religion, Imam.

I am first a man of truth, then a man of faith. I am sure my colleague, Rabbi, shares my vision.

Yes, I think we are both men of vision.

Gentlemen, thank you for your thoughts. We must now cut for a break, as the studio demands.

Chapter 164
The fourth interview: Plan for the Abolition of Applause and Demonstrations of All Kinds

Father Frank, may I first ask how you respond to the accusations?

First, I would like to note that in my answer I will not try to explain or excuse myself, or to manifest an intent to discredit the reports, which may be motivated by pure professionalism. I understand writers and reporters like yourself have to make a living, it's perfectly okay, however, it should not be at the expense of the truth. I have been accused of severe violations of social and moral conduct, and I will definitely not name them here, as they bring so much indignation, not just to me but also to the parishioners. What I find so annoying is that the accusations were essentially indirect, through allusions, based on so-called witness reports. Who are these witnesses? Their names have never been mentioned. Why the secrecy, why no references to concrete evidence? This is all so unsubstantial and severely lacks credibility. It can easily make the public believe that the church itself is a facilitator of such abominable crimes. It's absurd. Sure, we made mistakes, but they should not be generalized, because no human institution is perfect.

Faith emerges from revelations, but it needs to be sustained with trust. We all have to suffer if the church's image is affected by incorrect, incomplete, false accusations.

Thank you Father. One of our current affairs analysts has said recently, referring to the events in Town, and I quote, The expectancy for a favorable resolution to an extreme matter of life and death is rarely matched with immediate satisfaction, which may cause even more stress to the subjects. To wait is a way of dying. How do you comment?

I don't think you can psychoanalyze suffering. Suffering is reality. It simply exists. It does not have an intrinsic contingency. I know aid has been unfortunately delayed. It was hard for everyone, the believers, the nonbelievers, but we helped each other, through praying. We thank the government for its help.

How about those who lost their lives?

I pray for them every day.

I knew salvation would come, for one soul it came very soon, a girl who fell in the water—

Some say a man saved her.

We all did. It was a joint effort, although some claim it was their individual efforts.

What do you think it means?

I am not the one to make these kinds of judgments. I am a man of integrity. I am dedicated to my faith, and I seek the truth. There are unexplained events that befell us. The committee will review them and truth will prevail. But they must be careful with the so-called witnesses' recollections, because I think many are faulty. Yes, it can be explained scientifically. The lack of food and lack of water can severely impair the memory, the senses, and grave statements can be made. We should concentrate on the fact that it's a miracle that we survived that long. We should mourn the departed and help the reconstruction.

Father, many say they have lost patience with demagogic, empty, meaningless, long, boring, action-lacking statements.

True, true, I sympathize with those citizens, whoever might they be, believers and non-believers, by case. We will have elections soon, and I'm sure this will clarify many things and a sense of freshness will emerge in the spirit of the public.

Thank you, Father Frank.

My pleasure.

Chapter 165
The eighth interview: uncensored and uncut

This is a collection of various amateur recordings we have collected during the past few weeks from various official and unofficial sources. We apologize for the quality of the sound or video. We intervened with minimal editing, and if we did, it was with the sole purpose of improving the accessibility of the content. We advise discretion in accessing this information.

Is this thing recording?, Give it to me, Shut the fuck up, we dont have time for this.

Mom, Dad, I dont know where you are, I wanna show you this, everybody is crazy on the streets, please come come home quickly, Im gonna show you whats outside, everybodys running, theres a big wave coming, where are you?, I love you, Mom, I love you, Dad, its coming.

Dude, theyre gonna bust you for that, So what?, Everybody else is doing it, so why cant we?, Let's take the shit and run, This shit is expensive, dude, Are you recording now?, Its awesome, Dont tape me, theyre gonna find it, No they wont.

Its my turn, Shut the fuck up, watch out, Dont hurt her, I aint gonna hurt her, Tell her to shut up, You tell her to shut up, Man, I dont have a good feeling about this, I have a great feeling about this, Shut up, woman, Yeah, shut up, Come already, Give me a minute, will ya, Stop that camera.

What do you think this is, I have no clue, Do you think its worth something, What do I know about precious stones, I think its worthless, its a fake, Like you know shit, Im gonna record this and send it to a friend of mine, Like he can tell from a video if its real, youre a dumbshack.

As you can see, Town is completely covered with water, many houses are totally underwater, we found refuge on the roofs, I dont know how many died, Im gonna zoom in on those people, Hey! Over here!, See me? Hey! I dont think they can see me, Im gonna record till the battery dies, I have one hour and twenty-seven minutes left, Ill be back, Im gonna try to get to those people.

Father Frank, do you think we can find some food here?, I dont know, I dont know, I need to think, leave me alone for a few minutes, will ya, do you think this is easy for me, do you think I wanted this to happen?, Father, we didnt say that, were as scared as you, what are we going to do?, Leave me alone!, But, Father.

Did you hear what happened at the Bank?, No, its all gone, What are you talking about?, The money, man, its all gone, Of course it is, the flood took it, No man, it was somebody, How do you know?, I heard, You heard, You dont listen, we could have been part of it, Part of what?, Exactly, just my point, Stop that, Stop what?, Turn it off.

We cant call anyone, we dont know where everybody is, we are running out of food, of water, it doesnt rain, I dont know what to do, I saw a dead man, I saw a dead man.

Shes losing too much blood, man, what do I do?, Dont ask me, Im not a doctor, Is there a doctor around here?, ANYONE, Stay with us, Breathe, Im losing her, man, Here, tie this around her, I dont know how, man, Dont yell at me, Im trying to help, You do it, Fuck, I dropped my phone, Fuck the phone, shes passed out, Fuck, it was recording the whole time, Hold this, I think we got her.

Hes gonna say something, Folks, hello, FOLKS, may I have your attention?, the bad news is that the Citizens Guard left us here, AWW, what the hell!, I know, I know, thats not cool, not what we expected, Fortunately, EXCUSE ME!, theres also good news, they left supplies, YEAH!, We must be organized with this, fuck knows when theyre gonna come, Why did they leave?, How am I supposed to know?, They talked about some virus, What virus?, Folks, dont exaggerate, everythings fine, let us come up with a plan to see how were gonna deal with this, you in the back, stop that, come and help us.

Mom, Dad, hes coming again, he said that if I say his name hes gonna kill me, I cant say his name, hes a bad person, I saw him do things.

Mom, Dad, Im cold, We found food, they say its a miracle, I dont know what a miracle is, its cold, they say its gonna be fine but I dont know, I dont know what time it is, its dark all the time, they dont let us go outside, they say its dangerous, I dont believe them, because its so quiet, nobody comes, I miss you, Mom, Dad, the pregnant woman is crying, shes gonna be a mama, I have to close now.

Chapter 166
The eleventh interview

Mr. Mayor, there has been much speculation about your prolonged absence, some even say disappearance, many believed you left Town for good, which obviously is not the case, but your supporters never stopped believing in your return. Would you like to comment?

Thank you for honoring my invitation. With this occasion, I officially announce my candidacy for another term of Mayor of Town, now from a position of wisdom and awareness, as I have learned from the wrongdoing of the past, from the conflicts I had to manage. I'm sure the public wants to know what I've been doing recently. Let me explain.

Number one. I led a team of investigators whose purpose was to expose those responsible for certain misdeeds. The nature of this work was confidential. These four individuals are well connected. Yes, we caught them. No, it wasn't easy. No, they have not confessed. Yes, we have evidence. Yes, this will be a shock for the public, the flood was not necessarily natural, it was caused by human hands, we found traces of explosives at the mines, and similar chemical compounds in receptacles found on these four individuals.

Number two. We have rebuilt a significant number of houses, and created a significant number of jobs, the blood flows through Town's veins with more energy than ever, we are at the peak of social cohesion, we are heading into a bright direction, the suffering has awakened us to a better status.

Number three. We have repaired the crack in the exterior shell of the Church. It was a very delicate job, we had to preserve the architecture, the fine details, make it seamless, like nothing happened. I'm sure believers from all corners of Town appreciate our work and will happily return to the religious service with more enthusiasm than ever before. Traditions must be kept unaltered for the good warm feeling of home they give us.

Number four. The press has already reported on the looting at the Community Bank. I am happy to announce that we recuperated a significant amount of money, with the aid of the Citizens Guard. The cash deposits that could not be recuperated are insured by the government, so in the end nobody lost anything. Therefore, there's no need for concern.

Number five. My opposing candidate has maximized his public exposure at the expense of truth and actual accomplishments. After my reelection, I will open a public inquiry that will reveal his involvement with the so-called Club and the rerouting of public funds into his political group that was done under his signature, which I have right here, you can take a look at it, maybe you can zoom in on it, not to mention his counterproductive activities that led to public disobedience and delays in public projects. I am surprised by his daring endeavor to run for this office, not that I want to discourage the principles of free speech, anyone can do whatever they want, as long as it does not break the law, does not mislead the public, as happened recently. I urge the citizens of

Town to join my cause, to renew their support to help me and themselves with the revitalization of our great community.

Chapter 167
The twelfth interview

Mr. Lawyer, everybody was expecting you to run for Mayor, but many voices have expressed their disapproval. I've heard that one analyst even said that he was disgusted. How do you respond to these statements?

Let me thank you for inviting me here. I don't need to respond to statements or unsubstantiated allegations. I will simply let my beliefs and facts speak for themselves. Since I have announced my candidacy, I have worked hard to spread the word. At the core of everything I do, there is a big WHY. Why are we doing what we are doing? We are doing it for our children, for our belief that life can be good, that we can live in peace, that we can share hope through responsibility and compassion. This is my position, this is where I stand.

I will challenge the points raised by the opposing candidate.

First. It has been said that those four criminals were caught by, and I quote, a team of investigators. False. I provided the intelligence that led to their capture. I was collaborating with the Citizens Guard the whole time. Taking credit for this is preposterous. Plus, it was suggested that I would have liaisons with those four individuals. I cannot say enough how absurd this is.

Second. I acknowledge the opposing candidate's efforts to rebuild houses. Compared to our efforts, they are utterly insignificant. Numbers speak. You read yesterday in Town Chronicle how many units my party has helped get built. I have brought millions in private funding and numerous investors back to Town.

Third. Part of the Church was indeed built with money from the local budget, from whatever there was left. But no attention was given to the Mosque and none to the Synagogue. This violated at least two rules. The principle of secular administration and the unequal distribution of spending on ethnic criteria.

Fourth. I will tell you what money was recuperated from the Community Bank. Less than five percent. Five percent! To claim full recovery it is not only incorrect but an affront to the citizens of Town. I will tell you what really happened. The bank was severely damaged in the flood. When Colonel's team arrived, the vault was already open, ransacked by water and looters. Just a few bills were found scattered about, and they were in poor condition. Read the report. Check the photos. After my election, I will find those responsible and bring them to justice. It is not fair for the taxpayers to have to support this loss.

Fifth. I will not address personal character remarks. I find them below my dignity.

Let us go beyond the demagogy of the past and focus on the future. We need to build a different future for Town, a different way to interact with each other, a different way to achieve harmony. It is time for a fundamental change. It is time for an age of reason, compassion and assumed truth. It is time to turn the page on the policies of the past. It is time to bring new energy and new ideas to the challenges we face. It is time to offer a new direction to the Town we love.

Chapter 168
Epilogue: The final metaphor and what comes after

Iris returned the next day.

I cannot leave you, she said.

He hugs her for a long time. They cry and stay quiet for a while.

Look into the camera, Tim, I cannot focus on you, Iris says.

Don't point it at me. Stop talking, they'll recognize your voice.

They don't have to.

You don't want to be associated with this?

It's not that.

What is it?

The light that comes from within.

Are you going to show it?

We cannot deprive them of truth.

But we don't know what it is, Tim, she says.

I saw everything white, my father was there, he told me that everything real and unreal appears with complexity, it's driven by complexity itself, from the unreal within us to the intangible sun, to the violin. Is this all unreal?, I asked him.

He didn't say anything for a moment. Then he said that death is a stage, a transformation just like any other, like birth. He said that everything is entangled, that light is an illusion as much as it is a wave or a particle.

I asked him what an illusion was.

He said it's when consciousness is numb and it becomes its own phantom limb and you feel your mind amputated but you don't understand it.

He said death is irrelevant in itself, in time and space, in its esthetics, everything loops onto itself, one way or another, it's the meaning that transports desires, intentions, the craving for a purpose, that comes from nowhere, from light.

He said it with his white voice, my father, he was rowing in a white boat, with white oars.

The Lake was tranquil, windless, and impenetrable like the silence of awareness.

What comes after?, I asked him.

There is no *after*, he said, not like we normally understand the *after*, we continue in timelessness, we are absorbed back into the vortex, on a thread of light.

I told him I could not understand consciousness without individuality.

Then he said individuality is a manifestation of consciousness. The bullet killed just flesh.

I asked him if he was real, and he said he could not *tell me* that, language is a convention, truth cannot be withheld.

But we have made so much progress, we know so much more.

The journey to enlightenment is very long, we often take steps backwards, we drift on with the currents, we hesitate on the crest of the wave, because we don't know where we are, the real within us closes the circle, encapsulates us in the placenta, everything becomes illuminated with white powerful light that blinds us, makes us focus too much on the purpose, the purpose is not essential, don't worry too much about it.

What about life, father?

Life is also a stage, he said.

Why?, I asked.

Why is not a good question, he said, the *why* just links, it does not transform.

Is everything changing?, I asked. Does it have to change?

It has been always like that.

Have you met god?, I asked naively.

He laughed. That's also not the right question, Tim. Free your mind from itself.

He would not say anything, he would just stay still, in a trance, in a lotus position and breathe the white air.

Tim, I think we should open it. I don't think your father would mind. We don't have to say anything.

No we don't.

Do you think Gregoire is alive?
I saw him turning into a flaming snowman.

They will ask questions, they will want to know, Tim.
We will tell them we are no more different than they are.

Open it, Tim. Open the suitcase. Please.
No, not now.

Do you think the garden on the rooftop was a miracle?
If I think it was, then it was. If I don't think it was, then it wasn't.
You're just playing the card of relativism.
No, on the contrary, I'm *not* playing it.

Iris, I want to know you will be near me, for all time.
I will be near you, for all time.

The End

Made in the USA
Charleston, SC
06 June 2016